Jia Pingwa

Heavenly Rain

Panda Books

Panda Books
First Edition 1996
Copyright © CHINESE LITERATURE PRESS 1996
ISBN 7-5071-0346-3
ISBN 0-8351-3182-3

Published by CHINESE LITERATURE PRESS
Beijing 100037, China
Distributed by China International Book Trading Corporation
35 Chegongzhuang Xilu, Beijing 100044, China
P.O. Box 399, Beijing, China
Printed in the People's Republic of China

CONTENTS

Heavenly Rain — 1

The Good Fortune Grave — 124

The Regrets of a Bride Carrier — 199

The Monk King of Tiger Mountain — 305

Heavenly Rain

IT was the third month of the lunar year, when Tian Jian stood under a warm sun, smiling awkwardly at the handsome face of his young sidekick. "Can I really ... do this?" The wind gusted up suddenly, dried leaves whirled around and spun away, swirling clouds of sand temporarily buried Tian Jian's high-heeled black boots. His smile hardened as he asked again: "Can I really do it?"

The handsome youth keeled over with the sudden force of the wind, and fought to stand up by supporting himself against the wild peach tree to which his donkey was tethered. What a fierce wind! The peach tree swayed like a wreckless swarthy man. Clusters of wind blown petals merged with the clots of blood on the ground before taking off again with the surging current of air like rose-tinted clouds scudding across the sky. As he pondered Tian Jian's question, the young outlaw gazed out at the land, entranced at this strange hitherto unseen beauty. He spat out grains of sand that had flown into his mouth and, suddenly kneeling down, he assumed a very solemn expression. "Your excellency, I know you can do it. Why not? Who could possibly have doubts about you being the county magistrate?"

Tian Jian looked at his partner who remained kneeling on the ground. Yes, he could become quite used to being addressed as "Your Excellency". His head moved slightly, and first the two long shovel-shaped flaps of his hat were swept up and then his entire body seemed to rise into the air. "Aye-ya!" Tian Jian let out an animal-like cry. Did wearing an official's uniform mean he deserved to be addressed as "Your Excellency"? And was there really a place up river in the midst of this green and majestic mountain chain called Zhuyang County, where all the inhabitants were eager to meet him, their newly appointed county magistrate? Tian Jian grabbed a handful of sand and rubbed away the blood that had dried on his hands, and again glanced at the youth kneeling before him, whose handsome, fair and innocent face gazed back with total sincerity.

The wolf still lay on the opposite bank. The gloomy surface of the river in between had regained its composure after the corpses of the aristocrat and his servant had sunk below to the bottom. Only one tall reed protruded above the surface, but just at that moment it too, suddenly disappeared, snapping in half, and the protruding part dropped into the water where it was carried off on the current. Small waves continued to erode the base of the cliff, and one after another deposited bubbles of foam on the sandy shore. Tian Jian stamped on the bubbles as they rolled up against his feet, whereupon they burst and dissolved. All that remained was an empty silence, which heightened the undefinable and altogether unique sense of remorse that Tian Jian felt and was unable to explain. For years he'd been an outlaw, scouring the mountains and forests for victims. He'd already killed quite a number, and had cut off heads and pried open lips to get at gold teeth, yet had he eaten and slept contentedly. But now he felt as if he'd actually wronged the well-dressed aristocrat. As Tian Jian reflected his glance gradually lost its intensity, and he pulled off the stiff, uncomfortable official's hat that was beginning to numb his scalp and loosened the hair that had been tightly bound up beneath it.

"Older brother," the handsome youth sighed. "Are you really not going?"

Tian Jian shook his head in confirmation, took off the official's uniform, picked up the silver coins that lay scattered on the ground and put them into his pocket. "Little brother, move that flagstone over here, smear it with blood and write in it: 'Tian Jian killed the Zhuyang county magistrate.' I don't want the people of Zhuyang waiting for nothing."

The young outlaw made no move, so Tian Jian went to get the flagstone himself, but as he did so the back of his gown caught on the stubble of a young willow, inhibiting his movement and making it very difficult for him to lift the stone. "Yes brother, I've done you wrong. I know it's your ghost that's got hold of me, trying to make trouble. Damn! Tian Jian shouldn't have killed you, but was it not you who wanted to be a county magistrate? Too late now. Tian Jian will use this money to have headstone carved for you at a proper grave. Then will you forgive me? Little brother, go ahead and spit. Look up to the sky and spit as high as you can, so this dead spirit won't bother us any more." With great effort, Tian Jian dragged the flagstone into the shallows. He fell into the sand under its weight, causing a strip from the back of his jacket to be ripped away by the spikey roots of the young willow.

"Older brother," the young outlaw sighed again.

Tian Jian turned around and regarded that part of his gown now hanging from the willow. "This spirit is a pain in the ass! See, the wolf is still over there. That son of a bitch is definitely an evil spirit. He saw everything, and knows all."

The two outlaws were standing on the bank of a river which oddly flowed west rather than east. After their evil deed had been done, they had suddenly noticed a white wolf lying motionless on the opposite bank gazing at them. Tian Jian was worried the wolf would swim over to where they were and had raised his broad-bladed knife in anticipation. They'd shouted at it for a while and even thrown stones which had hit their mark, but the wolf showed no fear and did not move at all. Since the river stood between them and there seemed no danger of the wolf getting across, the young outlaw had apparently forgotten about it. When Tian Jian mentioned it again, he didn't pay it any attention, and continued talking.

"Older brother, you think you're not the right man to be an official because people hate outlaws like us?"

"No, that's not it."

"You don't think outlaws can be good rulers?"

"It's not that either."

"Older brother, you say it's not this and it's not that, so what exactly is the problem? Since you've already seen the uniform's a good fit, why can't you just go and take his place. An outlaw's life may be freer, but outlaws don't have the luxury of being decent and honest. Didn't we kill that aristocrat and his servant so we wouldn't have to kill again? Isn't it right to reform ourselves this way?"

A series of spasms twitched along Tian Jian's back which prevented him from twisting around, and instead continued to stare across the river at the wolf. At that same time, the young outlaw's gaze fell on the wooden knife sticking in the sand. The earthworm-like trickles of blood along the sticky blade hadn't yet congealed. Two teardrops slid from his eyes.

"I understand, older brother. You're worried someone will find out what we did, right?"

Tian Jian forced himself to turn around and fixed his eyes on his young partner who continued speaking: "I'm younger than you and know far less, but I do know that in this lousy world officials are the only ones who live well. Older brother, you now have a chance to live well too and you should take it. Only Heaven knows what happened today and it won't say anything. Spirits might be ugly and scary if you see them, but they don't talk our language. Only you and I could ever reveal what happened here. Once you've become an official, just don't get drunk and there'll be nothing to worry about. You started taking care of me when I was fifteen and I'll never forget that. You should know that even though I can wag my tongue, I can hold it too." And with that the youth quickly bent down, grabbed the knife and brutally slit his own throat. Tian Jian rushed over in a panic, but it was already too late. The young outlaw's head lolled back towards the sand, whilst his truncated body continued to kneel on the ground.

Tian Jian was terrified by the speed at which everything had happened, and for a moment lay prostrate on the sandy beach like a piece of driftwood, as still as stone. Earlier that day, they'd been waiting in ambush in the long grass under a bright sun, but by noon not a soul had come by. They'd both cursed loudly but swore that if they were successful that day, they'd go down to the village at the foot of the mountain, dine on a steaming pig's head and get drunk; and then rising after a long sleep, they'd head over to the gambling house in the city. Their victims arrived just as they considered topping the evening off with a visit to a brothel where they could relax after so much hard play. As soon as they spotted the man walking behind a heavily ladened donkey, they jumped out and blocked the road. Who could have guessed that the man shaking his official hat in an effort to impress and frighten them off, cursing them all the while as insane and ruthless gangsters, was the newly appointed magistrate of Zhuyang County.

They would have got more than enough reward for their labours if the man hadn't waved his official hat at them, but as it was that act immediately provoked another possibility. The youth had laughed: "Hey, older brother, this guy thinks he's a real big official. Why only rob him? Zhuyang's a small but new border county. Why not go and take his place as the county magistrate?"

Initially they hadn't planned to kill anybody, just to make off with whatever property they could get, but this unforeseen opportunity seemed too good to pass up so they forced the magistrate to tell them his name, age, hometown and a good many more details about his life before they knifed him to death. But now Tian Jian's partner was also dead, the cherished friend who'd become his companion as a fifteen-year-old boy.

They'd roamed the wild mountains and barren forests on windswept moonless nights, plundered and robbed, and visited street whores and brothels together. His agile and nimble, buffooning friend was gone from him for ever. Tian Jian had killed an aristocrat and his servant so he could become an official, it had never entered his head that he might lose his friend too. Now there was no turning back, if only for his partner's sake, he had to go ahead and do what they'd planned.

Tian Jian stood up and once again donned the official uniform. The long and broad, dragon-embroidered gown hung heavily over his shoulders making it difficult for him to straighten up. His arms and legs felt stiff and then numb. His mind was filled with uncertainty. "Does the act of putting on these clothes make me an official? And if it does, what kind of official will I be?" All at once Tian Jian's knees began to wobble and he sat down on the sandy bank to steady himself. When calm again he gently lifted his partner's head, with its eyes still wide open and staring out at him, then after washing his hands in the water, he carefully cleaned the traces of blood from the head of his friend and follower, removing the sand from the mouth, nose and ears grain by grain. As he lowered the now perfectly scrubbed body into the river, the white wolf stood up and slowly walked away.

"Little brother, little brother..."

Tian Jian grabbed the broad-bladed knife and hurled it into the river, then kowtowed three times on the sandy beach, the first for his loyal friend, and the other two for the aristocrat and his servant. He rose and walked over to the wild peach tree, loosed his donkey's reins and snapped off a branch from the tree. Peach tree branches being believed to drive away evil, he waved it around to dispel the fear and cowardice he felt deep in his heart.

After leaving the white sands and dark rocks of the Westward Flowing River, Tian Jian threw himself into the role of the newly appointed magistrate of Zhuyang County. At noon the following day, he arrived at a spot several miles south of Zhuyang City where the assistant magistrate, the prosecutor, chief clerk and county commander, and a group of local gentry had come out to wait for him, as they had been doing for the last three days. He was quickly ushered into an official sedan chair ahead of which were a number of attendants carrying signs that read "Keep Quiet" and "Make Way". As the procession moved toward the city, it was greeted by throngs of people standing on both sides of the road all ringing bells and waving batons. The procession finally entered the city gate at sunset and proceeded directly to the yamen. There followed three days and nights of feasting, innumerable bows and offerings of congratulations and a lavish presentation of gifts to the new magistrate. Tian Jian had convinced himself that his official clothes had dispelled any doubts about his background, and his earlier fears to the contrary disappeared. He could now relax and enthusiastically offer his subordinate officials the assortment of old wines, mature vinegars, silks and cottons, antiques, calligraphy, paintings and mountain products that had filled the donkey's packs and now filled a small room in the yamen. Naturally, this show of generosity earned him universal cheer and approbation.

Tian Jian had never been a great lover of sleep and was a regular early-riser. The county magistrate's bed was a wooden frame criss-crossed with coir ropes that were uncomfortable and hurt his back. In addition his flower-design cotton pillow was too hot, so on the third day after his arrival he substituted a brick which helped him sleep better and eliminated the morning redness from his eyes. When the night watchman on the street sounded his gong for the fourth time, Tian Jian would wake up, and still somewhat dazed, imagine himself under an altar at the Mountain Spirit Temple stretching out his leg to touch his young friend. But of course, his leg didn't touch anything, and after realising where he was Tian Jian would laugh to himself. This day, awake and glancing around, he discovered that the bright light filling his spacious bedroom came from a papered window, a light which reminded him of the white wolf lying prone on the riverbank. He quickly turned over and sat up. Lighting the wick of his lamp he began to feel more reassured once he could see the piece of peachwood hanging at his chest. Tian Jian had already had this vision several times, and it was always the same: a white wolf staring at him. All he had for protection was that small piece of wood he'd whittled from the branch of the peach tree. The unease that pursued him in his waking hours persuaded him it would even be comforting to have the charm under his shirt in the yamen courtroom. When he had this vision of the wolf and became frightened so much that he couldn't go back to sleep, he would throw on some clothes, get up and read official documents. In order to reform himself and pursue his new career virtuously and successfully, he felt impelled to familiarise himself with county affairs and the information needed to manage those affairs satisfactorily. But Tian Jian couldn't read very well and would soon lose concentration, seeing only rows of black ants crawling around on the pages in front of him. This was a great frustration and after cursing about it loudly, he would stroll out to the rear courtyard and exit the yamen gate.

Zhuyang City really couldn't be considered a city. There was no moat encircling it, no battlements at the city gate, and all that divided it from the surrounding area was a wall-like earthen structure held together by glutinous rice broth. The city itself was located on a plain ringed by mountains, and had only one narrow street. The day Tian Jian was carried into the city, this street proved too narrow to accommodate his large sedan chair, and the people who'd come to welcome him were all forcibly squeezed together on the stone steps of the wooden storefronts or into the doorways and windows of the adjacent houses. The base of the mountains to the south formed the southern boundary of the city, and from both sides of the yamen gate, which stood forward from the wall directly addressing the north, ran a low dirt wall that sloped down to the Westward Flowing River, and the street which ran in parallel with the wall made a strange detour and doubled back to the river forming a horseshoe. Every yamen Tian Jian had seen before faced south, only this one at Zhuyang faced north. Was this why the first county magistrate mysteriously contracted scabies and left before his term was up, and the second magistrate, he, Tian Jian, had had such an easy time assuming his position? On one hand, Tian Jian felt this smooth transition to be odd, but on the other he rejoiced at his good luck.

Tian Jian stood at the entrance to the yamen and ran his eyes from one end of the foggy street to the other, the sloping hills stretching out endlessly before him. The small arched stone bridge at the eastern end of the street curved around like the crest of grey and white waves, and the houses adjacent to the street appeared foreshortened and shapeless like floating ethereal pavilions. Tian Jian sneezed loudly at the thick fog drifting around him which was so thick he couldn't see clearly the dogs he knew to be stalking in packs. Where did the fog come from? From the Westward Flowing River, or from the Valley of Ghosts behind the city and then up through the hidden caves below the small arched bridge? Tian Jian had served at his new post for ten fog-bound days, a fog that settled over the city at dawn and lay like a blanket over the day. It weighed on him and so he was surprised by the crippled attendant's reaction to the strange weather: "What a wonderful fog! Your Excellency's appointment will surely bring prosperity to the people of Zhuyang County." Tian Jian couldn't decide how the fog could be considered either wonderful or fortuitous, and flushed slightly at the compliment. The attendant explained that the people of the region believed that if it remained foggy for an entire day, or it rained continually, it was simply Heaven and earth locked in an act of love. On these auspicious occasions, the best course of action for the living was to imitate nature and frequently engage in sexual intercourse so the women would be impregnated with male heirs.

Tian Jian laughed at this explanation, and then sighed deeply. "The inhabitants of Zhuyang County satisfy their lust on this foggy day while I, the venerable county magistrate, sit chaste and alone in my large room!" Of course, Tian Jian couldn't say he had no family. He'd come to Zhuyang in the name of the true magistrate Yan Xiyun, and in the swampy region south of the Yangtze River was supposed to have a lovely wife whom he'd recently married. In fact, at noon that very day he had written a letter informing his "family" of his safe arrival, and had personally given the letter to the crippled attendant to hand to the postman. "His Excellency must miss his wife," the attendant had remarked in sympathy.

For a while, Tian Jian stood looking out into the fog, but eventually grew bored at being unable to see anything. He was about to return to the yamen when he thought he heard the voice of a man quite close by him: "Sister Wang, can you not move a little quicker?"

A woman's voice replied: "I can't go any faster. You know I have beautifully bound feet. Why can't you put me on the back of a donkey, that will quicken our pace?"

"What donkey are you talking about? If I had a donkey I'd be able to exchange it for a wife and wouldn't need your help now, would I?"

"All right. Carry me on your back then!"

Tian Jian listened to the sound of footsteps followed by heavier steps.

"I can't do this."

The woman giggled. "I knew you couldn't."

Tian Jian wondered how it was that a man and woman who were not married and apparently unrelated, could be out in the fog talking to each other so freely. Were they taking advantage of the early hour so they could be together alone unseen? Tian Jian peered down the street but could not see anyone, but then he lowered his head and just three steps away from him near the eastern end of the low decrepit wall, he discovered a pretty face which startled and sent a shiver through him. He guessed the woman had been walking along the far side of the wall and had carelessly stuck her head through a breach. He also supposed that once she became aware of him staring at her, she'd colour with embarrassment, quickly withdraw her head and flee; however, as he continued to observe her the woman didn't budge, and instead smiled at him whilst humming to herself.

Although Tian Jian was a man of mature years, he'd never really been involved with a woman. During his days as an outlaw his most cherished wish had been to find a woman somewhere in the wild and remote mountains. Once during hold-up, when he'd held up a small sedan chair, he had raised the silk curtain assuming he would get away with a large cache of gold, silver and jewels, and a beautiful woman had rolled out. The beauty had neither fainted from fright nor cursed in anger, just stared back with her two glowing almond-shaped eyes fixed upon him. Tian Jian had no idea what to do, and unable to bear those eyes, his only response had been to turn and run away. He was so unnerved that he had dropped all the booty in the process. His handsome sidekick had teased him about it: "How can you claim to be a famous outlaw if you're even afraid of a pretty lady like her."

Currently, Tian Jian was an official, with the impressive status of county magistrate, and there was no need for him to fear anyone, but the woman still made him uncomfortable. He coughed once, composed himself, and then looked directly into her eyes for the first time. "You..." Tian Jian abruptly stopped, not knowing what to say. He found himself thinking of asking whether the dew in the wild grass had dampened her tiny shoes and long belt; whether she wanted to comb again her glistening hair which she'd obviously pressed down with saliva outside the city, embarrassed about it not being neat; why she'd just plucked a rose from somebody's fence and put it in her hair; and who it was she wanted to be seen by to be adorned like this so early and in such thick fog. But Tian Jian didn't say any of these things. Although he had yet to conclude that certain of Zhuyang's customs were immoral and should be censured, he did know that as magistrate he should not permit this wanton practice of couples engaging in fervent love-making on foggy and rainy days to continue. The greatest responsibility of a county magistrate was to enlighten the people through education, to propagate the virtues of the imperial court and thereby transform dubious local social traditions into an acceptable morality, and honour filial sons and women who died protecting their chastity. Shouldn't a practice that offended public decency be eradicated and replaced by a better one? That was another question.

Finally the woman spoke: "Are you the honourable county magistrate?"

That one sentence again rendered Tian Jian speechless. Dumbfounded he looked at the woman who tried to make herself taller by putting one hand over another on the dilapidated wall and pulling herself up, but the top of the wall was in bad shape and wouldn't support her. After raising herself a little, she found she couldn't go any higher. "You *are* the honourable county magistrate. I saw you the day you arrived. Do you remember someone throwing a string for lighting firecrackers at you. That was me. I recognise you."

"Yes, I remember that."

The sedan chair carrying Tian Jian had entered the city through a narrow pass in the mountains. There were no houses there and all the people were pressed together on the ridge of a hill row upon row watching the excitement. Tian Jian had lifted aside the curtain of the sedan chair and looked out, but saw only column after column of feet. At that moment Zhuyang seemed more like a village than a city and its people filled him with delight. When they had reached the main part of the street where it was lined with storefronts, a woman had squeezed herself through the crowd, holding aloft in one hand a large red firecracker, and in the other a string she was using to light it. She'd bent herself over backwards and as her body shook with the strain, she made several unsuccessful attempts to light the string before eventually it caught. Those around her shouted: "Throw it up to the sky!" but all the woman managed to throw was the string, which fell on the honourable county magistrate, while the firecracker exploded in her hand. If this woman really was the one who let off the firecracker, Tian Jian had much sympathy for her. On the other hand, how could a decent woman dare show her face to the county magistrate in public? It was evident that the women found in this wild mountain district weren't as civilised as those beyond the mountain.

"You don't recognise me?" The woman seemed disappointed that Tian Jian did not respond. "But how foolish of me, how could Your Excellency still remember me?"

Tian Jian again heard the sound of feet and also a man's voice: "Who are you talking to, Sister Wang?"

The woman motioned for him to come to her saying, "Come quickly, come here. It's the honourable county magistrate." The next moment a shining bald head emerged through the breach in the wall, faced itself towards Tian Jian for an instant, then grunted and vanished. "Hey, what are you doing down there," the woman burst out giggling, "bowing to His Excellency, or bowing to the wall?"

"What kind of talk is that?" Tian Jian demanded.

The laughter abruptly ceased and the heads of the woman and man who had stopped bowing and raised himself back up to his full height, stopped moving and remained framed in the breach of the wall, their two faces a stark contrast of ugliness and beauty. Could a woman like the one before him be in love with an ugly man such as this? Tian Jian assumed a stern expression. "Who exactly are you? And what are the two of you doing out together at this hour?"

"Your Excellency, let me explain." The man knelt again, bending down so far that he could no longer see Tian Jian and was forced to stand back up. "We aren't thieves. And even though it's very foggy, we wouldn't dare come out here to fornicate. My name is Yan Geda, and this woman is Sister Wang. We are acquainted but we've never been out together before. You see, today is the third anniversary of my mother's death, and I am duty-bound to apologise to my mother for being so poor that I haven't been able to marry. I wanted to hold a proper memorial ceremony so her spirit could rest peacefully in Heaven, so I gave Sister Wang ten copper coins to return home with me, to pretend to be my wife and weep at my mother's grave. Sir, I never expected to run into you here."

"Is this true?"

"Why not? I've done almost every kind of job there is to do, except it's the first time I've been a mourner for someone." The woman raised her hands which, in keeping with her task, held a mourner's clothes and hat. "I'm not really his wife, see, I'm only pretending to be. Your Excellency, you must think I'm not from a good family."

Tian Jian almost cried out in the cold fog, touched to find such a filial son in this remote area; a filial son too poor even to marry. Tian Jian scrutinised himself; a decent county magistrate would not immediately suspect them of immoral sexual behaviour. He decided his mistaken assumption about their activities on this lush foggy day was due to nothing more than deep envy. His face brightened and in a softer tone he said to the woman, "Since you were invited to be a mourner, shouldn't you have mourned by the grave last night?"

"I did mourn last night. But I'm not his wife, and it wouldn't have been proper to sleep on his *kang*."

"Why were you laughing if you're on your way to mourn again today? And why have you made yourself up this way?"

"Does the honourable county magistrate also manage these affairs? I am in fact, not made up at all."

"I should tell you, Your Excellency, that Sister Wang is naturally very pretty."

Tian Jian wanted to say she ought to be punished for having such a beautiful face but these words never left his mouth. Instead he sighed deeply. "Your mourning for another person is well-intentioned. I only wonder how well you can act the role of a real mourner?"

"I won't deceive you, sir. I sell my laughter and tears to whoever has the money."

"Whose daughter or wife are you? Why do you earn your living this way?"

"I don't have any family and if I didn't make money this way, the people of Zhuyang City wouldn't let me live here. And I don't think anyone should criticise me for what I do. I cried sadly in the mourning hall because I sympathised with this man and wanted to earn my ten copper coins, but I also used his family's memorial hall to cry for my own problems. Why should I be blamed for being a drifter?"

"A drifter?"

"I'll explain what she means, sir. Of course, Your Excellency just arrived here and wouldn't know about this." From the man's general description of the situation, Tian Jian learned the drifters were people who'd fled from the area of Hunan Province, and that now there were quite a number of them in the area. Not being native to Zhuyang County and without ancestral roots there they couldn't live peacefully with the local people. After Zhuyang became a county, the conflict between the locals and the immigrants sharpened, resulting in fights and injuries, and in some cases, even death. The first magistrate supported the rights and interests of the local people and regarded the drifters as wild and violent thieves and robbers. He ultimately issued an order stating that drifters could neither settle down nor live in, the cities and towns on the plain. "You shouldn't hate or envy the city people, Sister Wang. It was the previous magistrate who issued the order," Yan Geda concluded.

"What kind of stupidity is that," Tian Jian said, visibly angered, and then cursed aloud.

The man knelt down again. "Yes, you're right. I'm sorry."

The woman fixed her eyes on Tian Jian whilst grabbing the man and pulling him up. "Stop being foolish. His Excellency wasn't talking about you."

Tian Jian hadn't cursed Yan Geda, but was concerned at his criticism of the previous magistrate in front of these common people, and the exposure of the brutal side of his character. Indeed, he'd always found it very difficult to control his hot temper. He took one more look at the woman, turned around and began to walk away. He had taken but a few steps when the woman spoke again: "Is Your Excellency's family name Yan?"

Tian Jian's real family name was Han, but as he was passing himself off as county magistrate Yan, naturally this was the name to which he was to answer. "You're really, Mr Yan?" Tian Jian's heart started to beat wildly. Had his outburst caused this woman to see through his feigned identity? "Everybody in Zhuyang is talking about the dream of the provincial counsellor. In his dream the emperor had just driven his chariot into the great hall of the palace when the ceiling of the southwest corner collapsed. The counsellor feared for the emperor's life until he saw that protecting the emperor from being crushed by the ceiling were a number of bags of salt. When the counsellor awoke from the dream he remembered that the southwest corner of the main hall faced in the direction of Zhuyang County, and quickly searched for a man named Yan* to be county magistrate. Is this true, Your Excellency?"

This was the first time Tian Jian had heard this story and it made him think of his own extraordinary history and events that had led him to Zhuyang. Since the tale was apparently becoming popular among the people, he was eager to live up to all expectations associated with the name Yan and perform some great deed himself. But since his real name wasn't Yan for a moment he didn't know how to respond. He just laughed nervously, turned around and again started back to the yamen.

"Your Excellency, Your Excellency...." the woman cried.

The man apparently thought she should stop talking for he tried to restrain her. "Sister Wang, you talk too much. Haven't you said enough?"

"Oh, but his excellency is wonderful! I thought he would be older, but now I see he's quite young and still without a long beard." And then suddenly she stopped talking as if someone had put their hand over her mouth.

"Hey, stop biting my hand," the man shouted.

Back at the yamen, Tian Jian was once again

---

*The name Yan is homophonic for the Chinese word for salt.

greeted by deliveries of gifts of wine, musk and honey from wealthy families in the area. He decided it was time to call a halt to the practice and ordered the doorkeeper not to allow in anyone else bringing gifts. He'd been serving as county magistrate for more than ten days and saw no need for further congratulations. "However, if he's really rich and wants to bribe me, I..." Tian Jian got half way through blurting out this sentence to the crippled attendant before he caught himself and said no more, waving the attendant away with his hand. "Years ago when I was starved for money, no one would give me a penny, and now I have money they all take turns showering me with gifts! If you only knew about my nocturnal talents you wouldn't still be bringing me gifts," he mused to himself. And acting on this stimulating thought, and with little effort, Tian Jian leapt gracefully into the air, floated up and landed with ease at the top of a flight of steps. The attendant was startled to such a degree that his tongue stuck straight out. This demonstration of upright modesty convinced the yamen attendants that the honourable county magistrate had passed the highest imperial examinations and had been recommended and promoted to Zhuyang by the provincial governor himself. He was definitely an impressive and dignified official, not at all like the former county magistrate who'd bought his appointment and had come to Zhuyang County to make money. Tian Jian often sat at the stone table in the rear garden of the yamen drinking tea with the assistant magistrate, the county commander and the procurator, while the attendants stood at a distance with their hands at their sides. This time when the preparation of the tea was complete,

Tian Jian called for the attendants to join the gathering of officials. The attendants were greatly flattered by the invitation and rushed over; however, the officials were displeased and admonished them: "His Excellency has generously offered you a gift of tea. How can you run over here with your clothes hanging out everywhere?"

Tian Jian, himself no lover of overly refined men, spoke up for the attendants. On this occasion he wanted to find out what they knew about the local affairs of Zhuyang. "Pay attention to what they have to say," he announced to all present.

The clerks had not been party to the officials' prior discussion, so they just drank their tea, politely answered Tian Jian's questions, then withdrew to their former positions. Tian Jian then took up the subject of the drifters again with the officials. On several occasions, he had informed them that he intended to rescind the order prohibiting the drifters from settling down and living in the cities on the plain. Now, just as on each occasion, the assistant magistrate and county commander both shook their heads. The conflict between the local people and the drifters had a long history, they said, and though Zhuyang was but recently established, it differed from other counties in regard of its strategic location, its arduous working conditions, and its truculent inhabitants. If the counties were divided into those with minor problems, those with routine problems, those with significant problems, and those with the worst possible problems, Zhuyang would certainly qualify as one of the latter; if not, why would the county magistrate's salary be 1,600 taels of silver, five hundred taels more than that received by magistrates of other counties? Most of the drifters in

Zhuyang County were wanted criminals or impoverished refugees who banded together in groups for illegal purposes. They were generally regarded as defiant in disposition and as often engaging in immoral behaviour. The other officials present were of the opinion that since it was the previous county magistrate who had imposed the ban, it might not be such a good idea to reverse his policy.

Although Tian Jian wasn't persuaded by their arguments, still the image of Sister Wang flashed to his mind, and he wondered if all drifters were disruptive to the point of being almost ungovernable. Certainly such a disposition would explain why Sister Wang was more brazen than the average woman. Or was that a consequence of her own particular circumstances in life? Women who were fortunate enough to be brought up in wealthy and prestigious families and who never had to deal with the world directly had the luxury of appearing pure untarnished and innocent. Sister Wang had nothing in common with these women. How could Tian Jian not feel sympathy for a woman whose circumstances were so unfortunate that she was forced to sell her smiles and tears for a living? Indeed he himself had made his way in life as an outlaw. For that he had robbed and killed, but did that necessarily mean he was born with the propensity to rob and kill? Or was it just down to circumstances from which he could not flee until...

With this in mind, the county magistrate explained his position on the drifters' situation. Since the mountains and forests of Zhuyang County were abundant with drifters, it was unreasonable to think that they could eliminate the conflicts with the local people by prohibiting the drifters from settling down in the cities and towns on the plain. In this way, the mountains and forests naturally became dangerous, inhospitable places. If they kept the drifters bottled up there in order just to stay alive they'd be forced to become highwaymen, to rob and loot, or to engage in other criminal activities. This would only worsen the conflicts with the local people and further impair social order. Another point to consider was that in Zhuyang County the local people lived in sparsely populated areas where limited young blood led to much intermarrying which resulted in a profusion of dwarfs and idiots. Prohibiting marriages between locals and drifters would only perpetuate this problem, and inevitably find the local people unable to produce healthy and vigorous children. For the time being, there was no need for a ban against drifters in Zhuyang. What the county did need was a large and capable work force. "Even if the drifters are driven out to the mountains and forests, many of them would still survive because by nature they're a tough people," Tian Jian explained. "It's obvious that not all of them can be shiftless good-for-nothings. For example, the one who makes it her job to mourn for others...." This last point obviously took the other officials by surprise and Tian Jian stopped talking for a minute.

The county commander took the opportunity to ask: "Your Excellency has met Sister Wang?"

"One day I heard her crying outside the yamen gate. She seemed terribly upset but the man she was with told me that she wasn't his real wife but someone he'd hired as a mourner."

"I suspected that sooner or later that impudent

woman would try to present herself to Your Excellency," said the county commander.

Apparently, the assistant magistrate thought the county commander had spoken too sharply, and tugged at his gown as a warning, which Tian Jian noticed but ignored.

"What do you mean by impudent?"

"How could a decent woman pretend to be someone's wife and act sincerely as a mourner? If Zhuyang were the provincial capital she'd be working in a whorehouse!"

"The man was so poor he couldn't afford a wife," Tian Jian offered as defence. "Hiring someone to mourn was an act of filial piety. What was wrong with Sister Wang helping a filial son?"

The assistant magistrate appeared to be persuaded by this. "You're right, you're right. And the woman is quite beautiful. It's just a shame her nature doesn't live up to her beauty."

"Doesn't that bring us exactly back to what I was saying: a ban forcing people to live on the fringe of society is harmful?"

The county commander lowered his head and began fiddling with a bronze coin he'd taken out of his pocket. He couldn't directly show his disapproval so he cocked his head up towards the sky. "Are there no birds in the garden today?" Just then a cuckoo flew out of a clove tree on the left side of the courtyard. The county commander raised his arm and threw the coin at it, but neither hit the cuckoo nor frightened it away.

The assistant magistrate watched as Tian Jian stood up, sat down, and began to laugh. Then he focused on the bird. "It's hot today. The cuckoo's flight is surely a sign of rain," he said.

"All that squawking is a nuisance," Tian Jian complained and threw his teacup in the direction of the clove tree. The cuckoo fell without a sound, and the teacup smashed against the wall behind the tree.

The county commander's mouth dropped open in amazement, his face reddened like a glowing charcoal and several beads of sweat formed on the bridge of his nose. "It's hot today, Your Excellency," the assistant magistrate hurriedly said to him. "Let us loosen our robes. I think the county magistrate will not fault us for relaxing the regulations on this occasion."

"Absolutely!" came the reply and Tian Jian took the lead in loosening his robe, exposing the small piece of peachwood hanging from his chest as he did so.

"Your Excellency, how is it that someone in your position still carries around that kind of charm? Did your wife make it for you?"

"A teacher gave it to me. When I was young I studied martial arts from him, but he obviously didn't think I had much ability for he told me to go learn to read instead. I think he was afraid that I would never accomplish anything and gave me the club to remind me that I'd failed at martial arts."

"How can you say that, Your Excellency? The expert throw we just witnessed was not made by someone lacking in martial arts training. Zhuyang County is very fortunate to have for its magistrate a man who's master of both the pen and the sword. Your Excellency, your idea about rescinding the ban on the drifters is not without merit, and I support it. What is the opinion of the honourable county commander?"

"Rescind it."

"Fine. Since you both agree, I'll have it announced." Tian Jian asked the attendants to prepare a banquet table, ordered a special dish of stewed wild pigeon to go with the wine, then received the group of officials in the yamen to dine. The assistant magistrate and the county commander remained sober, but Tian Jian fell down dead drunk and had to be carried back to his bedroom on the back of the crippled attendant.

Tian Jian was so drunk, he didn't wake up until the following day, and when he did finally come to, he found the crippled attendant cleaning up the mess he'd vomited in his stupor. Tian Jian was immediately fearful that during the evening he'd blurted out something he shouldn't have and cajoled the attendant to recall all he'd said. The attendant told him he'd cried for a while, then laughed, but had said nothing at all. Tian Jian was relieved but realised he'd all too quickly forgotten his partner's warning about drinking too much. He rewarded the attendant with a bamboo fan tied around with a jade pendant, one of the many welcoming gifts he'd received, then gave him instructions for the future: "From now on, my limit is three cups. If I start on a fourth, I want you to give me a stern look."

"I couldn't presume to do that."

"If I tell you to give me a stern look, you do it. I'm here to govern the county, not to get drunk."

"There's no need to be so cautious, Your Excellency. The former county magistrate often got drunk."

Tian Jian was disappointed. "I would ask you not to compare me to other people. I am an official, but you're older than me and I trust you and that's why I want you to help me. Can you do that for me?"

The attendant knelt quickly before him, quite moved to tears, and from then on was totally devoted to Tian Jian, and in turn, Tian Jian, with the attendant's help, cut down his drinking.

As soon as he had rescinded the ban on drifters, Tian Jian rode out on his donkey, accompanied by a group of attendants, on a tour of the towns and villages in Zhuyang County. The county was made up of sixty percent mountain, thirty percent farmland and ten percent water. Most of the land was arid and Tian Jian had come up with the idea of constructing a large irrigation canal that would encompass the entire plain, which he wanted to consult the people about. Everyone welcomed the idea enthusiastically, but many were concerned that the relatively small and dispersed population living on the rather large area of land would be unable to complete the project in a reasonable period of time. There was further uncertainty as to whether the county magistrate could raise the necessary funds.

When Tian Jian returned to the yamen, he ordered a clerk to calculate the reserves in the county's coffers and found there was hardly any money to spare for the project. The most pressing question was how to raise the capital for the hard labour that would be required. That night, Tian Jian again turned to wine to escape his worries, but just as he picked up the fourth cup, the crippled attendant gave him an angry stare and he put it down.

"If Your Excellency wants something to drink, may I suggest some tea? If Your Excellency tries the tea from Sister Wang's teahouse, I'm sure you'll find it more satisfying than alcohol."

"Sister Wang? Would this be Sister Wang the professional mourner?"

"Yes, that's her, Sister Wang the drifter. After your excellency removed the ban on drifters she bought a two-story storefront on the left side of East Rock Bridge and opened a teahouse. Shall I visit her shop and have her bring over some jasmine tea for Your Excellency?"

Tian Jian could well recall that foggy morning scene. Sister Wang was quite astute in so promptly opening a teahouse and serving tea that had so soon established for her a well-praised reputation. As the attendant was about to leave, Tian Jian suddenly cried out: "I've got it! That's it!"

"What exactly is Your Excellency referring to?"

"Not all drifters are as adept at business as Sister Wang obviously is. There's plenty of land on the plain but not many people, so why not draft labour according to how many hectares of land each family owns? Those who can't do physical work will be allowed to sell part of their land, thus raising capital for building the canal, and the drifters can do the work. Those who work can then earn themselves a piece of land and will have an incentive to live in peace. Won't that kill two birds with one stone?"

"Your Excellency is truly a brilliant leader. Please let me send for Sister Wang before it gets too late and Your Excellency is left thirsting."

"I don't need to drink now." Excited Tian Jian stood up and zealously explained to the attendant that with this plan within a few years everyone in Zhuyang County would have a plot of land, and that the land would be productive even in times of drought or flooding. The men would till the fields and the women would sew, and a time of peace and prosperity would prevail. And then he paused: "Tell me something. Do you think that only an official who has passed the highest imperial examination can produce such ideas?"

"Of course sir, you're capable of doing amazing things."

"But what if I hadn't passed the highest imperial examinations?"

"Ah..."

"Then my idea wouldn't be any good?" Before the attendant could reply Tian Jian answered: "Not at all. Do you think only those who pass the highest imperial examinations are capable of great accomplishments? Even reformed criminals can make outstanding contributions and accomplish difficult tasks."

The attendant was completely baffled and didn't know what to say. But Tian Jian continued: "And since I have passed the highest imperial examinations, I ought to make even greater contributions and accomplish even more difficult tasks!"

Tian Jian hadn't expected the drifters to give him so much trouble after the ban on them was lifted. The first people to come down from the mountains and forests and settle on the plain on the banks of the Westward Flowing River worked very hard at cultivating the rocky sand-dunes and terraced fields. A number of those who followed later and found there was no land left to till, opened stalls or shops in the cities and towns where they sold bamboo, raw lacquer, medicinal herbs and coffins. However a large number descended on Zhuyang City where they loitered around doing nothing, which led to daily complaints of swindling, theft and robbery. The county commander was responsible for handling these cases, but all he did was report them to Tian Jian who became certain that the commander was shirking his duties because he had opposed the lifting of the ban from the outset. In the yamen, Tian Jian complained about his actions to the assistant magistrate. "If the county commander won't do what he's supposed to do, Zhuyang County can do without him. Years ago in..." Tian Jian was about to describe his years in the mountains and forests when no one in his band would dare challenge his orders, and anyone who tried to was driven away with one clap of his hand. He stopped himself. He felt dizzy and his head ached, and again the image of the white wolf appeared before him. Lapsed into silence, he stood next to the assistant magistrate, panting as if he was having trouble breathing.

Unsure of what Tian Jian would say next, the assistant magistrate quickly ushered all the attendants out of the room. "It's probably best if Your Excellency were not to say such things in the presence of others. Even though Your Excellency is the county magistrate and can promote and demote as you choose, it is still not advisable to offend the county commander."

"I may not be able to do anything about him myself, but I can still report him to the prefectural government and have them get rid of him!"

"His Excellency is probably unacquainted with the reason why the former county magistrate left before serving his full term. Officially it was because he was ill, but his inability to get along with the county commander was a significant factor. You see the county commander is the younger cousin of the prefectural magistrate's wife." When Tian Jian made no reply, the assistant magistrate continued less forcefully: "Sir, forgive me for speaking so directly, however I'm sure Your Excellency is aware from serving as an official for many years that this is how the world of bureaucracy operates."

His speech over, the assistant magistrate's beady coal-black eyes avoided Tian Jian's hard gaze. Tian Jian laughed coldly: "So this is really the world of bureaucracy?" He then span around and spat a thick ball of phlegm which swept along the surface of the table before spraying the office's red-lacquered pillar. The assistant magistrate was shocked and quickly took off his shoe which he used to rub the phlegm off the pillar. "Sir, I know you're angry, but I should perhaps point out that while your not paying attention to matters of form may be all right elsewhere, in this small county the people who work in the yamen are snobbish and arrogant. If they should see you acting this way, they'll spread rumours which will cause far more trouble."

"To hell with them!" Tian Jian blurted out in anger, but as soon as the words left his mouth, his face reddened and unconsciously he dropped the bare foot that had been stretched out on a chair and slid it back into his shoe.

Thereafter, Tian Jian paid more attention to his personal decorum which included a daily routine of washing his face, cleaning his teeth and dressing very neatly. Since his "wife" wasn't present and his parents weren't alive, he ate simple meals of unpolished rice with a bowl of cabbage and bean curd soup and, seated at the square dining table, he forced himself to chew his food as carefully and slowly as he could without making a sound. The magistrate's solemn and dignified appearance was well noted by the attendants both inside and outside the yamen, and had the effect of discouraging them from shirking their responsibilities. Tian Jian realised from the assistant magistrate's display of frankness that he was a shrewd and seasoned man, and regularly relied on his advice when he left the yamen on business. However he repeatedly refused the assistant magistrate's suggestion to visit the county commander who had kept himself home — feigning illness Tian Jian suspected — until one day, having finally run out of excuses, he got on his donkey and made the trip.

The county commander's family was one of the most wealthy and influential in the area, and his family insignia was inscribed all over the alley leading to his house. During the first meal Tian Jian ate with them, he counted ten servants in attendance upon them. As they ate, the county commander's mother sat glancing at lists of the family's tenants complaining that one family in the Western Village was short two bushels of millet due as rent. When she demanded someone make a thorough investigation of the matter, at least seven or eight more servants standing outside the dining room promptly volunteered to take care of it.

The county commander's home was very impressive, vastly more impressive than the county yamen, and Tian Jian and his donkey seemed doubly meagre by comparison. When the county commander first received Tian Jian, he'd sat him down in the drawing-room at an old-fashioned square dining table for eight, inlaid with jadestone. The inlaid portion wasn't particularly large, but when two husky servants tried to move the table, they were unable to lift it. At first, Tian Jian was surprised, but it didn't take him long to reason that the table was not all it seemed and that it probably contained a secret compartment chiselled out under the jadestone which concealed a number of gold bars. At that moment, Tian Jian felt a pang of regret at being the county magistrate, swearing that if he wasn't, the county commander wouldn't have a gold bar to his name come the following morning.

When Tian Jian left the county commander's house and made his way back along the street, many people recognised him. The more timid quickly ran back to their stores and peeped through doorways or the slits in their windows for a look at him. The more bold stopped and smiled at him as they politely waited for his donkey to brush by them, so closely they could smell it. Some even knelt in front of the donkey and cried out, "I wish His Excellency well." Tian Jian responded with a wave of his hand and moved on slowly. As he rode back to the yamen, all at once he noticed a man scurrying out of an alley with a woman in hot pursuit. The man was completely dishevelled, having already lost one shoe in his flight, and held a steamed bun in each hand which he was gulping down. After nearly colliding with Tian Jian's donkey, he stopped, turned back to face the woman pursuing him and spat on the bun.

The woman came to an abrupt halt and yelled out: "You'll get yours, you thief. If you try and come up the mountain for wood, you'll get thrown down so hard your head will splatter blood like a slaughtered goat's. And don't think you can go down to the river to draw water because if you do you'll be drowned or at the very least cut to pieces. Your family is rotten to the core, and if you ever have children I'm sure they'll be about as pleasant as shit!"

This was too much for Tian Jian. "What kind of foul woman is making such a racket?" he thundered down at her.

At that instant the man and the woman realised who was sitting on the donkey. The woman immediately kowtowed mumbling: "Your Excellency, I want to report that this good-for-nothing is a thief. I hadn't taken one bite out of the bun I bought when this villain grabbed it from me. These damn drifters are all over the city. There are hundreds crowded around the food shelter at the Eastern Gate Transformation Temple, and they're all robbers and thieves."

"Yes, yes," Tian Jian replied. "I know all about that. But as far as the matter in hand is concerned, I have decided to let the thief eat the bun. Is this enough to pay for it?" Tian Jian took a copper coin from his breast pocket, dropped it into her hand and then turned to the man. "The bun is yours, go ahead and eat it." The man wolfed it down straightening his neck as he swallowed it, and when he'd finished he looked up at Tian Jian from eyeballs that were more white than black.

"Are you full?" Tian Jian asked.

"No."

"Then come with me." Tian Jian gee'd up the donkey and rode off glancing at the shops on both sides of the street until he found one he wanted where he dismounted at the doorway. Someone had apparently used a bowl as a template to paint fourteen circles on the vermillion vertical scrolls hung on the doorposts. Tian Jian laughed as he shouted: "Shopkeeper, how about bringing us five steamed buns?"

The shop was rather small. Inside a total of five men were sitting and eating at four tables. When they saw the county magistrate enter, they quickly wiped their mouths and left, while the people on the street outside gathered on the steps to see what was going on. The main room had a side door that opened onto a rear courtyard where another group of men were sprawled around napping on straw beds. The people outside in the street continued to peep into the shop, and some of those in the courtyard, disturbed by the commotion, looked in through the side door. Tian Jian paid no attention and called out to the shopkeeper again: "Shopkeeper, let's have those steamed buns right away." In response, a woman pushed the curtain next to the counter aside, and walked out fixing her hair as she went. "Who is it that's so impatient? These buns have to be steamed until they're hot. And, what kind of glutton wants to eat five?" When the woman raised her head and saw who was standing in front of her, she let out a sharp cry, her hands instinctively raised in alarm causing her heap of heavy black hair to cascade down her back like a waterfall. "Oh, how can this be," she wailed. "Only if the sun rose in the west would I expect the honourable county magistrate to come to my humble inn to eat."

Tian Jian now recognised Sister Wang, whom he'd encountered that foggy morning as the woman standing before him, and immediately felt very ill at ease. He got up to leave, but thinking that this might be rude he just stood there in great confusion. Meanwhile Sister Wang bowed to one side with her hands folded and paid her respects. This attractive woman then leaned toward him with one leg slightly bent, the other raised with the small foot curled up and just touching the ground and said, "His excellency's presence in her shop, makes Sister Wang feel very important." The flower apron tied around her pink cheongsam accentuated her shapely body.

The crippled attendant had already told Tian Jian that Sister Wang had opened a teahouse, and now it was evident she also served food. "Does Sister Wang do odd jobs here also?"

"Fortunately for me, His Excellency abolished the ban on drifters and I was able to buy this two storey shop. I began by selling tea, but that didn't bring in enough money so now I also serve meals and provide a laundry service. Even though my business is modestly successful, the place is a mess and so dirty it must surely offend His Excellency."

Tian Jian, however, was very happy with what she'd done, and asked the cost of running the shop, and the number of drifters who were running eateries and inns as she was doing. Sister Wang answered each of his questions in turn, telling him the names of all the shops and shop owners along the street, and went into so much detail that he even learned whose family had one dog and three chickens, and which had roosters and which hens. "Oh, I've been talking so much I forgot to attend to the buns. Surely His Excellency has not tired of shark's fin and bird's nest soup at the yamen? Or is that why he has come in search of something new to eat steamed buns like us common people?"

"They're not for me. Give them to him."

The man Tian Jian had brought with him laughed scornfully.

Sister Wang frowned at his presence. "This is the kind of loafer that gives us drifters a bad name. He's been free-loading here for the past few days, so I had him go up to the mountains and chop wood. This he did, but then he spent all the money he made on alcohol, drank himself half dead and fell down flat on the steps outside the door where he slept the whole night. I had to use a rolling pin to wake him up." As she talked, she pulled at the man's trousers, exposing a hole where the flesh could be seen. "Just look at him. Maybe having a little money and some clothes is enough to get by on, but he has no more ambition than to pour wine down his throat. I'm surprised he doesn't drown in it. And you still want to give him these buns?"

"This time let him eat. If he stuffs himself to death that'll be the end of it, and if he doesn't he's going to chop firewood every day and save what he earns to buy some land, put up a house and settle down and raise a family. If I ever run into him again in the city drinking or stealing from anybody, I'll put him in jail and let him rot!"

The man shook violently, and Sister Wang put her hands on his head: "You're not even going to thank His Excellency?" The man kowtowed three times and Sister Wang shoved the five buns into his hands. "Since his excellency is not eating, may I offer him some tea?" She brushed off the table with a towel, went inside and came back carrying a bowl of strong tea. As Tian Jian reached out his hand for the tea a tiny bug flew in from outside and landed on a green wooden comb Sister Wang had set in her hair. Just a minute ago when she had recognised the county magistrate her hair had fallen into disarray. When did she have time to put it up in a bun and adorn it with a green comb?

Tian Jian drank a mouthful of tea, savouring its taste, and when he looked at her again he noticed the bug had folded its wings and that its red oval shell had seven small black dots on top. That the bug landed on the wooden comb rather than on her hair or clothes was a fortuitous omen and led Tian Jian to focus more directly on Sister Wang who momentarily appeared as a tantalising green-leafed flower.

Tian Jian stiffened with excitement and felt a dreamlike confusion take hold of him. He'd seen a number of women in his life, both beautiful and ugly, but he'd never seen one quite as beautiful and alluring as Sister Wang. What was it that gave her this provocative allure? The bug flew away, its tiny wings fluttering rapidly as it made three circles in the air, like some unreal visionary image, before dropping down to perch on the tip of Tian Jian's nose. For a moment, Tian Jian felt numb. He thought about extending his tongue and licking it off but his tongue wouldn't move. Sister Wang giggled with delight. Tian Jian sensed that both the group of people behind the side door and those in the doorway appreciated his embarrassment and were laughing silently with her. He coughed once, trying to conceal his discomfort as best he could and regain his official demeanour. The bug finally dropped into the bowl of tea. Tian Jian quickly stuck his finger in to pull it out, but the bug had already been scalded to death. Tian Jian was sorry to see the bug die and refused the second bowl of tea Sister Wang offered. Looking once more at the man, who'd already eaten three of the buns, he asked: "Where is the tea from?"

"This is tea we drifters grow in the reeds and gullies. It's not well-known at all."

"I like its taste."

"If His Excellency doesn't dislike it, perhaps he'll consider coming back for more."

Tian Jian laughed, told her to mark down what he owed for the five buns and present a chit at the yamen for the amount, and then got up to leave.

"Should I really bother His Excellency for money for five buns? I'm surprised and grateful that his excellency has visited my shop, and since he's here I'd like to ask if he'd do me the honour of writing in the circles on the doorposts. I can't write clearly myself. I drew circles with a bowl."

Tian Jian's reading had improved, but he still couldn't write well enough to complete a couplet. "Drawing circles with a bowl is just fine. What would a restaurant be without bowls? If only we had a bowl of food for each drifter who comes to Zhuyang City then this county magistrate will have accomplished all he intended."

Sister Wang called out in the direction of the side door: "Wu Sheng, Gao Yun, San Zhuzi, did you hear what His Excellency said? His Excellency wants to give you all an opportunity to make a living, and still you don't come out and pay your respects?"

The faces peeping in through the side door shrank back in unison when they heard Sister Wang's voice.

Several others pushed forward and took their places and three or four even stepped beyond the threshold of the door, but when those behind tried to push them forward they too shrank back.

"Do these people live at the shop?" Tian Jian asked.

"I don't have extra rooms for guests," Sister Wang replied. "They're all unemployed with no place to go. I have some extra space in the rear courtyard and let them spend the night there. During the day they go out and try to get food in whatever way they can. The ones who stay here are beggars who don't even do that much and just lie around in a daze. Come in. Come in. His Excellency is an official, not a tiger. Are you afraid he'll eat you? In future if you're hungry go to the yamen and the county magistrate will feed you. I don't have any more to waste on you."

No one dared enter the shop, so Tian Jian approached the side door and immediately all the people standing in the courtyard knelt down and kowtowed. Without saying a word, Tian Jian walked over to the counter, took down the blackboard and on it wrote: "County magistrate: 40 steamed buns." "Sister Wang, are thirty-five buns enough for seven people?" he enquired. "I know you'll come to the yamen to collect the money for forty buns. Are there a lot more people like this?"

"Yes, many."

"Let me suggest this. Have someone list all their names and ages and bring the list to me at the yamen. We'll think of a way to have them work for a living."

"Good idea. Everybody says that because His Excellency was the one in the dream who helped the emperor support the collapsing ceiling with the salt bags, he should be called 'the virtuous Lord Salt', just like the great judge Bao was named 'the virtuous Lord Bao'.'' Sister Wang escorted Tian Jian to the street where he remounted his donkey, assumed a stern expression and rode away without turning back. From a distance, he could still hear Sister Wang talking with the drifters:

"Was that really the honourable county magistrate? Why would he visit your shop?"

"Are you suggesting His Excellency is a fake?"

"Sister Wang, you dagger mouth! His Excellency was here and you didn't let me see him?"

"Do you want to kowtow to his excellency? His excellency sat on that chair, go ahead and kowtow to the chair."

"I wanted to bring a complaint to His Excellency. My family's three chickens have been stolen and I know it was a drifter who did it."

"Don't blame the drifters for everything. There's good shit and bad shit. What hillside doesn't have crooked trees? Yesterday at the market there were so many people crowded into the intersection of the street I couldn't move. All of a sudden I felt a hand creeping across my chest and figured it was some creep trying to grope me. I had never seen him before and after touching me for a few seconds he went away. At first, I didn't think too much about it: everyone knows a widow is no virgin. Then after I finally managed to squeeze out of the crowd to buy some spice for smoking meat, when I reached inside my shirt for my purse, I found it was gone. The jerk hadn't been groping me at all, he'd stolen my purse!''

Tian Jian calculated that he could employ approximately six hundred drifters for the project, and with that in mind formally announced the building of a canal across the plain. As expected, many families on the plain who lacked the man power agreed to sell a piece of their land to the government in lieu of labour, and the government then distributed the land among the drifters. Tian Jian himself travelled out to the villages and towns persuading the drifters to settle down and live on the land they were given. Then he assembled and organised them into a labour force and apportioned the construction work. Each village community was responsible for a particular section of the work and elected one person to lead its work brigade. These people were answerable to the canal supervisor who had overall responsibility. An auspicious day was chosen and a banquet arranged at the yamen at which Tian Jian personally toasted the canal supervisor who'd previously served as the yamen official in charge of the grain supply. The new supervisor was inspired by the grand inauguration ceremony and pledged in writing that if the canal wasn't completed in three months they could have his head. For his part, Tian Jian promised that if the supervisor was successful he'd award him three hundred taels of silver and have a stone tablet erected in his honour.

Although the granary supervisor was well-intentioned, he lacked the experience required for the strenuous work. Many of the drifters had become accustomed to living by their wits not work-skills, and soon started sloping off when the food supply wasn't as plentiful as they had expected. Although the canal was completed in three months, water had only run halfway along its length when a number of embankments collapsed. As soon as he heard the news, Tian Jian ordered the canal supervisor to come and see him. A short while later, instead of the man, he was presented with a bag containing a bloodied head which the supervisor, before his death, had directed an assistant to bring to Tian Jian. Tian Jian couldn't bear to look at the head; it reminded him of his partner's death on the banks of the Westward Flowing River and he burst into tears.

The county commander claimed that Tian Jian had chosen the wrong person for the job and that only his own men could control the lazy and cunning drifters. It was his suggestion that one of his outstanding subordinates from Xifeng Village in the western part of the county be appointed canal supervisor. Three months later, the northern section of the canal still hadn't been completed, and one third of the work force had come down with dysentery. An investigation revealed that the second canal supervisor had embezzled thirty percent of the funds collected from the villages, and that all the wheat set aside for food had been exchanged for corn, a portion of which was mildewed. Tian Jian was furious and immediately sentenced the canal supervisor to death, but not satisfied by this, he ordered the man flayed and had his skin stretched on a drum and hung on the city gate as a warning. The wind breathed on the surface of the drum for seven days and nights making an awful racket and frightening every one in the city. Debate raged about how the usually refined county magistrate could have been so cruel.

Tian Jian was determined that the canal be built, and cursed anyone who advised him to give the project up. Nevertheless, there were no volunteers to step into the supervisor's shoes, and no one responded to the notices he posted asking for candidates. Tian Jian became more and more impatient, he slept poorly at night frequently tossing and turning, and his dreams were constantly plagued by a bright white light which contained the eyes of the white wolf. One night, rising from his broken sleep, he lit a lamp and covered the only window in the darkened room with a sheet. When he returned to sleep, the image of the white wolf lying motionless on the riverbank again appeared in a dream. "Have I been too cruel? Should I really give up the canal? But if it is not built, how can the people of Zhuyang County prosper? How will the drifters be able to earn a living? And what notable achievements will I be able to claim as county magistrate? Perhaps I have acted too cruelly, but I swear if I didn't hold my office, I'd cut the county commander in half. Was his recommendation of that incompetent supervisor intended to wreck the project and make me look bad?" Tian Jian was constantly embroiled in these concerns, and regularly awoke in the middle of the night and dressed in his official uniform. He became aware that he felt his entire body itching, an itch that became more and more aggravating as time went on. One night after removing his uniform he discovered that the seams were infested with lice. This was very strange. He'd roamed the mountains and forests for years, eaten anything that was available and slept wherever he could, and never found a single louse on the one blue shirt he always wore. How was it possible that now when he regularly took hot baths in his nice tiled bathroom and wore such a splendid official uniform, that his uniform was lice ridden? Tian Jian ordered his uniform to be cleaned frequently, but this had no effect, for as soon as he put the uniform on it again began to itch. One day the crippled attendant observed: "This is odd. Why are there no lice in His Excellency's regular clothes? Can it be the lice also want to be infused with His Excellency's illustrious official spirit?"

Tian Jian laughed: "They just want to suck my blood."

"Sir, Sister Wang's shop also provides a laundry service. I hear she soaks the clothes in boiling water infused with chinaberry seeds, and then rice broth to make them soft. Perhaps this method will kill the lice. Shall we let her try cleaning your uniform?"

"That's a fine idea. I told her to come to the yamen to collect money for the forty steamed buns I bought, but so far she has not appeared. Why don't you take the money and at the same time have her clean my uniform."

The next day the attendant brought back the immaculately cleaned uniform and Tian Jian remained itch-free for a significant period of time. Ten days later, however, the lice reappeared, and the attendant fixed a regular time with Sister Wang to come and pick up the uniform.

One cold day after Tian Jian had finished adjudicating a case, he and the assistant magistrate discussed the lack of response to notices pasted for the canal supervisor job but came to no conclusion about what to do. Somewhat depressed, Tian Jian returned to his bedroom in the rear courtyard. After he'd lit a lamp and heated up a brazier of charcoal, the crippled attendant came in and announced that Sister Wang had brought over the uniform and was waiting outside the door. Tian Jian lowered his head and under the door curtain, saw the tip of a red shoe. Quickly straightening his lapels and sitting up stiffly, he said, "Have her come in."

Sister Wang walked in looking quite self-assured and paid her respects to Tian Jian. But after taking the seat he offered her, crossing her legs and glancing around the room, she sat still without making a sound as if ill at ease. A cricket began chirping on the wall behind her chair.

"Is Sister Wang uncomfortable?" the attendant asked.

"Sir, if you go to burn incense at the Transformation Temple, do you act as freely as you do at home?"

The attendant laughed and withdrew from the room, leaving the two of them alone and uncertain about what to do next. The cricket began chirping again.

"There are even crickets in the yamen?"

"Yes, the yamen has its crickets," Tian Jian replied laughing, amused at his comment.

Sister Wang still seemed uneasy. She stood up and went over to the lamp, then took a pin out of her hair and pulled the wick of the lamp to increase the light. "Does my coming here at this late hour reflect badly on me?" she ventured. "There are so many customers at my shop, eating, and drinking tea during the day that I can't get away. I had planned to come tomorrow but was worried that Your Excellency might be hearing cases then and would need his uniform."

"Thank you for your prompt service, Sister Wang." Tian Jian opened the bamboo basket she'd brought, took out the neatly folded and well-starched uniform, and noticed a package of tea at the bottom of the basket. "You also brought tea?"

"That was no trouble at all."

"Thank you. Since it now belongs to me, let me make a pot and we can drink it together." Tian Jian took out a kettle and had the attendant fill it with water. Sister Wang wanted to do it, but Tian Jian insisted she stay where she was. When the attendant rushed forward to take the pot, she requested him go to the well for fresh water. When he returned, he put the kettle on the brazier and Sister Wang who insisted on keeping an eye on the kettle, moved her chair closer to the brazier.

As the two of them sat together in silence, Sister Wang raised her head once and caught Tian Jian peeping at her and laughed to herself. Tian Jian had already witnessed her loud giggling laughter, the kind that engulfed her entire body and made it shake, but the silent laughter was something new, and drew his eyes to her more intently. Sister Wang had large cheekbones set half way down her face, giving it a round, plate-like smoothness. When she laughed small wrinkles appeared at the corners of her lips, and her two small dots for eyes were well matched and radiated a Buddha-like benevolence.

"Did Sister Wang use chinaberry seed water to starch my uniform? I am able to wear it for ten days without an itch." Tian Jian blushed at the thought of Sister Wang finding lice in the seams.

"Yes, I use chinaberry seeds in the water. As soon as the lice smell it they die."

To conceal a face burning even more brightly, Tian Jian raised the spout of the kettle and remarked that the water still hadn't come to a boil. Sister Wang immediately rose to adjust the fire, but the kettle must have been hotter than she thought and she knocked it over, causing the water to spray out on the burning coals with a puffing and a stream of vapour and dust to rise up quickly. As he raised his feet Tian Jian told her not to worry about it.

"Relax. The county magistrate is supposed to sit in court and hear cases while wearing an official uniform. But since I'm sitting on the edge of a bed and not wearing my lice-ridden uniform so Sister Wang must see someone other than the county magistrate."

"The county magistrate must think that because Sister Wang isn't bending down to kowtow and is pouring water for his tea and getting dust all over his face, she isn't one of his subjects."

Tian Jian began to laugh, and seeing him laughing, Sister Wang began to laugh too.

In fact, Tian Jian hadn't laughed so easily since he'd become county magistrate, and wondered why today in the company of Sister Wang he'd allowed himself to give freer reign to his feelings and abandoned the stern official image he'd worked so hard to cultivate for the past half year. He was quick to suppress the beguiling notion they had some affinity for each other, but did wonder whether he was connected by Fate with this woman in some inexplicable way. Otherwise, why would he have already run into her several times, on each occasion under such unusual circumstances? There was hardly anything extraordinary about drinking tea or laundering clothes, and couldn't understand why he found her tea particularly tasty, or why she was the only one who could properly clean his lice-ridden uniform. Could a dignified county magistrate actually become involved with a widow who was also a drifter and the keeper of a small shop? Tian Jian fixed his gaze straight ahead and no longer saw the image of the white wolf. He still was concerned about the recurrence of the roguish habits he'd developed in his lawless years in the mountains and forests, and knew he'd have to vanquish them completely if he truly wanted to change his fate by assuming another man's title as an official, and make important contributions of his own. When Tian Jian had first put on the official uniform on the bank of the Westward Flowing River, he had had no specific ideas about what he would do as an official, and now half a year later he was even less clear about it. He had no knowledge of what other people did when they became officials, and also couldn't explain how his meeting Sister Wang had begun to make him do things differently. Tian Jian realised he couldn't uphold his responsibilities effectively if he didn't act like an official in front of his subjects, but he also knew he was unable to deny his strong feelings for Sister Wang.

Tian Jian raised his head and stared boldly at the woman in front of him, an action which seemed to embarrass her. He couldn't work her out at all. In a crowd she was brash and outspoken, but here with him she was gentle and yielding, her face and ears blushing pink then bright red from bashfulness. If Sister Wang had been as outspoken now as she'd been when he'd met her before, perhaps she wouldn't have roused his interest to such an extent. Yes, her deferential quiet confused him profoundly.

The water in the kettle finally came to the boil, Sister Wang poured the tea and they began drinking. The hot tea warmed them and she got up again to open the window beside the bed. She sat for a while and then rose once more to close it, opening another window facing her so the cold air wouldn't blow on Tian Jian. Although this small detail made a deep impression on him and he silently praised her solicitousness, a vague worry crossed his brow and he sighed deeply.

"Is there something bothering Your Excellency?"

"No, I'm fine."

"Sir, you look pale. You must be worrying about something. All the other officials in the county are local people with families and relatives in the area. Your Excellency's family is far away in the south. Why not have them move here? Would your wife not like this small county? Or perhaps she is unwilling to leave the beautiful home you had built for her."

Tian Jian laughed. "Do you think I'm too cruel?".

"I'm sure you have your reasons for not bringing your family here. How could I dare suggest your excellency was cruel?"

"But I am cruel. Many people say I'm cruel."

"That's because you killed the canal supervisor, and had his skin used to stretch a drum."

"Is that why no one has paid any attention to the notice for a canal supervisor?"

"Sir, I said you were worried, I should have realised that it was because Your Excellency is so concerned about the affairs of Zhuyang County. The matter of the supervisor is not worth worrying about. Anything can upset people, like there being lice on this perfectly good uniform. If Your Excellency doesn't mind, permit me to say something else. I've heard people say your excellency shouldn't have used the canal supervisor's skin to make a drum, and that even outlaws who kill and rob people for a living don't do that. I know Your Excellency can't be compared to the likes of such outlaws, but this is what the family of the county commander is spreading around. Of course, it's my opinion that people who open their mouths like that should themselves be skinned, and their bodies boiled into soup to be eaten by everyone in the county. But what I want to tell you is that it isn't just that no one will volunteer to be canal supervisor, it's that that position is so very important. Those who have the necessary status are afraid, and those who aren't afraid and do have the ability are humble people who wouldn't dare to volunteer."

"What do you mean they wouldn't dare to volunteer? Don't all officials come from the people?"

"Well, if you really mean that, let me recommend someone."

"Who?"

"You already know him."

"I already know him?"

"Do you remember that morning Your Excellency saw me in the fog? The day I worked as a mourner? The man I want to recommend is Yan Geda, the man who couldn't afford a wife. I know all about him; since I helped him, he's constantly at my shop thanking me. He's decent, honest and is very able. Yesterday, he came to the shop and gave me a daylily. We started talking about the canal and he said Your Excellency couldn't possibly want him for the supervisor job. He thought the first supervisor was loyal but didn't know what he was doing, and the second was a bad guy who didn't understand farming. He took a look at the canal himself and thinks that the embankment collapsed because the five mile long site that was used for the construction wasn't a good stretch of land. If the canal had been built on more compact soil, a sturdier wall could have been built, but the red soil here isn't as durable so when the water ran through the embankments collapsed. If he were canal supervisor, he'd build the canal several hundred yards to the north where the soil is white and much stronger."

Tian Jian was very pleased to hear this and clasped his hands together in approval. "I'm very grateful to you for telling me this. Could you find Yan Geda early tomorrow morning and have him come to see me?" Tian Jian clasped his hands again and saluted her, and she quickly knelt down.

"Sister Wang, you've become one of my subjects again."

"Sir, you've become His Excellency again."

Yan Geda's first act as canal supervisor was to survey the land on which the canal was to be built. He assigned ten men to each work team with shared responsibility for supervision, and the engineering work proceeded without a hitch. Tian Jian inspected the project three times, and each time found Yan working very hard, setting an example for others. Besides running around and making sure the work proceeded smoothly, he would also help with the arduous physical tasks, like moving rocks from the caves which caused thick calluses to form on his knees. He suffered his worst injury when he ordered his men to use fire to clear the side of a cliff. To do this, the men first bore holes into the rocks, under which they lit a grass fire. They then ran cold water through the holes so the rocks would split more easily. Yan had a fall just as the cold water had been poured into the rocks and cut his right leg so badly that sores developed all over it. But his injuries didn't slow him down at all, he simply called for a sedan chair to carry him around, so he could still supervise the work. Tian Jian was very impressed by this and awarded him a large earthen jug of preserved wine. Yan refused to drink alone, and called all the drifters and local people working on the canal together, and poured the wine into a small clear spring so everyone could share in it. The wine was heavily diluted, weak and almost without taste, but his generosity moved everyone deeply.

Although most of his fellow officials were sceptical about the selection of Yan Geda to be canal supervisor, as the work progressed Tian Jian became more confident about the project and was certain he'd have the last laugh. To show the people of the county how strenuous and back-breaking the construction work was, Tian Jian had his attendants make daily trips to the canal area and gather all the broken wooden tools and mangled straw sandals and place them in piles at the entrance to the yamen. He also donated grain, meat, vegetables and clothes to those working on the canal. Whenever Tian Jian could make time, he'd either go to Sister Wang's small shop to drink tea, a habit which was approaching addiction, or lead his attendants out to the villages to inspect local agricultural and silkworm production. At night he always made tea from the tea leaves Sister Wang had given him.

Once when he was staying overnight in a wooden house in one of the mountain villages, he opened a bag of Sister Wang's tea, took out a leaf and had started chewing on it when he discovered a strand of brown hair on top of the tea. Sister Wang's hair wasn't the more usual colour of black lacquer, and the longer it was the lighter it seemed to become, still not blond but almost a light brown. If a dark-skinned woman had the same colour hair it would have been ugly, but as Sister Wang's skin was fair, her long, thick, tousled brown hair further accentuated her beauty; a beauty he attributed to her fleshy milk-white skin, star-bright eyes, and clean and even white teeth that sparkled whenever she smiled. It was Tian Jian's guess that she'd intentionally coiled the long strand of hair in a ball and placed it on top of the tea leaves. For a long moment he held the hair in the palm of his hand, staring at it as if infatuated, before slipping it into a pocket close to his heart, and staying awake all night drinking tea. He could hear the attendants snoring in the adjacent room, and the owner of the house and his wife and child whispering among themselves on the floor below after they'd turned out the light. Later still the boy mumbled something Tian Jian didn't catch, and the woman got up to urinate into a large empty chamber pot.

No one had ever treated Tian Jian as well as Sister Wang. The county yamen required his attention for a score of uncompleted projects, but they all seemed of little consequence compared with her haunting beauty. Lately, whenever he had time for a moment's reflection, he would silently express his gratitude to Heaven for allowing him to succeed in his deceit, though it would be more accurate to say this was because Heaven had furnished him with the opportunity to know Sister Wang rather than to serve as county magistrate. Tian Jian's lack of experience with women had led him to believe that they were either sacred Bodhisattvas or evil devils. Sister Wang seemed to be a remarkable blend of the two: fully capable of burning him to ashes. Even the assistant county magistrate was impressed with her. "If she'd been a natural born singer and dancer, she would have been a famous big city star. It's too bad she lacks those talents," he declared. Of course, how could the assistant magistrate know how soft she was, or that she was as pure and innocent as a mountain brook?

Tian Jian's mind ran apace, his body dry and hot. He developed the habit of holding his breath, closing his eyes and imagining Sister Wang's desirable form before him. He fervently hoped that when he was thinking about her she too was thinking about him. On his most recent visit to her shop, he had casually described a dream he'd had the previous night: He was standing on the north bank of the Westward Flowing River and suddenly saw Sister Wang walking across the bridge which spanned it, her skirt blowing up in a gust of wind, her pale white print pantaloons billowing out above cuffs that were tied with a white silk garter. She wore a pair of small and exquisitely made shoes which enchanted him. He didn't know why she was there and called out to her several times, but she neither turned around nor gave any indication she'd heard him. At one point he seemed to wake but wasn't sure whether this was real or a continuation of the dream. It was in this state of confusion that he asked her whether she had ever been to the banks of the Westward Flowing River. She laughed and replied: "That's strange. How is it I too dreamt I was on the bridge above the Westward Flowing River and saw you leading a group of men along the bank? I called out to you but you didn't answer, and assumed that when His Excellency is out on official business he has to maintain his official dignity and couldn't talk to a poor woman." When this conversation ended, they lapsed into silence again.

Tian Jian held his breath and closed his eyes and no longer saw the image of Sister Wang in the wooden house in the mountain village, but instead heard a row of ants crawling along the pillars of the house, and beyond the window-sill the song of roses blooming... It was early in the morning when he finally curled up in a chair and fell asleep, still wearing his clothes and boots.

The next day he was awakened by much noise, the sound of moving feet, and a voice calling softly from the floor below: "Your Excellency! Your Excellency!" Tian Jian rubbed his eyes and walked over to the balustrade circling the house. He looked down at his attendant who was sweating profusely and smiling. "Your Excellency, come out and take a look. You have to see this."

"What could there be to see in these forsaken mountains and forests? A two-headed snake? Or the tree with nine different kinds of leaves?"

"It's a leopard that gored an ox to death. No, no, I mean it's an ox that gored a leopard to death."

The attendant led Tian Jian to the entrance to the village where a large crowd had gathered: some were crying, others laughing, some recommending the skinning of the animals, while others wanted to dig a hole and bury them. A voice cried out: "His Excellency has arrived! Make way for His Excellency! Zhuyang County's oxen are all loyal to His Excellency." Tian Jian made his way through the crowd, and in front of a stone embankment saw leopard and ox hairs scattered everywhere as well as clots of blood like decomposed pomegranates. A white-haired, spotted leopard was standing up on its hind paws, pressed against the embankment, its front claws stretched out into the air and its fangs bared in an attitude of death. The head of a dead ox was lowered against the body of the leopard, its four hoofs spread wide, its back arched, and its eyes staring out vacantly. Everyone assumed that the leopard had slipped into the mountain village the previous night in search of food and had been challenged by the ox. Since it was late and everyone was sleeping no one knew how long the battle between the two had lasted. Although the animals might have been thought to be evenly matched, it appeared that the ox had driven the leopard into the base of the embankment and gored it to death. But it must have been unaware that the leopard was dead and kept it pinned there the entire night afraid to let go. Finally it had died of fatigue. Tian Jian was deeply impressed by this sight and astounded by the ox's courage and loyalty. The villagers praised it for goring the leopard to death and sacrificing itself precisely on the night when the honourable county magistrate was staying in their mountain village. For the villagers, this extraordinary act proved beyond doubt that the county magistrate was wise and diligent; and the fact that he had personally witnessed the ox's fortuitous death was a tribute to the ox. While its owner wept profusely, the ox was carried away and buried in a pit that was promptly dug for that purpose. The villagers then butchered the leopard insisting Tian Jian take both the meat and the skin. Tian Jian had no particular interest in the meat and had it boiled in a pot for his attendants to eat their fill, but he did keep the leopard pelt for himself knowing very well what he wanted to do with it.

Tian Jian was quite excited by the sight of the leopard skin spread over Sister Wang's *kang*, though initially he feared she wouldn't accept it. Although she never willingly took money from Tian Jian when he drank her tea or she cleaned his uniform, she still complained that he underestimated her moral integrity. She was poor in spite of being a good businesswoman, for she had no great love for money and only did what she liked. Hadn't she gone out in public and for only a few coins pretended to be someone's wife, and then full of tears and woe called out to the deceased as if she were her own mother? And what about the fact that she let so many drifters live in her cramped rear courtyard? Tian Jian had his own misgivings about giving her the leopard skin. She might think he was only paying her back for her kindness, or that he was using it as bait to entice her to be even more friendly, thereby transforming their feelings for each other into a mere exchange of commodities. As it turned out, Sister

Wang accepted the leopard skin with great delight, pressed it to her breast, and told him repeatedly she would use the skin on her bed to keep her warm at night. She counted up the black spots on the skin, and chanted: "Spotted leopard. Spotted leopard. Sister Wang will dream about your spots every night."

Thereafter, every night as Tian Jian lay down to sleep, he would imagine a particular woman stretched out on the leopard skin naked; or perhaps it would be more accurate to say a particular seductive woman mounted on the back of a ferocious leopard, also naked and an unsurpassably intoxicating sight. A woman who was a perfect blend of Bodhisattva and devil could easily subjugate such a savage animal, and provoked by this exciting fantasy, Tian Jian, alone in his half-empty bed, would unabashedly indulge in his old habit, and for a few torrid minutes imagine himself as that wild leopard.

Tian Jian's pleasure in these fantasies and his delight in Sister Wang's enthusiastic acceptance of the leopard skin, had a salutary effect on his confidence as county magistrate and strengthened his resolve to undertake great work. He had felt this way the first time he'd met Sister Wang, but had no idea then that he would come to know her so well. Now he believed himself capable of achieving almost anything he wanted to do, and his apprehensions about his disreputable past, about his ignorance of official business and the accompanying feelings of inferiority and timidity no longer bothered him. Clear proof of this change was that he was no longer harassed by the image of the white wolf. Tian Jian felt liberated from the maelstrom of uncertainty, and repeatedly declared to himself and to the people on the street that, unlike the two previous supervisors, Yan Geda would successfully build the canal. Acting on this belief, he ordered his subordinates to find the best stone-cutters they could and have work commence on an octagonal pavilion and a stone tablet which would be installed at the central intersection of Zhuyang City once the canal was filled with water. The assistant county magistrate seemed perplexed by Tian Jian's unequivocal confidence in Yan Geda. "Is His Excellency really so sure that the canal will be built properly?"

"Yes, I am. I have a very strong premonition about it."

Three months later, exactly as Yan Geda had predicted, the canal was completed and filled with water without mishap. As the large octagonal pavilion and stone tablet still hadn't been finished, Tian Jian personally decorated Yan with red silk and flowers, and on donkeys, one behind the other, they paraded the length of the long street and narrow alleys of Zhuyang City. Subsequently, Tian Jian let it be known he intended to promote Yan even before the pavilion was completed. The news spread, quickly becoming the talk of the town, with everyone trying to guess which position the county magistrate had in mind for Yan.

Late one night the assistant county magistrate came to the yamen to speak to Tian Jian about the promotion. "Sir, people are saying privately that you intend to dismiss the county commander and have Yan Geda replace him. The lesser officials in the yamen are all fond of gossip and quick to believe unreasonable rumours, and as they're aware that Your Excellency and the county commander do not see eye to eye, they assume you want to provoke him. Is this really possible? Won't this rumour further exacerbate the problem between the two of you? Let me put a lid on this gossip immediately, and if people continue to spread such ridiculous nonsense I'll have their tongues pulled out."

Tian Jian stuck his tongue all the way out. "Then pull mine out first."

"Sir, you…"

"You heard what I said. Tell me what you think of the idea."

"Yan Geda has certainly done a commendable job, and does have the ability to handle any position. He should be promoted, but do you think it would be wise to dismiss the county commander? I understand he has already heard the rumour and has been very critical of you in front of his family. It is said he has even written a letter to the provincial officials."

"You mean he isn't really sick? I visited him on several occasions, and each time he was lying in bed moaning. I assume he would not be back at work for a long time and didn't want his position permanently vacant."

"I think it's outrageous the county commander stooped to telling you he was sick and couldn't work because he and you are at odds," the assistant magistrate declared. "But his family is quite powerful and rich, and very well connected so what would you gain by offending him?"

"If he's so well connected why wasn't he chosen to be county magistrate? I'm the leading county official, and it's my responsibility to honour those who deserve to be honoured and get rid of those who don't.

Have you come here today on his behalf?"

The assistant county magistrate was sweating profusely as he got out of his chair and stood up. "Of course, His Excellency can run the county government any way he chooses, and I would add he's doing an excellent job, I've said as much."

Tian Jian laughed: "Good. Now I know what you've said."

In fact, Tian Jian wasn't particularly interested in what the assistant county magistrate had to say. Although his assistant was familiar with the world of officialdom, he was also spineless. Perhaps he'd come to talk to him because of the rumour, or perhaps he was worried about a number of things and wanted to feel the magistrate out. In any event, he seemed very certain about one thing: If Tian Jian removed the county commander the county commander would be offended, but if he wasn't removed, Tian Jian would be offended. The situation must have been worse than Tian Jian had thought, because over the next few days the chief clerk, the superintendent of education, a number of the wealthy gentry and the abbot of the Transformation Temple all came to speak to him on behalf of the county commander. Of course, they weren't as direct as the assistant county magistrate and tried to obscure their intention by first praising the county magistrate's perspicacity, his paternal love for the people, and his unsurpassable merit in completing several significant projects that would go down in the annals of history. Only after going through this litany did they then praise the county commander's knowledge of public affairs, and his honesty and incorruptibility. Although they acknowledged he was somewhat supercilious, they suggested he should be forgiven his occasional impoliteness, and that only a stern leader, forced to deal with thieves and robbers on a daily basis, could effectively maintain law and order in the county. Following these solicitations, one by one the leaders of each town's foot patrol presented Tian Jian with an array of notable mountain products including fox and mink pelts, porcelain, and various tonics which they'd either hunted down or collected. Initially, they claimed to have intended to enjoy these things themselves, but said that when the county commander heard about it he was furious. Zhuyang was a small county and it wouldn't be appropriate for them to indulge themselves in luxuries that the county magistrate couldn't enjoy. After considering the county commander's point of view, they ultimately decided to donate the merchandise to the government. Additional pressure was applied by the prefectural secretary and commander, as well as by neighbouring county bureaucrats, who all sent official letters to Tian Jian paying their respects to him and inevitably adding the following postscript: The Zhuyang county commander is my old friend, please convey my regards to him.

Tian Jian was troubled by all this. The promotion of Yan Geda had only been hinted at and already had provoked a great deal of controversy throughout the county and the province. The more Tian Jian heard about the controversy, the more eager he was to make the promotion a reality. "What does a county magistrate do anyway? Supposedly he's responsible for the moral cultivation of the people, trying cases and imposing punishments, giving advice on agricultural matters, collecting taxes and produce, registering households, building bridges and repairing roads, providing education and supervising prayer and sacrificial observances." Since he'd assumed office, what had the county commander done to help him fulfil these responsibilities? Tian Jian clenched his teeth in anger and ordered the doorkeeper not to let anybody else in the yamen who was to intercede on behalf of the county commander. He further asked that all gifts be refused but that a list of all the people who came and the gifts they brought be made, and all checked thoroughly for any improprieties.

Tian Jian had no strength to stand up from his magistrate's chair after his subordinates left, and all at once the pillars in the courtroom began whirling around, the stone steps at the entrance to the courtroom rose straight up, and the ball of white light again appeared followed by the image of the white wolf. Tian Jian clutched at the small peachwood charm for a moment and eventually calmed himself. Had he misjudged the county commander? Was the entire problem down to the fact that he'd undervalued and failed to recognise his achievements? If the county commander really was well connected in the prefectural government, how could his own political career succeed without his help? And if he didn't have that help, wouldn't his fervent wish of becoming an outstanding official come to a premature end, and the murder of the two innocents and his friend's sacrifice on the banks of the Westward Flowing River be for naught? Although Tian Jian withdrew his order prohibiting anybody who was interceding on behalf of the county commander from entering the yamen, he resented doing so and still couldn't see how they could ever cooperate in governing the county after he had been let off so easily. Nevertheless, Tian Jian felt as if he had no choice. In view of his assumed identity, he didn't dare show his face outside the county, nor did he have a network of connections in the prefecture government or the neighbouring counties, or even in Zhuyang to fall back on. His reaction to this stressful situation was to sit alone in his office in the yamen, anxiously rub his hair and watch it fall to the floor strand after strand.

Tian Jian eventually became ill. The first to discover it was the yamen cook when he carried away the well-prepared noon meal he'd brought for him untouched. Tian Jian lay on his bed with a distracted expression in his eyes, his face drawn and blanched, and the only thing he wanted to eat and which he managed to force down was a few mouthfuls of lotus seed soup.

"Sir, do you wish to visit a doctor?" the cook asked.

Tian Jian shook his head.

"Would you like something else to eat?"

Tian Jian again shook his head.

"Then His Excellency should get some sleep." The cook adjusted Tian Jian's quilt and after he'd put the pillow under his head, Tian Jian indicated he wanted something brought out from under his bed that was wrapped in a paper bag. The paper bag was very heavy and the cook imagined there was a small box inside filled with gold and silver. After Tian Jian put his head on it, the cook left. Tian Jian was very tired and needed sleep, but just as he began to doze off he heard someone knocking on his door and the assistant magistrate walked in.

"Is His Excellency ill?"

"I'm a little sick, yes."

"Have you seen a doctor?"

"No, it's not necessary. A bowl of lotus seed soup and a good night's sleep are all I need."

"You look exhausted and should get some rest. If you want anything to eat or drink, let me know and I'll take care of it."

"Thank you, I appreciate that."

After the assistant magistrate left, the chief clerk came in. "I heard His Excellency was ill."

"I feel as if I'd lost all my strength."

"I'll call a doctor."

"I don't want a doctor."

"Do you want something to eat?"

"I don't want to eat, I just want to sleep."

"Well, you should have some rest, that's best." The clerk sighed deeply, expressing unbounded sympathy, before taking his leave.

Tian Jian closed his eyes and his whole body began to relax. First he felt his legs disappearing and then he felt his hands disappearing and just when he was about to lose consciousness he was again jolted awake by a noise at the door. "Your Excellency. Your Excellency." Tian Jian opened his eyes and saw it was the crippled attendant. "Your Excellency, are you really sick?"

"If one eats too many different kinds of food, one gets sick," Tian Jian replied, now red-eyed. "It's not serious."

"Do you want something to eat? My wife can make some hot and sour soup. Let me go home and have her prepare a bowl."

"I'm really not hungry, just very tired."

"Get some sleep then. Rest is good for hundreds of illnesses."

This pattern continued for the rest of the day as a succession of high and low yamen officials came to visit. Toward evening an even larger number arrived including the surveyor, a group of trainee officials, the superintendent of education, the rich men Zhang Lian, Han Tao and Li Ming, between ten and twenty village heads and almost everyone from the county commander's office. The visitors seemed to think that if they came in groups they would make no impression on Tian Jian; and when they came alone they inevitably would ask how he was feeling and what he'd like to eat, and Tian Jian would uniformly reply his illness wasn't serious and that he didn't feel like eating, and before leaving they, in turn, would advise him to get some rest. This continuous procession of "good will" kept Tian Jian up tossing and turning half the night, the lack of sleep aggravating his illness.

When Yan Geda heard that Tian Jian was sick, he too rushed to the yamen to enquire after his health, and was surprised to find an angry and frustrated county magistrate who sat up in bed and complained: "Have you all come to take my life? Everyone tells me I should rest, but how can I rest with this endless stream of visitors? Get out! Get out!" Yan was greatly frightened, and lowered his head as if to leave. "Who are you?" Tian Jian demanded. Yan immediately turned back and knelt down in front of him. After a moment's silence, Tian Jian propped himself up on his bed and said, "You just arrived. Why do you want to leave right away?"

"Your Excellency, I only just found out you were ill

and came over as fast as I could. I didn't know his excellency was unable to get any rest. It's late. Please sleep. I'm happy his excellency's sickness isn't as bad as I'd feared."

"Am I really an 'excellency'. I'm afraid this 'excellency' is a useless idler. Why didn't you visit me at the yamen the day I gave you the silk and flowers?"

"Sir, I've always been grateful to you for your kindness, but when I heard rumours that his excellency wanted to promote me I didn't dare to visit. What kind of person would Yan be if he presumed to have crazy illusions about being promoted, after already being lucky enough to be chosen by his excellency as canal supervisor? Everywhere people are talking about this. Late at night someone even left a basket of ugly toads at my house as a curse on me for imagining a man as lowly as myself could be promoted to such a high position; someone else dug a hole in my mother's tomb to break the flow of my family's ancestral fortune; and tonight when I left the house, a paper figure with needles all over its body was stuck to the tree trunk at the gate. I could put up with all that, but when I heard people were complaining to his excellency I was afraid something would happen to him. I felt terrible when I heard His Excellency was sick so I had to come and visit him, sir."

Before he'd finished speaking, Yan was already lying face down on the edge of the bed, weeping. Tian Jian helped him up and they sat together silently for a while, then Tian Jian tried to console him. "It's all right. Go home now. In future if anybody threatens or insults you, let me know. His Excellency after all is His

Excellency."

Yan Geda left early the next morning, and the more Tian Jian thought about what had happened to him the angrier he became. Tian Jian was not in a position to succumb to sickness, and criticised himself for not acting like the county magistrate he was. "His Excellency after all is His Excellency." Was this really true? Did his words truly ring with the authority of Heaven, or were they like raindrops falling into a deep river: superfluous and without effect? Of what value were his words if he couldn't reward who deserved to be rewarded and punish those deserving of punishment? Was it the case that the county magistrate couldn't support the virtuous and remarkably able Yan Geda because of his lower social ranking? These tormenting questions eventually produced a headache. "Stop thinking about it," he shouted at himself. "Don't think about it anymore!" Though he did finally succeed in putting it out of his mind, he was still unable to sleep, now distracted by the image of Sister Wang. Why hadn't she been among the multitude of people who'd come to visit him? Didn't she know he was ill, or did she think it improper to visit because she was a shopkeeper and a young widow? Tian Jian hoped that at least a few of his visitors were sincere about their concern for him. Although he was the highest ranking official in the county, he had no one he felt he could talk to. Naturally, out of so many visitors there must have been some who truly cared among those who didn't, but even the few who were concerned were subordinates whose solicitude was driven by ethical obligation and a generalised sense of sympathy rather than deep feelings of friendship.

The cock had crowed at dawn before Tian Jian finally fell into a sound sleep. He didn't know what time it was when he became aware of a whimpering sound and opened his eyes to find Sister Wang sitting in front of his bed on a low chair. Her hair was oiled and neatly combed, but her face was worn and her eyes red and puffy like mouldering peaches. "Sister Wang," he said as if still dreaming, unconsciously pushing himself up. A hot wet towel fell from his forehead.

Sister Wang let out a cry of pleasant surprise: "His Excellency has awakened!"

When he realised this was not a dream his face flushed deep and long with embarrassment. Sister Wang insisted he try and sleep a little more and alternately added warm and cold water to a third pitcher, testing it with her hand until it was the right temperature, then wet the towel and applied it to his forehead a second time. Tian Jian's illness was born of worry, and his recent sleep, although brief, made him feel better. Sister Wang's visit refreshed him even more. "Why did you come now? When did you get here?" He removed the towel and sat up. "Why didn't you visit when everyone else did?"

Sister Wang blushed and a couple of tears trickled down. "Are you really feeling better? Your Excellency, you have had so many people taking care of you, I didn't think you needed me too. I was this morning so worried when Yan came to the shop and told me you were sick. I got rid of my customers right away and ran over here right as soon as I'd locked up. It was raining hard and the yamen was shut so I knocked on the door. Luckily the attendant was there,

I asked him to give you some tea I'd brought and he let me in.''

"It's true I didn't want any more visitors, but that didn't mean Sister Wang couldn't visit. Didn't you get wet from all the rain?"

"My clothes have dried now. You slept for such a long time. I had no idea how sick you were and didn't want to wake you. When you're sick like this you really need your wife with you. Since she isn't here to take care of you, and you are all alone, I started to cry."

"How could this minor illness possibly be worth your tears? All I needed was some sleep. I'm not sick at all." Tian Jian pushed back the quilt and got out of bed, still wearing the clothes he'd worn the previous day. Only his hair was dishevelled. Sister Wang quickly looked around for something he could put on his head and, not finding a cap, had to settle for his official hat. This he refused, complaining that such a hard hat was uncomfortable at the best of times.

"Hats are important to men, and this is an official's hat," Sister Wang began.

"What difference does it make whether it's an official's hat or not? You're here today and I'm putting my official's hat aside, so we can talk as friends."

Tian Jian was quite exhilarated sitting together with Sister Wang and, caught off guard by this feeling, had some trouble maintaining his composure. Sister Wang covered her mouth to conceal her smile at his manner, but a moment later her eyes turned red.

"What are you crying for now?"

"Sir, I'm crying because His Excellency has given me such a nice welcome... I won't cry any more.

There, I've stopped."

Her eyes, however, became even redder and tears streamed down her face, which intensified Tian Jian's excitement.

"You're very pretty when you cry. Everyone says Sister Wang is an iron lady, but you're quite brittle underneath."

Sister Wang gazed at him ardently for a moment, pursed her lips and flushed red. "Could His Excellency be the one who's changed this wild woman?"

At this moment they heard someone calling from outside and the crippled attendant came in. "Sister Wang, you're still here?"

"His Excellency has just got up."

"Sir, you look much better after your sleep. Would you like something to eat now?"

"What time is it?"

"Almost noon."

"Tell the cook to make two bowls of light noodle soup. Sister Wang should eat too, and since she was drenched by the rain, ask him to add some ginger and peppers for her."

"Your Excellency, I can't eat with you."

"Since His Excellency has invited you, you can't refuse to eat with him. While it continues to rain like this, you can not possibly go home," the attendant admonished and then left the room.

"I'm still not going to eat with you here."

"You claim you're not afraid of anything, and yet you won't even eat with me?"

"All right, if you're not worried about breaking the rules, neither am I. I serve people food everyday, so today it'll make a change to be the one who's served."

"Ah, that is the other Sister Wang talking again. Would you dare walk outside with me?"

"Yes, I'd do that too." She blushed as she spoke, and her eyes narrowed and twinkled for an instant before fixing on the tips of her toes. Tian Jian's heartbeat quickened, and a flood of words came to his lips where they got stuck. His eyes gazed in wonder at Sister Wang's feet which were exquisitely bound, like a pair of soft and sticky rice dumplings, and delightfully lodged in a pair of low, black embroidered boots with buttons which were stained with mud although she'd tried to wipe them clean with a stick.

Tian Jian wanted very much to touch her feet but couldn't do it. "Are your boots soaked through?"

"It's not important." Sister Wang raised her feet from the ground to look.

Tian Jian was flustered further. "Your feet are beautifully bound."

"No, not really. When I was young my mother did it for me. She told me my feet had high arches which made them difficult to bind."

"Your mother was wrong. Women with highly arched feet are very much admired. In fact, all really beautiful women have high arches on their feet." Tian Jian now reached out toward her foot, at the same moment that Sister Wang reached down to it. When his hand was about two inches away, he could only point as if he was going to touch it, before her foot moved slightly and withdrew. Tian Jian raised his head and glanced through the window at the sheets of rain pouring from the eaves of the yamen. "Yes, feet with high arches are particularly pretty." Sister Wang again extended her foot, rubbed her instep, made a circle with her toes and then began massaging again. At that moment the crippled attendant entered carrying the noodle soup.

The attendant stood by until Tian Jian and Sister Wang finished eating, then he removed the dishes and poured some boiling water in with the tea leaves she'd brought. After he left the room the two of them sipped the tea in silence. "I ought to go now."

"Why leave in this rainy weather? You're not going to have any customers at your shop to eat. What are you worried about?"

"You're ill. Tiring yourself out won't help you. I'll come another time. I still have to clean your uniform."

"All right, but if you insist on leaving, I'll escort you out."

Sister Wang laughed. "Do you think it's proper for the county magistrate to walk out with a common woman?"

"I'll see you to the gate." They walked into the living room and paused for a moment looking out beyond a folding screen into a cluster of water-soaked bamboo in the small rear courtyard at the pouring rain. Beyond the courtyard was a gravel path bordered by flowers. The path had been soaked by the rain, and the earth on either side was becoming liquid in puddles full of bubbles which floated up to the surface and burst. "See how hard it's raining," Tian Jian declared.

"Yes, it's as dark as night."

"And you're still set on leaving?"

"Yes, I'm still leaving."

Tian Jian took out an oilcloth for her to wear. Sister Wang went to wrap it around her herself, but Tian Jian wanted to do it for her, and extended his hands, raising the oilcloth which moved like a cloud above them before falling down over her head and back. Sister Wang's warm sweet breath caressed Tian Jian's face and the hair on her forehead brushed gently against the bridge of his nose. They were so close he could clearly see the contour of her delicate milk-white forehead and how the strands of her fine narrow eyebrows unfolded one after another. He wrapped the oilcloth firmly around her and embraced her, a moment they'd both longed for. Eventually their burning mouths found each other and pressed tightly together. Lost in the heat of their kiss they began to caress each other excitedly until the oilcloth dropped from Sister Wang's body. A little while later their mouths separated and, standing face to face and panting heavily, they both looked into a foreshortened image of themselves in the other's eyes.

Tian Jian took her in his arms again. "My dear, my dear. I adore you. I love you. Let me kiss you. Let me hold you." Sister Wang struggled for a moment like some weakened insect caught in a web, yet the more she struggled the more tightly she pressed against him. "I feel the same way, your excellency, I love you also... But ... but ... the yamen must be full of ... people ... during the day."

"Why didn't you tell me before? I've felt this way for so long ... I was afraid you had no feelings for me and feared offending you. Don't worry about other people. Every day I take a nap at noon and no one will disturb us now. I love you so much. A minute ago all I wanted to do was rub your small delicate foot, but I was afraid of being crude and hearing you accuse me of using my position as county magistrate to force you into consenting to it."

"I could sense you wanted to touch me and hoped you would take my foot in your hand, but you were too shy."

"If you were thinking the same thing, why did you move it away?"

"I didn't dare let you do it."

Tian Jian kissed her again and felt a fleshy thing come out of her mouth which he sucked on forcefully as if wanting to pull it out at its root, swallow it and make it a part of himself. He'd never made love with a woman before and felt such joy at the prospect, akin only to the prodigious ferocity he'd formerly needed to kill and rob. It seemed to swell his body to gargantuan proportions. Sister Wang responded immediately to his exhilaration and softened against him, unsteady, like a frail blade of grass. Tian Jian embraced her tenderly, and with one hand supporting her neck and the other sweeping up her long slender voluptuous legs, he carried her off to the bedroom in the rear courtyard.

The rain continued to beat against the window, enveloping their world in darkness. "This lush rain is magical."

"Yes ... yes, it's good, good..."

"But it came very late."

"Yes, it did arrive late... But it's here now."

Sister Wang lay next to Tian Jian in a daze and seemed completely drained by their love-making.

The rain continued for ten straight days and during this period Zhuyang County was the site of a number of unusual incidents. First there was more than the usual shooting off of firecrackers to celebrate weddings, festivals, pregnancies and engagements, as well as an increase in the number of irritable and anxious young men and women visiting the large hall at the Transformation Temple for silent prayer. But the truly perplexing events came to Tian Jian's attention from the daily reports he reviewed in the yamen courtroom. One example involved a married women in a certain village who had hung herself. On the sixth day of rain the woman had visited the Spiritual Temple to offer incense to the Buddha: "Please give me a child, Goddess of Mercy. If I'm not capable of having one, how could I have given birth in my mother's house when I was younger? And even if there's something wrong with my husband, well ... I've had another lover and that didn't work either." The woman believed she was alone in the temple and never expected a painter, who was at work up on one of the beams in the roof and happened to hear what she said, to throw down a bowl of paint in anger and splatter it all over her. On her way home, the woman hung herself from a tree in shame. A report from another village described a marriage arranged by a family on behalf of their son. On the wedding night, the wedding party played the usual jokes on the bride and groom, then the young husband and wife had eaten date soup and gone to bed. In the middle of the night, the groom had abruptly passed out in the bride's arms and except for a full erection looked as if he were dead, causing the bride to flee in terror. After the boy's family found out what happened, they dragged the bride back to the room and put their unconscious son on top of her in the same position he was in when he passed out. The woman started making love to him again, and their son revived. Still a third report involved an even more bizarre incident. In another village a man and a woman were caught fornicating in someone's mill, and when the facts came out it was learned they'd been at it for two entire days. When someone caught them in the act, instead of fleeing they'd burst out in tears and begged to be forgiven, but curiously the two remained locked together and couldn't be separated. The villagers were enraged by this abnormal and hideous scene and cut them apart with a knife, tied them both up in a bamboo cage and sunk it in a deep pond. And still a fourth report stated the unusual downpour had inundated and destroyed a total of thirteen thatched houses, and in Zhuyang City had caused the collapse of four walls which crushed to death a cat and a bitch in heat as well as two spotted snakes twisted rope-like around each other. Tian Jian chuckled at these fantastical accounts, not knowing what to say about any of them. Simultaneously, he and the assistant magistrate looked at each other in tacit understanding.

"It's the rain," said Tian Jian.

"This rain..." the assistant magistrate responded.

"The rains have come somewhat late this year."

Ultimately, since there was nothing they could do, they let the reports stand without taking further action.

Nevertheless, Tian Jian did have the inscription on the small round gate of the yamen's rear courtyard changed to read "Heavenly Rain", and whenever it caught his attention he'd recall all the details of that wondrous afternoon with Sister Wang. He'd received the gift of her heart and body at his most despondent moment, and now when they were together he was so filled with joy by the incongruous juxtaposition of the world's immense possibilities and their brief but fated encounter that he forgot all else. This newly-found, deep satisfaction gave him the strength to overcome all obstacles to Yan Geda's promotion. Regardless of opposition from his fellow officials and other influential people in the county, Tian Jian could still see no good reason not to appoint a filial son, known across the entire county as the person responsible for successfully supervising the building of the canal, to replace the current county commander. In his current frame of mind he wasn't the least bit worried about the likelihood of the county commander appealing his dismissal, and was certain the provincial governor would support his decision if a thorough investigation was made. And even if Tian Jian failed and was forced to exchange his purple official's robe for the blue clothes of a labourer, what of it? He'd be more than content to take Sister Wang with him to some remote outpost, plant bamboo and vegetables, and raise their children. But despite his resolve, the image of the white wolf again began to plague him, and glancing at the new "Heavenly Rain" inscription on the small round gate in frustration he muttered: "Enough of this. Enough."

When the rains eased, Tian Jian issued an order to speed up construction work on the octagonal pavilion. When it was finally completed he rode out the yamen gate to take a look at it. He had barely taken in the scene when he was made acquainted with such appalling news that he fell off his donkey: Yan Geda had hung himself.

Tian Jian couldn't understand why Yan would kill himself and initially didn't believe it was suicide. Yan had told him how he'd been threatened and his family's grave desecrated, and Tian Jian suspected the county commander's subordinates were responsible. He immediately sent out some of his own men to investigate. They quickly reported back that Yan had hung himself from the beam of a room, and was found with rope burns on his neck and his tongue protruding, thus they concluded the rope had not been tied around his neck after he died. He died wearing new clothes, and had left half a jug of old wine on a table, suggesting he was very upset before his death and had prepared himself for it by numbing himself with alcohol. His clothes had been removed and no other wounds found on his body, nor any nails stuck into his head or the bottoms of his feet, which might suggest murder. All these facts proved he had taken his own life. What was strange was that on top of Yan's family altar there was not only an image of the Goddess of Mercy and the memorial tablet of his deceased father and mother, but also a plank of wood with Tian Jian's name inscribed on it. A pile of ashes on the cabinet showed he'd burnt incense just before he'd hung himself. "His dying in this way was either a rash act or he was crazy," the sheriff observed. "Sir, you're still alive, why did he write your name on the wood and put it on the altar as if he were worshipping the tablet of a dead ancestor?"

"I pushed him to do it," Tian Jian cried out, his eyes filling with tears.

The sheriff had no idea what Tian Jian was talking about. "How could you have killed him? Perhaps his fate didn't allow him the good fortune to accept his excellency's promotion." Tian Jian was certain Yan's suicide resulted from the threats provoked by the prospect of his replacing the county commander, and Yan's desire that the county magistrate neither be harmed or embarrassed, as well as his not wanting to explain this to him. Tian Jian was grief-stricken and enraged, and detested himself for his impotence. A man had given his life for him, and even as county magistrate he hadn't been able to protect him. He'd be indebted to Yan for the rest of his life, a debt he would never be able to repay. He immediately issued an order stating that the county would buy a first class coffin for Yan and that his internment would take place at the octagonal pavilion, exactly nine days after his death, as was appropriate.

Tian Jian assumed this decision would be opposed by some, and that the county commander would be the most vociferous dissenter. Regardless, he still proceeded with the appropriate preparations, insisting that Yan be buried at the octagonal pavilion with his name carved in large letters on the monument to the canal, and that the pavilion and grave be set forever at the centre of Zhuyang City. On the day of the burial and unveiling of the monument, Tian Jian ordered twelve cannons to be fired simultaneously. A huge crowd had gathered and included county officials of every rank, as well as the wealthy. The one prominent absentee was the county commander. Tian Jian laughed aloud twice and intentionally shouted: "And where is the county commander? Why hasn't he come?" Just then the sound of funeral music rang out from a small alley at the eastern end of the street, and a group of eminent local musicians emerged arranged in rows and dressed in white mourning clothes. Eight men walked behind the band, carrying a beautiful shroud, and following them were two other men also dressed in white who were holding up a third man whose head was bound with a mourning scarf. The man seemed absolutely grief-stricken and was weeping so hard he was shaking. The crowd encircling the grave turned around to look as did Tian Jian. Yan Geda had lived along so who was distraught family member taking part in the funeral procession? When Tian Jian looked more closely, he realised to his amazement the mourner was the county commander who continued to weep as he marched along, seeming so distraught he had to be helped to the side of the grave where he leaned over the coffin and cried out: "Yan Geda, my beloved friend. You rendered a great service to Zhuyang County, and are a tribute to its glory. How could you have died? Because I was ill, I was unable to help you build the canal. When you died, His Excellency, the county magistrate, purchased a coffin for you. I would now like to offer you a shroud for your coffin." The county commander was so consumed by tears he actually passed out several times, and nearly everyone present seemed truly moved by his expression of grief.

Someone came forward to assist the county commander saying, "The honourable county commander's appreciation of those who are talented moves us deeply. With His Excellency the county magistrate and the honourable commander as its leaders, the county has been blessed as have its people. This is also the reason the county could produce a genius like Yan Geda. Indeed, Yan Geda is most fortunate to have such important men as yourselves to bury him. But though Yan was a capable and virtuous man, he wasn't an official, neither can he return, so His Excellency the county commander shouldn't overwhelm himself with grief and risk injury to his own health.''

The county commander wiped his eyes, turned and bowed to Tian Jian. "Has the honourable county magistrate named the pavilion?"

"We've named it 'Canal Pavilion' to commemorate the building of the canal."

"'Canal Pavilion' is certainly a good name, but since Yan Geda supervised the construction of the canal and His Excellency is having him buried next to the pavilion, what does His Excellency think about naming it 'Yan Pavilion', in memory of him?"

Tian Jian regarded the county commander as a treacherous individual capable of all manner of trickery, but still was surprised he could act with such duplicity in front of the inhabitants of the county. Of course, his performance helped his cause immensely, and even people who'd detested him seemed convinced he'd found his conscience after observing the depth of his mourning. How could Tian Jian deal with him now? "Yes, that's an apt name. You've improved it considerably. Let's call it 'Yan Pavilion'."

After burying Yan, Tian Jian never again raised the subject of demoting the county commander, and in his turn, the county commander suddenly announced he was no longer ill and was ready to resume his job of maintaining law and order in the county. Tian Jian, disheartened by this new turn of events, excused himself from hearing cases for several days and delegated his authority for handling all official business to the assistant magistrate. He felt incompetent and out-manoeuvered, and even considered resigning. For days he walked around in a trance, and at night, constantly harassed by the image of the white wolf, he slept poorly. He did resume his visits to Sister Wang's shop, and though he saw her more often than he had previously, he was unable to tell her directly what he was feeling. During his visits, they would talk, drink tea, and when no one else was around, again indulge themselves in the physical pleasure they'd already once shared. When he was lost in the ecstasy of their passion, Tian Jian forgot all the worries that were assailing him, but once their love-making ended, he would inevitably withdraw to his burdened distressed state of mind. Sister Wang assumed that he was working too hard on county business and would flatter him every way she could to alleviate his stress. "If His Excellency really likes me, we can be very happy together here…"

"When Sister Wang is hard she's like iron, and when she's soft she's like water. That combination is very alluring. How happy I'd be if we were together every day!"

"I'm a middle-aged widow who isn't as pretty as she was, and even if some people still consider me attractive, in Zhuyang City alone plenty of women are younger and better-looking. His Excellency has become more and more eloquent, but please tell me what you mean by 'very alluring'?"

"Beauty alone isn't enough. There are a number of beautiful women working at the silk and yarn store at the west end of town whose faces are much prettier than Sister Wang's. I have had a good look at them, and do you know why I didn't fall in love with any of them? A beautiful woman's capacity to excite a man lies in her charm and powers of seduction. If a woman is both charming and seductive the effect is like a burning fire, a hypnotic light or a mesmerising jewel. Sister Wang is precisely that kind of woman. As soon a man sees her, he can't stop thinking about her and would gladly give his life to possess her."

"I didn't know His Excellency understood women so well. I have never heard you talk like this before."

"I have always thought you were very alluring, but until now I didn't know why. The day before yesterday the magistrate of East River County sent me a book written by Li Yu. As I read the book I realised you were both a charming and seductive woman, and therefore extraordinarily alluring."

Sister Wang didn't know who Li Yu was but pretended to be displeased and rolled over into Tian Jian's arms. "A few years ago I went to the provincial capital and saw a play. There were two lines the actors recited that I didn't understand then, but I think I do now."

"I'm listening. What were the lines?"

"One line was 'Everyone wants to fall in love, but when they do they're consumed by it'. And the other was 'as soon as a person is infatuated with someone, they're compelled to think constantly about their lover, even if they don't want to.'"

Tian Jian was quite moved by her recitation and lifted her into the air.

Tian Jian's frequent visits to Sister Wang's small

shop eventually provoked a good deal of speculation about their relationship. Whenever he prolonged his stay there and was needed at the yamen, the assistant magistrate would send an attendant for him. The attendant would stand on the street calling out for him, but Tian Jian would ignore him and have Sister Wang reply that he wasn't there. When the attendant returned to the yamen, the assistant magistrate would again search for Tian Jian in the rear courtyard, and unable to find him there would send the attendant to the shop again where Tian Jian would once more give him a hard time. Even Sister Wang was concerned about this. "Your Excellency, the attendant has come for you several times. They must need you at the yamen for something important, something that only the county magistrate can take care of."

"It's enough that other people are harassing me, without you giving me trouble too? What do you mean 'county magistrate'? County magistrate, bah. What a lot of nonsense."

Sister Wang quickly closed the doors and windows. "You shouldn't let other people hear you talking like that. Being county magistrate isn't an easy job."

"What's difficult about it? If I wasn't an official I'd still be myself, and I'd probably be much happier." Tian Jian almost let slip what he constantly tried so hard not to reveal, buttoning his lips into silence. The image of the white wolf again appeared before him and he walked back to the yamen in a daze.

For the next few days, despite being quite anxious about Tian Jian's state of mind, Sister Wang was overjoyed that he loved her so much. What greater wish could a woman have? As they saw more and more of each other, aside from being targets for rumours Sister Wang also became a regular source of comment and discussion. Some people were very envious of her, whilst others regarded her contemptuously. Sister Wang, however, was neither frivolous nor resentful, she paid little attention to the gossip and was mostly preoccupied with running her shop. Only one question continued to pain her: Was his excellency neglecting his official responsibilities because of her? He came frequently to her shop and it bothered her that the attendant often had to come for him. On the other hand, if his excellency was happy in her shop and could find refuge there from the demanding and unpleasant county business wasn't that to her credit, and a large enough contribution to the county to free her from any guilt?

A woman had approached her on the street and asked: "Sister Wang, how do you manage to look younger and younger every day?"

"You're eight years younger than me. Why are you teasing me?"

"I may be younger, but my husband's a real bully and you can see how it's affected me. People often say a woman is like a lute whose sound depends on the man who plucks her strings."

Sister Wang was startled by her frankness, but the saying pleased her. "Perhaps, your husband is a bully who tramples all over your flowers, but at least you have a husband. As for me, what do I have? A lute that's covered with dust from lack of use."

The woman pouted. "Ah, see how pleased you are with yourself for saying that. But I want to ask you something much more interesting. Do you think the older or the younger of the Li brothers living down at the Eastern Bridge will win the boundary dispute?"

"That's for the county court to decide. How would Sister Wang know?"

The woman was put out and for a moment didn't reply. "How could Sister Wang not know?"

Sister Wang knew very well what she meant being aware of the numerous rumours circulating about her. She was beginning to feel more and more responsible for Tian Jian ignoring his official business. A good woman ought to deepen her man's interest in his work, and she feared she was being self-indulgent.

The next time Tian Jian came to see her, she ventured to tell him what was troubling her. He seemed to come to some sudden realisation and cried out: "My love, please wait for me. I want to marry you."

After that visit, Tian Jian didn't return to her shop for quite some time. Accompanied by his crippled attendant, he made a trip out to the lower reaches of the Westward Flowing River and burned ten piles of paper money under the thickening peach tree. Tian Jian explained to the baffled attendant that he'd been in the county for a year already and during that time hadn't returned home to perform the appropriate sacrifices for his dead mother and father. He'd dreamt about them the previous night and when he woke up he'd decided to go to the county border and make the proper offerings for their spirits. As the paper money burned, clouds of smoke rose up like flocks of black butterflies, covering the branches of the peach tree. Tian Jian thought of his loyal friend and was filled with remorse for nearly failing to live up to the promise he'd made to him. Tian Jian was suddenly very grateful to Sister Wang for bringing him to his senses about his official duty. After praying for Heaven to protect and bless the spirit of his friend and his lover, a gust of wind suddenly swirled up around them. The thick smoke and burning ashes rose quickly forming a column in the air, but Tian Jian, his attendant and the peach tree seemed unaffected by the curious gush of air. The attendant's face paled with fright, but Tian Jian smiled knowingly. "He has answered me. He answered..." As Tian Jian was about to leave the riverbank, he looked carefully at the opposite bank from one end to the other and rejoiced in the absence of the silent white wolf.

Travelling away from the banks of the Westward Flowing River, it took them five days to circle the base of the Tianzhu Mountain. They passed through twenty-three villages, checking the canal's irrigation system, local agricultural production and the cultivation of silk worms. The day after Tian Jian returned to the yamen, Sister Wang came to visit. She neither brought tea nor picked up his uniform for cleaning, but just took a folded paper from her sleeve, and said, "Your Excellency hasn't been to my shop for so long. I came to ask about you once and they told me you'd gone to the countryside. Since you're so busy with government work, I didn't think it would be right to bother you. Last night I went to the south gate and asked the fortune teller to prepare this for me because I wanted to tell you these things. Perhaps I've been impertinent in writing to you, I hope you won't laugh at it."

Tian Jian took the letter over and began to read. Tears covered his face even before he'd finished it.

"Your excellency always laughs at me for crying. I see you enjoy crying too."

Tian Jian didn't respond but stood gazing at Sister Wang for what seemed like a long time, until all at once he was struck by her resemblance to his young partner. Yes. Her forehead was as narrow as his friend's, and she had a large light coloured mole on the left side of her nose just as he did. "Are Sister Wang and my old friend the same person? Have they been sent from the heavens to guide me?"

Tian Jian had decided he wanted to marry Sister Wang, and to bring this off smoothly he began laying the necessary groundwork. First he let it be known in the yamen that he'd sent numerous letters to the south to his wife asking her to come to Zhuyang County, but she was so well-taken care of at their home she found the idea of living in a remote mountain area disdainful to her. Did it have any theatres? Could one dine on steamed squid, boiled sea cucumber, stewed lobster or fried fresh water crabs? Could she buy Hunan or Suzhou style embroideries in Zhuyang, and were there any clothing and accessory shops with fine clothes? How could she endure the cold winters and put up with wearing heavy and uncomfortable clothing?

Tian Jian would openly complain about this to the assistant magistrate, procurator, director of education and cultural affairs, and the comptroller. "That woman could never leave her rich indulgent father. In her eyes, the position of county magistrate here isn't as desirable as manager of a big pharmacy in a southern village."

The officials were all sympathetic to the county magistrate's predicament, and the assistant magistrate observed: "It seems as if your wife has been given everything all her life and regards Zhuyang County as a barren mountain enveloped in a noxious mist, an altogether uninhabitable area. Perhaps if she actually came and saw it for herself, she might like it.''

"Women who've been given everything compare poorly to heroines like Meng Jiangnü who travelled nearly a thousand miles to find her husband, and wept so deeply for him when she found out he had died that a part of the Great Wall toppled over.''

After Tian Jian completed the first part of his plan, he next publicised the contents of a letter he was sending to his wife stating that it would be better to dissolve the marriage contract than live a thousand miles apart in an empty marriage, and he saw no alternative but to divorce her. The yamen officials quickly spread this news around the county, and it provoked varied reactions. There were those who complained that the southern woman was short-sighted, and though she was from a prominent family she still couldn't escape her destiny as a woman which was unavoidably linked to a man. Others commiserated with the county magistrate. They'd heard the southern woman praised as being as flawless as the purest jade and as graceful as the celestials: it was regrettable to have to sacrifice such a beauty to his position as Zhuyang County magistrate. Still others were pleased with the news. If the county magistrate was single, perhaps there could be a young local woman whom fortune would smile on and make his wife. And on this point, someone was heard to remark: "His Excellency frequently visits Sister Wang's small shop for tea and she is quite beautiful.''

"Sister Wang is a harlot who should work in a

whorehouse," someone else snickered. "If His Excellency wants to visit a brothel and drink that's one thing, but how can anyone suggest her as a good match for him? His wife should be graceful and dignified, and should neither expose her feet when she walks nor smile with her mouth open..."

Whilst these gossiping men and women ridiculed Sister Wang on this bright sunny day, she was sitting in her shop by an open bamboo window which faced on to the street, embroidering a marital shawl. The window had been covered with a new green gauze screen, through which Sister Wang's freshly oiled hair and upper body could be seen from the street. There was a suggestion of a smile on her delicate swan-white face, and the flower in her hair, which at first had attracted attention with its faint movement, had now fallen into a state of shimmering quietude. Several of the women were deeply moved by this beatific premarital state, while others were envious or suspicious of it and didn't believe a marriage between Sister Wang and the county magistrate would ever come to pass.

All the inhabitants of the city kept close watch for a newly whitewashed storefront with a red lantern hung outside for good luck and strings of firecrackers made ready to be set off, all hints of a forthcoming marriage. The officials in the yamen gave much time to guessing the situation from Tian Jian's expression, but half a month passed and his intentions remained a great mystery to all.

One bright moonlit night, a cool gentle breeze carried the light sweet-scented fragrance of plum blossoms through the city, suggesting as perfect a time for passionate embraces in the bedroom of "Heavenly

Rain" as on all those rainy, foggy nights. The assistant magistrate brought a bottle of Lord Jade sweet wine to Tian Jian's room and sat with him by the brazier. "Sir, you're the highest official in the county. It's not appropriate for you to remain unmarried forever, and the yamen is too big for one person. I know it's all commotion during the day, but at night it must be awfully lonely for you here in this great space."

"But I don't have a wife."

"Have you considered finding one in Zhuyang County, or would you prefer someone from your hometown?"

"Someone from here would be better."

"Your Excellency has been here for a while. Is there anyone that has caught your eye? If you have, perhaps I could arrange it for you."

"That's not necessary."

"Are you suggesting you have a sweetheart?"

Tian Jian had already had several glasses of wine and was slightly drunk. "You might say that."

The assistant magistrate winked at Tian Jian, and for a moment seemed lost in thought as if trying to deduce which of all the eligible women from the city's rich influential families she might be. "May I ask who she is?"

Tian Jian laughed slyly. "I'm not going to tell you now, but you'll find out when the time comes."

The last month of the year passed quickly as did the new year celebrations. Tian Jian's birthday fell in the second month of the lunar year, as the same month Sister Wang who was six years younger. It was in this month when the apricot blossoms would be in bloom that Tian Jian chose a day to bring his bride home. In anticipation he decided to have the bedroom of "Heavenly Rain" renovated and whitewashed and was filled with joy during the Spring Festival; he was soon to be married, water was running through the canal, and the spring harvest had been very productive. During the festival, each of the village communities organised themselves into teams and put on daily performances which were enjoyed by the officials and the people. On the first day of the new year, Tian Jian prayed to the heavenly deities, before embarking on a round of daily trips to the city and county with his attendants to take part in the festivities. The county commander was busy ensuring every police station was manned, and also had his men patrolling the county to prevent fires and theft. Tian Jian saw this as an excellent course of action and showed his appreciation with some new year's gifts.

At noon on the tenth day of the new year, the yamen arranged its yearly collection of donations for the harvest festival. Even though the previous year had seen a bumper crop and there were two hundred and thirty-seven families donating, Zhuyang County was situated in a remote area and had relatively few wealthy families, thus the average donation per family was only seven to eight bushels. According to the rules of the warehouse, fixed awards were distributed according to the amount of grain donated. Tian Jian had them amended so that local officials could award special dividends to families who contributed more than ten bushels. On the seventh day of the new year, approval for the revision was given and in addition, Tian Jian handed out generous bonuses which further gained the people's trust. He had the main hall decorated for a large banquet at which three rounds of alcohol were served accompanied by much kowtowing. When it was over he escorted everyone out of the yamen to the beating of drums. When the donations had been collected, he made a speech praising the virtuous, and called to the bench all commoners and officials who throughout the year had been admired and respected in their communities, had been observed doing good deeds for others or had earned official or educational degrees. After an active and tumultuous day, Tian Jian returned to his newly decorated room, and was sitting down to a relaxing cup of the jasmine tea Sister Wang had sent him when the county commander burst in to inform him of a disturbing incident that had just been reported from Niuzhai Village involving a son who'd beaten and injured his father. The villagers were shocked and clamouring for action to be taken right away so the county commander immediately went to investigate. He found that the offender had already been arrested and was being detained in prison. The incident coincided with Tian Jian's presentation of awards for virtuous behaviour. It was perhaps for this reason that the county commander advised him to act expeditiously to offer moral guidance for the people and reduce the likelihood of further trouble. Tian Jian agreed and quickly went to the court where he had the offender brought for trial. Tian Jian found himself confronted with a young man brutal in appearance who knelt down before him, and an old man on the verge of death who had to be carried into the courtroom on a wooden plank. Tian Jian cursed the man kneeling before him. How could he be so unfilial and disrespectful as to beat his own father so badly, more so on a day when the whole county was joyously celebrating the new year? Even a beast would not be so insubordinate.

"His Excellency only knows that the son hit the father. Why doesn't he ask the father what he was doing to deserve a beating?"

"What was he doing?"

"He was playing babe-in-arms with my wife!"

"What did you say? I've never heard a son speak so obnoxiously about his father. If you talk like that again I'll have your face slapped."

An attendant rushed forward and prepared himself to slap the son's face if necessary.

"Your Excellency, listen to me, I only suckled her boobs once, and you see how vicious he was to me. He suckled my wife for three years, and I never said a word to him about it."

Tian Jian had heard more than enough, so the old man's last comment really infuriated him, and smashing down his wooden gavel, he yelled out: "You disgusting cradle-snatching old letch! You actually have the nerve to open your mouth and admit you violated the law against incest."

"Sir, since you've already heard that, I'm not afraid of you hearing the worst. Ask him what else he did," shouted the son.

"Well?"

"My current wife is my second one. Not long after I took my first wife home, I was hired to go and work on the plain. I was away for a year and when I returned my wife was pregnant. At the time we drifters weren't permitted to settle on the plain and our families lived alone deep in the mountains. You ask him how my wife got pregnant."

"Tell me the truth, old man."

"It wasn't me. I only peeped at her naked."

"Are you saying a ghost did it?"

"His wife was ferocious. A tiger couldn't get near her. I told him, at night we kept a pisspot in the central room. I was sleeping in the east room, and when I woke up to take a piss, I couldn't stop myself from giving my John Thomas an airing, and maybe I was unwittingly aimed in the direction of the pisspot. When your wife woke up in the west room and went to use the pot, maybe she sat on the spot if you know what I mean. That was her problem and had nothing to do with me. He can't accuse his father without having any proof."

"Your excellency, can you really believe what he's saying?"

Tian Jian's entire body began shaking with anger. How could this shameless pair howl at each other in his courtroom like wild animals. The fact that this vile offence took place in Tian Jian's county was sure to make him look bad. "You old bastard, I want to hear the truth, now!"

The old man continued to deny that he had had sex with his son's wife so Tian Jian ordered an attendant to beat the truth out of him, but after receiving one hundred and twenty strokes of the cane the old man died.

"Your Excellency, he's dead."

"He's dead?"

"Yes, he's dead."

Tian Jian regretted his action but didn't want to admit it. "Actually, he just died a little ahead of schedule, because if he hadn't died now, I would have had him paraded through the streets before being beheaded." Tian Jian then had the son thrown in jail.

The entire incident was disposed of very quickly, and no one could have imagined that the prisoner would try and bribe the jailer with a promise of three hundred taels of silver into taking a message to Sister Wang asking her to talk to the county magistrate on his behalf. "Sister Wang tries to help everybody she can, but how can a common widow help you out with the county magistrate?"

"I understand Sister Wang and the county magistrate get along very well. Her talking to him could be helpful."

"Even if Sister Wang and the county magistrate are on good terms, considering what you've done, who'd want to help you?"

"My relationship with Sister Wang is unusual."

"Is she related to you?"

"I wouldn't call her just a relative. You see, Sister Wang was my first wife. Yes, I beat her and forced her to abort that bastard child, and then got rid of her, but with me locked up in this rotten jail how could she not remember what she once felt for me?"

The jailer immediately reported what he'd heard to the county commander who, in turn, told Tian Jian whose entire body immediately weakened under the weight of this staggering news. A moment later he let out a cry of despair and passed out.

Of course, Sister Wang didn't ask Tian Jian for clemency for the offender, for the jailer did not inform her what her former husband had said, but the scandalous matter became the talk of the town and Sister Wang was thoroughly humiliated. Everybody knew she was a drifter, a woman who had not had an easy life, and now all of a sudden it appeared there was an ugly, incestuous skeleton in her closet. Even though Sister Wang was a good talker, there didn't seem to be anyone she could talk to to clarify this mess. After the incident she'd spent several miserable years trying to forget and by the time she arrived in Zhuyang County she had almost succeeded. Now she was without hope and felt as if she were falling deeper and deeper into a bottomless pit, the stench provoked by the charge of incest worsening each time it was mentioned. She detested her bitter fate: A fresh and ripening plant had been crushed to bits by a dirty, odious old man, its tender leaves devastated and defiled. And who was it should she hate? Her lying impudent father-in-law or her stupid, brutish husband? She hated them both from the bottom of her heart and now hated herself as well. After she'd fled the hell that was the prison of their home, she'd led a pleasant and carefree life as a widow. Perhaps there were people who regarded her as cheap, wild and immoral, but these condemnations were infrequent and did not give her much cause for concern; they certainly hadn't inhibit her from getting on with her life reasonably well. But she had become involved with the honourable county magistrate and he was deeply in love with her. His attentions he had heaped upon her had given her a feeling of self-worth that she'd never had before and a far different understanding of what her life could be like, and then just as she was about to become the county magistrate's wife, she'd been hurled back into her seamy disreputable past. What would the county magistrate think of her now? And how would the people of Zhuyang treat a county magistrate who had such a wife?

The pitiable Sister Wang stayed in bed for three successive days and nights, trusting to her fate and hoping the man who'd assaulted his father wasn't her former husband. "If it really was him, how could he have dared to ask for my help?" And if it wasn't, all the slanderous gossip would be proved groundless, merely the lies of vindictive people. Nevertheless, the posters on the street announcing the sentence handed down to the offender all had her former husband's name written clearly on them; and soon after the sentence was posted, the county commander sent one of his men to inform her she had to close her shop, and had sealing tape pasted across the main entrance facing onto the street to keep everyone away.

Sister Wang became desperate. She feared going to the yamen to try and explain to Tian Jian what had really happened, and lost all hope of him coming for her in a big sedan chair in the second month of the lunar year and taking her away as his bride. She spent the days alone in her house weeping, with the doors and windows shut and the embroidered shawl wrapped in her arms.

Tian Jian had some reservations about imposing the death penalty on the unfilial son, but at the moment of sentencing decided the crime was too great for leniency, and if he didn't have him executed Tian Jian's own anger would never abate. After the execution he returned to "Heavenly Rain", and disregarding his pledge, drank one flask of alcohol after another, his body eventually numb to the point of inertness though his mind was crystal clear. He had no doubt that Sister Wang was the prisoner's former wife. She'd told him she was a widow, but he had never asked her how she'd become a widow, and could not imagine how much she had suffered. Had she really committed incest with her father-in-law as her former husband had charged? Tian Jian sighed with regret. The old dog had admitted everything except that, but now that he was dead and as the dead don't talk there was no way to know what really happened. What remained was an unsolved mystery only Sister Wang could clear up. And what about Sister Wang? This was a matter of great importance regarding her and she hadn't come forward with an explanation. Didn't that alone suggest she had a guilty conscience about it and that the accusation was in fact true?

If the facts were as the husband described them, what was left to Tian Jian's imagination was a harrowing scene: Late at night in an isolated house deep in the mountains a vile old man gropes his way to the west wing of the house where his daughter-in-law is sleeping... This thought made Tian Jian sick to his stomach. But, but... Again and again Tian Jian analysed his feelings. If the father of Sister Wang's child was her father-in-law, he had been beaten to death for his crime. It occurred to Tian Jian that from Sister Wang's perspective, how did he and her father-in-law differ? Was it right for her to be subjected to such intense public humiliation and for him to condemn and abandon her? No. No. The father-in-law had acted despicably, but he was equally despicable for ceaselessly doubting and scrutinising her.

Thus did Tian Jian forgive Sister Wang and rack

his brains to find a way to help her. Finally he decided to pay a call at her shop. The street was quiet and almost empty, but as he neared Sister Wang's shop he found that a fairly large crowd was gathered in front of it. The entrance was still sealed with tape and the poster announcing the prisoner's sentence was pasted on one of the wooden beams. When Tian Jian arrived a number of people were scattering ashes over the front steps. One of the crowd told Tian Jian that Sister Wang was so repugnant to the neighbours that they had decided to put a circle of ashes around her store to ward off evil spirits. Tian Jian's anger burst out but there was nothing he could do to change the situation, and after gazing long at her small, now frail-looking shopfront, he returned to the yamen and ordered the crippled attendant to go back when no one was around and bring Sister Wang to see him. The attendant did as he was told but returned alone carrying a bag of chinaberry seeds and three bags of jasmine tea. He explained that when he got to her shop the front door was shut, so he went around to the back and shouted for her several times, but she didn't respond. He could hear her crying inside and continued to shout until she dropped the seeds and tea from the back window, but she refused to show her face.

"She won't come to see me?" Tian Jian stared vacantly at the chinaberry seeds and jasmine tea, his eyes reddening. "Perhaps, Sister Wang did sleep with her father-in-law and is ashamed to face me, but she still remembered that I need my uniform cleaned and enjoy drinking jasmine tea. My dear, my dear, you're too ashamed to come here, and I feel too guilty to come and see you."

The first month of the new year passed, the second hot on its heels. It should have been a time of great joy, but for Tian Jian the period was marked by desolation and grief to the point where he lost all interest in eating and grew considerably thinner, and made no effort to trim his unkempt beard and moustache. The county commander brought him a bag of ginseng and enquired as to the cause of his drawn and sallow face. On several occasions Tian Jian wanted to ask the county commander why he thought it necessary to close Sister Wang's shop, but felt too conflicted about his own feelings for Sister Wang to mention it. He simply said he had caught a cold.

"The problem is that there's no one here to care for Your Excellency when you're not feeling well. Sir, if you don't mind I would like to offer a suggestion but don't know whether it's appropriate at the present time."

"What could you say that wouldn't be appropriate?"

"Sir, since your arrival in Zhuyang County you've proved yourself to be a wise leader and are unanimously acclaimed. At home my mother often lectures me on the merits of emulating His Excellency, but thinks it's sad His Excellency lives alone. Thus has she spoken of the possibility of my younger sister caring for His Excellency, which, I would add, would be a great honour for the Yao family."

Tian Jian listened patiently to what he had to say, then smiled: "I deeply appreciate your dear mother's solicitousness, and please tell her I'll never forget her kind intentions, but I've just divorced my wife it wouldn't be proper to remarry immediately. If she doesn't mind waiting half a year or so, I would be pleased to reconsider her offer at that time."

Although he had put the county commander off, Tian Jian felt remorseful about abandoning Sister Wang. The sordid matter that had recently come to light was a thing of the past and of no importance to him. During the time in which they'd become involved, he had learnt little about her past, and his deep-felt interest in her, to the point of wanting to marry her, was due to her endearing feminine charm. It was also true that she had reacted passionately to him.

"What would happen to her if our relationship ended? How could she let that happen? She will be terribly hurt if we don't marry. What would have happened if my disreputable past had been exposed instead of hers? What would I do if Sister Wang treated me the way I'm treating her?"

Tian Jian dressed himself neatly, called for his donkey and rode again to Sister Wang's shop. When he arrived, he looked up directly into the piercing sun and saw that the windows were closed and the green gauze curtains drawn. Reluctant to call out to her, he coughed loud enough for her to hear, and eventually the window opened slightly. Tian Jian couldn't see her through the small opening in the window, but assuming she could see him, he tried as hard as he could to force a smile and even winked seductively, but the only response was for the window to be gently closed.

Tian Jian ordered the donkey to remain where it was, and momentarily glanced down at the shadows himself and the animal projected on the ground. He was on the verge of despair when he heard someone call out to him, and the county commander approached with a big smile on his face. Behind him he led a white horse draped with a saddle cloth of red felt.

"What are you doing out here today?"

"I was bored in the yamen, and since the weather is so good I decided to have some air."

"Walking is good for your health. I was just on my way to the yamen to see you. I didn't expect to run into you here. What do you think of this horse? They are not bred in Zhuyang County, all we can manage are donkeys. One of my relatives in the provincial capital gave it to me, but I didn't think it proper for me to ride it. My mother wanted me to present it to you and had my younger sister make a saddle cloth for you. Sir, please accept this gift; the magistrates of other counties would surely mock us if the Zhuyang County magistrate had only a donkey to ride."

Tian Jian couldn't easily refuse the gift. He agreed it wouldn't be appropriate for the county magistrate to ride a donkey while the county commander rode a horse, and after profusely expressing his gratitude to the commander's mother, they exchanged the two animals there and then. Tian Jian led the horse around to view its form. As he started back for the yamen, he suddenly turned around and yelled out: "You come and see me. Definitely come and see me." The county commander clasped his hands and bowed. "As you wish, Your Excellency." Of course, Tian Jian's words were more particularly intended for Sister Wang.

Three days later, Sister Wang still hadn't appeared at the yamen, so one night Tian Jian went once more to her shop but was not rewarded with a view of her. In his office he felt frustrated, sitting and doing nothing. Finally one night he again made for her shop and ripped the sealing tape away from the entrance, kicked away the circle of ashes, and was about to beat on the door when someone passed by on the street and he fled in panic. The next day the county commander reported to Tian Jian that a villain had dared to rip the sealing tape from Sister Wang's storefront the previous night, raising a security problem in the city. He was sure one of the drifters had done it. Tian Jian ventured to ask whether it was worth sealing up the shop again and even suggested letting Sister Wang reopen for business. The county commander disagreed: "The people have been behaving well since His Excellency was appointed, and considering what she did we are being lenient enough by not forcing her to leave the city; if we let her continue to operate her store, people might complain the county authorities are covering up for immoral men and licentious women!"

Tian Jian disagreed but held his tongue. When he returned to his room and thought about what the county commander had said, he became infuriated. What the hell did he mean by "immoral men and licentious women"? I'm a bandit and I was born of bandits, and I think it's time everybody had a good look at this excellency's true talents. That night, Tian Jian reverted to his former profession, and masked and suitably attired, he spent the nocturnal hours leaping over walls and slipping through gates. By the time he'd finished, he'd acquired the ten bars of gold the county commander's family kept hidden in their jadestone inlaid dining table, a jade ornament and an incense burner owned by the wealthy Zhang family, and a shroud made for the parents of the superintendent of education. The next night he carried away a box of jewellery owned by the wife of the dean of education and an embroidered dress from the silk yarn store. Finally on the third night, he took two hundred taels of silver from the chief archivist's home, fifty taels of silver from the Wang family pawnshop, and even seized goods that three night workers were carrying on their backs, scattering the mountain grown walnuts, tree fungi and mushrooms all over the ground. For three consecutive nights, Tian Jian was more exhilarated and happy than he'd been in a long time. He had been afraid he'd lost his talents, and although he wasn't quite as nimble as he once was, everything still came off just as he intended. After all, Zhuyang City was just a hick border town with no one who could stop him from coming and going at will. Tian Jian realised that his old profession was ten times, or a hundred times, more gratifying to him than being county magistrate.

Of course, the entire city was panic-stricken during these three days, and the families who were robbed flocked to the court shouting and complaining about the intrusions. Tian Jian played the role of investigator and listened attentively to the particulars of each burglary, but when the image of the white wolf appeared again and again, he developed a terrific headache and fainted on the courtroom table. Those who witnessed Tian Jian faint concluded that it was due to his anger and grief at the crimes, and they massaged his chest and forced water down his throat until he came to. A little later he asked for the county commander to come to see him, and when he arrived he immediately knelt down before Tian Jian and criticised himself for being negligent, suggesting that the thefts were the work of a notorious bandit who must have recently come to Zhuyang County.

"Zhuyang is a small city. What would a big-time outlaw be doing here? Have you made a list of who has been burgled and what was taken?"

The county commander handed over a detailed list. The only thing that wasn't noted down were the ten gold bars taken from the county commander's house.

"Is this everything?"

"Yes, that's all."

"I notice no gold was stolen. Do you think a major thief would come to Zhuyang just for these minor goods? You have lived here for quite some time, how is it that you still haven't rid Zhuyang of even small-time thieves?"

The county commander acted as if he didn't know what to say and could only repeatedly mumble "Yes, sir yes" in reply.

On the fourth night, Tian Jian sat drinking tea in the "Heavenly Rain" bedroom and began to worry about what he'd done. That day the image of the wolf had returned to haunt him several times, for him a portentious omen which helped him control his restive temper. Although he'd taken advantage of the opportunity to reprimand the county commander and delighted in his worried expression and sweating brow, he knew he'd acted ridiculously and should abandon any further illegal activities. How could a reformed bandit turned dignified county magistrate do what he'd done? When Tian Jian reassumed his role as county magistrate, his anguish at not seeing Sister Wang returned too. He again left the yamen and rode to her shop, and after again finding it closed and not catching even the slightest glimpse of her, he rode back frustrated and unhappy. This became a nightly practice, excursions which eventually provoked the assistant magistrate's interest and praise. "His Excellency is an honest and wise official. Zhuyang's first county magistrate never conducted nightly patrols of the city."

Tian Jian laughed to himself whilst announcing: "Three provinces converge on the border of this small and remote county. The people here are a complicated mix and the crime rate is high. These recent burglaries have been a great embarrassment to me, and since I have a horse, I can well ride around at night and try to rid the city of thieves." Tian Jian's patrols thus ironically became a point of virtue. Several days later he left all the articles he'd stolen, as well as the ten gold bars, under the small arched bridge at the east end of the main road. The stolen property was discovered the next day and turned over to the yamen, and Tian Jian immediately returned each item according to the list the county commander had prepared, and since the gold bars hadn't been reported stolen, he deposited them in the county treasury. All the inhabitants of the city were consumed by this matter, and universally praised the county magistrate for his night patrols which had led both to the suppression of theft and return of everything that had been taken, in addition to the gift of the gold. In tribute to Tian Jian's efforts, a plaque was made for him, inscribed "Just and Honourable" and, with great celebration, it was carried to the yamen and presented it to him.

The more the people of Zhuyang County hailed their county magistrate the worse Tian Jian felt. On his nightly patrols, he'd often see a light in Sister Wang's shop and would drop his reins, letting the horse walk up to her shopfront, only to see the lamp go out immediately. He'd then jerk up the head of the horse, which would abruptly stand still, kick up its front hooves and neigh loudly before slowly walking away. At a distance from the shop, Tian Jian would turn back his head and again see a light in the window, but if he rode back it would again go out. It was obvious to him that Sister Wang could tell when he was approaching from the hoofbeats on the road, but he couldn't decide if the lighting and extinguishing of the lamp meant she didn't want him to visit her.

If one night Sister Wang had waited for him on the street or opened the window and waved to him, perhaps Tian Jian would have suddenly recalled the ugly things she was reputed to have done and which were causing him such great distress. But her avoidance of him only intensified his regret that he had not visited her immediately after the incident with her father-in-law became public; and the more tender thoughts he had of her the greater was his desire to see her.

The seasonal rains returned, bringing sexual chaos with its oceans of muddy water. Tian Jian couldn't get Sister Wang off his mind, and each night as he mounted his horse, he threw over his shoulders the same oilcloth he'd once wrapped around her. He was full of hope each time he went out to see her, but inevitably returned disappointed and this particular night was no exception. All along the quiet city street windows were closing early and lanterns were set low, and the air reverberated with the sounds of sweet laughter and the squeaking of beds. With the return of the rainy season the people of Zhuyang County once again honoured Heaven and earth and drowned themselves in love-making. How cold and lonely his loved one must be on this rainy night, he thought as he returned to the yamen alone. With his head hung in gloom he entered "Heavenly Rain", held up the oilcloth and, recalling that earlier tempestuous scene, felt his body first burn with desire, then grow cold with sweat, and finally sink in on itself, as if awarded a reprise of his ardent feelings for his lover.

"Oh, my dear love. My dear Sister Wang. Would we have allowed ourselves to fall in love if we'd known it was going to end this way? You haven't come to Tian Jian for so long. Have you decided to forget him? Yes, you've forgotten him and there's nothing he can do about it."

The rain gradually eased, and in his uncertain state, Tian Jian began to blame the rain as well. If they hadn't made love during the rainy season and Tian Jian had never experienced the softness and tenderness of a woman, would he be so despondent now? Why was that? Why?

Tian Jian agonised over these questions for quite some time, coming to no clear conclusion. He could only lament that he was a mere mortal with male genitalia and sexual desire. Why did man have these demanding genitals? They were there for procreation, for the continuation of the male line, but Tian Jian wasn't particularly interested in spawning descendants. He couldn't understand why Heaven had implanted such desire in men for this made men highly attracted to women. And why was it impossible, even in dreams, to escape this tragedy? Tian Jian was deeply in love with Sister Wang, a love so strong it rendered him completely indifferent to all other women, and now she was lost to him. The only way Tian Jian could escape this bitter love was to excise the carnality he was born with, and the more he considered this possibility the more he was impelled to do it. Finally, this night in a moment of madness he pulled off his pants, covered his genitals with the oilcloth, and with one thrust of a knife forever did away with the harrowing burden of desire. Tian Jian fainted from the pain, but when he came to and saw his truncated organs on the ground covered with blood, he just laughed coldly. "Sister Wang, my dear Sister Wang. This finishes us, doesn't it?"

Using illness as a pretext, Tian Jian remained in bed for several days to care for his wound, and intentionally injured his arm to dispel any suggestion of what had really happened. When the doctor applied medicine to his arm he asked for an extra supply, and secretly used it for the wound at his groin. Now that he lacked his carnal organs, he no longer felt that peculiar, uncontrollable desire for Sister Wang that had so overwhelmed him. All that remained was a detached feeling of sympathy and pity for her fate. After all, Sister Wang was just a woman, and weren't all women essentially the same? Tian Jian knew that if Sister Wang was appraised objectively, no one could say she conformed to any female norm. She was sarcastic, impatient and bold in speech and action, and though her shortcomings weren't repellant to others, her behaviour certainly didn't match that expected of a woman from a high-ranking family. Why had he become so infatuated with her? Had it been a mistake? Had he been bewitched by her? What was the fatal attraction between men and women? Tian Jian had the answer: it was a trick played by Heaven in giving them desire. This was like eating. If the sense of taste didn't exist and eating was only necessary for survival, eating would be a highly unpleasant process. To obtain food, man had to plant and harvest; to eat he had to chew and swallow; to digest he required a stomach and intestines; and if that wasn't enough he had to defecate and urinate: What an exhausting bore! But since man had a sense of taste, he willingly endured this laborious process. Wasn't it the same with sexual desire? Just one single act of intercourse was a painful monotonous event, but because of Heaven's artful trap of desire, mankind readily submitted to the ordeal for a fleeting moment of ecstasy. Tian Jian had seen through this great ruse and for him the innocence of the world was restored. In fact, he was overjoyed he'd finally come to his senses and laughed at his futile efforts to visit Sister Wang. He was even able to console himself with the peace of mind that accompanied the amputation of his desire.

Through his action, Tian Jian had exposed the sexual desire for what it was and no longer felt bound by it. Nevertheless, he didn't intend to enter Transformation Temple and become a monk, he still had a great deal to do. By assuming the position of county magistrate, he'd abandoned his life as an outlaw and reformed himself. Now after many bitter years and no longer hounded by sexual passion, at last he could fully devote himself to being a virtuous official.

Tian Jian was decidedly more relaxed after he recovered from his injury. He attended court every day, dispensed with his cases easily and read when there was nothing else to do. Whenever he reached the point of working himself to exhaustion, he'd lie down on his bed in "Heavenly Rain" and gaze at the four beautifully calligraphed hanging scrolls that Sister Wang had given him. One by one he'd examine each precept on the art of being a virtuous official, reviewing he'd accomplished and that which still remained to be done, then mutter to himself "Sister Wang is a good person" before falling into a sound sleep. One day he suddenly realised that he'd castrated himself he hadn't seen the image of the white wolf. And his uniform which Sister Wang was no longer cleaning, was no longer plagued by lice in the seams. Thus, he asked himself whether Sister Wang had alleviated his distress or provoked an endless string of troubles?

The new Tian Jian couldn't help shuddering at the presence of women in the world. If men wanted to conquer the world, it was equally obvious that women wanted to conquer men. The spirit of a cunning fox was metamorphosed in a pretty woman, and the more alluring she was the more harmful she became, like ripe, bright-coloured poisoned berries or a calm bottomless pond. In fact, Tian Jian was grateful to Sister Wang for helping him understand women, so well that now he disliked them and regarded them all with contempt. What difference did it make if they were beautiful or ugly, they were all just bodies. He particularly disliked women who were promiscuous but if he could, would behead them all! He subsequently issued an order prohibiting the arranging or celebrating of marriages, all rendezvous, and even normal sexual relations between spouses on rainy or foggy days; and set aside particular days on which the people of Zhuyang

County should offer sacrifices to Heaven and earth, drink the local alcohol, and stroll around at temple fairs. He also divided the people in the countryside into village units of one hundred families, with each ten families forming a special tax community called a *li*. The heads of both the villages and the tax communities were responsible for patrolling and supervising their respective units. The county commander was responsible for maintaining law and order in the urban areas, and those who committed offences were summarily taken into custody with no questions asked. In this way, bad practices were to be rectified, Zhuyang County would again become a peaceful place in which to live, and Tian Jian would finally be satisfied.

Although Tian Jian ceased his nightly patrols, he still enjoyed riding around on his horse during the day, and became very fastidious about his appearance. Before leaving the yamen, he would look at himself repeatedly in the mirror to make sure his hat was on properly and his clothes were neat. Whether he went out on foot or on horseback, he was always very attentive to maintaining his official demeanour, and ordered his attendants to follow behind him at precisely the appropriate distance. When he rode he would sit ramrod straight on his horse, with his head cocked, his chest out and his eyes gazing into the distance, one hand lightly tapping the saddle to the rhythm of the hoofbeats. Staring at his shadow under the bright sun, he offered the world a smug and complacent look.

When all the wheat was harvested, the village communities had no further work to do and families began visiting each other to offer their regards and present gifts, and the county yamen itself was the recipient of many donations. At first the gifts were sent from a few private individuals, but then one day, to the sound of gongs and drums, the people of Three Fork Village presented Tian Jian with a wooden tablet. They were followed by the people of Dragon Bridge, Windblown, Bamboo Forest and other villages all doing the same. After twenty-three wooden tablets had been hung in the yamen meeting hall, Tian Jian smiled and said to a group of officials: "The people of Zhuyang County are good people. If you treat them well, they won't forget it. Unfortunately, I see I still haven't fully carried out my responsibilities in ten of the villages." When this news reached the ten villages concerned, the village leaders panicked and stayed up all night making tablets that they could present to him too.

That night Tian Jian ordered the assistant magistrate to distribute monetary rewards to the rural villages. An embarrassed assistant magistrate suggested that the money might be hard to raise, so Tian Jian had the comptroller take out the account books to determine the amount of funds that had been received from the livestock, head and land taxes as well as monies raised for supplementing salaries to keep the officials honest. He also checked the salary and living expenses provided for the chief archivist, and the salaries of the yamen guards, the errand boys, sedan and umbrella bearers, granary keepers, street patrolmen, jailers, chief cooks and grooms. After examining these figures, he ordered a little more than one tael of silver to be deducted from each of the individual amounts. The county commander, however, immediately challenged this idea. "His Excellency doesn't need to worry about giving monetary rewards to the rural villages. The county magistrate is an intelligent ruler, and it goes without saying the villagers are very grateful. On the other hand, has his excellency considered reporting Zhuyang County's prosperity through the past half-year to the prefectural officials?"

"Oh, oh," Tian Jian exclaimed, immediately understanding what he meant and recognising his own oversight. As a consequence, he quickly withdrew his order to give money to the villages, and instead deducted one and a half taels of silver from each of the public funds intended for the county magistrate, the head of the military, the food for the poor, the spring and autumn offerings to the Confucian and martial arts temples, the sacrifices for rain in the fourth month of the lunar year, the rural entertainment expenses, the sacrificial articles to the martial arts temples in the fifth month of the lunar year, the official salaries for education officials, and the stipends and expenses for twenty trainee officials. Tian Jian gave the deducted funds to the county commander, who compiled a list of names and corresponding gifts.

Five days later the county commander had twelve donkeys loaded with silk, animal pelts, crude lacquer, medicines, alcohol and meat ready for transporting to the prefectural capital. Tian Jian personally saw the chief gendarme off, and holding up a glass of wine in both hands, wished him a successful journey. As the loaded donkeys rode out of the city gate, the crippled attendant whispered something to Tian Jian which shocked the warm smile off his face.

"Dead?"

"Yes, she's dead."

"When?"

"She was found this morning, but as yet we don't know the precise time of death."

Tian Jian muttered to himself: "Dead? Why did she want to die?"

"Your Excellency, she has already been put in a coffin. This afternoon we'll dig a grave at the foot of the mountain by the river. Although we don't know the exact time of death, the neighbours are saying she died on an ominous day and because of that the burial can not take place until a half year after the grave has been dug. You should go and see her. She can not refuse to see you now."

"Yes. I will go."

That night when the moon was full and there were few stars in the sky, Tian Jian left his white horse at the yamen and passed through the city gate on foot, accompanied only by the crippled attendant. They walked past the Westward Flowing River and quietly approached the foot of the mountain. Sister Wang's coffin lay in a small adobe-like hut surrounded by a dark pine forest. While Tian Jian waited, the attendant moved aside the rocks that served as a door to the hut and went in. The coffin still hadn't been nailed shut, and the lid was tied down with a rope. "Your Excellency, do you want to come in?" Tian Jian entered the hut without speaking, and stared at Sister Wang lying in the opened box. Although the coffin wasn't particularly large, her body filled only half of it, giving her the look of an emaciated child. Tian Jian had seen many dead people in his life, but none like her. She must have been dead for many days, for her flesh and bones had withered greatly. Could she have been dead this long without her neighbours detecting the stench of decay because she was completely dehydrated? The attendant told him that just that morning it had suddenly occurred to an old woman that Sister Wang's back door hadn't opened for several days and wondered if she'd been able to draw water and eat. Several other neighbours had noticed this too and they tried knocking. When there was no response they assumed something was wrong, immediately raised a ladder, climbed over the wall into the rear courtyard, and entered her house. They found her in bed already dead from lack of water.

"They say Sister Wang had died in bed, sir. I noticed a mirror at the head of the bed which, from a crack in the window, reflected the street below. Your Excellency, the neighbours all said she must have been quite fastidious about her appearance to have the mirror placed where it was. They didn't realise that she probably spent her time watching the mirror, waiting to see you when you passed by on your nightly patrol."

"Waiting for me?" Tian Jian mumbled. After castrating himself, he had discontinued his patrols. Sister Wang was indeed very strange. "When I rode over to visit her she wouldn't see me. Yet after I stopped trying, could she really have been waiting day and night to hear my horse approach and see my reflection in her mirror?"

Tian Jian put his hands in the coffin and held up Sister Wang's head, and for a moment stared at the wrinkled face, the mouth and eyes that resembled three hollowed-out caverns, then lay it down again. As he did, he noticed someone had placed the leopard skin under her body. Could her neighbours have wrapped her corpse in the leopard skin when they moved her from the bed to the coffin? Tian Jian couldn't bear to think about what had happened between them. He turned away, searched inside his shirt and pulled out an object that was wrapped in the oilcloth and gently placed it under her body.

"Your Excellency, did you give Sister Wang a keepsake?"

"Don't talk so much."

The attendant seemed embarrassed, and said to the corpse: "Sister Wang, you're very fortunate, His Excellency came to visit you."

"I want you to keep returning here in secret for the next six months and make sure no wolves or wild dogs destroy the coffin. I'll also give you money to hire someone to dig a grave so she can rest peacefully in the ground."

The attendant seemed distressed. "Your Excellency, you're the county magistrate. You shouldn't kneel before a common woman. Let me kneel and kowtow to Sister Wang instead."

Tian Jian walked out of the forest in great despair. "Don't tell anyone what happened today," he said to the attendant as he stuck out his hand and felt raindrops. He had no idea when the moon and the stars had disappeared under a layer of storm cloud. The muffled ring of thunder sounded in the distance.

Although the plum blossoms were in bloom, except for a few drops, the seasonal rains hadn't yet fallen. Ten days after Sister Wang's death, Tian Jian ordered the expansion of Yan Pavilion, and to make it a truly wondrous sight, had each village community transplant its prettiest vegetation and trees there. The following summer, Tian Jian received the vacationing prefectural magistrate on the banks of the Westward Flowing River. The magistrate was extremely impressed with the display of flowers around the pavilion, and after his visit, Tian Jian collected additional taxes and again expanded the pavilion square to a circumference of six acres by tearing down the surrounding houses. He also commissioned a rockery to be built from oddly shaped rocks which he had transported from the far distant Tiger Head Mountain in Luoxi County, and the strange varieties of bamboo and flowers that were transplanted from Tianzhu Mountain. All this effort transformed the pavilion into the centrepiece of a large garden. A year later, Tian Jian married the county commander's younger sister, but never invited her to accompany him when he escorted guests from the provincial capital or bureaucrats from neighbouring counties to the garden. One day he suddenly decided that Yan Pavilion itself was too small, of poor quality and crude by contrast with the large, southern style garden he'd fashioned on the square, so he had it rebuilt in the form of a flowered pavilion with twelve pillars. Tian Jian was very pleased with the new version of the pavilion, but it struck him that Yan Geda's burial mound didn't really belong there any more and so he ordered the county commander to have some of his men level the mound and replace it with a large raised flower bed. Henceforth the main intersection of Zhuyang City won great fame as a beautiful scenic spot and was renamed Zhuyang Garden. A year later Tian Jian was cited by the prefectural magistrate for his outstanding achievements as magistrate of Zhuyang

County. The prefectural magistrate also submitted a report to the provincial governor recommending that Tian Jian be promoted to general commander of all twelve counties in the province. It was after Tian Jian heard this news and was awaiting final approval that the heavy rains finally came to Zhuyang County and continued without cease for three months. Mildew began to spread itself over clothes, shoes and hats, and the ceilings and walls of all the houses in the city were eventually hidden behind a layer of green moss. It was at the height of this season that the wound Tian Jian had inflicted upon himself in the act of castration flared up again. Tian Jian eventually died from the unbearable ache caused by the itching.

Translated by Richard Seldin

The Good Fortune Grave

HAD Gou Baidu kept his mouth shut that night he'd been at the bottle, Liu Ziyan would never have been chosen to select the burial ground for Proprietor Yao's aging parents. There was no refusing it now, for Gou had arrived to collect the geomancer. This footman from the Yao house swaggered through the door, his bleached cotton gown rippling behind, then kicked off his shoes and flung himself into the deck chair.

"Brother Liu!" he yelled, "you've got some dough to make! My proprietor in Northern Terrace is waiting for you!"

"How come? He doesn't know me. Northern Terrace is eighty *li* away — that's too far for me to go," Liu said.

Gou plucked a hair from his naked chest, raised it to his lips, blew it away, and then chortled, "You are right, His Excellency doesn't know you, but I do. I've brought a donkey and a rope with me. Which do you prefer, sir, making the journey by donkey or with your arms roped behind you?"

Outside, the donkey was rolling on the ground, kicking up a cloud of dust. A rope was coiled around Gou's waist; at a flick of his hand he sent the rope whizzing up into the air until it hung languorously down from the roof beam. Then he pulled it down, showering the feathery dust on Liu Ziyan's head.

So, off went the geomancer with the butler of the Yao house, his friend Gou.

The passage way that fringed the Yao house was lined on one side with latticed windows in the pattern of golden chains threading through clusters of plum blossoms. Behind one of the windows was a table for eight with four men wearing mandarin jackets over long gowns sat around it drinking and chatting in the midst of a finger-guessing game. They glanced sideways at Liu Ziyan as he padded along the corridor outside. One of them spat, and the thick phlegm barely missed the geomancer as it flew out the window. Liu shifted the long knapsack on his shoulder and bent down to take off his shoes one at a time to shake out the grit that had been hurting his feet, smiling all the time as he staggered on one foot. A chicken scurried in and pecked at the sputum.

The April sun shone radiantly in the sky. Gou Baidu had gone inside to report to Proprietor Yao some time hence and there was still no sign of him. A feather, obviously that of an eagle, came scudding and drifting in a series of arcs in the air before it skittered over the courtyard wall and disappeared out of sight. A dog had sneaked up on him and started barking. Liu was torn between shouting it down and leaving it alone when a voice called out from inside the house: "Let me see who the gentleman is who has arrived." The voice was liquid soft and ringing, and Liu immediately found himself wondering how a shrivelled old man like the proprietor could have sired such a dainty daughter. The sky seemed to brighten up when the woman emerged at the top of a flight of stone stairs like a puff of rosy cloud. Liu had hardly made out her face when the sprightly voice was heard again: "Ah! A smooth-faced greenhorn! Are you really a good geomancer?"

The men at the table stopped their finger-guessing game and once again darted their eyes at the stranger. There was a burst of guffawing when one of them said, "Aren't you the brother who sang love songs at the temple fair the other day?"

Liu blushed deeply, blushing not at the jibe but at the sight of the woman, who gazed at him with eyes that reminded him of the sun suddenly staring from the skies and blinding him with simmering rays of all shapes and sizes. A sense of inferiority surged through him, and his legs trembled.

At length the proprietor called from inside the room: "Let the gentleman in!"

The dog kept snarling and despite Gou Baidu's coaxing, refused to get out of the geomancer's way.

"Tiger!" the woman called out, and in one single step pinned the hostile animal between her knees. In the meantime something icy-cold landed on the nape of Liu's neck. Removing it with his fingers he found it was the husk of a roast water-melon seed that had been in someone's mouth long enough to remove the seed. The woman tossed a foxy smile at him.

The proprietor greeted him while puffing on an opium pipe. "I've invited you because Baidu said you were good at it," he said in a tone appreciating and warm. "For generations we Yaos have been good-natured people. I'll reward you handsomely if you can find an auspicious site for my parents' grave. Even if you don't find one I'll thank you for trying all the same, in what small way I can."

Humbly Liu replied, "As your servant, sir, I'm afraid my talent is but slight, however I'll do my best."

"Right! Think of yourself as the egg of a louse: Just produce a flea large enough to do justice to your size." Laughing, the proprietor asked Gou Baidu to wine and dine the guest in the ante-room. Liu, who was not much of a drinker, brushed off the offer. The proprietor, half rising from his seat, pushed the opium pipe to him and he declined again.

A gentle breeze sent the curtain hooks clinking. It swayed, revealing underneath a tiny foot sheathed in a narrow white shoe. Liu knew who it was behind the curtain: the proprietor's daughter. As he mentally prepared for her to emerge, he saw the tip of the shoe shift its position hesitantly for a moment. Then it disappeared. In no time the geomancer was led through the back door towards the foot of the hill behind the house.

The nape of his neck itched as he tramped about the slope in search of what was supposed to be an auspicious location to site the Yaos' grave. The itching grew so intense that several times it stopped him, absent-minded, in his tracks. Each time it happened he pinched his face with his fingers and cursed himself, "You ridiculous fool!" Then he would break into a trot up and down the gully until he was quite out of breath. All the while a foot-weary Gou trailed behind him, stopping now and then to adjust his shoes. "The hell with you!" he shouted. "You don't smoke, that's okay, but why didn't you accept the pinch of opium and give it to me! What kind of a man are you? Even a donkey has a pipe dangling between its hind legs, and you don't know how to smoke!"

Liu stopped and sat down at the bottom of a ridge. "The sun hasn't set yet. Why don't you go and bring His Excellency here. His good fortune grave is right here."

When the proprietor appeared the western hills had been tainted red by the setting sun. Liu Ziyan set his compass and ascertained the directions. Then, pointing a finger across the river at a horizontal mountain ridge in the distance, he started explaining his findings to his client. "The horizontal ridge is as flat as a desk," he said, "with the peak to the left looking like a hat and the one to the right a writing brush. In front of the 'desk' stand two round boulders, one resembling a drum, the other a cymbal; as percussion instruments for festive occasions, they augur well for the family's luck in officialdom. The contour of the mountain behind the grave site now pitches precipitously down, now rolls gently in curves large and small — these are the markings of a real dragon. The dormant dragon is not alone, for it is attended by servant dragons on all sides, with a large retinue in the front and a band of musicians in tow. A contingent of courtesans stand ready to answer the dragon's questions and attend to its needs," the geomancer said. "Wherever the dragon goes, there is someone greeting it. Within a circumference of several hundred *li*," Liu concluded, "no grave site is as majestic and awe-inspiring as this one."

Immersed in his geographical divinition, Liu became quite carried away with himself. Using the tip of his foot he marked out the four corners of the burial site and asked that wooden pegs be driven in. The workers started with the northern corner, but the peg refused to go down; they dug into the ground, only to find a peg had already been planted there. Moving to the southern corner, a second peg was found. The same happened to the two other spots. The proprietor laughed. "Mr Liu, you are terrific! To tell you the truth, I had already invited four experts to seek a site, who spent seven days finding this one. You were invited to see if they were right. Now, sure enough, this is the auspicious site for my family!" Liu Ziyan slumped to the ground, so panic-stricken by what he had been told that he broke into a cold sweat.

That night, Liu railed at Gou, who was making the bed for him in the wing-room of the Yaos' courtyard. "Gou Baidu, you bloody thief! You're supposed to be a friend of mine. Why didn't you tell me that they wanted me here only to confirm the site? Are you trying to ruin my career?"

"Brother Liu," Gou replied, "don't be so damned ungrateful! Didn't I give you a chance to show yourself off? So I pulled the wool over your eyes, let me treat you to dinner to make up."

With the palm of his hand the geomancer pushed open the back window. A dark world greeted him. Somewhere cats on heat were caterwauling. Under some roof a chamber pot resounded with the straggling sound of a woman urinating. A lantern emerged in the depth of the darkness, accompanied by an eerier voice: "Come home, come home..." and Liu heard Gou ask, "Hey, who are you?"

"It's me, Uncle Gou!"

"Are you the guy from the Western Gate. It's so dark out there. Have you come to rob His Excellency?"

"Uncle, don't talk like that, please. My kid is running a high fever — he is as feverish as burning charcoal. I've come to summon his soul!"

"Did your child catch cold when you and your wife were at it and dislodged the quilt?" Gou laughed and then said, "The geomancer has come and chosen the grave site for His Excellency. Why haven't you sent gifts?"

"Ah. I really didn't know about it. I'll hand in two bushels of millet first thing tomorrow morning."

"That's all right, you needn't bother. Just as long as you are loyal to him. I'll smooth things over for you with His Excellency, so keep the millet for your child. You may as well just give me a chicken right away and get it over with."

"Thank you so much, Uncle Gou!"

"Not at all. I'll wait here. Just tap the window when you've got the chicken."

Gou Baidu turned to light the stove in the corner of the room. The flames were just rising nicely when he heard the expected knock. The window was pushed open, and a chicken, its wings fluttering, was tossed in.

'Wow, a hen!" Gou shouted to Liu. "How lucky we are to get something nice to eat at this hour of the night!"

Before he shut the window he popped his head out and asked, "Hey you from Western Gate, what have you got in your hand?" The neighbour replied that the hen had been behaving strangely over the last few days, laying eggs at night instead of in the daytime, and it had laid an egg on the way there. Gou waxed angry. "Now that the chicken belongs to His Excellency, how dare you pocket his egg? Give it to me!" At these words he snatched the egg from the man, cracked it open against the windowsill and sucked its content dry.

The hen was plucked alive and, without being gibletted, pierced with an iron rod and placed on the fire. Gou, while chiding the hen for its desolate cackles, showered pinches of salt over it until it started oozing oil. "Uh, smells good!" He tore a leg off and handed it to Liu Ziyan.

Suddenly the door was flung open with a bang, letting in a draught which blew out the lamp in the corner of the room. "My goodness! Baidu, whose dog have you stolen and are eating over there?"

From the voice Liu immediately knew who the intruder was and so scared was he that he spat the chicken out and shifted himself into the shadow of the stove.

"Fourth Mistress," Gou crowed, "I knew the aroma of chicken would bring you here. I've prepared a leg for you — and some toothpicks as well."

From the shadows Liu observed the woman's body glow beautifully in the light of the fire. Fourth Mistress? The way Gou addressed the woman confused him, for he had mistaken her for the proprietor's daughter. How could the old man's fourth concubine be so young?

The mistress spotted Liu as she reached out for the chicken. Her eyes flicked and then, composing herself, she said, "My goodness! The gentleman also likes to take food on the sly. Is stolen food particularly tasty?" Liu was embarrassed, but the woman's eyes bore into his. "Women from Northern Terrace all have single eye-lids, but you, Mr Liu, have double lids. Why don't you let me share what you are eating?"

Liu answered, "Certainly Fourth Mistress, help yourself."

"All right, let me eat your meat!" The woman took the chicken leg from Liu. She screwed up her lips and opened her mouth to take a nibble. "Is it too hot?" Liu ventured. The woman answered, "I was afraid of smearing up my lipstick, that's all. Is it still there?" The mouth was pushed together, red and round like a cherry.

That night sleep evaded Liu, who by nature was a man of composure. He tossed and turned in bed, feeling hot and dry all over. All the while Gou Baidu talked glibly on topics from chicken meat to his personal dietal history. He bragged that he had eaten all things with a plumage except the feather duster, and all legged animals except stools. "How about you?"

Liu said no, he had not eaten all of these things. His wide open eyes fixed on the flickering lampwick, his mind as chaotic as the elusive, shifting shadows the lamp threw on the wall. Sleep usually came swiftly to him and on an ordinary day he would have fallen fast asleep the moment his head touched the pillow, especially after riding eighty *li* on the back of the donkey and spending an entire afternoon tramping up and down the hills. Now a hundred things came crowding into his mind. He thought about his life as an orphan, apprenticed to his master in the Xuanwu Mountains at the age of eighteen, and recalled his long career as a geomancer. Having taken roads that no others dared take and seen people he wasn't supposed to see, he was still amazed by the unexpected turns in life. Take what happened today as an example: It was hard to explain how a man like Gou Baidu could have coerced him into coming here to meet the proprietor, known far and wide as a rich and powerful man. And yet here too, he met this fourth wife, a stunning beauty.

The mere thought of Fourth Mistress brought echoes of her shrill giggles ringing in his eardrums. Charged with an audacity only children are capable of, the giggles imparted an unaffected ease and even an inconceivable boldness to this young woman from a rich family, and give the youthful Liu Ziyan the sensation that he had run into a dainty small animal in a newly reclaimed forest. For his sake, the woman had restrained her dog between her legs. Whilst she was doing this, her body leaned sideways in such a graceful pose where one of her legs appeared drawn taut like a bow string as gravity pulled at her entire body. To keep her balance, the other leg bent backward slightly from the knee down, and her arm hung in the air all the while, her hips perfectly sculpted by her white brocade cheongsam which, embroidered all over with tiny red plum blossoms, faintly hinted at the milky-white skin of her calf. One shoe was half-off a foot which looked feeble but supported her body weight admirably. Yes, it was this beautiful foot, plump but not fat, which later pointed out her presence to him by revealing its tip beneath the door curtain. In his mind's eye, Liu could see the five toes with their tender knuckles and jade-like toenails inside the shoe that was embroidered with a peach flower which looked so fresh he could almost breath its fragrance.

To Liu, the presence of this woman came as an

unimaginable miracle, for he had never seen a grey and shrivelled man in the company of such a young, delicate wife; a woman who set his heart pounding at first sight. The nape of his neck where the melon seed moistened with her fragrant saliva had landed, still felt itchy. Since that moment that patch of skin had seemed to gain a life of its own. But there was more for when darkness had fallen that night, she had praised him for having double-lidded eyes. He had heard this flattery almost everywhere he went and it had never had any meaning for him before. But when the words came from this woman, they had thrown him into panic, and unaccountably, beads of sweat had formed on the tip of his nose.

Thinking back, he knew he'd behaved like an ignorant country bumpkin. "With my handsome face and unrivalled skill in geomancy," he thought, "I certainly deserve a woman with regular features to be my wife and life-long companion. But to this day, having travelled all over the country with my compass and cloth bag slung over my shoulder, I've got nothing but an iron lock for the door of my house! I would take my pre-ordained bachelorhood lying down if I had just stayed home planting crops and grazing cattle. But who am I? I've seen so many of the things to be seen in the world and, as luck would have it, I have chanced to see the maidenly concubine of this wizened old man." It suddenly dawned on him that his career was much like that of a beggar, but all his hatred for it gave way to a deep sigh in the isolated wilderness of the night.

He blew out the oil lamp. As the wick glowered on the verge of extinction, Liu willed himself not to get lost in thoughts of the past. Outside, darkness was gathering. The dog was still barking in the yard. A voice called, "Tiger!", then came the faint clinking of a metal chain. Holding his breath subconsciously and remaining quite still, Liu knit his brows tight as if waiting for his third eye to open on his forehead so that he could perceive what was happening in the yard. The woman had changed into a short, collarless night gown which gave her a tenderness and charm quite different from that he had seen in daytime. In a subtle way the gown revealed the lines of her protruding collarbone at the base of her tender neck. Fourth Mistress was perhaps the singular epitome of feminine beauty: Her chest and hips were as fleshy and well-rounded as any should be, and her back and waist were slim without being skinny. She was walking her dog. The chain-leash was more than her delicate strength could bear, so that it dragged along, softly scratching the ground as she padded past the bedroom of her bed-ridden father-in-law and the prayer room in which her vegetarian mother-in-law was murmuring incantations. Would she retire to the bed she shared with the proprietor? He imagined the pair of red-tipped white shoes once emptied of their contents, would look like a couple of small boats moored to the riverbank that had just transported two flowers fresh with morning dew to the embrace of a tree full of patent signs of decay. At the thought Liu's eyes stared wide into the darkness, and despite himself these words came out: "Gou Baidu, your Fourth Mistress is so pretty!"

"Every good woman in this world has been laid by dogs!" Gou said. Obviously, he too was sleepless and, moreover, was enraged by something which gnawed away inside. "Have you taken a fancy to her, too?" he demanded.

This single line tainted Liu's fine feelings. He regretted having roused this vulgar, ugly man. But it was too late, for the man was already striking the flint, wanting to relight the lamp. In the glow of the tiny sparks that flew up from the flint, Liu could see Gou's stark naked body in the bed with his manhood menacingly erect between his legs. Disgusted, Liu turned his head away. "Pass me the kindling paper, which is in the hole of the wall behind your bed," Gou said. Instead of reaching out for the kindling, Liu took out a roll of flint rope. With a "Here you are!" he tossed it over, and at a flick of his hand deliberately toppled the lamp. Gou, cursing and abandoning the flint, started talking about the proprietor's state of impotence. "Despite heavy dosages of ginseng and pilose antler," he said, "the man remains limp and can do no more than fondle his fourth concubine's hips, and more than once his flap-skinned face has been left with bloody scratches."

Liu, bored by this soliloquy, pretended to snore. "I won't say any more if you're not going to listen to me," Gou said. "Brother Liu, why don't you spike your ear with the mat straw? Then that thing under your belly won't bother you about her any more. Let's stop thinking about her. You are here to choose the best grave site, is it really so important?"

"If it were not," Liu answered, "why should His Excellency invite so many people to find the most auspicious site?"

"Four gentlemen chose the same place, and again your findings coincided with theirs. Does this mean the

Yaos' grave site is the best?"

"Yes, it does."

"Are there any other good sites?"

"Of course there are, but at Northern Terrace no site can beat this one."

"Damn it! Then the Yaos will be rich generation after generation and have the best women for the choosing?"

Liu rose early the next morning, and stood in the yard squinting at a jujube tree. It was April, and young leaves were growing on the gnarled, thorny branches and twigs, which cut the sky in downy, zigzagging strokes. Fourth Mistress was hanging out quilts on a clothes-line in front of the corridor. Her soft cough startled Liu. Looking over his shoulder he saw her fair-skinned face smiling radiantly at him from between two green quilts. The scene, so wonderful to him, reminded him of a lotus flower protruding from the surface of a pond. He stood there, mesmerised.

"You're up so early, sir!"

Liu replied to the pleasantry in the same convivial vein.

The woman ducked over from under the quilts and started complaining. His Excellency, she said, had spoiled her sleep. He had got up at dawn to see the other geomancers off and collect money from village shops along the way.

"You've been watching the jujube tree for such a long time," she said, her liquid eyes meeting and holding his for a lingering moment. "Have you seen any flowers in the tree?" In no time she was standing by his side.

The question threw Liu off balance. Desperate for words to camouflage his inner turmoil, he suppressed the smile creeping towards his lips and said, "Do you see the date up there?"

The woman saw it as well. It was dangling at the top of the tree, shrivelled and frost-bitten, but warming in a deep reddish way. Obviously it was the sole survivor of the previous season's harvest.

"I want that date!" she said.

Liu shook the tree. The downy patterns of the sky above became blurred, but the jujube failed to drop.

"I want it! Pluck it down for me."

By now Fourth Mistress was acting like a spoilt child before a man her own age. Forgetting his place as a temporary employee, Liu plucked up courage and jumped, seizing the branch with one hand and picking the dried date with the other. When he offered her the date, his palm pricked with thorns, instead of taking it, the woman said happily, "You are a honest man!" And with a ripple of laughter, she turned and made for her room.

Liu stood dazed, embarrassed. The woman mounted the stone steps and turned to wave at him. "You blockhead, why don't you come and have your thorns picked out?" Sheepishly, Liu entered the sitting-room. The woman was nowhere to be seen, so he stopped where he was and picked the thorns with his teeth. There were so many thorns, he had trouble removing them all. "Come on in," came the woman's soft voice from the adjacent eastern room.

Liu took a few steps, lifted the curtain and stepped in. It was dim inside, the window curtain undrawn. There was a faint fragrance in the air. The woman was lying on her side on the bed, with two silk floss-padded pillows, laced with water chestnut-leaf patterns, cradled under her head. The curves of her body rose and fell softly, her silvery-white gown was drawn up to reveal two slender, shapely legs. Liu, his heart pounding frantically, was about to beat a retreat when the woman asked again: "Don't you want your thorns picked out?"

When Liu replied that he had solved the problem of the thorns, the woman rolled off the bed, took his hand and asked him to sit by the bed. "You may not need my needle for the thorns now, but I have a favour to ask of you," she said. "Since you know all about the workings of *yin* and *yang*, you must also know something about medicine. Would you please take my pulse — I'm having terrible trouble getting to sleep." At these words, she stretched her hand and laid it on his knee. Liu did not know the first thing about medicine, but in spite of himself he seized hold of her wrist with three fingers. The woman's pulse was throbbing audibly, but the blood in Liu's fingers was beating even more violently. Sitting so close by the woman and having her hand in his grasp, Liu could have felt the flow and ebb of her pulse if he really did know anything about the activities of the pulse. But could he tell her the truth; that the cause of her overnight insomnia was much the same as his? They were obviously thinking the same thoughts, but should he make any kind of reference to it? What if she really was sick and seriously seeking a cure? Liu regretted his pretending the knowledge of a doctor, and he had trouble withdrawing his hand. Shutting his eyes he was suddenly seized by self-hatred. "Why should I harbour such amorous desire for Forth Mistress? How despicable I am, knowing nothing about medicine but stooping to such fraud in order to play out my one-night unrequited love this far?" Sweat broke on his brow from nervousness, self-remorse and doubt about his moral conduct. "To see a beautiful woman and fall in love with for the first time in my life," he reasoned with himself, "I certainly can't be counted as being a despicable man; if, at the sight of such a beauty, I remained cool as if nothing had happened, I wouldn't be the expert geomancer I am reputed to be, I would be but a block of wood or a chunk of stone. Now that the woman's slim wrist is in my grasp, I might as well read her pulse as if I really knew the ropes."

Having regained his bearings, Liu started to feel for the pulse. He discovered that hers was now beating in rhythm with his. He cocked his head to read it more accurately, but his self-control was undiciplined and soon his thoughts went astray once again. Though his head was hanging low, he could still feel the woman's eyes darting now and then at him. A ray of morning sun penetrated the window curtain, setting light to the myriad tiny particles flying in the air and transforming the woman's downy facial hair into an ethereal aureole. A large mouse appeared furtively from the corner of the room, paused to strike a prancing pose and then at another rustling sound, disappeared beyond the threshold. He heard himself ask, "Cat?"*

---

*The Chinese text reads "mao" meaning cat. The word is homophonic with "mao" meaning hair, hence Fourth Mistress' misunderstanding.

"Hair?" The woman was slightly confused. Her hand suddenly swelled in the man's grip. Liu raised his head. The woman, blushing, answered, "Not much... only a little..."

Liu immediately knew she had, to his dismay, misunderstood his question. "How could I ask such a seemingly unsavoury question?" he asked himself. "What if she, feeling obliged to answer it, thought me lascivious?" But instinct told him that the woman liked him. "At least she has not found me repugnant, or else she would have not let me read her pulse in the privacy of her room. If she could so easily mistake my questions for lewd intention and change her attitude, then she would not have spoken to me in the first place."

Hurriedly, he tried to explain: "I, I..." The woman, however, seemed to be struck by something else. Still flushing, she withdrew her hand and, coiling it into a tiny soft fist, drummed his shoulder. "What are you up to, sir? What are you up to?" she asked, smiling, a little out of breath. Her coiled hair had come undone. The dishevelled jet-black strands tumbled down, covering Liu's forehead and eyes. When her soft body sagged limply and she seemed about to lose her balance, Liu stretched out his arm to support her. The woman melted into his embrace.

All this had happened unexpectedly. For Liu, it was like a dream, in which he had jumped down a sheer cliff, and the deafening sound of the impact of his body against the bottom of the ravine brought his heart to a standstill. This isn't real, he told himself. When his eyes fell again on the woman in his arms, her eyes half shut and her lips quivering, a question flashed through his mind: "Why does she give herself so willingly to me? Is she really in love, or just a promiscuous whore who has an axe to grind hidden up her sleeve? If she were not the proprietor's wife but an unmarried woman from a common family, then all this would be perfectly logical. But here, as a poor, lowly man hired by the Yaos, how can I do such an immoral thing? Is the woman, just like Gou Baidu said, so hungry for sex that she wants to use me as a tool to satisfy her pent-up desire?"

Honest Liu, who was still a virgin, was dazed by this flood of thoughts; he was totally at a loss about what to do with the woman. Glancing at her, he saw the woman's eyes open, flashing fire, her cherry-red lips parted slightly and the tip of her tongue quivering between her teeth. Blood surged to Liu's face, and his worries evaporated into thin air. Again, he held the woman tightly. Subconsciously he sensed he had been proffered a cup of invitingly red, poisonous wine, but at this moment his thirst was unquenchable.

He laid Fourth Mistress on the bed, and unbuttoned her gown. She was stark naked underneath, a bright red undergarment barely covering her soft, white abdomen. "Don't look at me there!" she demanded. Liu undid his trousers but found to his consternation that he could not get an erection. The woman was already gyrating and moaning, but no matter how hard he tried he could not enter her. Sweating profusely, he slapped his head forcefully and, pulling on his pants, fled out of the door.

The rising sun had half of the courtyard in its warm glow. A magpie with its angled tail was chirping merrily in the jujube tree. In her tiny room Fourth Mistress was smashing chinaware and toppling the stools. A clump of something was tossed out the window. Then came the woman's cry. Liu saw it was the woman's red undergarment, its ribbons torn apart.

Liu returned to his room feeling like a thief. His heart pounding, he hated himself for being the guttering candle of a man. "Though I haven't had any physical contact with a woman, I'm not a weakling! See how rigid I am now! But why did it fail me like that then?"

The dog's barking broke Liu's remorseful reverie. Gou, returning from the village river with a full pair of water buckets dangling from his shoulder pole, was shouting: "Fourth Mistress, could you please restrain your dog?" The shout made Liu feel some small relief about what had happened and found reason to celebrate that his abortive tryst had saved him from being discovered. Once again he became suspicious of the woman's intention. Was she out to land him in a vulnerable situation by offering her sexual favours in broad daytime, so that when he was caught on the spot he would at the very least loose all payment for his labour? Was it possible that with her sexual desire unfulfilled, she would become so vexed that when the proprietor returned, she would accuse him of raping her?

Time tipped away slowly. By the time he was summoned to the proprietor, he could only stand there stiffly and dared not take his seat.

"Do sit down. You have selected the grave of good fortune for me and I want to thank you. Will this be enough?" the proprietor said, pointing to a table with five columns of silver dollars stacked on it.

The money, shining with a cold sheen, set Liu's mind at ease. From the walnut-like face of the proprietor, he saw no trace of a hoax, and he instantly knew the woman had not betrayed him. "Why," he muttered, "I can not take so much money. I'm happy to have done something for you."

"That won't do," the proprietor said. "I want to show my gratitude anyway. Well, let's do it this way. You may pick up whatever you like under my roof."

The words turned Liu's thoughts back to the woman. He loathed his self-defeat as much as he prided himself on being desired by a woman of extraordinary beauty. As he relished every detail of their secret meeting in his mind, he felt he had been given a supply of food enough for a lifetime's consumption. The train of thoughts, however, took a drastic turn. His heart ached as he thought that it must have taken a mountain of dedication and courage for the wife of a rich man to secretly fall for a poor and humble geomancer like him. "How shameful, how despicable am I, to receive her love but at the same time find faults in her! All my worldly wisdom gained from travelling so many prefectures and counties has come to naught, so has my knowledge of geomancy! Rubbish!"

"Misgiving, suspicion, timidity, fear... all these have cost me a refreshing morning. An irretrievable morning, for that matter." Liu cast a sidelong glance at the adjacent room. The curtain hung there as usual, but the woman behind it was nowhere in sight. Even if she appeared to see me off, he thought in despair, how could I look her in the eye again? His gaze drifted out of the window and into the sun-washed courtyard. Beneath the beetling stone lay a soft mass of red cloth — the undergarment the woman had tossed away in her fit of frustration. At length he said, "Since I've had this chance to visit Your Excellency, such a wealthy man, I would like to carry away a piece of your family's good luck. If you'd allow me, I'd like to have that piece of red cloth over there and use it to wrap up my compass."

Seven days after the proprietor had had a twin-chambered grave dug at the chosen site, his bed-ridden father died. His remains were buried in the left-hand chamber. During the next three years, the Yaos' stars shone forth. Five more shops were added to the family's burgeoning business. Whatever the family shipped down the Luohe River from Nanyang unfailingly brought in profit. The four patches of land in Northern Terrace gradually merged into Yao land, and almost all the families which had fled famine from further down the river became the proprietor's tenant farmers. Eight years later, his mother died. All members of the family donned the white robes of mourning. The twin-chambered grave was about to be completed.

Gou Baidu remained with the Yaos as a butler. He deliberately did without a chamber pot in his bedroom, so that during his night forages to the outhouse he could stop by the window and eavesdrop on the proprietor and his fourth wife in bed. Back to his quarters he would spend the rest of his sleepless night masturbating, smearing his sperm on the wall.

Now, observing the family code, he had to don a coarse hemp robe in mourning for the deceased lady. As a servant he was not supposed to sit on the straw mat and observe the wake in the parlor, nor was he allowed to stand by the front gate greeting and seeing off mourners and offering them tea and cigarettes. He was nothing but the head of the household's roustabouts; to his chagrin, all he was asked to do was dispatch his charges to build stoves and make the fires, fetch water and wash rice, peel scallions, mash garlic and so on. The plaintive notes of the funeral music played on *suona* horns perturbed him deeply, filling his heart with sadness as to his own fate.

In the crowd he spotted Fourth Mistress, who stood on the top stone step of the parlor and watched sacrificial offerings changing hands. There was something unusually bewitching about her in her mourning attire. Why, Gou thought maliciously, didn't death seek Proprietor Yao out?

Gou's thoughts were interrupted by the proprietor, who asked him to go and open up the conduit to the right-hand chamber of the grave for the interment of the coffin. Though bone-tired by now, Gou dared not disobey his boss. On heading towards the door with a pickaxe on his shoulder, he daubed his eyes with saliva and said to Fourth Mistress, "Don't you be too sad, Fourth Mistress. You have to watch your health!"

"Bah! Gou Baidu, are you saying I'm not crying?"

"How dare I say so?" Gou retorted meekly. "As a matter of fact, the passing away of Her Reverent Ladyship is a blessing in disguise. After the remains of the Reverent Lord were entered into the grave of good fortune, the Yaos have been showered with riches for all these years. Now Her Reverent Ladyship is going to join him. Doesn't that mean that the sons and grandsons of the Yaos will become officials one after another?"

"Can that stinking mouth of yours utter nothing decent? Are you making fun of me for not having had any children? Don't forget you're son-less too? Or else, your son would end up waiting on mine."

This struck Gou dumb the entire way to the grave. Impotent anger seethed in him as he worked on the tomb. Inwardly, he let off every vile obscenity at the proprietor and his fourth wife, cursing Liu the geomancer for choosing the lucky grave site for the Yaos, and blaming himself for recommending him. If this isn't being rewarded with less than nothing for my good deed, what is? he asked himself in exasperation. He worked alone for the entire morning until he had opened the entrance to the left-hand compartment of the tomb's twin chambers. Wrath suddenly gripped him. "Isn't it this auspicious site that has kept money rolling in to the Yao family? Your Excellency has more than enough to eat and wear besides possessing such a charming lady, though I am nothing but a tattered coat upon a stick, and as if that is not enough, you even want each bed in your house to be provided with a good lay and keep it that way through the generations." At this thought he threw his pickaxe at the wall which sealed the left-hand chamber of the tomb. With a crash part of the wall collapsed, and an eerie, bone-chilling puff of vapour poured forth with such velocity it threw him to the ground. The vapour turned white in the fresh air, and spiralled skyward in a column as thick as a finger until it dissolved itself into a mushroom cloud and vanished into thin air. Gou, who was bold in the extreme, ran a hand through his hair and without hesitating stomped into the chamber. The coffin, still in good condition, was covered with spider's webs in patterns akin to a lotus flower or an official crown minus its flaps. Gou had heard people say that spider's webs or ant hills were both signs of an auspicious grave, and that the pattern of the web and the shape of the hill determined the exploits that later generations of the family could accomplish. Slow realisation came to him: by entering the tomb he had undermined the lucky geomantic omens by which the Yaos could thrive and lord it over the local people from generation to generation. The realisation filled him with trepidation. Involuntarily his hand rose and touched his neck as he imagined himself being beheaded by the proprietor. But horror soon gave way to a roar of laughter. "Proprietor Yao, you old turtle," he mused aloud through clinched teeth, "I, Gou Baidu, won't be your slave any more! I helped your family locate this burial ground with all the bliss it brought you. Now, I'm the same man who has ruined your geomantic luck."

It was but a short time before the Yaos' fortune started to go downhill. First, the family's dye-works in East Township was looted by bandits. Then the accountant who worked for the noodle shop in Western Gully was kidnapped for ransom, and a boat berthed at Huishui Habour on the Luohe River caught fire and was burned to ashes consuming a full load of silks, hemp and lacquer. The proprietor attributed all this to the evaporation of the good portents from his family grave. The mere mention of Gou Baidu would set him fuming. During one outburst of animosity he raised his knife and chopped off all four corners of the table in the parlor. Gou Baidu had fled Northern Flat without a trace. All the proprietor could do in revenge was to hire a team of shamans at great personal expense, whose incantations and magic drawings had caused, or so it was believed, Gou's mother to lose one of her eyes.

About three years later, during the time of year when paddy rice was flowering, Proprietor Yao's period of mourning for his mother drew to an end. One night, after a quarrel with his fourth wife, he was smoking opium on his bed when a villager rushed in with the report that he had bumped into Gou Baidu on the paddyfield ridge outside the village. According to the report, Gou was clad in a robe of black tussah and sported gold-filled teeth, with a rifle polished to a shine flung over his shoulder. The villager had greeted him saying, "Gou Baidu, nice to see you again. Where have you been all these years?" Gou had snapped the bolt of his gun by way of an answer. The villager, his face pale as ash, had asked, "Oh, Old Gou, so you've become a Chinese Robinhood?"

"Call me Detachment Commander Gou. Commander Tang has appointed me one of his team leaders."

Commander Tang, whose full name was Tang Jing, was a notorious bandit whose headquarters were in White Rock Hamlet in the northern mountains.

The villager had immediately insisted, "Commander Gou, why don't you come into our village? Every family will treat you to a cup of wine — if they don't have wine at hand they can at least offer you boiled eggs." Gou had replied that he was waiting for someone.

"Who?"

Gou then lost his temper. "Keep you mouth shut! Are you asking for a bullet! It's none of your business. Leave me!"

Upon hearing the report Proprietor Yao jumped to his feet and snatched a sword into his hand. Then he put it down. His forehead was filmed with sweat for it suddenly dawned on him who had robbed his shops and burned his boat, and whom the footman-turned-robber was awaiting outside the village. Colour drained from his sallow face. Grabbing his young fourth wife's hand he decided he had to flee for his life.

"I won't leave," the woman said. "Who was Gou Baidu anyway? I don't think he has the audacity to manhandle me!"

The proprietor jumped out of the window and hid himself in a pond on the slope, covering his head with a gourd ladle.

Gou waited until dark. "Let the son of a bitch live for a few more days," he said and went away. Only then was the drenched proprietor carried home on the back of a family servant.

The following evening, the village was aroused from its slumber by the sudden barking of dogs. The watchman rushed over from the entrance to the village to say that Gou had come again. There were three men with him this time, each of them carrying a gun. The proprietor was on the verge of taking to his heels when the report of a gun sounded outside his front gate. Opening the door he spotted Gou sitting on a stone mill on the threshing ground. Now that his route of escape had been blocked, the proprietor became uncharacteristically calm. He changed into a suit of new clothing, preparing to meet his death and, with a lantern in hand, stepped out of the door. "Who is out there? Oh, it's younger brother Baidu!" he exclaimed. "All the years you've been away, I've missed you younger brother. Why didn't you say goodbye to me when you went away? Have you come all this way to visit me?"

"Commander Tang received report that some bandits had been observed in Northern Terrace," Gou replied. "He sent us here to arrest them. Have they done any harm to Your Excellency?"

"With Detachment Commander Gou's protection, who would dare to come here! Wouldn't they be too scared to show their faces round here? Come on in, gentlemen, for a smoke — I've just acquired a batch of opium!"

Entering the parlor with his men, Gou kicked off his shoes, flung himself into a reclining chair and reached out his hand for the opium. But his hand froze in the air, for as he raised his eyes, he saw Fourth Mistress emerge from behind the curtain and lean against the jamb of the door one leg crossed over the other so that one touched the ground with the tip of her foot. With a pop of her lips she spat out the melon-seed husk she had been chewing.

"So Fourth Mistress! You still look so young after all these years," Gou said. "As I remember, today's the third anniversary of Her Old Ladyship's death. Why aren't you wearing your mourning clothes which made you look even more delightful?"

"What a good memory you have, Baidu — you still remember what day it is today," the woman replied.

The proprietor made haste to reproach his young

wife for her flippancy, and asked her to prepare a pipe of opium for Gou. The woman, placing another melon seed in her mouth, walked slowly over to the opium lamp. In the shadow of the lamp Gou pinched her leg. The woman swung around in shock and, in doing so, knocked over a plate, flipping its content — deep-fried doughnuts — to the floor. Gou went to pick the food up when the woman stopped him. "It's dirty. Let the dog eat it," and she called her dog into the room.

Gou flushed purple at this loss of face. "Does Tiger still listen to you, Mistress?" As he said this he raised his gun and shot the dog in the head. The parlor was instantly filled with the smell of gun powder, and the members of the Yao family shrieking in panic. The proprietor said with a forced smile, "A good shot indeed, which has whetted my appetite. Tonight I'll treat you to succulent roast dog meat and sorghum liquor. Brother Baidu, why don't you take the hide for your bed?"

In a nonchalent, condescending tone, Gou answered, "I won't take it right away. You may have the hide cured and sent to White Rock Hamlet some other day."

A few days later, the messenger who took the cured dog skin over to Gou, returned with the message: "Gou Baidu does not want a penny from Proprietor Yao; he wants only to become his relative — the proprietor will become Gou's respected elder brother if he agrees to marry Fourth Mistress to him."

A red letter of consent was immediately dispatched. Ten days later, Gou arrived on the back of a beribboned black steed. He dismounted, gathered Fourth Mistress into his arms and installed her on the saddle. Then, remounting himself, he turned to bow to the proprietor: "My kind brother, good-bye. Please don't bother to send me off..."

The woman cut in: "Old man, I'm leaving. After being my husband for so long, don't you feel you should come over and put my hair in place?" Tears came rolling down the proprietor's face as he stepped forward, wanting to bury his head into her chest for a hearty cry. The woman spat at him: "Pooh! You heartless cuckold, letting a former footman of yours rob you of your wife like this!" The proprietor fell in a dead faint on the stone steps.

The steed, its smooth black mane gleaming in the sun, dashed like lightning across Northern Terrace to the cacophony of croaking frogs. In that beautiful, sun-bathed morning, an ugly but muscular Gou Baidu was intoxicated by a monumental joy. Instead of making for home at White Rock Hamlet, he drove his horse down a flagged path which led to nobody knew where. By the time the fiery sun had scaled the summit of the mountain in the distance, the horse was already sweating profusely. Only then did he gather in his reins and turn towards home some fifty *li* away. His red-tasselled black velvet hat which he had worn as a bridegroom had rolled off and landed in some grassy depression along the way. Feeling hot he unbuttoned his coat and let it flap noisily in the wind. The tight strap of his shiny rifle cut into his broad chest and his body began to emit the odour of perspiration. He held the reins with one hand and with the other pinned the woman tightly in his embrace. The woman, held motionless as if entangled with a snake, shrieked non-stop until, spent by the jolts and tosses of the bumpy ride and the strangling effect of the strong arm around her, her screams tapered off into faint moans.

"Fourth Mistress," Gou said, "no, no, my wife, please cry and shout to your fill — you can kick at my belly and bite into my arms. That is what I like in you, your hot-temper! It made me feel so good when you spat into the face of that old bastard. You make me feel good by working off your anger upon me! Don't you know that I used to call your name in my dreams every night during the years when I ran errands for the Yaos? But you'd rather fondle the dog than extend a single finger to me. But now, at last, you are my wife."

The woman came to, only to find the nape of her neck being nibbled by a slobering mouth and saliva running down her spine. Her left breast was being kneaded by the cattail-leaf fan of a hand, with the nipple pinched between two fingers. She realised that she had fallen prey to a ferocious wolf. During her dozen years with the Yaos, she had no reason to complain about the food she ate nor the clothes she wore, but she despised the skinny, invalid proprietor who was so old that even his beard had lost its coarse vitality. Because of this she had vented her spleen at will, breaking plates and throwing bowls, shouting at whoever came in sight, all the while gleefully anticipating the taste of what it might be like being subdued highhandedly. But when the suppression came in the form of Gou the bandit, she was overcome by terror and sorrow. The prospects of being molested from this night on by this man, ugly of face and filthy of body, terrified her to the quick. She regretted her laughter of false relief and glee at the proprietor's painful decision, and she also regretted the fact that instead of making good of her silent escape or killing herself when she had the chance, she had meekly allowed herself to be carried away on horseback. Her regrets brought her thoughts back to the Yaos, and made her pity the emaciated proprietor. In an outburst of wrath, she sank her teeth into the hand that was clenching her left breast. Blood appeared down the corner of her mouth. No sooner had Gou loosened his grip than she swung back and dealt a battery of boxes on the ugly face whose every pore she felt was oozing greasy sweat. She then unleashed a torrent of hot words: "See what you are! A pig-like dog craving me for your wife. But are you worthy of me? You are nothing but a piece of charcoal which can never be washed clean! Neither inside nor out!"

Gou was stunned by this sudden onslaught. The familiar submissive facial expression resurfaced inadvertently, as befitting a long-time and lowly servant of the Yaos. But in a split second the bandit let go of his reins. With one hand he grasped the woman's lower jaw and with the other he loosed a right hook to her belly. The heavy impact sent her lying flat against the horse's back, and she started shrieking and cursing madly once again, her four limbs flailing about in a frenzy. Gou pinned her down and sank his fists into her body, his finger ring cutting into her skin. The sight of fresh blood, running across the ivory-white belly like a crawling crimson earthworm, sent his adrenaline to a high. His muscles shuddering in a peal of guffaw, he acted every bit like a slaughterer pinning a dainty wild deer to a chopping board and slitting its throat while feasting his eyes on its four slender legs dangling in the air. Slowly he untied the woman's belt, pulled away her clothing, and pressed the entire weight of his body upon hers.

All the while the horse galloped at full speed. So scared it was by the turmoil taking place on its back that it ran in a vain attempt to escape. The jumble of mountains flashed past one after another. The hoofs shot swarms of locusts up into the air from the grass, splashing some of them against the shoulder stock of the rifle and leaving a thick green patch on it. Gou, his mouth gasping for air in an eerily loud panting, eventually consummated his sexual relationship with the woman after so many years of frustrated attempts to possess her. The blood that had seeped from her belly congealed on his chest, forming a crust which refused to be rubbed off. The woman, in the first major crisis of her life, had tossed her body this way and that like a slender willow tree caught in the throes of a tempest, managing to stand straight each time it was pushed to the brink of destruction. The countless pounding she had received had tested the willowy resilience of her body to the extreme and, paradoxically, aroused in her such physical pleasure as to leave her half-dead. She was, after all, a woman. What had happened had robbed her of her sharp-tongued ferocity and the volatile caprice which she had used so often in dealing with her former husband. When the horse finally slowed to a gentle trot, she was dazed, utterly speechless. After what seemed an eternity she rediscovered her tongue. "A bandit, that's what you are!" she said at last. "Take me to the river. I want to wash."

Gou reined in his horse and let go of her. He behaved like a husband, so sure of himself that he did nothing to prevent her from escaping. Idly, he squinted his eyes first at the shining sun overhead and then at the woman, who by now had reached the river and was scooping up water with cupped hands. The water slipped through her fingers like strings of silvery pearls. Judging from her silhouette in the river, she was pondering how her shadow could remain still at the bottom while the water flowed on. She squatted, as if to urinate, but actually she was douching herself thoroughly with the determination to eradicate all that was alien to her body.

At this juncture a solitary man emerged from the small gully on the other side of the river. The woman cast a cursive glance at him and, pulling up her pants, lowered her head again to wash her face. The labyrinth of mountain trails in the gully resembled a web of ropes, and she had the impression that the man was towing the web down the gully behind him, or rather, one of the ropes was dragging him down. "Oh," he exclaimed as he paused by the riverside, and in bewilderment, he called out, "Fourth Mistress!"

The voice, skimming across the surface of the water, sounded muffled and trembling as if bedraggled by the river. The woman reacted as though stung by a hornet. The voice sounded intimately familiar yet strange — familiar because it was the very sound which had roused her from many a dream, sitting up to look around puzzled. It was strange because, with the passage of time, it had become so elusive that she eventually became numb to it and forced it from her mind. Now, having deserted her for so long, the voice returned like the draught of a gentle breeze, a bubble resurfacing from the depths of the ocean, and it made her heart ache. By the time she raised her eyes to see the man again, Gou Baidu, on his mount, had already recognised him. He yelled boisterously, "Mr Liu! Liu Ziyan! Fancy meeting you here, you son of a bitch!"

The shout directed the geomancer's attention to the man on horseback with the rifle slung over his shoulder, and stopped him short on legs which would have carried him across the river but which got stuck then and there in the sand like wooden sticks. "Oh, it's you, Gou Baidu," he said. "I heard you'd become a Chinese Robinhood, a detachment commander under Tang Jing. No question about it! It is really you. Where are you going?"

"Liu Ziyan, let me tell you. I got married today. You are the first man to come to congratulate me."

"Married?" Liu, his gaze caught by Gou's gold-filled teeth glistening in the sun, felt the urge to make fun of him. "Who's the bride? What woman deserves to be the wife of such a powerful brigand leader?"

"Come and see for yourself. You called her 'Fourth Mistress' just now."

By now the woman had stood up and kept her eyes riveted on Liu across the river. He was wearing a long gown topped with a short jacket, and a knapsack on his back. He was no longer the young man he had been, though he was just as handsome as she remembered him. The woman, her heart beating violently, wanted to say something but failed. The change of expression on Liu's face, however, was not lost on her. When Gou had said he had married her, his smile had frozen, just as she might have hoped, and he had remained silent for a long time, his foot sinking deeper in the loose sand so that he looked shorter than usual. The water in the river swelled, soaking his shoes and the legs of his pants. "Mr Liu!" she sputtered, but her voice failed to register on her own ears. Liu apparently didn't catch it either, for he just stood there, bedazed. When at last he stole a glimpse at her, misery was palpable in his eyes.

"You've married Fourth Mistress?" Liu asked in a modified tone. "Do you mean you've shot His Excellency?"

"A wedding is a red-letter event. How could I kill anyone on such a day? Don't you think I deserve a good lay?"

At the words the geomancer hung his head and turned to leave, but not before casting an involuntary glance at the woman across the river. As he stumbled up the mountain trail, he tripped repeatedly over the pebbles on the path. Wherever he fell he rose at once to resume his escape.

In the bright sun on the opposite bank, the woman plodded her way back to Gou. "Let's go," she said, and with Gou's helping hand mounted the horse. Gou, muttering Liu's name in a playful tone, loosened his reins and whistled the horse into a trot. Soon the land reverberated with the clattering of hooves amidst the singing of birds on the wind and the gurgling of water from the river. Lashing out his arm he grasped the woman by the small of her back. Suddenly, she snapped, "I want Mr Liu!"

Gou reined in the horse. "You want Liu Ziyan?"

The woman turned her torso, repeated her request. She stared at Gou, her tiny mouth mutinous, her slender brows knitted tightly. The bandit, rough and rash, was confused for a moment, and then became heartened by her capricious temper. Wasn't she just throwing her tantrums about becoming his wife? Wasn't it a resurgence of the spleen she had often vented on the proprietor as his fourth wife, or an indication of her transition from stubborn resistance to meek obedience? Gou took great delight in subduing women like breaking in a raging wild horse; nothing pleased him more than the sight of a horse, once subdued, shaking its head, perking up its ears or snorting for no reason at all. A sense of humour hit him. "You want Mr Liu — are you infatuated with his pale face?" he asked.

"Mr Liu is the first man to have seen the two of us together, but you let him go without allowing him to say a few words of congratulations," she answered. The reply brought Gou to his senses. He turned his horse around and raising his rifle let off a shot into the sky. The sharp report shook the river valley and sent Liu, who had been stumbling along in the distance, collapsing to the ground. This time he didn't get up immediately. The impact, which caused the loose pebbles to roll down the cliff, also lifted him from the cloud of confusion and brought past memories to his mind. During all the years since he left the Yaos, he had never met another woman as charming as Fourth Mistress, and was still madly in love with her. After all, who would have cared for a down-and-out man who knew nothing but geomantic omens? He felt sad for his lot and for the loss of her love. He was still wearing the red silk undergarment which embodied her frustration and unfulfilled desire — he wore it as a symbol of her love. He could feel the warmth of the fabric on his body. The softness with which the undergarment had enwrapped her body, and now his, made him feel dizzy with happiness. He had repeatedly travelled on foot to Northern Terrace in the hope of meeting her once again. If Fourth Mistress had happened to be drawing water from the stream, he would have lifted her into his arms, and it would not have mattered if in so doing he had smashed the earthen jar to pieces; if she had happened to be picking mushrooms on the mountain slope, he would have laid her down in a grassy depression and let the grass blades shake a thousand times around them. His secret longing for her had grown to such miraculous proportions that whenever he saw the stone castle, the vestige of an ancient battlefield on the mountain ridge behind Northern Terrace, his entire being would plunge into a dream world. He had dreamed of walking hand in hand with her into the castle and lying down there side by side on a night when the moon was full and bright, mindless of the wind rustling long and loud through the small windows, mindless of the dew which wetted their eye lashes, shoes and socks and trouser belts, just lying there for eternity. Each of his day dreams, however, was broken by the cock-a-doodle-doo of roosters from the village at the foot of the mountain; and each time the smoke-stack of the Yaos came into sight pouring forth its smoke, he would sit down and weep in solitude. On such occasions, he had wondered more than once if all feeling had not been fossilised in him.

Earlier that day, of all days, he had been on his way to Gourd Vale, where a family wished to consult him on a matter of geomancy. There was a road which ran directly to the vale, but in spite of himself his feet had carried him on to the mountain trail towards Northern Terrace — he had been making a detour of several dozen *li* just for a peep at the place where his lover lived. He had never expected to meet the woman across the narrow strip of river.

The meaning of the encounter sank in painfully — she had turned from Fourth Mistress to the wife of a bandit. Deep in his heart, he still loved her. But the possibility of her becoming his wife for the rest of his life drifted away like the cloud which always managed to keep him at arm's length even if he had scaled the mountain closest to it.

In the long bygone days, with each of his solitary visits to the mountains behind Northern Terrace ending up in the hopeless quagmire of unrequited love, his burning affection for her had gradually cooled and consigned itself to the back of his mind. "Oh, fate is so unkind to me!" he would lament. The only recourse left to him was to turn her image into a desiccated pickle in the salt pot of life and wash it down his throat with liquor. Whether the woman had remained as Proprietor Yao's concubine or become the wife of some official did not matter any more to him. But the problem was she had now become the wife of the swarthy, stinking Gou Baidu, a fact he could not stomach. Grain robbers, mountain bandits and rural tyrants — don't they live on the same thing; the rifle which is capable of devouring life and drinking blood! When moments earlier, Gou Baidu, his pugnacious, ugly face shining like black lacquer, was making a show of himself, Liu's hand had itched to pick up a stone and mash his brain into pulp. It was only the man's tall steed and black gun that had kept him from doing so, and forced him to swallow his tears for the woman's fate and for his own weakness. He had wanted to get away as quickly as possible, for every minute he delayed, the more ashamed he became of his own helplessness to deal with the ugly man. He was even more ashamed of this than his abortive attempt to make love to her. He had better never let the woman who had once desired him see him again.

Now, as he lay on the ground, it suddenly occurred to him that the gun shot was meant for him. Now that the woman has become Gou's wife and seen my dilemma, he thought, she must have laughed at me and inadvertently told her bandit husband about what had happened between us. Gou is a bandit. Like the miser proprietor, he won't tolerate what a geomancer did to his wife.

The horse, its hooves whipping up a cloud of choking dust and sending pebbles flying in all directions, was galloping towards him. Gou was shouting: "Stop! Stop!" All of a sudden Liu turned and started running. This incensed Gou, who let out a torrent of abuse. The horse vaulted over Liu's head and blocked his way ahead.

Sensing his death in the air, Liu asked: "Gou Baidu, you want to kill me?"

"Why did you run?" Gou said. "My wife has something to say to you."

Liu, surprised, stared at the woman, who dismounted and walked towards him until she stopped under a slender willow tree about seven metres away. Her hair, in disarray, floated in the air behind her like a black flame.

"You go away, just like that, without saying anything to me?" she asked.

"Congratulations," Liu said.

"Say it again!"

"Congratulations to you on becoming the wife of a bandit ring leader."

The woman, giggling lewdly, leaned her body against the tree, which shook suddenly under her weight.

Liu jerked around and started to stumble away.

"You go away just like that?" The woman suddenly became hysterical. She reached out and pulled down a branch and, her face distorted by rage, asked once again: "You go away just like that? Walking away like a cuckold for the rest of your life?"

In a frenzy she flung herself at Liu, who stood dazed and perplexed as all of a sudden the branch rained blows on his face, sending leaves flying in the sky like tiny bits of paper. Liu stood motionless. He had a foreboding that his life was drawing to an end now, but he'd rather be beaten to death by the woman he loved than die by Gou Baidu's gun. He felt no pain, and somehow he remained standing despite her stormy rage. In his imagination the willow branch was actually a sharp knife, and in the next moment he would lose one arm, then the other, then his head, neck, waist and legs. Panting breathlessly, the woman flailed her willow branch, leaving bloody welts smarting across his face. Fragments of the branch flew into the sky, along with the strands of hair it had dislodged and touched down on the surface of the water until only a foot-long stub was left in her hand. But her rage knew no bounds, and she tore apart his coat with a feverish rip. The sight of the red silk undergarment on his naked torso rooted her to the spot. Then she collapsed to the ground and started wailing.

Liu, his body covered with bruises, fell into the sand with her, tears running unbidden down his face. He suddenly realised she was still in love with him. Gratitude surged from inside him as he watched the blood trickling down from his face splash on a pebble and dissolve into what looked like a cluster of splendid peach flowers. He rose and bent over to pull the wailing woman to her feet. Gou, misinterpreting his move for a counter-attack, roared down from the horse's back, "Liu, you dare lay a finger on my wife and I'll smash your skull with my gun!"

Proudly, Liu raised his head. "How could I?" he retorted. "Gou Baidu, now my formal congratulations to you!"

"Why didn't you say it earlier? Now you can go."

Liu didn't budge an inch. The woman said, "I won't let him go!"

"Have you got it, Liu," Gou said, "that she won't let you go? Why don't you kneel before me and wish her all happiness?"

"I want him to go with us," the woman said.

Gou was puzzled by the request, his brows knitted tight.

The woman continued, "Mr Liu is a geomancer. I want him to go with us so that he can choose a burial place for us. Do you want my future son to be like you, doing footwork for the Yaos for the greater part of your life?"

Gou guffawed. "Well said! Mr Liu, here is my invitation. Please go with us and locate the site of good blessing for my family. While the wealthy Yaos could award you with a table-load of silver coins, all I have is the gun — but with it I'll secure a woman for you."

The three of them thus took to the road together.

They started the journey, with Gou and the woman riding the horse and Liu walking behind. As they threaded their way across bridges and sparkling streams and past ancient-looking trees on precipitous cliffs, the woman continuously dropped her handkerchief and asked Liu to pick it up for her. Or when she saw a blossoming peach tree she implored him to fetch a spray for her to savour its aroma. Several miles into the journey, she started complaining that the jolting of the horse was tearing her bones apart. Gou asked Liu to carry her on his back. "Willing or not, you've got to do it," he said.

This was just what Liu wanted. When the woman had wrapped her arms around his neck and hitched herself onto his back like a flying leaf, he felt the heat emanating from her body, soft and warm as winter clothing. Delicate warm breath drifted from her aromatic mouth and filtered through the back of his skull. A tendril of soft hair fell from behind her ear and touched his forehead, which evoked a memory of their previous bedroom tryst. He did not know if he was walking with a burden on his back, or hovering in the air propelled by a tousle of mauve cloud. The woman, having been carried kneeling on his back for some time, now shifted her body piggyback fashion, with her legs drooping down on both sides. When Liu had stretched his arms and pinned her thighs in position, he caught sight of the two familiar tiny feet, plump but not to the point of being fat, encased in a pair of red shoes. His heart missed a beat, and he swallowed hard. The swashbuckling Gou wasn't watching; he was whistling on horseback. Liu managed to release a hand and, grasping one foot, pinched it time and again. The woman was delighted. "You've got guts!" she said, giggling. When Gou turned to see what was going on, she had one hand innocently pointing at a goat grazing atop a razor-sharp cliff, while her other hand, hidden, lightly jabbed at Liu's back.

Past the Wuthering Vale, the three of them reached Gou's house which stood on a hillock. It was a three-room construction, built of slate with a thatched roof, where Gou's one-eyed mother lived alone. Pleasantly surprised by the return of her son with a pretty woman, she laughed until her toothless mouth became a large "O" and her face as wrinkled as a walnut. Then, raising a lamp in her hand she scrutinised the woman from head to toe. In a whisper she asked her son where he had come by her. "The woman's hips are plump," she told her son, "just the right type for bearing children, but her breasts protrude too much to produce enough milk." At nightfall, Liu was put up in the old goat barn beside the house. When the mistress came out to see him, Gou followed close behind her and tossed him a goat skin pillow stuffed with hay. "If you feel lonely you can hug it," he declared and then he bent over and gathered the woman into his arms and carried her to the *kang* in the eastern room.

Having been smitten by the day's happy journey

Liu Ziyan suddenly found himself alone in the cold and isolation of the sheep shed. He closed the heavy wooden door and listened to birds chirping in the otherwise hushed silence of the mountains. Their chirping only served to enhance the emptiness of the night. In the corner of the barn the lean, pallid flame of a pine torch planted in a block of stone was belching black smoke. "Is the pine exhaling smoke," he thought, "the only thing it could emit when it failed to burn luminously? While I lie here in this shabby shed, the woman I carried here is sleeping on the other side of that wall. She loves only me, but it is Gou the dark-skinned bandit she sleeps with. If this is not cruelty in the extreme, what is!" When these wild thoughts became unbearable, he grabbed his knapsack and flung it at the pine torch. The fire died down with the thump.

From inside the slate abode he could hear Gou Baidu puffing and panting like a bear and the woman's occasional gasps of pain. The old woman, sleeping in the western room, knocked at the lid of a trunk with her long-stemmed pipe. "Baidu, what's wrong? Are you fighting?" she asked. Her son retorted, "Mum, go to sleep! Stop acting like an old fool!" After that everything quieted down. Then the rats started gnawing and nibbling at something, and Liu heard the door of the house creaking open. The woman, complaining of loose bowels, scampered past the sheep shed and squatted near the door. Straining his eyes Liu peeped through the seams in the wooden door; what he saw was a blurred shadow, which then stood up and went away. When the woman made a second foray into the open, Liu suddenly realised that instead of having loose bowels, she was bracing the bitter cold in order to see him! Tears rolled down his cheeks. He opened the door silently and waited for the woman to appear again. Sure enough, she came up and squatted near the door a third time. Liu had hardly muttered her name in a soft voice when a naked, beastial Gou rushed out and, immediately after she had relieved herself, lulled her home again. Apparently he didn't want to waste a minute of the time he could be relieving himself in her body!

The next morning, the three of them gathered by the brook in front of the house to wash their faces. All looked thinner than the previous day. In silence Liu watched the woman, who returned his glances with the passionate longing of a bird just snatched away from its warm nest. The eyes of both moistened.

Breakfast was a heap of potatoes baked in the brazier and eggs boiled in a pot hanging above it. Gou gave Liu an egg and climbed up the scholartree in front of the door to draw honey from a beehive. He spread the honey on some eggs to feed his new wife. "Am I a child?" she protested. "Instead of feeding me, why don't you do something about your running nose?"

A string of snivel was hanging precariously from his nostrils. Gou passed his hand over his nose and daubed the stuff on a pillar. The woman pushed her bowl to Liu. "Mr Liu, please eat mine. I don't feel so well." Liu took the bowl and saw five eggs in it. A warmth welled up from the bottom of his heart.

Liu knew what to do; he would choose a burial site with every conceivable bad omen for the bandit, so that he might fall while climbing a mountain, be drowned whilst near the river; that his horse would perish for no reason at all, and failing all else he would die of sickness or from a gun-shot wound. However, Gou was not easily fooled; he had seen so many geomancers in action in the years when he worked for the Yaos. "You've got to do me a good job," he said to Liu. "It is said if you plant a bamboo stalk in an auspicious site at night, it sprouts up the next morning. A place that can make a bamboo sprout — that is what I want."

When Liu had chosen the location, Gou planted a bamboo there, and lo, bamboo shoot sprang up overnight. A beaming Gou offered to see him off for five *li* over the mountain trail. When Liu bade good-bye to the woman, she said, "Mr Liu, now you know where my family is, do drop in whenever you're passing by!"

"Sure," Gou butted in, "do drop in, for I love to see my friends."

The woman walked the two men down the mountain. Tearfully, she said, "The wind in the mountains is so chilly, be careful of your stomach — don't catch cold!" Liu patted his stomach and felt the red silk undergarment underneath. Gou laughed: "See what happens? She can't leave me for a moment now! You might have realised, Mr Liu, life with a woman is quite different from life without."

At an isolated mountain valley twenty *li* into the journey, Gou made an obeisance by cupping his hands on his chest and hiccupped his promise that he would never forget the geomancer or his good service. Liu muttered his thanks and started climbing the mountain. When the geomancer was about to reach the top, Gou took out a bullet, rubbed it on the sole of his shoe and dabbed it with saliva before loading it into his gun. With one deafening bang he sent Liu tumbling down the other side of the mountain. "Now that I, Gou Baidu, have found the site of good blessing, I won't allow you to choose another site for anyone who could outdo me," he said to himself.

A year passed, and Gou Baidu was no longer his old shabby self. One early summer day, he was sitting in the courtyard behind the lobby of his spick-and-span house and shooting at an apricot tree. He offered one apricot after another to the woman while talking glibly and proudly about the good fortune of the burial place Liu had chosen for his mother. He certainly had reason to feel proud. Right after he had wrapped up the remains of his mother — who died from a fall down the mountain slope — in white silk and buried them in the grave of good luck, he left White Rock Hamlet, took control of another mountain area and emerged as a local despot. Now, like Tang Jing, he was a commander in his own right. The change of status, and the power that went with it, earned him the respect he had craved for. In no time he was owner of a mansion complex of brick-and-tile houses, where even the chamber pots were made of fine, blue-glazed porcelain. Wealth came pouring in, so that he never ran short of big trunks of meat, large bowls of liquor as well as ample stocks of linen, homespun silks and brocades. What was more, the woman, who had failed to conceive in all her years in the Yao household, was now a pregnant wife whose simple favourite food was sour apricots. That son of a bitch Liu was indeed somebody!

The woman, fed up by the endless boasts of wealth, stood up and left for her room. The mention of Liu

Ziyan caused her heart to ache, like the pungent apricot the mere mention of which made her feel sour. In spite of her longings, Liu had never set foot on the place again after he performed his service for Gou posterity. "Do all beautiful women under Heaven have the same misfortune?" she asked herself. "Why does the man I hate ravage me like a growling wolf, and the man I love act as soft as a sheep?" The only consolation for her sorrow and distress was to sit behind the window alone, and watch the green wooded mountains bathed in moonshine. The green mountains, where white poplar trees stood solemn and aloof, were radiantly lush without loosing their wild beauty. There was something elusive about these divine green mountains and poplar forests, a quality which was tranquil, bewitchingly mysterious and rueful.

A peaceful, moon-lit night like this allowed no gun shots. Whenever Tang Jing's vassals raided White Rock Hamlet, Gou, who did not have enough guns to square them off, would have his wife carried up the mountain and hidden in a cave. The hideout had all the everyday amenities — sitting room, bedroom, grain storage and water-tap — and once the stepping plank was withdrawn with a hidden mechanism, all Tang's men could do was to rain a layer of tiny bullet marks on the wall of rock outside.

A moon-lit night like this tolerated no dog barks, for each canine clamour would herald the triumphant return of Gou's underlings with bulging parcels. As they started untying cloth-wrappers on the tables and tossing copper coins and silver dollars into baskets, the moaning of a hostage could be faintly heard from the solitary cell tucked away in some corner.

A moon-lit night like this was alien to liquor, for whenever Gou Baidu had drunk until every pore in his skin oozed alcohol he would wax proudly about his possession of a beautiful wife. Imagining the way some remote emperor satiated his lascivious lust, he would remove the straw mat from the *kang*, spread peas on it and top it with a wood plank, on which he could turn his insalubrious fornication into a swaying pleasure ride.

May this very moon-lit night be preserved for the woman alone, so that sitting by the window she could think about Liu Ziyan and blame him for his betrayal, and lament their ill-fated affair, an affair which was like a trellis of calabash plant which allows the glory of its golden blossoms to come to naught. But on a previous night under the moon, she had perceived something meaningful in the poplar tree towering over the gully hard by the window. How closely did the cicatrices on its trunk resemble a man's unblinking eyes! It must be Liu's eyes! He's watching me everyday! she told herself.

Since then she had kept the window open so that she could see eye to eye with her lover whenever she tossed her glance in the tree's direction. However, eyes are but eyes. "Liu, where are you? Are you really never to return to me?" These questions would bring tears rolling down her face. Placing her hands on her swollen belly, she slowly directed her loving heart to the child she was bearing. "You'll grow up to become an official, believe me," she said to the fetus, "because your mother trusts Mr Liu's ability. When you become an official, you should go and find him and bring him back to me, even if it means going to the remotest parts of the earth!"

Actually Liu was still alive.

The bullet, daubed with Gou's saliva, had torn his leg apart and thrown it into the depths of the mountain. Liu himself was flung into a thicket of wild rose on the other side of the mountain. As he lay helplessly in a pool of blood, a local woodcutter had found him and carried him to his cottage. Convinced by the geomancer's promise that after his recovery he would improve the lot of the woodcutter's family by finding him a propitious grave site, the woodcutter kept him under his roof and nursed his wound with pumpkin pith until six months later Liu could prop himself up on his single foot. After he honoured his promise to his savior, he was carried back to his home village. In his attempt to walk again with the aid of a crutch, his handicap threw him to the ground time and again, and he broke two front teeth in the process. When he was able to hobble around, he often stood by the crumbling stone wall of his courtyard, gazing fixedly at the mountains which spread out in the distance like a two female brows, and listened to the gurgling brook that flew past nearby. At moments like this, his thoughts would wander to the woman he had promised to see again. However, thus crippled, he had no hope of making the journey to her abode. Neither did he have a gun, so even if he could get there, he could not prevail over Gou.

It was a smoldering summer day. Having lit incense sticks in honour of Buddha, Liu sat on a straw mat and prayed for safety and good luck to be bestowed on the woman he yearned for. His incantations were interrupted by a flurry of footsteps. Turning his head he saw a litter being carried into the gate. The man who emerged was none other than Proprietor Yao. "So he's still alive," Liu thought, "despite his senile liver-spotted face." The old man bowed to Liu. "I've been looking for you for ages," he said, "but I was told you'd died at the hands of Gou Baidu. Then someone else said you were still alive. I decided to come over and see for myself. Sure enough, you are in perfect shape, as young and handsome as I remembered."

Speechless, Liu smiled and stood up. The absence of one leg surprised the proprietor, who threw out his hands to shore Liu up while letting out a torrent of abuse at the bandit. "He has destroyed you and me. He is our common sworn enemy," he said.

Thus for a second time Liu was invited to visit Northern Terrace to choose for the proprietor a new family grave site with the most propitious topographic slew. This time, rather than ride a donkey, he was taken there in a crate borne on the back of a footman.

Sitting in the small room where the woman had given him her love, Liu sobbed bitterly. When the proprietor asked him what was the matter, he answered that he was thinking about Fourth Mistress. "The room and its furniture remain the same," he said, "but I can no longer see her."

Tears ran down the proprietor's haggard face as he exhorted Liu not to worry about him. "Though Fourth Mistress is a beauty and it is simply not possible to find another dainty woman with her charming features, I won't cry my heart out now that she has become a bandit's wife."

"Do you have any news of her lately?" Liu asked.

"I had expected that, being snatched away like that, she would have stabbed her scissors into that bandit or died by her own hand. Who would have thought that she would still be alive! I was told that whenever she goes out, she has two bodyguards following her — she's now a dyed-in-the-wool bitch!"

Liu felt wrath surging through him. "What are you anyway," he thought, "a rich man wallowing in money, an old turkey who shouldn't have taken the young woman in the first place! You surrendered your wife to the bandit so submissively, yet have the cheek to blame her for having not sought her death for chastity's sake! Were you worthy of her even after being her husband for so long? Are you worthy of your reputation as a landed gentleman in Northern Terrace?" Having seen through the ungrateful proprietor, Liu no longer felt sympathy for his misery at the hand of Gou Baidu, and this more than made up for all his years of uneasiness over his own brief affair with Fourth Mistress. In his abomination against the proprietor, he started cursing the man's meanness; yet in the proprietor he saw his own ugliness. He cursed himself, in the old man's stead, for he too had failed to keep the woman out of harm's way. "She didn't love the proprietor who, after all, was getting old, but did I do anything for her?" he asked himself. Turning his head and looking out of the window, he saw the jujube tree once again. In sadness he mused aloud, "Not a single dry date is left on the tree this year."

"Can any date remain on the tree for so long?" the proprietor chuckled. Suddenly a question came to his mind and he asked, "Mr Liu, did Gou Baidu find a good burial place with your help?"

"Yes, if it can be counted as a good one."

"Does this mean he will amount to something? You know that to have that lucky grave occupied, he flung his mother into a valley and having thus caused her death announced that she had died from a slip of her foot... Can the corpse of a blind old woman really maintain the grave's good omens?"

"Let's not talk about the bandit," Liu interjected, "I'll find you another auspicious place where you can move the remains of your parents."

The proprietor, delighted by his promise, called out to ask the serving maids if the wine had been heated. "I am not in a hurry, Mr Liu," he said. "You can drink your fill for three days. And if you like any one of these serving girls in this courtyard, just ask for her services."

This time, Liu let go and drank himself into a stupor.

That night when the two men were lost in the brash words of drunken nonsense, the explosive news was brought to them that Gou Baidu had been snatched away by the Dragon King. Grabbing Liu into his arms, the proprietor burst into a fit of laughter and cries, and started praising god for upholding justice: "Why, the bandit chose to die on this day, of all days, when Mr Liu is going to choose another site of good fortune for my parents' remains! This must have been preordained by the grave of good fortune you are to locate for me." He wanted the messenger to repeat his account of Gou's death in minute detail until he was rock-sure that what he heard was true.

According to the messenger, it had all happened

three days before. Gou, whose sphere of influence had by then extended far and wide, had left his mountain stronghold to smoke opium in the house of a moneyed man at Dragon Mouth Terrace. He had been puffing at the pipe for three hours but had still not had enough to satisfy him. As his host and cohorts listened, Gou bragged about his heroics.

Once, he said, Tang Jing sent a thug to kill him. The man, a sharp shooter and deft sword wielder, did not know the fact that he, Gou, was someone even Tang himself could do nothing about. When the thug had arrived, Gou, bare fisted, was squatting beside a brazier at the door, smoking tobacco. The man asked, "Who is Commander Gou?" Gou answered: "I am, why don't you join me in a smoke of tobacco." "Ah, a black eight-litre pot!" the man exclaimed. Gou replied that he was indeed ugly and, lowering his head, continued to smoke. When the pipe went out, he tucked his bare fingers into the brazier, picked up a red-hot piece of charcoal and pressed it onto the pipe. The visitor, aghast, closed his eyes. Gou took the burning charcoal down after lighting the tobacco. Instead of returning it to the brazier, he placed it on his knee. Soon the air was filled with the sizzling sound of burning flesh. As if nothing had happened, Gou asked the visitor, "The tobacco smells good. Wouldn't you like to try some?"

The visitor had fallen on his knees. "Commander Gou," he had said, "you are man enough, indeed. Now, you may either chop my head off or let me join you as one of your men." At the words, he tossed his dagger to the ground.

"Just accept a man like that, Gou?" the host had

asked.

"Nothing doing! If a highwayman dares not kill people, what do I want him for?" Picking up the proffered knife, he had said, "What a sharp blade!" Before anyone could react he had sent the thug's head rolling on the ground. It took place so suddenly that the brows and eyes of the head were still knitted in a smile. Gou then cut off the corpse's penis, stuffed it into its mouth and had the head sent to White Crag Hamlet. Everyone present was dumbfounded. Only Gou was laughing madly. He had hardly finished laughing when the sky suddenly blackened. A puff of cloud flew over and hovered above the rooftop. Then came the deafening volley of a thunder. A ray of lightning flung open the windows and, penetrating the room, and struck everyone inside unconscious. When they came to, they saw that everything inside the room was intact, only Gou Baidu was missing. Rushing out of the door, they saw something fall from the sky with a thump — it was Gou Baidu been burned into a chunk of charcoal less than a metre long!

This traumatic ending to the story elicited another spasm of laughter from the proprietor. "What a pity," he said.

"Do you mean it was a pity that the bandit died?" the messenger asked, puzzled.

"I heard he had two large gold-filled teeth which cost a fortune. They must have melted away."

"Nay! They weren't burned away. His hatchetmen knocked the teeth down before they wrapped up his corpse in a piece of white cloth. Because of this they dared not see Fourth Mistress — the bandit's wife — and they each went their own ways. It was the host of Dragon Mouth Terrace who buried the remains."

"You were right to say Fourth Mistress. I'm going to fetch the woman back. And when she's back, you'll continue to call her Fourth Mistress."

Proprietor Yao left in haste to arrange for the return of Fourth Mistress, leaving Liu dazed by the unexpected events. "Fourth Mistress, my fair lady," he mused as he sat alone in the room. "Can I see you once more? Only fate can bring us together."

When the proprietor and his men had left for Wuthering Vale with torches and lanterns in hand, Liu's rekindled hope gave way to sadness for himself and for the fate of Fourth Mistress who, having become the bandit's wife for the last three years, would end up returning to the bed she once shared with the senile invalid, her former husband. Was it because she was such a stunning beauty that she had so easily fallen prey to one wolf after another? On both occasions he was her witness, and each brief meeting with her left him with a bad taste of lingering sorrow and misery. Was Fate just cruel to this poor woman or, rather, to Liu who had lost his limb for her? "If all this is the hand of Fate, then my love for her, a love within reach yet unattainable, is a self-inflicted crime — on no account should I bring this to bear on her," he said to himself.

That sleepless night Liu, who had caught cold and was running a high fever, made up his mind not to be there to see Fourth Mistress again when she was brought back. He thought: "If she does not see me, her heart won't be disturbed and she may spend the rest of her life in peace and quiet."

As the first light of dawn inched above the horizon, Liu packed and leaning on his clutches, went out. He was met by a litter carried with all haste up from the threshing ground below. In it sat the proprietor, his face ash grey, his brows locked in agony. The woman was nowhere to be seen. "Where is Fourth Mistress?" Liu asked him. The old man made no answer; the exuberant joy he had worn on his face as he departed the previous night had disappeared without a trace.

"You didn't bring her home?" Liu ventured again. Proprietor Yao snorted impatiently by way of an answer. To his men who had just set the litter down and were about to leave, he said, "Send food and utensils over there and keep her under close watch. Shut the front and back doors. Make sure no one is allowed to enter, and nobody in the household leaves." He then stumbled his way through the parlor and into his room.

Liu realised that he could not leave without permission. As he looked on puzzled, someone headed out of the gate with bedding and food containers. Then the door was locked with a bang. Serving maids and footmen whispered in corners and dispersed the moment someone came in sight. Liu, who dared not talk to anyone, slipped back to the wing room. He surmised that Fourth Mistress hadn't been brought home because she had either died or fled Wuthering Vale. From the outhouse facing his room across the yard came the rustling of soybean stalks; then someone emerged on the far side of the waist-high wall. Liu knew it was the proprietor's first wife, using soybean leaves in lieu of toilet tissue after she had relieved herself.

Over the wall of the outhouse, First Mistress waved at him. "Come over, Mr Liu!" she called out. "Don't you want to hear the news?"

When Liu came out, the fat woman, whose waist was as thick as a rice barrel, emerged from the outhouse. While hitching up her pants, she asked, "Do you want to know what happened to that young whore?"

"Fourth Mistress?" Liu asked impatiently. "What has become of her?"

"Huh! The old slug always wants to feast on tender meat, but the wench is still infatuated with the bandit who dragged her off to the hills — she refused to come back even though the bandit had died."

"So, she didn't want to come back," Liu guessed. "She's refused to return?" he asked aloud.

"Will the old slug let her off lightly because of her pretty face? That her body has been polluted by someone else does not bother him at all — what bothers him is the bandit's baby she's carrying. She's far gone in pregnancy, and I'm afraid abortion is out of the question even with a heavy dosage of chinaberry-seed potion."

Liu was stunned. "Fourth Mistress is having a baby?"

"Yah, when the old slug saw her like that, he literally hit the ceiling. He had wanted to kick the bandit's baby out then and there, but didn't for fear of killing her. The witch tried to jump down the gully. When she was pulled back she bumped her head on a stone, making quite a hole in her skull. The old slug was furious, and cursed, 'Why didn't you jump the cliff at the very beginning — in that case I have had a stone tablet erected to your chastity. Now that I've come to take you home, you threaten me with death!' He then had the whore carried home by litter. I'd rather see her die."

In earnest, Liu asked, "How come I didn't see her carried back?"

"You mean carried her back under the Yao family's roof and allowed to bear that seed of the bandit? Who are the Yaos anyway? But that would make us the laughing-stock of everyone, and induce evil spirits to descend on us and ruin the Yao residence. You want to know where she is? She's been thrown into the stone castle. When she has given birth to the bandit's baby, firecrackers will be let off for three days, and her body will be cleansed with water boiled with Chinese mugwort — only then can she enter the Yaos' gate by riding a donkey facing backwards."

The fat lady finished her tale and, hand on mouth, giggled. Liu's mind was in a turmoil. His face filmed with tears, he gazed beyond the yard wall at the ancient castle atop the hill, legacy of the ancient battleground. He recalled again how a few years earlier he had, on his surreptitious trips to Northern Terrace, imagined what it would be like to meet Fourth Mistress there on a moon-lit night. Never had he expected that several years later she would be locked up in the solitude of the building. He could imagine the dilapidation of her cell, where wild grass straggled and the stench of wild-dove droppings choked the air. How could the pretty woman be left there waiting for her labour day and then take the life of her new-born with her own hands?

Liu had no idea when the fat First Mistress retreated inside. Digging his fingers into the surface of the wall, he hopped along on his single foot. His finger-nails cracked, leaving streaks of blood on the stone. He kept hopping in this fashion until he landed himself at the foot of the stone stairs that led up to the parlor. Now he had changed his mind: Instead of going away, he wanted to see Fourth Mistress. He would stay with the Yaos so that he could see her, and she him, for ever. He leaped up and down the stairs until he collapsed and in doing so broke his front tooth. The noise drew the proprietor out of the door, and Liu said to him, "How could you lock up Fourth Mistress in the stone castle? You shouldn't treat her like that!"

Bewildered, the proprietor said, "Mr Liu, I think highly of you. Don't you butt in my family's private affairs."

"No!" Liu jumped to his single foot and stood there like an awl with its tip drilled into the ground. "I certainly should not stick my nose in your private matters. But you know you've invited me to choose the lucky burial site for your family. To obtain such a site the most important thing is to accumulate virtue. Not a single man of virtue and personal integrity has ever failed to gain a lucky piece of land. Gou Baidu died an ignominious death because he was an unscrupulous evil-doer. That is why he laid a fortuitous grave to waste."

The proprietor said, "Not that I don't want to do as you advise; it's just that the woman is carrying the bandit's seed. Wouldn't I bring disgrace to my ancestors if I allowed her to make a mess of my family by having that child under my roof? If I didn't intend to treat her nicely I would've slashed her belly with my knife at Wuthering Vale. Mr Liu, I'm afraid you are still suffering the hangover from last night's drinking. Come, servants, help Mr Liu back to his room and treat him to a bowl of lotus seed soup!"

A number of footmen virtually carried Liu to the wing room.

Lying on the *kang* Liu wept in silence. His pleading for the woman who would soon return to the proprietor as his fourth wife had incurred the man's rebuttal and rancour, and he felt his bravery had got him nowhere.

The day seemed maddeningly long and he hated himself for not being a bandit. "Had I the muscle of a bandit and a gun," he thought, "I wouldn't have put up with the old dog like that!" The thought made him regard Gou as a real man. What a pity he had died; the woman would've fared better as the wife of a bandit than as Yao's fourth concubine.

Day gave way to night as the four surrounding mountains cast their dark shadows over the courtyard. The moon rose. It turned out to be a fine moon-lit night, tailor-made for romance, for lovers to go to the mountains and take a stroll along the winding footpath leading to the stone castle, and in doing so let the moonlight soak through their snow-white silk clothing and chisel at their delicate faces. It was a night made for silky dreams, for unspeakable thoughts that flew forth like a stream, for a thousand and one words of mutual understanding and prayer. But the grim reality was that the woman wept in the stone castle; only she knew how many tears she had shed.

Liu was suddenly apprehensive at the thought that

the woman would perish over the prospects of witnessing her own child done to death. Yes, she will die, for even a woman with the strongest character will succumb to desperation and disillusion. The thought and Liu's taut nerves brought him to a sweat. In his mind's eye he could see the woman screaming, her hair dishevelled, but nobody could hear her, for her screams were muffled by the wind; then she quieted down and looked woodenly at a colony of happy ants marching along the stone wall. If only she was one of the ants. May god incarnate the soul of the woman into a free ant! Can she peep out of the crack in the door and see the billowing mountains under the moon, the plank road hewn into the rock face and the stone corridor enveloped in the ethereal cloud? No, she can't, for the stone castle presses down on her like a dead weight, incarcerating her like a cage. What meets her eyes is a field strewn with greenish jack-o'-lanterns.

Then an ancient legend came to Liu's mind. It was about a heroic general who for all his life's exploits ended up besieged in the castle. It too was a moonlit night. The dead bodies of his soldiers lay about. Only the general and his wife and a loyal bodyguard remained alive. As the enemy soldiers swarmed up the hill, he killed his beloved young wife with his sword, not wanting her to be humiliated at the hands of the enemy. Hugging the dead woman in his arms, he burst into a fit of laughter. "Now," he said to his bodyguard who was dazed by his act, "that my life as a hero has come to an end, let me do you a favour. My enemy has set a price of three hundred taels of silver on my head. My faithful man, you may take my head to see them." His long hair fluttering in the wind, his armour glistening in the light of the moon which hung in the star-spangled sky, the general clutched his hair with one hand and beheaded himself with the other. While his head dangled from his hand, his truncated body stood rod straight.

As details of the tale went through the geomancer's mind, he surmised that Fourth Mistress had heard the howling of the ghosts and seen the heroic general and his wife. That must have prompted her to ask, with a sigh of sadness, "Who's my hero?" She must be thinking: "The wife was the happiest woman in the world because although her heroic husband could not protect her in life, he protected her in death." She must be saying, "I have lived with stinking men because of my maidenly looks. Today I could not even die under the knife of someone I love."

This train of thoughts sank Liu into an abyss from which he had no way of extricating himself. Past scenes of his impotence, weakness and endurance came back to him, combining to arouse the manly bravery in him. "I'm your hero," he said between gritted teeth. "Yes, I am!"

With the hero awakened in him, Liu pushed open the gate and went hobbling up the hill.

All was quiet, for it was the dead of night. The mountain trail was bumpy, and he tripped over numerous times until he was reduced to clawing his way towards the top, his clothes torn to threads, his leg and arms grazed and bleeding. But all this was irrelevant now, for in his mind he was planning how, after reaching the castle, to open the portal gate and in what proper manner to call out her name so that she could be willing to meet him. He would beg her not to cry and waste time relating her heartfelt, pent-up love to him. For she had to make haste and leave the castle. Even if she couldn't go far because of the dark, she should hide herself somewhere and he would join her later, or if she preferred to go alone, help her flee to a faraway place.

Hardly had he climbed to the canopied plank road below the castle when he was discovered by the man taking the watch there. The old man, who ran errands for the Yaos and therefore knew who Liu was, asked him why he'd come there in the dark. Liu told him of his intention, knowing that with this man on guard, he'd never be able to pull off a one-man rescue operation. At great length he told the watchman about the woman's trauma, hoping to talk him into helping him saving the woman. He promised to pay the watchman handsomely for his cooperation and find him a burial site with all the major auspicious omens to bless his family with perpetual peace, happiness and prosperity. The watchman consented, but he dissuaded Liu from going up the mountain by himself. "Passing the precarious plank road takes all the strength and caution of a healthy man," he said, "and it is an impossible proposition for a man handicapped such as yourself. Trust me, please, sir. I'll go right up and help Fourth Mistress get out of here. If His Excellency asks tomorrow, I'll just say that she disappeared while I was in the toilet. His Excellency may bind me up with a rope and flog me. He may take all I own, but that will be all he can do to me."

Moved, Liu kowtowed to the old man repeatedly and said he would never forget his great kindness the rest of his life. But he didn't take his leave and climb downhill until he reeled off a host of exhortations for the old man to be careful.

The sky had started to turn pale when Liu returned to his lodging at the Yao family mansion. Acting as if nothing had happened, he had himself borne by a family servant out of the door. On the way he met another servant fetching water from the river. "Please let His Excellency know I've gone to prospect for the lucky site at the foot of the back hill. Tell him to come and have a look."

He worked there until noon, but the proprietor didn't appear. Liu wasn't in a hurry to go back, and he lay down on the sun-warmed ground, wanting to take a good rest from the fatigue of his trip to the stone castle the previous night. He wondered what the proprietor was doing at that moment. The stupid man must be ignorant about his fourth wife's escape, he thought, still less the fact that it was masterminded by a crippled geomancer. But where is Fourth Mistress hiding? A mountain cave, or a pine-tree forest? No matter where she is, she must be feeling grateful to him and yearning for him. He couldn't wait to join her, and for that matter he had to finish his job with all haste. He wondered if the honest old watchman would seek him out after he returned to the Yaos and tell him her whereabouts? Liu finally relaxed and dozed off. In his dream a strange feeling came over him, a faint sense of foreboding mixed with a subconscious pride for the heroic rescue mission.

Then he felt himself being nudged, and heard someone calling, "Sir, wake up. Here comes His Excellency!" Opening his eyes he saw the proprietor approach and stop a dozen metres away. "Why the hurry, Mr Liu?" he said loudly. "Why don't you rest for a few more days? I don't know how to repay you for what you've done for my family."

"Don't stand on ceremony, Your Excellency. Come over and have a look. This site is indeed very good."

"Isn't it so? How did you manage to find it so fast? Why, you are hurt. See, there's blood on your hands."

Blushing, Liu said hastily, "I fell down the ridge accidently a while ago. It's not serious. Now that you've come, why don't we settle the position of the burial site and have pegs driven into the four corners?"

What he heard next was the least he had expected: "You seem in a hurry to go? But this time I won't let you go so soon, for I want to entertain you the best I can. It's lunch-time now. Let's go home and come back tomorrow."

Liu was carried back, not to the dining room for lunch but straight to the parlor. The proprietor threw himself into an easy chair and started smoking one pipe of opium after another. All the while he avoided Liu's eyes and remained silent. When Liu rose to his foot, wanting to return to his room, the proprietor suddenly said, "Mr Liu, are you in love with my fourth wife?"

Blood drained from the geomancer's face. Leaning against the table, he sat down again. "How could you say that, Your Excellency? Did I offend you anyway?"

"Something odd took place last night," the proprietor said. "Someone went to the castle and wanted to spirit my woman away. You, sir, are a capable man.

Do you think it was Gou Baidu?" These words threw Liu into a panic and led him to think that the woman had fled the castle and that the proprietor wanted to track her down. The thought of the woman's flight to safety filled his heart with pride.

Regaining his composure, he said in affected surprise, "Now that Fourth Mistress has been brought home, whoever would've gone to the castle, and for what reason? Hasn't Gou just been snatched away by the dragon?"

The proprietor sneered. "It is true Gou is dead. Some one else wanted to emulate him, but unfortunately he didn't have Gou's muscle. Deshun, come in!"

A man entered the parlor. He was none other than the man who had watched over Fourth Mistress the previous night. He stole a glance at Liu and dropped his head.

"Among the Yaos' servants," the proprietor said, "Gou was the only biting dog. Nobody else has ever been disloyal to me. Deshun told me everything. Now I only want to ask you one question: Do you love my fourth wife?"

Suddenly Liu felt as if the sky had turned upside down. His heart burned with hatred for the man called Deshun. Why didn't the dragon have it out with this doggy Deshun instead of Gou Baidu? he thought bitterly. My entire heroic attempt was spoiled by the hand of this despicable servant. With the full truth laid bare before him, Liu groaned inwardly for the woman who, for his own stupidity, was sure to receive more severe punishment. "Now that everything has gone absolutely wrong, why should I conceal anything and why should I be so timid?" Glaring angrily at the proprietor, he burst out: "Yes, I'm in love with Fourth Mistress! I fell in love with her the first time I came here. You may take my life for it, Your Excellency!"

The old man tossed his pipe away and guffawed until his body and easy chair shook violently. "What a candid man, Mr Liu! You may also want to know: not only you have fallen in love with Fourth Mistress, she, too, loves you."

"No," Liu said, "this has nothing to do with Fourth Mistress. If you want to kill someone, kill me, for all this is my fault."

"Fancy your loving the woman so deeply. You are my distinguished guest. I want to thank you. With what? I'll give Fourth Mistress to you. I loved her, lost my family fortune for her, and brought her home even after she became the bandit's woman. However, after meeting her in the castle this morning, I've decided to give her to you."

Liu let his eyes meet and hold the proprietor's for a lingering moment, incapable of fathoming what the wily man meant. He stood there, motionless, waiting for the man to change his face and call in his robustious hatchetmen. Unexpectedly, the proprietor said, "Mr Liu, don't you want to thank me in return?" Liu could not believe this turn of events. It was as if all of a sudden an overcast sky had broken into bright sunshine, a rough-and-tumble river had hit a gentle stretch or a tornado had died down. Lowering his head he said smilingly, "I'll be very grateful if Your Excellency really means it."

"In return, I want you to see that you find a grave site of extreme good fortune for me. Yesterday you wanted to decide the location without working really hard on it — that I won't accept. Let's do it this way: I'll ask Fourth Mistress to stay in the castle for a few more days. You'll leave with her whenever you've finished your job."

Toiling for six full days with business-like intensity, Liu selected a grave site that met with the proprietor's satisfaction. When at last, he climbed up to the castle, the woman who appeared before him had changed beyond recognition. A few days earlier, having been lashed by the proprietor with a whip, she had given birth to a baby which was instantly thrown to its death on the ground. The woman had picked up a piece of sharp-edged stone and, as the proprietor looked on, had defaced her features by carving four scars from left temple to right cheek. To the man she had said, "Didn't you love my face? Now, with heart and soul, let me be your Fourth Mistress."

Despite himself, Liu aahed and sagged to the ground at the sight of the woman's ruined face. The proprietor, looking triumphant, said in a seemingly apologetic tone, "I shouldn't have kept you in the dark about this, Mr Liu. Please forgive me. When you marry a woman, you marry her face. If you dislike her like that, I'll give you a servant-maid with a pretty face, someone really charming." Liu jumped to his foot and flung his arms around the woman.

Liu hired a donkey and returned home with his woman. Having stuck her wounds together with downy chicken feathers, she was no longer the bewitching beauty she used to be. Four red welts ran across her face in a diagonal tack. Yet Liu's love for her remained as fervent as ever. Embracing his wife who had eventually fulfilled her own wishes after going through indescribable trauma, he was no longer the impotent man he had been. He was her husband and performed his duty as such.

Five years later, they produced a son.

With the advent of the boy, the couple felt they had had enough of the humble life. They wanted to live in the world with dignity and with everything going the way they wanted. To attain that goal, they believed that their son should become an official when he grew up so they decided to select the best grave site for themselves. For the better part of his life Liu had made his services available for the happiness of many others; now it was high time to do something for his own family. Thus husband and wife, with their hair already flecked with white, took to the road on the back of a skinny donkey. Eventually, on the noon of a fine, rain-cleansed day, they found the place where they wanted their own grave to be. His mouth foaming with excitement, Liu explained to his wife the beauties of this fortuitous plot.

In geomancy, he said, a mountain is regarded as a dragon, because only a dragon can assume such richly varied postures, its body can shift in different positions and the way it is revealed or leaps forward is unpredictable. Spittle splashing from his mouth, he continued to babble about the prodigies of *mai*, equivalent to arteries and veins which make it possible for vital energy and blood to run through the human body. He whose body has a clear-cut network of *mai* is of noble stock; he whose *mai* is vague is of a low breed; he who has propitious signs will live in peace; he who has ill omens will meet his wretched end. The same goes for the topographical *mai*, he said. As a dragon, the mountain should have vivacious contours and fine-looking *mai* with deeply hidden pores, and the vital parts of its body all clearly present, its minor parts should be openly visible and its fluid flows gently. The dragon should have two ears that point to the sky and a crab's eyes with shrimp's barbels protruding from both sides; there should be adequate space for the dragon to stretch its limbs.

Liu's geomantic interpretation, full of archaic phrases and jargon, was Greek to his wife, who pestered him with questions about what their own burial site really entailed. Liu, carried away with his findings, told her that the site was situated in the semi-circle contour of the mountain below a horizontal ridge, in the rear of which another mountain formed a full circle. Though the place lacked the portents of five mountain peaks, rising to the skies and four springs encircling it, and twin green dragons embracing an imperial certificate of official rank, it was a typical lucky site under the foliage of a Chinese parasol tree. The dragon, with an evenly developed body and limbs, looked as if it was in the embrace of a pair of outstretched tree branches, whose twigs formed a heart-shaped space — the phenomenon entailed absolute bliss which had descended on the ancestors and would be bestowed on sons and grandsons of the family. "Enough, enough!" the woman cried in joy. "I don't understand your explanations. What I want is simply a site which could help propel our son to officialdom!"

Liu had lost his parents as a child and was brought up by his master. Not knowing where his parents were buried, he placed a wooden tablet to their memory in the grave, in which he had twin chambers dug. Then he announced that he had retired from his career as a geomancer.

When their son grew to be twelve years old, he was old enough to carry out his father's will. One morning, the couple took a bath in water infused with chrysanthemum flowers and put on new clothing. "My son," Liu said, "we won't see you grow to be thirty or forty, nor can we bequeath to you a great mansion of brick-and-tile houses, a hundred *mu* of high yielding farmland or generous family assets. But we will help you to become an official. From now on, forget your parents, leave this place, and go out to do what you like. The world is so big that you will never feel lonely. You have many important things to accomplish."

The son, a clever, handsome boy, took his parents' advice, kowtowed to them with a bang of his head on the ground, and left their mountain abode.

His mother was getting on in years, but she had taken good care of herself. Impeccably clad, she covered her head with a chequered handkerchief so big it hung down and hid her face. "Today it's rather warm and there is no wind. Why should you hide your face like that?"

"I look so ugly without it."

Liu scanned her face. Despite the web of wrinkles, her features looked as mellifluent as usual. Behind the four red scars he felt he could glimpse her beauty of bygone days. "You don't look ugly at all," he said. "You are an angel who once lived in Heaven. But when you descended on the human world, the peach blossoms hated you, the spring wind hated you, and so you had your fill of misery. Only with these four scars can you have peace. The sun is so warm, and we are going far away. Why should you hide your face?"

The woman accepted her husband's advice. When she was about to mount the donkey, Liu extended a helping hand, and in doing so pinched her pair of tiny feet. He then handed her a willow twig she could use as a whip. "One more pinch, and I'll whip you," the woman said. This reminded them of what had happened between them long before. Their eyes met, and both smiled in the broad daylight.

With the woman riding the donkey and the man following behind, they arrived at their burial site. Having got inside the tomb, they moved stones and bricks to block the entrance until not a trace of wind or light could penetrate it. "Tonight there'll be rain," Liu said, "and the earth will fall down from the top of the tomb to bury the entrance of our tomb. So let's sleep in peace."

But how? the woman asked. The thinning of air in the darkness was yet to take effect on them. Like a child, she wanted Liu to lay her down on the ground and hug her tightly, so that she could rest her head on his chest. To all her requests Liu obliged. Then they heard, in the outside world, the roar of wind sweeping past their tomb and the metallic rustling sound of withered grass. Ants were singing, so were the earthworms. Millepedes, creeping on the damp wall of the tomb, smelled of ginger and onion. Past events returned in minute detail to their minds. Liu regretted having not brought along a bottle of wine to be drunk with something as delectable as salted, sun-dried pork slices: recollections. In the darkness, Liu fumbled for the old red silk undergarment, so threadbare now as to break at the slight tug, and started untying it. The woman couldn't see, but felt what he was doing. Extending a hand she pulled at the undergarment and laid it on their faces.

"This is the flag of our honour," Liu said.

"A flag like that should be inscribed with our life's exploits," the woman said.

"Don't you see the blood stains — aren't they our own handwriting?" Liu said.

"Can our son become an official?" the woman asked softly.

"Sure, for this is a grave of good fortune."

"What kind of official will he become?"

"A great one, believe me. A ranking official!"

Ten years later, an actor from the local Hong-Family Theatrical Troupe rose to fame for his skilled performance in the role of Lord Bao, an upright Song-dynasty court official. He turned out to be Liu Ziyan's son. Liu had spent his whole life in search of propitious burial places for others. When time came for him to choose one for himself, however, he mistook a bad site for good. His son, instead of becoming a high official with power and influence, ended up impersonating one on the stage.

Translated by Ling Yuan

The Regrets of a Bride Carrier

THE dogs are aroused. Ever since Slacker Flat they've been barking and nipping at the feet of the bridal party. Funny how dogs are just like people, getting excited about the same things. It's that horn — its brassy, raucous whining drives everyone mad. The carriers are powerful young lads who could easily cut a swift swathe through the canine mob, and yet they claim the dogs are stymying their steps, that they can't possibly go any faster, and they perpetually complain of exhaustion. It's just too unreasonable, they say, to expect them to carry this stuff — trunks, bedding, a brazier, stools, pillows, lampstands, mirrors, and two porcelain bowls filled with wheat — the whole fifteen miles to Rooster Village without a break. "Whew! We gotta rest!" they pant, and they draw to a halt.

"No! No!" Wang Sao, the matron of honour, exclaims in dismay. She throws glances at Wukui through the pock-marked mask that is her face. Wukui reminds them of the chaos of the times, that bandits might well be preparing to pounce upon them. But the lads scoff at the idea. They puff themselves up and jostle about with boisterous bravado, boasting that there's nothing to be afraid of. They espy a thatched shed — the autumn crop sentinel's shelter — and acquire from it some hefty sticks, and start yelling at and beating the dogs. The dogs though, continue to swell in number as newcomers bound out of nowhere to join the pack. The horn's sonorous and haughty cacophony whips them into a frenzy, and they fling themselves into the air, thin, yellow, loptail bodies arching upward like bows. Or they raise a hind leg and produce streams of urine for all the world to see. Two of them lock themselves together in a long, drawn-out coupling that elicits bawdy shouts from the lads: "Hey! Horny dogs! Horny dogs!" Ostensibly hollering at the dogs, they in fact are ogling the woman on Wukui's back. The blood rushes to Wukui's face. He comes to a standstill. But he doesn't put the woman down.

The bride is forbidden to set foot on the ground during this journey. Wukui, well-versed in bridal protocol, fumes, "His Excellency'll really give it to you good!"

"Well, of course we're not like Wukui," the lads say with a leer. "We're carrying dead things that get heavier and heavier with every step. So, Wukui, since you're so tough, you can just go merrily on by yourself!"

Wukui's face glows red as burning charcoal. "You're just a bunch of trouble-makers!" he retorts. But as there's only one of him and many of them, he is hostage to their whims and so he leans his carrying frame against a rock. The woman shifts her weight, and two supple white hands grasp his shoulders. His neck goes stiff; an alien unease shivers through his body.

The lads are not themselves. They're behaving like a bunch of rowdies. Bridal expeditions in the past had always found them harkening to the siren call of the cigarettes, food and liquor waiting for them at the end of the line, and they invariably covered the distance with no-nonsense alacrity. Today, though, something has filled them with devilry. Wukui knows what it is: It's this particular woman he's carrying.

As the string of firecrackers was snapping and popping back there in Slacker Flat, Old Yao, cigarette pinched between his fingers, had welcomed them into his house to have a drink. They'd had a glimpse of the woman, face bathed in tears, sitting on the adobe *kang* in the inner room. But none of them had laughed or whooped it up as usual, because that woman was the most beautiful thing they had ever set eyes on. It was truly a miracle that such an angel should have come out of that humble thatched house. Up to that moment they'd felt their coming to pick up the bride was an onerous task imposed upon them by the Lius, those habitual abusers of wealth and power. But suddenly they felt privileged, as if a favour had been bestowed upon them.

Whenever it came time for maidens to leave the protective custody of their parents and go to the bed of another in matrimonial bond, their faces were always bathed in tears. But this woman was unlike any other crying bride they'd ever seen. She cried adorably. Her mother and her matron of honour were comforting her with words of encouragement. They pulled her hands away from her face and re-powdered that visage so utterly divine. They dipped her comb into fragrant oil and combed her hair until it shone. Wukui saw her there, sitting at an angle on the *kang*. She had one leg curled under her, while the other languidly stretched at a slant along the edge. Her tiny embroidered shoe, looking crafty, as if about to expose her foot, revealed the shape of her heel. At that moment he knew this was a woman worthy of the prosperity and prestige that accrued to the Lius, that such as she had a righteous claim to the life of ease they could offer her. Not only that, she should ride over in style in an ornamental sedan chair whisked along by eight bearers; only, unfortunately, in this land of furious topographical turmoil, there is no road that can accommodate a sedan chair, so she has to suffer being carried piggyback by Wukui.

By the age of sixteen, Wukui was already a strapping specimen of a man, precisely suited to the role of bride carrier. Due to the rarity of men so qualified, bride carrying soon became for him a career of sorts. In the past ten years, he has probably carried thirty or forty brides to their new homes. He knows the weight, body type, and even the scent of every bride in Rooster Village. But never has he carried such a stunningly beautiful woman before. She truly made him forget his mission. When he walked over to the *kang* and bent down to allow her to climb on his back, he had suddenly broken out into a sweat. By the time she knelt upon the carpet of the carrying frame, he had gone into a daze. Only after the Yaos painted his face red with a paste of cinnabar, and the shout to set out had been sounded, did he finally realise he was supposed to walk out the door. Now on the road he's suffering the pangs of regret, for she who is on his back is not for him to see, though she can see him up close and in detail and is probably smiling to herself at his foolish appearance.

The lads back-packing the trousseau right behind are capable of walking to the ends of the earth without a rest; they could walk until the last day of their lives and they wouldn't feel the least bit tired. But they really have no desire to draw this facile fifteen-mile journey to a swift conclusion, and that is why they can afford to let fly their excitement and indulge in garrulous idiocy. That's why they're looking for excuses to tarry. Though she who's the bride belongs to the Liu family, as long as she is on the bridal route, she is still not really a Liu. Thus they can get away with saying just about anything, and they are taking advantage of this; for once she enters that family, it'll be a rare day indeed when they'll be able to see her again. Wukui well understands that the lads should feel this way, since he too is smitten and is at this very moment bemoaning the fact that he'll never again have the chance to be this close to her.

Therefore Wukui goes along with them and leans the carrying frame on the rock to rest.

On the mountain road, the August sun shines with seasonal brilliance, while a leisurely wind ruffles the feathers of chirping birds loitering along the way. To Wukui everything shimmers with unusual beauty. For the first time in his life he actually enjoys looking upon the rolling hills and the road winding to the top. If there were in fact a broad public road that could accommodate a sedan chair or even a horse in elegant trappings, then the most he could hope for would be to serve as one of the trousseau carriers. He opens his mouth to unleash the song that is bursting in his breast, but all that comes out through his white teeth is laughter.

The matron of honour approaches and peers at him anxiously. She goes back to the trousseau, undoes the brass lock on the dowry trunk and takes out walnuts and dates. These she distributes to the lads. Generally it's for the carriers themselves to get into the trunk and partake of these goodies prepared for their refreshment on the road, but now the matron of honour herself is taking the initiative to serve them. Everyone knows what she has in mind.

"It's getting late," the matron of honour says.

"We'll be on time for the entry into the bridal chamber," the lads reply playfully. "Look how beautiful this weather is!"

"Yes, beautiful weather..."

"Aren't you afraid of bandits?" Smirks and leers.

"Who's afraid of bandits!" The matron of honour doesn't want to say anything unlucky. "You can take a rest, but Wukui will be exhausted!"

"Wukui will never be exhausted!"

If anyone's ever spoken the truth, it's that lad, Wukui thinks. Indeed, he could never be exhausted. And then he thinks, what a scream — they're jealous! Every time he carries a bride, they always derive the greatest of pleasure from making fun of him. Today, though, they're eating their hearts out! But what is she thinking? She hasn't said a word since they set out. Maybe she's thinking about what happened yesterday. Her people would've taken her out into the yard about noon and removed all those tiny little hairs on her face and neck with a pair of silk threads. Couldn't have been too comfortable. But he's never really dealt with a woman before, so he hasn't got the slightest idea what she'd be feeling. Not about that, nor about what's running through her mind as she draws step by step ever closer to wifehood. Through the thin layer of her clothing, he can feel her heart beating. Her purity is palpable. She's got a lot on her mind, that's for sure, because the women he carried before either laughed every once in a while, or cried the whole way; but this one's doing neither. Either she is just as anxious as the matron of honour, or she understands the significance of her beauty and knows well what's filling the heads of these lads. She's just not saying anything about it, that's all.

Silence: the virtue of the woman who knows how to be a woman.

Okay, then, Wukui thinks, it won't hurt to worry her a bit. Let them all be worried — the bride, the matron of honour, and especially the groom cooling his heels at the pass outside Rooster Village. At this point Wukui — ever well-behaved, ever the good little boy — is rebelliously snatching a measure of delight from the joking and the silliness. At this excruciating pace, the woman destined to live in luxury on the Liu's adobe *kang* won't be able to eat or drink or relieve herself for the whole morning, and this will cause her untold suffering. You might wonder how Wukui could possibly enjoy that, but here he's got a yen for revenge — for the sorrow he feels over his own impoverished existence. It's her beauty and its impact upon his seat of affections that has reminded him of this sorrow.

But now another thought crowds in to demolish this desire for revenge: Who was it who determined that he should be a pauper anyway? It's not simply a case of being deprived of a beautiful woman like this. It's that he can never have any woman, not even the ugliest. And even if he could get this one, could he feed and clothe her properly? A horse is saddled with the saddle that befits it; a tree attracts certain kinds of birds to its branches. This is all arranged by fate. That he should have the opportunity to carry this woman is already a piece of good fortune, and so he is satisfied! Thus, he forgets his pleasure in revenge and instead conceives a growing displeasure with the lads and their endless dawdling.

"Okay," he says, "we've rested enough. Let's get going!"

But the lads are flirting with the matron of honour. The real object of their amorousness is, of course, the delectable bride, but hers is a beauty that not merely fills them with rapture, it is forbidding and demanding of their respect and self-control as well. They are thus reduced to getting their jollies out of teasing the aging matron of honour. They say how pretty she is and they pick a wild flower for her to stick in her hair. Wukui turns his head to take a look and sees the matron of honour is having fun, and this translates into a feeling of happiness for him too.

Yes, it's true, the matron of honour, who's always been a wallflower, ignored and undesired, has forgotten for the moment her disfigurement as the lads rambunctiously show off for her. That such a gorgeous bride should choose this pock-marked woman to be her matron of honour clearly reveals her intent to set off beauty with ugliness. But then again, maybe she'd intended no such thing, for she truly is of surpassing beauty; maybe it only happens that this beauty makes the matron of honour's face seem all the more unsightly.

When Wukui steps away from the rock and into the sun, a surge of exaltation courses through his veins, sparked by the sight of his shadow and hers merged into one. He hopes she'll say something like, "This must be very tiring for you." She doesn't though, but he's sure she's thinking it. He's going through all this trouble for one reason and one reason alone, and that's so she'll remember the one who carried her today.

It really is getting late, but the lads are still dallying, as if they've no will to get the bride home before the sun glows like a copper basin and drops with a clang behind the mountain. When they finish horsing around with the matron of honour, they retrieve their cudgels from among the pack of dogs and walk up to Wukui. They brandish the cudgels under his nose and poke fun at his cinnabarred face to cover their own sneaky peeks at the blushing woman on his back.

Wukui's only recourse is to wheel upon them. He scampers away with the urgent, foreshortened steps of a man committed to speed but hampered by a load.

Their impudence, though, hasn't been lost upon the woman. Overwhelmingly shy, she pretends not to see by feigning intense interest in Wukui's cowlick.

He can feel the scalp under his cowlick itching. In fact, it's not been as normal right from the start, when they'd set out on their journey. In the first place, there was the possibility that though he'd washed his hair, lice might climb up from his collar. And even if there were no lice, still that cowlick's not a single cowlick, but a double cowlick, and if a man's double cowlick indicates he's a loser, then how would the woman regard him? Later on he feels air softly filtering through this clump of hair. He wonders if it's his own anxious soul pouring out of there like smoke, or if it's the woman's delicate warm breath. Or maybe she is gently blowing on his head to cool him off. That seems a likely explanation, for she can surely see he's dripping with sweat. Not daring to wipe it with her hand, she's trying to make him more comfortable by favouring him with a little cool breeze!

Absorbed in such thoughts, Wukui imagines himself a fine steed whose master is stroking his mane. He plunges forward on his clippity-cloppity hooves. The lads behind take up the challenge and exchange their loitering for a hastened catch-up pace. The sounds of the horn gyrate into the air, more joyful and frenetic than ever. As he speeds along with a spring in his step, he can feel the woman bouncing up and down on his back, her two plump breasts hidden inside her clothes pressing upon his back, emanating waves of heat. Locusts fly out at the two figures from the roadside grass like wind-driven rain. A bee takes notice and pursues them closely.

"A bee! A bee!" the woman suddenly exclaims in a low voice.

The bee settles directly upon Wukui's cowlick.

When he hears her warning, he braces himself and refuses to raise his hand to brush it away. He says breathlessly, "It's come because of your sweet aroma." The bee gives him a whopping sting, and that spot on his scalp immediately erupts into a burning hot welt.

"Wukui, you've been stung. Does it hurt?"

"No! Not a bit!" he lies.

She dabs her finger with her saliva and rubs it on his sting.

Wukui will be forever grateful to that bee. It had been attracted by her sweet scent, and she in turn had daubed his head with her most excellent sweet saliva! She's capable of affection for a lowly bride carrier. This is his reward. His feelings of inferiority vanish and in their place there arises a fantasy at once romantic, frightening and, at the base of it, wicked. He's hoping — horrors! — that there will suddenly appear a gang of terrifying bandits for this would annul his task of bearing this woman to the Lius. But even if it didn't, even if he still had to fulfill this obligation, he would have to take a circuitous route picking his way through gullies, ascending and descending slopes, negotiating an endless craggy, riverine terrain, all to escape the bandits. Thus he could carry her and bear her until he was thoroughly exhausted and thoroughly satisfied.

Perhaps the wishing makes it so, or perhaps fate decreed it long ago, for about five miles outside Rooster Village, out from the wild profusion of grass and weeds leap seven or eight rough looking fellows dressed in white from head to toe. These fellows fan out in front of the bridal party. The matron of honour screeches, "White Wind Village!"

White Wind Village, once a bustling gathering point for downriver people, is twenty miles from Rooster Village. Two decades ago, a man and his wife moved there from deep within the mountains. The wife was already quite advanced in years, a mismatch for her much younger husband. The two of them and their four children quietly set about scratching out a life for themselves by reclaiming some fields in the mountain forest. The husband had an extremely bad temper, and he frequently beat his children. One day three of the children roasted and ate some soybeans that were intended for seed. Enraged, he took a leather-thonged bullwhip to them, lashing them with a severity that unravelled the very integrity of the whip itself. When the mother heard what was going on, she rushed to the scene and screamed a torrent of abuse at her husband:

"How can you be so cruel? Those are my sons. And for that matter, you are my son as well — so who do you think you are pulling rank on them?"

The wife's words quite literally dazed her husband such that with a crazed scream the man smashed his head into a chestnut tree and killed himself.

When news of this incident spread and people learned that this husband and wife were originally mother and son, they seethed with righteous indignation. Though the wife had revealed merely what was in those days a desperate recourse to survival in the wilderness, it proved to be a monumental slip of the tongue. For by it she had lost all semblance of wifely and motherly virtue. The people tied a millstone to her feet and hung her by the neck from a branch of the chestnut tree. They seized as well three of her four children and right before her eyes as she hung there in the waning moments of her life, beat them to death with hammers. Overnight, the weight of the millstone pulled upon her hanging body until the neck became skeletally detached. It pulled out to a thread, and the body fell into a deep pool under the tree while the head remained dangling like a bell clapper from the noose.

The youngest of the four children somehow escaped his brothers' fate. He simply vanished. One day twenty years later, a fierce and ambitious young man named

Tang Jing cataclysmically altered the political landscape of White Wind Village when he routed the local government and pitched his camp there. With White Wind Village as his base, he performed many dramatic deeds of heroic banditry that made his name synonymous with terror throughout the surrounding areas. But the White Wind villagers themselves and those people within a several mile radius supported him, for to them he was not a terrorist but a protector. Neither government forces nor marauding bandits from anywhere else could touch a blade of grass or a single stone in this place.

This man, who was both a product of and a maker of legends, had taken a very beautiful wife. He always dressed himself in white and made his men and even his wife wear white as well, all year round. The White Wind villagers, wishing to please him as their village head, emulated this sartorial peculiarity, turning white into a symbol of place as well as of conduct. Thus, whenever the inhabitants of those places that were subject to Tang Jing's harassment would see someone dressed in white, they would react just as if they had bumped into the god of the plague. Eventually the ordinary villagers who advocated the wearing of white, though they stood aloof from actual acts of banditry, came to be regarded as just as guilty of unpardonable evil as Tang Jing himself.

The matron of honour has made a very astute observation: The ones blocking the road are indeed from White Wind Village. And they are not just any ordinary villagers either, but Tang Jing's own men. They were originally out to intercept a shipment of grain tax from the county seat to the provincial capital that was supposed to have been sent along a new route. But their information was inaccurate and they waited a whole day without seeing a trace of it. Angry and frustrated, they had withdrawn, discussing how the recent bad luck of White Wind Village was all on account of the bandit chieftain's wife, who was now deceased.

They deplored how this beautiful wife had been perfect in every way except for a mole on the bridge of her nose that had marred her reputation. But even worse, why was it that she had always been able to swing to a height that was level with the beam to which the swing was attached without her hand slipping; but right on the sixteenth of July, which was the village head's birthday, when so many people were gathered round to watch the swinging contest, why was it that she had to insist upon competing for first place? Why was it that just as the swing was about to reach a height perpendicular to the beam and everyone was oohing and aahing about how wonderful it was, why was it that the cord holding up her wide silk pants had to break, and the pants fall down, giving everyone a good look at what was not supposed to be seen?

The village head had never been the least bit embarrassed about his own murderous, plundering behaviour. Whenever he would distribute huge amounts of grain and clothing to the villagers, he would expound upon the fact that it was "rightfully ours". He would even pull out from his bag a dripping bloody head and announce that it was Official So-and-so or Rich Guy So-and-so. Nevertheless, he could not countenance anything within the area of his own jurisdiction that was inconsistent with the traditional ethics of human relations. He raised his gun and with a sharp report shot his wife on the swing, spattering her blood into the blue sky, practically dyeing the clouds red. And this beautiful wife of his dropped from the swing and onto the ground. He was the first to walk over to her body. He put the pants back on her properly and tied the string tight. He took off his outer garment and added a second covering over her lower body. The swing, inanimately obeying the law of inertia, hit him in the back of the head.

Now his men have stopped to block the road. Maybe it was because they were in a bad mood and the jubilant notes of the horn grated upon their sensibilities. Or maybe the colourful, generous trousseau aroused their avarice. Whatever the reason, they've decided it's time to put the power they have arrogated to themselves on proper display.

Geologic movement here shattered the lower stratum of rock and thrust the pieces upward so that they haphazardly puncture the surface of the rough and tumble terrain with black monoliths. By this time mist has gathered thickly in the ravines where the narrow road shoots over this hard barren ridge like a filament of light. The bridal procession has fallen into disarray, though its members make a credible effort at flaunting the overwhelming power that presumably backs them up: "So, it's robbery in broad daylight, is it?" one of them bellows. "Well, this one belongs to the House of Liu in Rooster Village!"

The ones blocking the road smile. With an air of self-possession they sit down, take off their shoes and shake out the sand and stones. One of them crooks his index finger, beckoning the victims to approach. "Come here," he says. "I say, come here and tell me all about how great and powerful the Lius are."

None among the bridal party responds to his beckoning, but from among its members the following information is volunteered for the edification and mollification of the bandits: "The eight ravines of Rooster Village all belong to the Lius, and His Excellency's brother-in-law is an official in the provincial capital. Today Young Master Liu is getting married, and all of you good fellows should come along and join in the banquet!"

The one who had beckoned them sneers, "So, old Mr Liu is a powerful 'Excellency', you say. Well, we don't have time to attend banquets, but I'm sure that the wealthy Lius won't miss the trousseau, don't you think?"

The lads, who at this point have nearly exhausted their options, are rapidly slipping into the vice-grip of fear. Hands rise to scratch heads in subconscious gestures of worry and perplexity as they glance nervously about. The slopes drop away from the ridge precipitously and bristle with bloodthirsty rocks. They begin disburdening themselves of the loads on their backs, setting the trunks and chests, bedding and pillows on the road in preparation for flight. The matron of honour, however, is an exemplar of bravery among the weaker sex. She flings the wild flower from her hair, smears her face with a fistful of dirt, walks over and kneels down. "Uncle!" she says. "This ring is solid gold. It's yours, uncle, if you'll only depart and let us pass unmolested." She holds out her hand. Upon the middle finger a chunk of gold glints.

The bandit approaches her, intent upon removing the ring. An unknown impulse makes him glance off to the side. Just at that moment the bride raises her head from Wukui's shoulder to take a look at the ring, and their eyes meet. She drops hers instantly and withdraws into hiding behind Wukui's back. The bandit laughs.

The matron of honour says, "Uncle, this is a whole ounce of real gold. The trousseau is really not worth anything, just a few symbolic items for luck."

The bandit says, "Now that's really a shame!"

"If only you will let us go, uncle, this ring will be a token of our appreciation — enough for each of you to buy a round of drinks!"

"Such a good female to be wasted on the Lius," the bandit is saying. "You mean all it takes to get a good woman like this is money? Well, if your young master can have one, why can't we in White Wind Village?"

He turns his head toward his confederates who are scattered on the ground: "Did you see that female? A good piece like that would be wasted on a moneybags — she'd be put to much better use as the wife of our boss!"

His confederates leap up in excitement.

The matron of honour scrambles to her feet. "You can't do that!" she shrills in agitation. "You can't do that!" She waves her hands about wildly as if she would block their path. The bandit draws out his knife sweepingly. A long narrow wedge of light flashes before her eyes, followed by something arcing up into the air. She focusses upon it to see what it is as the bandit catches it in his hand: It's half a human finger encircled with a ring. Only then does she discover her own middle finger is missing, a clean-cut, sharp-edged stump where it used to be. The stump isn't even bleeding yet. She falls to the ground in a dead faint.

"Okay, everybody, listen up!" the bandit announces loudly with authority. "This bride is still a bride, only now she's our leader's wife. Liu's a big excellency, so he's lucky we don't go over there and confiscate his property and cut off his head! There's no sense in this woman living a short life as a young mistress — she's far better off living a long life as the wife of our leader!"

Wukui doesn't wait for him to finish his speech. He whips about and starts running, retracing the road along which they have come. He ducks behind a big rock and veers off into an expanse of cogongrass. Then going for broke he heads for the ravine. The bride in mortal fright wraps her arms and legs tightly around him like a vine strangling a tree. He runs blindly. He has no idea where the route he has chosen will take them. As he dashes madly along, the woman slides and bounces lower and lower on his back. He keeps hiking up his shoulders in an attempt to shift her into a higher position. With each upward hitching movement, a new wave of sweat bursts out upon his skin and peppers off onto the ground. Finally he circles his hands behind him, clasps the woman about her waist, and says, "I'm going to roll!" Tucking up like a hedgehog, he rolls down a slope smothered in brambles and cogongrass, leaving a swathe of flattened vegetation in their wake.

They roll to a stop before a river spanned by a lashed willow bridge. Its waters run deep as the countless whirlpools lining up like rivets along its length reveal. Wukui lifts his head from the ground and looks up toward the top of the mountain. The ridge is obscured from his view. It occurs to him that if he should cross the bridge now, whoever is up there would be able to see. He purses his lips and nods toward the left, indicating a cliff that juts out starkly from the wall of rock, like the beak of an eagle.

"There's a cave over there," he says to the woman. "If we hide there, nobody will be able to find us, not even a ghost!"

He sets about rising to his feet, but finds they have rolled into a grassy depression that hinders his movement. That the woman's arms and legs are still clamped tightly about his neck and waist does not help matters. He tries negotiating the move by arching his body, a tactic that fails several times. Finally the woman says, "Here, let me get off."

This simple utterance — this mere pragmatic suggestion — transforms the crisis into the unfolding of a new horizon. The fear that possessed Wukui lifts and vanishes, replaced by confidence in the safety of this place in which they find themselves. He congratulates himself on his bravery and resourcefulness as a panoply of ideas explodes and jostles in his mind. Just think, this woman who is nothing short of an angel is now on very intimate terms with him! Here is a woman whom he won't, once she becomes Young Mistress Liu, be able to look straight in the face. Huh! For that matter, even if she were still a maiden in Slacker Flat, richer and stronger men than he couldn't lay a finger on her. Yet here she is now, with her arms and legs wrapped around his body making the two of them one and relying upon him in every possible way.

He looks down upon her white hands with their

fingers interlaced in front of him. They are scratched and bleeding. He bemoans the fact that he had been unable to protect them from the thorny malice of the brambles when they ploughed that pathway down the slope. And one of her embroidered red shoes is fractiously threatening to abandon her foot. How utterly embarrassed she would be had it snagged on a tree and left her with one foot bare. How guilty he would feel! He brings out one of his hands and readjusts the little shoe, reseating it firmly and properly where it belongs. The action staggers him. Electrifying awareness engulfs him. Throughout his body the blood in his veins gurgles and leaps. None of this shows on his exterior, however. The woman, for her part, is as impassive and accepting as a child as he manipulates it with especial attentiveness.

"Wukui," she says, "you have saved me. You have done a good deed!"

Such words as these coming from her mouth bloom expansively in his heart and trigger a surge of heady inspired effort. With one exhilarated arch of his body, he stands up.

"I've seen lots of bandits, and the one who can outrun me hasn't been born yet."

He has his plan clearly mapped out. All he need do is hide for a while under the eagle-beak cliff. The bandits won't be able to find them and they'll give up and go away. Then with the woman still on his back he'll cross that bridge and follow along the bottom of the ravine for about seven miles, circling round to Rooster Village. He could get her to the Liu's house by dusk. No disaster, this robbery. No disaster at all. Quite the contrary, for now he has extra time in which to carry this woman, just as he had wished. The thought of the bandits arouses no animosity in him. In fact, he feels as if he and the bandits have had a tacit understanding all along.

"I wonder what happened to Sister Wang?" This question from the woman on his back interrupts his reverie.

"What happened to her?" he echoes, suddenly reminded. He sighs, rapturously, at the woman's solicitous concern for another. The scene of the bandit slicing off the matron of honour's finger replays in his mind as a wave of pity wells up from the centre of his chest, leaving a hole. Perturbation fills it: She shouldn't have offered the gold ring in the first place. Hellava thing to do, trying to appease bandits. Her image — sallow, pock-marked face, severed finger and all — flickers before him. Would the bandits carry her off in lieu of the bride, a sort of consolation prize?

"This is all the fault of those bastards!" He begins cursing the lads. Dammit, they talk so big, but when it comes right down to it, it is all just a lot of hot air. If it hadn't been for him, Wukui, escaping like that, then this woman would've been fodder in the bandits' bed by tonight!

"All that matters is you're safe," he says. "I'll get you to the Lius in one piece, don't you worry about that."

The bandits might have carried off the trousseau, they might have even left a few bodies in their wake. News of this would reach the Lius, and they would undoubtedly be fretting and worrying about the bride. Or they'd be weeping, wailing and gnashing their teeth. Or they'd be organising a posse to descend upon White Wind Village to demand her back. Or they'd simply be there wringing their hands in despair. But then right in the midst of the commotion, he, Wukui, would appear bearing the bride safe and sound. Just think how grateful they would be to him in their ecstatic happiness! But then of course he's not basing his actions upon the prospect of the Lius' gratitude. All he asks is that the bride remember him. But then again, even if she doesn't, even if she should forget this whole event, he, Wukui, would still have accomplished the protection of a beautiful woman. This in itself would be enough to make him a heroic and satisfied man!

Under the eagle-beak cliff, he still doesn't put her down. He says he's not tired. He says there's nothing to be tired from, that he could carry a one-hundred-and-fifty-pound bundle of firewood more than fifteen miles down out of the mountain nonstop, that he could wrap his arms around one of those monstrous stone rollers and move it to wherever one might wish.

"I'm in perfect shape!" he says expansively. Revelling in his burgeoning physical prowess, he jumps up into the air, exultantly, demonstrating her virtual weightlessness. Instead of landing on his feet, however, he crashes clumsily to the ground. The impact loosens the woman's grip, and she too falls to the ground a yard or so away from him. Wukui's face burns with ignominious blushes. Raising his head to check upon the woman, his eyes fall upon three knife-wielding bandits. So — he hadn't screwed up after all. They had done it for him, smashing a stone against the back of his knee and making him fall like that.

Wukui rushes over to shield the woman with his own body.

"Heh, heh!" The bandits laugh. "Shrimpy, you've really got a pair of legs on you!"

"Don't take her — how can she possibly marry a bandit? Just tie me up and be on your way. How about it?"

One of the bandits kicks Wukui down. He leans down to pat his face: "And just why should I keep you alive?"

Wukui grabs the bandit's hand and leaps up at him. The bandit deflects his assault with another squarely placed kick. With face awash in blood, Wukui undaunted rushes for the bandit again. The bandit is phlegmatic. "This guy's really a pest!" he says as he raises his knife and brings it down like a chopper. The woman's scream splits the air: "Don't! I'll go with you!" The falling knife flips and the back of its blade smashes onto Wukui's neck. For Wukui, everything goes black.

Having barely escaped with their lives, the trousseau bearers deliver their burdens to the Lius' house, complete and intact. But this fails to ameliorate the Lius' disappointment at the absence of the bride. The crowd swarming at the portal of the Liu mansion had set off three thousand firecrackers upon the approach of the bridal party, but now the poles suspending the strings of firecrackers are thrown to the ground and the resounding crepitations stamped out. Excellency Liu's water tobacco pipe that he's been hugging to his chest slips from his grasp and goes clanking to his feet. Obese, balding Mrs Liu slumps wordlessly over the dinner table. Her entourage of attendants ministers to her for a seemingly interminable length of time before she finally begins to revive. The young master, sporting his festive red flower, bursts into laughter. Everyone stares at him gape-mouthed.

This is the laughter of tragedy, suffused with a wretched tone that plumps up the silence and charges the atmosphere with dread. It freezes the knot of humanity into uncertainty, stilling tongues preset to waggle with words of consolation. It becomes apparent that the appropriate reaction is to laugh along with him, but before anyone has time to react to this realisation, the young master turns upon one of the members of the bridal party. The hapless fellow, standing there respectfully with hands hanging meekly, receives a relentless beating about the head and ears. The blows ring through the dead stillness that remains oppressive both inside and outside the main gate to the Liu mansion. The young master drains his wrath upon the young man, turns upon his heel and stalks to the east wing room. The crowd continues to hold its breath.

It's only natural that Young Master Liu should fly into a rage. This scion of wealth and power is a highly disciplined young man. Unlike many others of his status, he eschews over-indulgence. Far from having destroyed his health with insalubrious eating habits, he has forged himself into the biggest, strongest, most robust man of Rooster Village. Yet in spite of his economic might and physical superiority, his new wife has been brazenly snatched from him.

He wastes no time in useless lamentations, but rather strides instinctively into the house to get his shotgun. He loads it with shot and iron filings and climbs atop a high bench to retrieve a bamboo basket that hangs from a pillar. This basket contains explosive paraphernalia for hunting foxes and wolves, bombs fashioned out of powder, shot, and porcelain shards wrapped in chicken skin. These bombs are ordinarily planted in places frequented by foxes and wolves, where they have taken the lives of countless curious wild animals. Now he has hatched in his mind a plan to lead his men on a shortcut to intercept the bandits. They will scatter the bombs about the mountain road upon which the bandits will be obliged to pass. When the bandits approach, they will shoot the bombs. In the noise and confusion created by the explosions, the bandits will abandon his bride and run off.

Young Master Liu lifts the bamboo basket off its high hook with both hands. As he shifts his weight to step back down, one of the bench legs breaks. He loses his footing, the basket falls, and he falls on top of it. There is a deafening explosion. The crowd outside comes pouring into the room to find Young Master Liu lying in a pool of blood. They pull him to a sitting position, but when they loosen their grasp, he flops back over. Only then do they discover that Young Master's legs are no longer attached to him: One is behind the door, the other is on the table.

The tragic events that have struck the Lius send the entire village into shock. Wukui's old father, upon learning his youngest son will not be coming home, goes out to the sunny side of his house and squats there, smoking a handful of tobacco. When only ashes remain, he calls his other two sons and says, "Take the mat off my *kang* and bring me back Wukui's body." Without a word the brothers take the mat and a carrying pole and trace their way to the scene of the robbery.

On a ridge about five miles away, there is a ball of swarming buzzing flies. The brothers approach to take a closer look and find the object of the flies' interest to be a chubby finger joint. Wukui's body, though, is nowhere to be seen. Puzzled, they follow the path of flattened cogongrass down the slope. At the bottom they discover Wukui sitting there looking about in a daze.

"Wukui! Wukui! You're alive!" The brothers are ecstatic.

Wukui starts wailing.

"You're alive, Wukui! You didn't die!" The brothers believe Wukui is suffering from shock.

"Wukui is thinking of Father," one of them ventures.

Wukui says, "The bride's been snatched away. She's been snatched right out of my hands!"

His brothers pull him up to take him back home. They say that if bandits take it into their heads to snatch a bride, what can you possibly do about it, Wukui? Even if there had been ten other men they would have all forfeited their lives. But you, Wukui, you were not killed, so let's go home and you can have some ginger soup and cover yourself up and have a good sleep and then the nightmare will be over.

But Wukui insists: "I'm going to find the bride!"

His adamant tone convinces his brothers more than ever that his terrifying experience has addled his brain. They slap his face to bring him back to his senses. To

Wukui, this is an unpardonable provocation. He returns the attack like a foaming madman, wildly punching the air so that his brothers can't get near him. Then he drops his fists and runs. Like a wolf he bolts out from under the cliff and sprints for the top of the ridge.

"It was I who was carrying the bride," he shouts, "and it was I who lost her, so I must get her back!"

His brothers at the bottom of the slope bellow at him angrily: "Wukui! Wukui! You blockhead! It's not your woman?"

Wukui runs on, heedless of their shouts and oblivious to all danger as he turns his steps in the direction of White Wind Village. Under his breath he mutters: No, it's not my woman, of course it's not my woman, but is this just any ordinary woman? If she marries into the Lius she can enjoy life. How can she possibly be the wife of a bandit?

Besides that, she and he had rolled down that slope together and she had been so close so tight to him, trusting him completely, he who was only Wukui, the ugly pauper Wukui, wasn't this reason enough? Anyway he'd failed her, she'd trusted him to protect her and he'd failed and in fact it had been she who had protected him, snatching his life back from the bandit's blade, and now that he was alive and his heart was still beating in his chest, he could not just simply leave her to her fate! Idiot! Such an idiot! Posing like a hero back there showing off for her when he should have crossed the bridge without a moment's delay and torn up the planks behind them, and then could the bandits have caught them? But no, he'd been so wrapped up in his own cleverness in discovering a hiding place under the cliff and had been so full of himself that he'd just waited there like a dumb bunny not even paying attention and letting the bandits sneak up on them like that. Wasn't this just the same as if he had handed her right over to them?

Ravine after ridge, Wukui runs, slipping and sliding down, scrambling and clambering up, until his body screams with fatigue.

He runs along a river flowing through a ravine as the declining sun dyes the water red. The brilliance of this sun gradually but perceptibly fades until there hangs in the sky a huge smouldering orange disk. The writhing water captures its image in various mesmerising permutations that get smaller and smaller the further he advances along. Steeped in wonder he pauses to watch the last of the waning rays as they withdraw into nothingness, their wispy tips drawing his thoughts into the realm of their reality: If he is to die, then so be it. It doesn't matter just so long as he can see her one more time and make her know the truth about himself, just so long as she can see the evidence of what is in his heart, the final traces glowing as gloriously as the final traces of this setting sun as he dies willingly and happily before her.

By the time Wukui gets to White Wind Village, it is nearly midnight. White Wind Village, it turns out, is not a mountain fastness surrounded by a fort of granite slabs and topped with towering battlements. Under the vague illumination of the moon it appears just as any ordinary village. A line of ridges and peaks resembling a colossal rooster comb stretches across its southern end, the tallest pinnacle vaulting up into the obliterating obscurity of the night sky. The base of the mountain slopes to a gentle pitch and is strewn with the inky shadows of boulders whose chaotic disposition contrasts with the inky shadows of persimmon trees lined up in smart rows like the thousand-armed Buddha. Among the boulders and the persimmon trees crouch unassuming dwellings whose lantern lights flicker jauntily in the gloom. The river that squirms around the base of the mountain bristles along its bank with houses that manage orderliness within confusion.

He passes into a lane that runs through the most concentrated section of houses, crosses over a humped stone viaduct, and comes to a tamped earth square. Rising from the east side of the square is a spacious alfresco theatre platform set upon a high brick foundation. The place is now awash with activity. Drums and gongs are banging out their gaudy dissonance amidst crowds of people milling about. Wukui has misgivings. This does not seem at all like the place he is looking for. Yet the sign above the stages swaggers with three out-size characters that gleam a lurid white in the dancing incandescence of twelve huge oil lamps: White Wind Village. He has always imagined White Wind Village to be a nest of bandits whose inhabitants barged about with dishevelled hair, dirty faces and glaring murderous eyes. Here before him, though, are nothing but simple ordinary people of both sexes and all ages immersed in a carnival atmosphere, pressing eagerly toward the stage, pelleting the air with naive shouts of excitement.

The stage accommodates a solitary man whose sole acquiescence to dramatic disguise is an artificial beard that adorns his chin and flows down his chest. He is lazily drawling, "At the crack of dawn I arise to burn a stick of incense," He sets up an incense stick on the table beside him, then sits there in apparent boredom. At length, he intones, "Sitting before my door, I watch the celestial phenomena."

The audience begins shouting: "Get outta there! We want to see 'Cotton Caper'!"

Wukui realises this is just the prologue to the regular play coming up. He is struck by the exceeding strangeness of this dramatic scheduling: Here it is, practically the middle of the night, and the play hasn't even started yet. The beard on the stage, intimidated by the audience, scurries to the exit. Someone else enters and launches into a short speech:

"Today there has been a very happy event in White Wind Village, and we have been celebrating it with performances. We've already done 'Mu Guiying Seeks a Husband'. The Village Head and his entourage have already left. This was supposed to be the end of the show. But now according to popular demand, we will perform 'Cotton Caper'. We've had to change the costumes and make-up, so now if everyone will just stay calm, we'll start right away."

With this, the curtain closes, re-opens, and the actors step out upon the stage. Wukui's interests, however, lie outside the performance. He makes a few inquiries as to where the Village Head has pitched his camp, but reaps only brusque expressions of annoyance or antagonised glares. Afraid of exposing himself as an outsider, he retreats into the anonymity of the crowd. He cocks his ears toward people's casual conversations, waiting for floating snippets of information that will reveal the location of Tang Jing's bandit nest. He pretends to watch the play. It's a comedy about a young matron who uses her wiles to filch cotton wadding from an itinerant cotton peddler even as she is conducting a transaction with him. He accuses her of stealing and she in turn accuses him of lying. But then she is subjected to a body search and wads of cotton are drawn up out of the crotch of her trousers. The cotton has been pretreated so that when it is squeezed, red water drips out. Gales of laughter envelope the audience in renewed waves of good cheer, and Wukui soon finds someone who divulges the coveted information. He extricates himself from the jostling mass of humanity and plunges into the shadows beyond the reach of the theatre lights. He heads toward a certain high spot at the base of the mountain.

Here in this place where lanterns run riot over the breadth and length of the slope, there is one place where they burn more brightly than anywhere else. As he mounts toward this conspicuous affluence of light, there looms ever larger a soaring gateway arch hung with lanterns of outlandish size. Blazing in concert with their glowing emanations are two unshielded oil lamps set atop wooden piles erected on either side of the arch way. They are certainly filled with wild boar oil, for the wicks are thick as ropes and black smoke pours up into the air from the ephemeral tops of their lusty flames.

People are coming in and out of the main gate in steady streams. Wukui decides it's too risky to try to gain entry that way. As if to confirm the wisdom of this decision, two figures silhouetted against the glare turn their steps in his direction. Instantly he drops down into a hollow. As he hugs himself against the earth, a conversation at the edge of the hollow ensues.

"The woman the Village Head got is gorgeous!"

"I just knew you'd fallen in love with her, the way you were looking at her. But you should take a look at yourself; are you a village head, or are you a seller of sesame seed buns?"

"Actually, she looks just like you."

"Oh, yeah? In what way?"

"Come here and I'll tell you."

The interlocutors close the gap between them. One produces the sound of a loud smacking kiss. "Watch out! Someone will see!" the other rebukes.

So! Wukui thinks. These young puppies have come out to catch a glimpse of the stolen woman. Boy, you can really tell this place is run by bandits. Tang Jing kidnaps a woman and the whole village goes wild — everyone comes out to celebrate and they put on performances and everything, and people come running to see and they take a look at the Village Head's woman and get all excited and head for secret trysts in the wild.

The girl says, "Go over there a ways and keep watch — I gotta pee."

The boy obeys, but not in earnest, edging away for only a nominal distance. The girl reprimands him, then crouches down and urinates.

As luck would have it, the urine lands right on Wukui's head.

Angry, hate-filled epithets leap to his lips, but he swallows them. He doesn't dare to make a peep. As he strains to discipline his tongue, a consoling thought comes to mind: Isn't it said that to get peed on by a dog is lucky?

At length, the boy and the girl leave. Wukui impulsively pops his head up out of the hollow to watch their departure, to see them off with his gaze, as it were, for he has conceived an admiration for them. Just think! This tender fledgling knows how to get some enjoyment out of life. And I? What have I to show for my life? But, he realises, he does indeed have something — he has the warm-hearted regard of the Liu family's bride. She had treated him with kindness, with consideration, with sincerity back there. The glowing good feeling she had elicited then returns to him now, if anything, in even greater measure. His heart swells with it, it bursts out and envelopes him in tenderness. He congratulates himself for having done the right thing — for having come to this place.

The population in and around the gateway arch, however, has not diminished. Wukui follows along the enclosing wall toward the back of the residence, looking for a spot he can breach easily. The wall is very high. Moreover, every inch of it is in good condition. There are no damaged or crumbling parts to accommodate his design. Then he comes upon an outhouse right in the back corner, built over a pit with a raised edge. There are two brick pillars supporting the wooden plank floor with its convenience holes where the squatting takes place. He looks up at the exposed floor in surprised delight. This outhouse has been built just for him, he says to himself. He takes off his jacket and drapes it over his head. He leaps up and catches the edge of the board with his hands. Straining his muscles, he lifts himself up and shimmies through the narrow opening, barely squeezing his buttocks through. He throws away the jacket and removes the filth from his hands by wiping them on the wall. A faint light thrown off from a lantern in the center of the courtyard reveals to him that he is in the corner of the back garden.

Like a thief, Wukui slips along the wall until he comes to the central garden. Here he conceals himself behind a tree. From this vantage point he can see into the large, five-room main hall of the residence. The three central rooms have no wall dividers and are demarcated only by the pillars that hold the structure up. People are sitting around a square table for eight, drinking liquor. The rooms on either end of the hall are walled in. The windows and door of the west room are dark, while a window of the east room is propped open with a bamboo pole. The light inside reveals a figure lying aslant across the *kang*. Wukui has to stifle his impulse to call out, for the one lying on the *kang* is none other than the bride herself.

He plucks up his courage and strides vigorously to the entrance. His footsteps fall heavily, prompting an inquiry from within: "Who goes there?"

He walks directly in and asks: "Which one is Village Head Tang?"

The men all stop their drinking and stare at him. One says, "Have you come to congratulate the Village Head? It's very late and he and his wife are about to go to bed. You can turn whatever gifts you have over to the front hall. Someone there will accept them and enter them into the record and give you a drink."

Wukui says, "I'm not here to present any gifts. I have something to say to the Village Head."

He hasn't noticed that two of the men seated at the table had been among the raiding party that captured the woman. These two now jump up and pounce upon him. Each one grabs an arm, and they throw him to the ground. Pinning him there, they turn their heads in the direction of the table: "Boss, this guy's that bride carrier! Somehow he's managed to find his way here."

A tall man with a pale face rises from the table. Wukui can feel it in his bones: This is Tang Jing. Their eyes meet for a second, a very long second. Tang Jing waves his hand and has his men release him. With a cold edge to his voice, he asks: "Did you come alone?"

"Yes. There's only me."

"What a good bride carrier! I am Tang Jing, and I want to thank you. Come. Pour our guest a bowl of brew."

Wukui declines to drink anything.

Tang Jing laughs. "You're wasting an opportunity for a good drink. Well, there's no doubt about it, when they talk about he-men, they're talking about guys like you. But the lone hero act is a bit foolhardy, don't you think? If you want to snatch the woman back, the only way to do it is to bring along about a hundred of your friends."

"I didn't come to snatch the woman back. I've come only to tell you something."

"Tang Jing has no secrets in White Wind Village. Go ahead and tell me."

"If you don't want me to talk, then that's very easy — all you have to do is have someone cut out my tongue. But if you want me to talk, then whatever I have to say is for your ears alone."

Tang Jing laughs again. "You certainly have guts.

Okay, then, everybody — time to go home and rest."

All the men take off. One of them, however, doubles back almost immediately, takes his knife out from his waist, and offers it to Tang Jing. The latter waves it off: "That's okay. I don't need it." He closes the door with a clang.

Wukui stands there frozen to the spot. He marvels at the fact that the person in front of him is really Tang Jing. The outside world is rife with stories about how the bandit chieftain's a monster with three heads and six arms. But here it turns out he's a handsome young man with pale, translucent skin and delicate features. And amiable. And polite. From his tongue to his legs, Wukui is petrified. Then instinct takes over, buckling his knees and dropping him into a kneeling position.

"Sir!" he croaks. The words gradually flow more smoothly. "Wukui is just a lowly bride carrier who has so crudely and so impudently barged in on you here. I have been disrespectful of you, sir."

"Anyone who comes here is a guest. Let's just say for now you are my bride carrier. And if you have something to say, just go ahead and have this drink as you talk."

Wukui accepts the crystalline liquor and studies Tang Jing's face as he drinks it. He sees in it no sign of treachery or intrigue. He hesitates: Is this a man who deserves to be lied to? Look at it this way — the guy's a bandit. He might not look like a demon, but a bandit's a bandit. What's he going to do with the Liu family's bride, anyway? Turn her into a bandit chieftain's wife, for chrissake! The whole purpose in coming here was to save her from that!

He sets aside his liquor bowl.

"Sir, I'm only a bride carrier, and as such there's really no reason for me to come chasing over here on account of this bride of the Liu family. If the woman had been snatched by anyone else, I wouldn't go through this trouble, because it doesn't really matter who a woman is married off to. And anyway, it's not my woman. But you — what kind of a personage are you? I may not be a citizen of White Wind Village, but I've often heard your illustrious name. So for your sake, I've come to tell you only one thing. You in fact can have any woman you want, so why does it have to be this particular one? She may have some merit, beauty-wise, but — she's a white tiger star."

Wukui's speech is long-winded. Throughout its duration, Tang Jing has been looking at him with a steady, bemused smile. But with the revelation of this last, most important point, the smile suddenly vanishes, wiped clean from his face. He leaps to his feet: "A white tiger star?"

"Yes, she's a white tiger star."

A white tiger star refers to a woman who has no pubic hair. In the mountains it is firmly believed that such a woman is the worst source of evil that exists, guaranteed to bring ruin upon any man she marries. If the family doesn't break up and the business go into bankruptcy, then her husband will get sick and die for no apparent reason. Even if such a woman looks like an angel and is worth millions, once a man finds out what she is, he'll want to have absolutely nothing to do with her.

Wukui sees in Tang Jing's face the effect he had

hoped for. He adds the final touch to his story: "Of course, if you're a blue dragon, then the situation is ideal."

A blue dragon is a man with thick, luxuriant chest hair that runs all the way down to his apparatus and back up again to the small of his back. The woman who is a white tiger and the man who is a blue dragon make the ideal couple. A marriage between them is a marriage made in heaven. Not only can neither harm the other, but they are perfectly compatible as well, and they would thus have the happiest, most fulfilling marriage in the world.

Tang Jing is not a blue dragon. He doesn't even have a beard on his delicate white face. Tang Jing stares at Wukui, stunned. Wukui's controlled exterior barely hides his internal quailing. He feels his line of defence begin to crumble beneath Tang Jing's riveting gaze. The silence draws out taut, then suddenly snaps with Tang Jing's abrupt inquiry: "How do you know she's a white tiger?"

Wukui has anticipated this question. He says this woman is the daughter of the Yaos in Slacker Flat, and that he, Wukui, has a female cousin who also lives in that village. When Young Master Liu of Rooster Village became engaged to her, he mentioned it to this cousin once when he went to visit her, and she quietly told him of the woman's peculiarity.

As Wukui spins this story, he proceeds with caution and makes a mighty effort to keep calm and to maintain consistency throughout. Suddenly — and he doesn't know why he hadn't thought of it before — he recalls the legend concerning Tang Jing's origins and the horrible ordeal he had been through as a child. Of course, he has no way of verifying whether or not this formidable man is the son of that woman who was hung twenty years ago. But still, supposing that he were — then he would be sure to have a taboo against women involved in incest.

"That's what my cousin said," Wukui continues, relating how one time his cousin and this woman went up into the mountain to pick mushrooms, and they got hot from the exertion and so bathed in a spring in the middle of the woods, and that was how she had made the discovery. Then she began putting two and two together and realised why it was that that young man of the Yao clan had fallen down the slope that time and was killed when he was cutting firewood in the mountain; before it had been said that this woman and this brother of hers — actually her first cousin — had been very close in such and such a way. So — his life had been cut short because she was a white tiger star. Of course, his cousin had not dared to broadcast this affair. But the Liu family had always mistreated Wukui's family, and Wukui has always felt outraged but impotent before this abuse — that is, up to now. When he found out that the Lius had arranged this marriage, his cousin had gleefully told him that wicked people reaped the fruits of their wickedness, and just look at how cruel the Lius have been!

"There really must be something to it," Wukui says, "because every year Rooster Village contracts so many marriages, and I've been the bride carrier in every case, but never before today have I run into kidnappers. It can't be for nothing that this should have happened to the Lius — it's got be because they've brought in a white tiger star, and this is just the beginning of their ruination."

Tang Jing says, "And what if I don't believe a word you are saying?"

Wukui lowers his head and appears to go into abstraction. The question, in fact, has hit him broadside, and he feels himself hurtling into panic and confusion. How could Tang Jing not believe it? Will he want to verify it for himself? He had been set to take possession of the woman this very night, and if he does indeed carry out his original intent, it will be immediately apparent as to whether or not she is a white tiger star. But, but... Wukui thrashes about in his own private abyss, blindly seeking a handhold, something that will get him out of this jam. And then he remembers how it is said that even if a man doesn't engage in sexual intercourse with a white tiger star, but only lays eyes on that thing, the result would be the same. Yes! That means that Tang Jing wouldn't dare to put himself in such peril. On second thoughts, though, he could have one of his underlings make an inspection for him. But then again, could a man of his position and prestige tolerate an underling scrutinising his own woman? If he could shoot his wife on the swing because her trouser string broke, he certainly would not be willing to have the private parts of this woman exposed to a subordinate. Thank heaven he remembered Tang Jing's little hang-up. Still, the sweat pours off him as if he has resolved nothing. He has never reconciled himself to lying, for any reason, and thus is unskilled — quite inept, in fact — in the art of duplicity. If Tang Jing should probe deeper into his story, he would be sure to uncover its flaws. Maybe he's already seen through the lie. Maybe he'll turn about at any second now and kill me, just like that! Well ... then ... if that's the way it is ... then that's the way it is. He'd already anticipated the possibility he wouldn't get out alive, so nothing has really changed. A drop of his sweat splashes upon the floor. He has only one thing to regret, and that is he hasn't yet seen the woman face to face.

"Whether you choose to believe it or not," he says with a ponderous sense of helplessness, "is up to you."

Tang Jing whirls about and strides to the west apartment. He re-emerges forthwith holding a liquor cup. He asks Wukui: "I assume you're under the employ of the groom's family?"

Wukui, the weight of trepidation crushing his breath, fails to reply.

Tang Jing says, "You're just the bride carrier — you're not responsible if the bride is kidnapped. And the groom's family wouldn't blame you, now would they? It doesn't really matter much to you as a bride carrier whom a bride marries and whether or not she gets kidnapped, isn't that right? Logically, you wouldn't be particularly enthusiastic about coming to White Wind Village to retrieve a bride for some rich and powerful family. And yet here you are! So either you've come to save this woman; or — you really have a genuine concern for me. But how can you make me believe your sincerity? Here I have a drink for you, and to be frank, it's been drugged. If you have come to save the woman, in consideration of your extraordinary bravery —being that you are only a bride carrier —I will let you go in one piece, without harming a hair on your head. And let it be known that Tang Jing always keeps his word. If, on the other hand, you have truly come for my sake, then drink this liquor. It has the power to make you deaf. And once you are deaf, I will have a very important task to entrust to you. Are you willing to drink?"

He places the cup on the table. Wukui's face floods with the straining turmoil that spills over the sluice gates of his self-control. He ponders Tang Jing's words and comes to appreciate the effective, if unusual, tactics they represent — no wonder this pale youth has got the world all shook up! Now he must decide. Admit to having come to save the woman and be sent on his way? Or avow he'd spoken the truth and drink the poisoned liquor? The rock and the hard place, the goddamned rock and the hard place! But would Tang Jing really let him go if he revealed his sympathies were with the woman? And suppose he did —to what end then would he have come if he left like that empty-handed? Then again, if he wanted to demonstrate his intentions had been purely aimed at the welfare of Tang Jing, he would have to take that drink and lose his hearing, and then wouldn't he simply be a victim of the punish-the-good-deed syndrome that bandits wallowed in? Okay, then, he'd come to save the woman, and if he can't extricate her, he'll just not leave. He'll go deaf — yes, he'll just go deaf, and insinuate himself into this place and wait for an opportunity to get her out!

Wukui takes up the cup with both hands, raises his head, tosses down the liquor. Immediately he falls to the floor in preparation for the ravaging effects of the poison.

But he feels nothing. His ears are as sharp as ever.

Tang Jing says, "So, Wukui, you did it for my sake after all. Now I'll tell you that there was no poison in the liquor. You should know, as well, that I had nothing to do with the kidnapping of this woman. My wife recently died, so ... I really have no desire to take another, at least not for now. But my good men brought me this one, thinking they were doing me a favour. I figured since she was already here, I would disappoint the men if I didn't consent to have her. But I'm not of a mind to consummate the marriage right away. I was simply going to keep her here and support her until a year had elapsed and then get married. Such being the case, I'm perfectly willing to let her go. And then, of course, Tang Jing will have averted a reputation as a kidnapper of brides, right? But I do have one hope, and that is that you'll remain in White Wind Village to serve as one of my soldiers. What do you say to that?"

Wukui's whole body suddenly feels transformed into a giddy pulpy mass. His hands and feet begin to shake violently. He kowtows to Tang Jing, knocking his head upon the floor numerous times, and says, "Wukui doesn't know how to be a soldier, I only know how to plant the fields."

"Then you can simply come here to live."

"I have an elderly father, sir. He can't leave the land he's been on all his life. He too attached to it. Just let me go back home if you would, sir."

"Such a fool you are! But that's all right. We'll just wait until your father has passed away, and then if you want to come and live in White Wind Village, just come and see me."

Tang Jing extends to Wukui an invitation to stay

overnight. He can take the woman back in the morning when he is rested and refreshed. Wukui, however, begs leave to depart that very night. He goes directly to the east apartment to take up the woman, who is happily surprised. Just as he is about to go out the door, Tang Jing pours two cups of liquor and hands one to the woman. He drinks to her and says, "Some day we'll meet again!" Unable to resist, he reaches out and pinches her cheek.

Tramping his way through dark, inhospitable territory, and fighting his fatigue, Wukui endures all torments to carry the woman to the Lius. But his narrative of how he sneaked into White Wind Village, drank Tang Jing under the table, and spirited the woman out on his back, reaps him only a third of a bushel of black beans, a basket of radishes, and a meal of plain millet washed down with brew. As if this is not disappointing enough, the Lius are full of suspicion.

They suspect not Wukui, but the woman.

She is not installed in the bridal chamber. Nor is she permitted to see the young master. Instead, she is locked into the wing room. Sometime after darkness falls, Mrs Liu brings in a cushion, sets it down, and covers it over with a piece of oilcloth. Upon the oilcloth she scatters a pinch of lamp wick ashes. She makes the woman strip naked and squat spread-legged over the cushion. Mystified, the woman holds the undignified position without moving a hair. Her mother-in-law hands her a chicken feather, ordering her to stick it in her nose. This elicits a violent splattering sneeze. Nonetheless, the lamp wick ashes don't fly off. Her mother-in-law says, "Ok, you can get dressed now."

Once she has redressed herself, her mother-in-law brings over a covered wooden basin. She lifts the lid to let out a turtle. The woman recoils in fright, every muscle fibre crackling into action. She whirls about and leaps onto a stool.

"That's enough!" her mother-in-law reproves her sternly.

The woman, compliant, timid, climbs back down.

"Stand on the turtle's back!"

Terrified, she places her foot upon the turtle and attempts to hoist her weight in place. Success eludes her, as she can not maintain her balance. Determined, however, to please, she rejoices that the turtle is at least as still as an insensate rock. She takes aim and steps quickly and squarely upon it. There is a snapping sound. The turtle's shell cracks. The woman tumbles to the floor.

A deliberate, satisfied laugh toddles out of Mrs Liu's throat: "Wukui told the truth — nobody else has stuck his plough into my son's earth!"

The woman shudders: Her mother-in-law has been giving her a virginity test! Her face flushes with embarrassment, anger mounts in her throat and chokes her breath. She has made a death-defying escape from the clutches of bandits, and all the Lius are worried about is her chastity! — What about her personal welfare? What about how she is feeling?

In point of fact, when the Lius learned she had been kidnapped, they had simply written her off. Her rescue and restoration to them have been from their point of view an anticlimax, a totally unexpected turn of events.

Which means, if the bandit Tang Jing had actually

ravished her...! She is seized with consternation. During the sneeze test, air would have rushed through the broken hymen, scattering the ashes; the turtle's shell would not have cracked because of her loss of that crucial weight —and how would her mother-in-law have treated her then? Two hot tears course down her face.

"Now that you're here, stop your snivelling!" her mother-in-law snaps. "And don't ever, ever breathe a word about having been in White Wind Village. Just say Wukui carried you into hiding under a cliff. Can you remember that? Remember it!"

Her mother-in-law leaves the room. After a moment someone brings her some ginger soup and presses her to drink it. Then someone else comes in with burning incense and circles it three times around her head and whole body. A third person carries in a tub, fills it with chrysanthemum water, and has her immerse herself in it.

A storm of firecrackers goes off outside. Seven or eight people swarm into the room leading a donkey decked out in colourful silk streamers. They set her astride the donkey, backwards. When she twists about to reseat herself forward, the person leading the donkey tells her: "You have to ride backwards because that's the only way to counteract disaster and exorcise evil."

The small congregation spills out of the room and into the courtyard. They turn with the donkey around the courtyard eighteen times. With each revolution they stop to light a stick of incense at each of four wooden pilings erected to mark the four directions. This ritual goes on and on until she is swooning with dizziness. They take her down, and the next thing she knows, she is sitting on the *kang* in the bridal chamber.

But the reed mat is missing. That mat is an essential accoutrement of a bride's first-time entry into the bridal chamber. Instead, the *kang* is overlayed with thick, soft red bedding topped with a green quilt. Under the quilt fast asleep is her husband, Young Master Liu.

Wukui tucks himself in and sleeps ponderously for three days and three nights, as unconscious as death itself. At dusk on the third day, a glorious choreography of his exploits crowds onto the formerly blanked-out screen of his mind. His fear now abolished, he savours his new identity as a legendary figure and warrior hero.

Then he learns that Young Master Liu has lost both legs and is condemned to lie on the *kang* for the rest of his life, an irredeemable amputee.

He plunges from the height of elation into the depths of remorse. He beats his breast, he stamps his feet, he flails about in agonising grief. He had stared down death to snatch the woman back. And for what? — so she can play nursemaid to a ... a creature, a thing that doesn't even look human. If he hadn't gone to save her, if he hadn't made up that monstrous lie — the first and only of his entire life — then she today would be the wife of the bandit chieftain of White Wind Village, infamous maybe, maybe even reviled, but then so what? At least Tang Jing is young and handsome and virile — a real man! Wukui's searing conscience wrestles with the question that brutally, relentlessly mocks him: Has he done a good deed, or has he committed an unpardonable sin? His anguish explodes in dolorous moans and drenching tears.

Why should this be? The injustice of it all! An angelic woman whom none can help but love on sight is matched to the best of all possible husbands, granted the best of all possible situations where she can enjoy wealth and ease as she deserves. But fate is so cruel and arbitrary, and right when she's supposed to become a real woman these kidnappers come along so when she finally gets to her new home it's to find a cripple for a husband. Just think how many men would be indignant to hear of it! Think of Tang Jing heaving deep sighs in White Wind Village. You idiot! You contemptible despicable idiot! Look what you've done to her! Just think what she must have felt when she entered the bridal chamber and found waiting for her a legless lump of meat. Oh, how horrible! The vigorous vital flame of her maidenhood splashed over like that with cold water what was she to think whose yearning for conjugal bliss had all at once come to naught — Oh no! Oh no! Could she doubt his motivations? Yes, what is he — just a lowly pauper, a bride carrier who really had no reason to go out and crash a nest of bandits to save her since he's unrelated to the Lius. She's bound to think Young Master Liu's debilitation came first and that she'd been acquired as a wife afterwards and that when she'd been kidnapped he Wukui had been paid handsomely to carry in the ransom and bring her back. Oh yes, it's true she can't possibly think otherwise all of his heroism's nothing but a big fraud in the perpetration of a conspiracy and he Wukui is in her eyes a demon, a vile character, someone to curse for a lifetime!

He must, as soon as possible, go to the Lius and apprise her of the facts.

But he has no reason to go to the Lius. Except in the case of weddings and funerals, a poor devil like him can't just go walking any time he feels like it into the Liu family compound. He takes up the practice of gathering animal droppings at the crack of dawn.

He contrives to pass the Lius gate numerous times. There's a large open space in front of it, so — he imagines — nobody will take it amiss. Or he stands afar on the opposite bank of the river that flows past it, watching the comings and goings.

Finally one day, before the sun has arisen, when the entry-way to the village and the river as well are both bathed in a luminous bluish mist, he sees the woman carrying a basket of laundry to the riverbank. She's as pretty and charming as ever, though her face is paler than he remembers. She rolls up her sleeves and thrusts her arms, white as lotus roots, into the water and sloshes the laundry about.

Her hair, which has been done up in a bun, is coming loose. It's puffy, like a black lotus blossom. After a while, a bunch of it falls down, completely hiding her face, its tip extending all the way into the water. From time to time she lifts the loose hair and flips it behind her head. Or she might hold it there with her hand as she gazes motionlessly upon the surface of the water.

If she would just raise her head a little higher, he thinks, she would be able to see him crouching on the opposite bank watching her. But she does not alter her posture.

He glances all about him. From a distant ridge, the mooing of cows comes wafting through the air. Downstream, the mill's waterwheel is turning. Above the edge of a field, a kite flown by three small boys hovers lazily. Emboldened, he picks up his manure basket and moves with a light step closer to the edge of the river. The sun's rays have just spilled over the top of the mountain. They cast his reflection onto the surface of the water, right where she would be washing the laundry if she were not at the moment fixed in a state of abstraction.

When she lowers her head, she sees in the water the image of a familiar face. Thinking it to be an hallucination brought on by too intense a daydream, she flushes a discernible red. She plunges her hand into the water and stirs it up. She renews the washing of her clothes, throwing herself into it with unusual vigour. At length, she lapses once again into meditation, and the image of that face reappears in the water. Startled, she jerks her head up. Her hair spills over her face like a black waterfall. She parts it with dripping fingers. Her mouth, slightly agape, utters no sound.

"Young Mistress Liu," Wukui says, "you're out awfully early doing the wash."

"Yes."

Already he's run out of words.

"It's you, Wukui. I haven't seen you for a long time. Don't you live in the village? How come you never drop by?"

"I live on Three Way Lane. The Lius' dog — I don't dare get near it."

She smiles. There's something different about her smile — it's not as dazzling as it was on the road when he'd been carrying her as a bride. Her eyes are red, even a little swollen. He knows why, and his heart weighs in him heavily.

"Wukui, how've you been?"

"I, I..."

He thinks of the terrible thing he's done. "Young Mistress Liu, I know all about it... I really didn't know at the time how things were... How're you doing?"

She lowers her eyes and two tears plop into the water. She laughs, softly, and says, "Not bad. His injuries don't hurt anymore."

Only now does he notice that it's not clothes she's been washing, but cotton bandages stained with blood and spots of medicine. While they're talking, one slips off the rock and starts floating away on the current. She reaches out to grab it, but misses.

An impulse to help her retrieve it impels him to bound across the river's stepping-stones. They are unstable against the force of the downflow, threatening to topple him into the water.

"You won't make it!" she calls out, signalling him to go back. "You won't make it!"

The notion that Wukui can't do something is a challenge to his pride; he just has to prove otherwise. With a burst of gathered strength he propells himself forward and leaps across in one bound. Still, he fails to retrieve the absconding bandage. Frustrated, he stamps his foot.

"Forget it," she says. "If it's gone, it's gone. So..., you live on Three Way Lane. When shall I come over to thank you? Do you and your elder brothers not live together?"

"Yes, I live alone. That place of mine is filthy dirty and there's no good place for you to sit."

"In that case, you can come to my home to have a

cup of tea. Come as often as you like. You performed a great kindness for the Liu family... From now on, when I hear the dog barking, I'll come out and bring you in."

With this, she arranges the bandages in the basket and heads back to the house. When she steps upon the slope leading to the open ground in front of the gate, she turns around to see Wukui still standing there watching her. Her exuberant hair veils half her face, her one exposed eye curves delicately, charmingly upward as she flashes him a smile, regaling him with an image to cherish forever.

She continues on toward the house, but now her steps have become stiff and self-conscious, as if she knows he's still following her with his eye. But this just serves to enhance her loveliness.

He turns at last to return to the opposite bank and resume his manure gathering. His feet somehow refuse to set firmly upon those recalcitrant rocks. He blunders and sloshes his way across, all semblance of virile competence gone, soaking his shoes and trouser legs.

About ten days later, Wukui, always the bride carrier, never the groom, performs his specialty once again for another family in the village. As usual his face is painted red with cinnabar. Before he has a chance to wash it off, Excellency Liu, who has been invited to the wedding banquet, approaches him.

"Wukui, you performed a meritorious service for us Lius, and I've been meaning to reward you further, as you deserve, but I've been so busy I haven't got around to it. If you like, come to my house to take care of the cows. You'll be provided with all you can eat and drink as well as two bushels of wheat. Heh,

heh! We'll just take you to be another Liu family dependent."

Wukui is flabbergasted. The proposal flies in the face of all his assumptions. Then he thinks, the Lius have eight cows. Bedding them down, cutting their fodder, and cleaning out the manure would be exhausting work. So even if he had all he could eat and drink and received two bushels of grain a year, in actuality he'd be no more than a hired hand. Where'd the excellency get off saying he'd be "another Liu family dependent"?

He's about to turn down the offer when it occurs to him that were he living inside the Liu family compound, he could see Young Mistress Liu every day. And not only that, the Lius have been very sudden about this proposal, so it must have been instigated by her. He gets down on his knees, knocks his head on the ground, and thanks Excellency Liu with a sufficient show of abject gratitude.

That he will only be a cowherd does not diminish the mystique of taking up residence within the Liu family compound. His bridal buddies gleefully seize the opportunity to rag him and torment him with their pranks. First this one walks up to him and pats him on his newly shaven head. Then that one, too, finds his head eminently pattable. Soon they all strive boisterously for the same pleasure.

"What are you doing?" Wukui growls. "Rubbing your mother's titty? Don't you know 'men's heads and women's feet are only for looking, not for touching'?"

Chortles and hoots. "Look at Wukui—he's climbed up so high he's even gotten himself a brutal mouth!

We're patting your head, so maybe some of your luck will rub off on us!"

"You better watch out — what might rub off on you is my athlete's foot!"

"Wukui's got athlete's foot all right — he got it from running around carrying brides. But now he's part of the Liu household, so he can't do that anymore. When're *you* gonna hire a bride carrier, huh, huh?"

"My bride's probably still up her old man's leg!"

"Ho! You're such a kidder, Wukui! Such a kidder! But you can't get out of it — we've heard there are eight of them waiting for you right now. It's just too bad their frames are a bit big. And if they weren't so stubborn and didn't find men so ... unsatisfactory ha! — you'd really have your work cut out for you!"

The ruthless japing at his expense has worn Wukui's patience thin, and now this crack about the cows has him sputtering in rage. But riding a high tide of hilarity, they pay his ire no heed.

The next day at noon, Wukui moves his bedroll into the cowshed inside the Liu family compound. He dons a big oilcloth apron and leads the cows out into the sun and scrubs them down. Warmed by the sun and languorous after the good scratch he's given them, the cows lie down in the dust and moo contentedly. The sunshine fills Wukui with lassitude as well. He sits down and leans against one of the cows. He can feel tiny movements inside his clothing.

Lice.

He's on the verge of taking off his jacket to catch the little critters, when he hears the young mistress laughing.

There she is, looking at him.

She had come out into the courtyard to gather from the clothesline the bandages she had washed as usual early that morning. There she sees Wukui and the cows lying together, the cows flicking flies away from their eyes and from Wukui's body too with their tails. This scene she finds immensely amusing, and so she laughs.

Wukui jumps to his feet: "Good day to you, Young Mistress!"

"Did you come at noon? Did you have your lunch?"

"Yes, I've eaten."

"Did you have enough?"

"Yes."

"You've got a hard job, so you've got to eat well."

"Um."

His eyes begin to sting. The only other person who's ever shown him such solicitude was his mother, and she's long been dead. Poignant words of gratitude well up in his throat, but this woman is the young mistress of the Liu family, and he must keep his place.

"Thank you very much, Young Mistress. Taking care of these few cows is not very much work. Whatever Young Mistress would like to have done, all you have to do is give the order."

The brilliant sun barely allows the woman to open her eyes. She says, "Wukui, you've grown distant. You're not like the Wukui who carried me that day."

The scenes of that day flash through his mind. He swallows hard. The smile he gives her whimpers a tinge of bitterness.

From this time on, Wukui is the first in the compound to rise every morning. He begins his day heating water to mix the fodder. Then he bangs the mixing stick against the feed trough while he observes the activities in the compound. This becomes a virtual ritual. Only at about this time do the members of the Liu household begin to stir, making trips to the outhouse, primping before mirrors, pouring water to wash faces, carrying quilts out to hang in the air. The rooster, having been let out of the chicken coop, flaps its wings and chases after the yellow-combed hen.

Wukui's interest, however, lies primarily in the whereabouts of the young mistress. She generally occupies herself at this hour with taking the bandages to the river or with bringing the sheets out to hang in the sun. He can sometimes contrive an opportunity to say a few words to her. At other times, he can only look from afar. It takes only a look, though, to put him into a good mood for the rest of the day. On such days he can be heard talking nonsense to the cows. A morning which passes without her putting in an appearance is, by contrast, a prelude to gloom, and throughout the day he is as agitated and absent-minded as if his soul has wandered off and left his body to fend unaided for itself.

Winter arrives. The cruel west wind freezes the river shallows solid. Now when he fetches water he fetches extra bucketfuls. When he heats the water, he divides it between the cows fodder and the large wooden tub in which the Liu family members take baths. He sees the young mistress heading for the river with the bandages. He waylays her and tells her the river is too cold and that there is warm water in the tub.

She looks at him for a long time.

Not embedded in habit, she begins doing the washing in the tub. He goes back to the cowshed for a smoke. When it's time to change the water, he reappears with another bucketful, already warmed.

"Wukui, this is wasting water."

"It doesn't matter, there's a whole riverful of water."

"You shouldn't work so hard."

"I'm strong — very strong. Really — I can even lift up that stone roller."

"Wukui not only knows how to feed the cows, he knows how to tell tall tales too."

Rising to the challenge, he walks over and embraces the stone roller used for tethering cows that is presently lying on its side. Squatting down, feet firmly planted on the ground, he gives a "Hai!" and lifts it to an upright position.

"Don't! Don't!" the woman shrills in alarm. "You'll throw your back out like that."

He's itching to show he can do more. He turns his attention to another of the stone rollers. As he squats into position, the knees of his trousers suddenly rip. This accident sends him running to the cowshed. There he hides, not daring to come back out again.

After lunch, when the Lius are taking their naps, he puts on a vest, rolls up his trouser legs to hide the ripped knees, and sets about shoveling manure out of the cowshed. He is working assiduously, head and face sheeted in dripping sweat. The young mistress comes to lean on the fence. She calls out to him. Hastily he wipes his face.

"Don't work so hard. If you can't get it done today, there's always tomorrow. I fixed up an old pair of Young Master's trousers. Since he won't be needing them, you can wear them. I figured they'd be a bit long for you, so I shortened them. I don't know whether they'll fit or not. I've already put them on your bed."

She withdraws from the fence to return to the house, but then she turns back to add: "I've already spoken to His Excellency about it, so go ahead and wear them — nobody'll say you stole them." A smile accompanies her disclosure of this information. Her left eye curves delicately upward like that other time as she turns away again to leave.

Just at that moment, one of the cows eating at the trough decides to toss its head and flings off a glob of fodder that lands directly upon her face. Wukui rushes over to pull upon the cow's head, but by this time, the woman has wiped off the offending mass and walked away.

Wukui's heart is bursting with passion. It is an orphan passion with nowhere to go and no hope of ever expending its energy in the exhaustive tenderness it demands. He grabs a wooden cudgel and goes after the cow. Attempting to evade the blows, the panicked cow turns about the post to which it is tethered. Wukui pursues, beating it with frenetic ferocity. The post sways, the dust flies, the chickens squawk in terror, the dog pelts the air with its barks. Excellency Liu awakens from his nap in the parlor. Clutching his pants, he heads for the outhouse. The scene of abject violence stops him cold. He berates Wukui:

"What the hell's got into you? You think as the cow's not your cow, you need have no mercy on it!"

"Excellency, this cow's been bad!" Wukui throws away the cudgel and savagely kicks it into the corner of the cowshed.

When he has purged his aggression and flayed his passion into abeyance, he devotes his attention to Young Master Liu's trousers. He tries them on. They are old, of course, but for Wukui they are the newest he can ever hope to own. They fit him perfectly. This in spite of the fact that the young mistress had not taken his measurements when she'd shortened them. He is surprised at this — and immensely pleased. He takes them off. Then he puts them back on — and takes them off again. He's too embarrassed to go out of the cowshed with them on.

When the young mistress sees him, she asks him why he's not wearing those trousers. Her interest ratchets up his courage. When he re-emerges from the cowshed with them on, he doesn't know where to put his hands. He walks with stiff, splayed legs.

"Excellent!" the woman extols. "It's the saddle that makes the horse and the clothes that make the man — now Wukui is so much more handsome!"

He relaxes into naturalness.

He wears these trousers all the time now: When he cares for the cows, when he performs miscellaneous tasks around the compound, and when he leads a cow out to the public roller stone to husk rice.

On this particular occasion, Excellency Liu has nothing to do. To dispel boredom he wanders out to the public roller stone. The people there are all admiring

Wukui's trousers.

"It's all thanks to His Excellency." Wukui wants to give credit where credit is due.

"Wukui is just like a member of the family!" Excellency Liu is magnanimous. "At the end of the year we'll be making up a new suit for him as well."

When they return to the compound, Excellency Liu says, "Wukui, those trousers may have been worn by the young master, but they've been washed only once, and four silver dollars went into the cloth out of which they were made. So I'll be taking four quarts of grain out of your two-bushel allowance — and that's still a bargain for you. As I said, Wukui is like a member of the family."

Wukui doesn't breathe a word about this to the young mistress.

Whenever he sees her out in the sunny courtyard doing needlework or beetling and starching fabric on the beetling rock, he changes into his new trousers and comes out, leading a cow to the earthen square on the pretext of giving it a rubdown. This way they can converse under the cover of work. This way, his nervousness and inhibitions recede.

Today the young mistress indulges in some good-natured ribbing, teasing Wukui about his naive little eccentricities. That's not all she indulges in: He catches her looking at him. Consciously or not, her eyes have been glued to his form. At first he figures she's savouring the sight of her handiwork, the pants of perfect proportions displayed to greatest advantage. But then her face clouds over. Anxiety floods her eyes.

Poor thing, he thinks. She probably sees me wearing

these trousers and it makes her think of how the young master must've looked before he became a cripple. Here I am running around in these trousers while their true owner will never wear trousers again.

His own heart echoes the ache he imagines is in her heart. His mood plummets. He ought to go back to the cowshed and remove the trousers, but he can't bring himself to leave her alone when she's feeling bad. He asks: "Young Mistress, are you okay?"

"No, I'm not okay."

This answer is not what he'd expected. He'd meant his words to be consoling, he thought she'd rise to the convention and say she's fine; that certainly would have made him feel a little better. Now he dangles in uncertainty, brain numb, all possible replies stifled in the depths of its unyielding recesses.

She looks at him, tears trickling down.

Chagrin. Humiliation. His impulse to do something helpful blocked by his incompetence before a woman's distress. The incompetence of inexperience. A chunk of wood, that's all he is, an inarticulate chunk of wood.

He hangs his head.

At his feet is a tiny little ant carrying something — what is it? — it's another ant, another ant that's dead. This dead ant must have been the husband or the wife of that little ant — such a fragile little entity carrying a body as big as itself, struggling so valiantly along its journey of affliction. Surely it has a wound in its heart many times bigger than its own body. His tears make little wet craters in the dust.

"His Excellency's coming!" The woman's voice rasps low — a loud urgent whisper. Her hands fly to her face, effecting the motion of rubbing away fatigue, a pretext for destroying the traces of her tears. "Wukui," — her voice now elevated in crisp, resonant clarity — "how old do you reckon this cow is?"

The question awaits no answer. Already she has bounded to her feet. She pivots and flits over to her father-in-law, asking him what he'll be having for lunch — she has to inform the cook, you know — thereby averting his approach to the scene of mutual misery. Wukui is left to the solitude of his falling tears.

That night his tireless companion, insomnia, enthralls him with vivid visions of all his encounters with the young mistress, from that first day to now. There is no doubt: she cares for him. Her angelic beauty, her saintly virtue, her nurturing, motherly kindness lave him like a salubrious balm, immerse him in a happiness that no words can express. That she'd confessed her distress to him this noon, said she was "not okay", cried right in front of him, elevates him to the heights of exhilaration, like flowers blooming and reblooming in perpetually renewing resplendence. She's treated him like someone to whom she can open her heart. She regards him as a relative or an intimate friend. But what can he who is a servant, the keeper of the Lius cows, do for her? If he could trade his legs, he would readily give them to the young master so that she could be happy. But how is that possible?

At least — and the thought provides some solace — at least the Lius are the biggest, richest family in Rooster Village. That makes up a little for the conjugal bliss denied her. She's got position. She's got status. All the servants and even all the villagers respect her. Unlike other young wives, she doesn't have to go out to the fields to plough and sow and fertilise and reap, nor up into the mountains to cut grass and chop firewood. And though her three meals a day don't consist of delicacies from distant seas and remote peaks still she has white rice and refined flour to eat. What the village women, all green with envy, wouldn't give for this happy lot.

Jealousy and loathing have always slathered village souls at the mere thought of the Lius. Time was when Wukui too felt exactly the same way. Now he hopes for their continued prosperity. Now he cowkeeps with total dedication, repudiating the slack-off example of the other retainers. He envisions the day when they'll have a whole herd of cows and their coffers will be bursting with grain. For this would all one day become the property of the young mistress—let His Excellency and His Excellency's wife and even Young Master Liu, who will never be a whole man again anyway, let them all hasten to their graves! Then if she should find another handsome young husband to join her, he, Wukui, would forever keep the cows for her. Even after he died, he would strive to come back as one of her cows so he could serve at her command.

For her part, the young mistress surreptitiously strives to improve his lot. She might find, for instance, the supper chicken to be too tough. As her father-in-law throws the head and the feet to the dog, she suggests it be given to the servants. She carries the left-overs out to the servants, who are eating cornmeal mush in the courtyard, and proclaims loudly, "Come, come, my father says you can all have a taste of these things." But she gives the whole lot over to Wukui and says, "Don't turn your nose up at it — it's still better than what you have in your bowl." In consideration of her kindly intentions he pops the left-over meat into his mouth and chews it on the spot to please her. He even says, "Don't worry about me. If only you eat well, I'll get fat on plain cold water."

He is delighted to discover he is able to say things that please her. Once when he is talking with her, she reaches out her hand and presses her finger on his forehead, saying with pouting lips and a precious drawling voice, "You know how to say just the right thing, don't you?"

This flirtatious gesture sweeps away his inhibitions. He becomes bold, vivaciously audacious. Words career off his tongue like drunken butterflies. He yearns for her to bestow this measure of spoiled preciousness upon him every day. But it never happens again.

By March, Young Master Liu has convalesced to the point where he can be carried out to the courtyard to take some sun. Seeing him for the first time since his accident, Wukui recoils at the sight. Dishevelled hair. Puffy, pasty face. Like a raised loaf of raw bread. He lies there on the lounge chair contemplating the sailing clouds and the soaring birds, all wrapped up in a blanket, pitifully resembling a wax gourd. On the little table before the lounge chair, the young mistress has placed tea and his water tobacco pipe. She is sitting there cracking walnuts, placing each walnut meat she frees from its shell into his mouth.

Wukui walks over, bows, and says solicitously, "Young Master, I see you've come out to take some sun."

Young Master looks up at Wukui's towering height.

He opens his mouth as if to say something, but nothing comes out. He closes his eyes.

The situation is awkward. It seems to Wukui inappropriate to leave, yet staying is no more appropriate.

"Wukui, how about coming round here and cracking some nuts."

He realises she's concerned about the effect a servant standing tall before the young master will have upon him. Compliantly, he squats down. As expected, Young Master reopens his eyes. Smack before his line of vision are his very own trousers wrapped around the haunches of Wukui.

"Eh!" His eyes narrow as he turns his head and looks interrogatively at the woman.

"Father said he could have them," she hastens to explain.

Young Master explodes. He bellows at Wukui, "Get the hell out of here! What am I — your cow? Did I tell you to come over here and feed me?"

The woman bites her lip and looks at Wukui. Wukui rises and leaves. As he departs, a rising crescendo of imprecations hurled at the woman assaults his ears. The walnuts, according to the shouts, have been cracked too small. There is a crash. Wukui turns to take a look. The young master has overturned the table and he's throwing walnuts at the woman's face. She begins wailing. Mrs Liu tumbles from the parlor into the tumult, yammering rebuke: "What are you blubbering about? He's your husband — don't you know he's mentally traumatised?"

Wukui flees the scene and runs back to his room in the cowshed. He throws himself on the bed and buries his head in the quilt. Silently, secretly, he sheds tears.

Thereafter he observes the young mistress daily emerge from the house, carrying in her arms what appears to be a baby with a hairy and enlarged head, its globular proportions incongruent against her delicate and graceful form. She deposits this being, her husband, in his lounge chair in the courtyard. She feeds him food and water. During his daily sunning, no other person save his parents and his wife is permitted to walk in the courtyard. This rule is eventually expanded to include — or rather exclude — cows and sheep and pigs and dogs — anything with legs. Otherwise he twitches, gasps, trembles and seethes, and generally relapses into mental incapacity. Soon the courtyard denizens dwindle to little else but stone rollers, rocks, and the occasional cattail cushion.

At length, Excellency Liu announces his son is completely recovered. Shortly thereafter two burly slave girls appear among the domestic staff, acquired exclusively to minister to the young master's needs.

The next opportunity following their arrival, Wukui remarks to the young mistress: "Now with the slave girls, things should be easier for you."

A wail. A most uncharacteristic and nasty eruption: "Shut up, will you! Just shut up!"

This is the first time she's ever lost her temper with him. His face falls. Devastated, he retreats to the cowshed and sits crumpled in a solitary timeless stupor.

Unable to reconcile himself to her anomalous hostility, he puzzles over it for many days. The nights now grip him with intense consciousness, hour after hour unrelieved, unsupplanted by the restorative blankness of sweet sleep. He gets up and goes out to sit on the edge of the feed trough. To a nocturnal symphony of regurgitations and cud chewings he wrestles with the elusive genesis of the woman's virulent outburst.

A new motif insinuates itself into the cows' digestive fantasia: crying, very faint, wafting from some indeterminate direction. He trains his ears upon the sound. It's coming from the apartment to the left of the parlor. It's infused with the ethereal substance of the young mistress. He walks over in that direction and slips behind the chicken coop, the back wall of which faces the window of the young master's bed-room. The glow of the window resonates with the now unmistakable sound of the young mistress' choked sobs. The young master's voice stabs through it with stentorian hysteria: "You're my wife! You're my wife!"

A slap studs the butt of his shouts. A swaying shadow totters upon the window paper. Feminine sobbing rises and falls in fits and starts, desolate in the dead of the night.

In the dawn only Wukui stirs. As the morning begins to age, the first person he runs into is the young mistress. Bloody scratches rankle across her face, her eyes are swollen. The rebuke he had received the other day stands as sentry at the gate of his compassion, bonding his tongue to the roof of his mouth. Thus muzzled, he turns to leave.

"Wukui, Wukui, are you going to ignore me too?"

Her plaintive query startles him to a standstill. "Young Mistress, what happened? Did you have a fall?"

"I was ... beaten."

The muscles of his face, from the largest to the most

minute, contort into the lineaments of distress: "I heard you crying last night."

"So — you knew?"

What he doesn't know, what remains unfathomable and mysterious, is the reason for the marital altercation. The ensuing days stretch their sunny, sunning rays into the extinguishing tyranny of darkness as the young master grows and nurtures a peculiar, malevolent temperament, transforming whatever pity Wukui harbours for him into palpable loathing. Night after night, creeping into the hours of deepest gloom, the grim weeping of the woman punctuated by raw shocks of slaps and punches strengthens the grip of his insomnia.

On one of those sun-drenched days, Wukui, banned as usual from the courtyard during the invalid's daily solar therapy, is spreading earth in the cowshed. Young Master, he observes, is directing Young Mistress in the performance of feminine toilette. Now she must comb her hair, now she must rub oil into it, now she must powder her face and apply rouge. Her compliance is carried out with meticulous obedience. Young Master laughs and asks the two slave girls, "Is Young Mistress beautiful?"

"Yes, she's beautiful," they chime.

"How beautiful is she?"

"As if she's stepped down from a painting."

"Have you ever seen a young wife more beautiful than Young Mistress?"

"No, never."

He orders her to walk ahead a few steps, turn around, walk back. He laughs with malignant satisfaction. The woman doesn't crack a smile. Indeed, since the beginning of the mandated grooming session, her every move has been mechanical, as spontaneous as the impersonations of a wooden puppet.

Thus, when the dog comes trotting in through the main gate, it's like the kiss of life, instant transmogrification from doll into human being.

"It's at the gate!" she exclaims. "How did it get in? I'll go tie it up." With this, she walks off.

The young master orders: "Take me back in!"

The two slave girls comply. From within the house, one of them calls out: "Young Mistress, Young Master wants you."

"He wants a drink," Young Mistress calls back, "go ahead and pour it for him."

"He doesn't want a drink — he wants to do that ... thing!"

The young mistress pays no heed. Without a falter in her step, she continues toward the gate.

The other slave girl runs after her shouting: "Young Mistress, Young Master is getting mad!" As if to confirm the truth of her words, a wolfish howling emanates from the bedroom. Still the young mistress walks along, disregarding the commotion.

She is confronted at the gate by a glowering Mrs Liu coming in from the outside: "Disobeying your husband? Get back to the room, this instant!"

The young woman pulls up short. She throws her arms around a tree and says passionately, "I won't go! I won't! I won't!"

Mrs Liu slaps her face and shouts: "Don't you disobey me! You've been brought here as a wife — get it? — a wife! What are you saving your ... for someone else?" With that she slams the gate door shut and orders the slave girls to drag her back to the house. The two slave girls seize her and take her across the courtyard by force. Mrs Liu follows along behind, cursing her and pinching her backside.

At length grievously piercing cries traverse the courtyard from the bedroom and invade that shady sanctuary intended for cows. Vividly, viscerally, Wukui comprehends the terrible thing they are doing to her.

Snuffed out from this moment is his abiding desire to see her. The sight of her no longer laves his heart with gladness but rather rouses the guilt that had been lying quiescent in the pit of his being: It was his error that dumped her into this misfortune. Her pain and misery shoot out at him through the windows of her eyes. Thus, except when he must fetch water, transport dirt, or bring in the fodder, he keeps himself hidden in the cowshed. Or he works the hayshears.

Standing on the frame of the hayshears, he savages the handle, grittily pouring his strength into its operation. An old riddle runs through his mind:

"She's seventeen, she's eighteen, she sleeps with legs apart,

He's young, he's strong, he presses score times four,

He's old, he's weak, just one press — can press no more."

The answer to the riddle is "hayshears". On the surface, though, it slyly describes sexual intercourse. Oh, how much better off she'd be had she married an old man! This young master — what's he got going for him? Two hulky slave girls, that's what! If Excellency Liu hasn't bought them to hold up that lump of meat as he works off his lust, then what else for?

Horrible.

The crying in the night wafts into his space, enwraps him in rebuke, suffocates him like an invisible spirit. In the day, the slave girls holler, "Young Mistress, Young Master wants you!" and he breaks out into an anxious, febrile sweat. He runs into his sleeping room, pounds the walls with frustrated fists, loosening the mud plaster, sending pieces smattering to the floor.

One day he brings down an exceptionally large piece of this mud plaster in an exhausting bout with the wall that leaves him physically drained and thoroughly enervated. As he sits slumped and immobilised on the floor, there is a deafening crash, as if a bundle of firewood has tumbled to the ground. It is in fact his door, which has been pushed open brutally, with a stertorous bang. Hair in wild disarray, the young mistress bursts through the opening and falls to the floor, weeping wretchedly.

Startled, he cries out and rushes to her, raising her up to a sitting position. She presses her head upon his chest. The volume of her crying increases, her tears soak his shirt. He holds her in his arms like a father comforting a child devastated by his absence. From her comes a heartbreaking torrent of anguish: "I can't stand it anymore! I truly can't stand it any more! You brought me here, now take me away! I'll go and be a nun, I'll go and be a beggar, but I won't be the Liu's young mistress anymore!"

"Young Mistress!" He is alarmed — and terrified — he, a servant in the Liu family compound, right here with the young mistress in his arms! He struggles to peel himself away from her, he leaps back as one would from a charge of electricity. Now on his feet, her words ring in his ears, but his vocal chords are paralysed. What can he possibly say?

Brilliant rays of sunshine flood in through the open door. She looks at his moronic, stupefied expression and wails even louder.

"Shhh! Don't cry!" he says nervously. "They'll hear you and know you're here."

Her crying stops. "Take me away! Take me away!" Her now blank eyes fix upon him.

How could she be so childish? Who is he that he would dare take away a young mistress? How would he do it? Where would he take her? What would he do once they got there?

He looks at the woman, then looks out at the courtyard. The fever-pitch of his anxiety squeezes into his tears, and those tears start from his eyes.

The woman clenches her fists and begins beating, ruthlessly, her own exquisite small feet. She has no wings, nor even feet on which to flee. She gouges her fingernails into her face. Already there is blood. He grabs her hands: "Don't do that!"

She snatches them back: "It's all because of this face! I'll make it ugly, he'll cast me off, he'll send me back home!"

He catches her hands again. This time he doesn't let go.

The patch of sunlight guarding the door blinks an ominous alarm. Excellency Liu appears, heading up a pack of others. Wukui throws off the woman's hands and scuttles off to the side. Helpless, passive, he hears Excellency Liu's rantings: "Never, ever, in all these generations, have the Lius been party to such a disgrace! Tie her up and beat her to death, the shameless hussy!"

Instantly the woman is swaddled in ropes. Wukui falls to his knees: "Excellency! It's not Young Mistress' fault. If you beat anyone, it should be Wukui!"

"You!" Excellency Liu's attention shifts to Wukui. "You ingrate! And I — I've been blind! I'd beat you to death, too, right here, you bastard, if you hadn't done a thing or two for us —so get yourself out of here! And never darken our door again! And I tell you, if you go around telling stories about how the young mistress was with you here, I'll shove your mouth all the way down to your asshole! Now get out!"

Wukui rolls up his bedding, tucks it under his arm, and walks out the door. Outside, he turns and looks at the woman and says, "Okay, Excellency, I'm leaving. But Wukui has one last thing to beg of you: Release the young mistress ... if you don't want to kill her ... she's still one of your own!"

Excellency Liu kicks out at him, catching him square in the buttocks. He departs to the sound of a shoe sole slapping and slapping on skin — tender skin — undoubtedly the face of the woman.

It's been three days since Wukui has returned to live in his old house. Today the rumour-mongers are out in full force.

They say that Young Mistress Liu is sick. They say she's paralysed. They say she spends the entire day lying on her back in bed. Someone remarks that the Lius are really having a lot of bad luck — first the young master loses his legs and has to spend all his days in bed, and now the young mistress too is condemned to bed even though she has legs. Someone else observes that the Lius love to collect antiques, and now that the young mistress has become a Sleeping Beauty, they have a talking knick-knack to admire and enjoy.

Wukui knows why she's been turned into a paralytic: So Young Master, with the help of the two slave girls, can use her anytime he wants — no resistance, no struggle, just pure, trouble-free indulgence. Wham, bam, not even a thank-you ma'am. His blood boils at the thought.

Regret raises its sorrowing, accusatory head. She'd begged him to take her away, and he'd not done it. Why? Why had he not granted her request? There had to be some kind of karma at work here. Otherwise why would a servant like him have so many uncanny connections with such as she? He was such a dolt he'd failed to notice or heed it. The first time she'd told him to do something — to cross the river and escape — he'd not listened. And now this time, when she told him to take her and escape the Lius, he failed to listen again. All he'd done was to watch — with wide-open eyes — her slippery, sliding descent into the abyss of misery and affliction. He'd not lifted a finger to help. How detestable you are, Wukui — how frail, how puny, how ... repulsive!

In the night as he lies on his bed, he hears someone calling to him: "Wukui". The voice is ardent, then resentful, then utterly wretched. He knows this is just a hallucination, nonetheless it is vivid and persistent and gives him no peace for the entire night. Indeed. What is she thinking the whole long day as she lies on the bed, she who has become a tool for working off sexual desires, a literal sexaid? She'd known very well that to run crying to his quarters was mortally dangerous. Yet she'd taken that risk. She'd unleashed her tears in his arms because she'd been driven beyond the limits of human endurance. It had taken a lot of courage to do that. She had regarded him as a man, in the virile, capable, protective sense of the word. She had placed her faith in him. But Wukui, what did you do, Wukui — feckless, good-for-nothing Wukui...!

Loud bangs of skull upon adobe. Knocking, knocking, knocking, his head pestles the edge of the *kang*, he must punish himself, he must immolate himself, for the crime of betraying a woman's faith.

No longer can he remain sitting still in his room. Enshrouded in a personal fog, he goes rambling through village lanes. Nothing he sees pleases him. He chases chickens from his path, he beats dogs who happen in his way, he curses, even smites, anyone who speaks to him. A lugubrious moan billows up from the inhabitants of Rooster Village. They're all convinced he's crazy. They all bemoan that mysterious skew in the topographical layout of the place — it's always turning people weird.

During this period when the villagers live in the terror of uncertainty, yet another disaster hits the Lius. There is a wide open space just outside the entry to the stockaded village, and on that space sit three mountains of hay that belong to the Lius. One evening all three mountains catch fire. The ensuing conflagration emits light so intense that half the sky glows red and it spews smoke enough to envelop all of Rooster Village. The Liu family compound disgorges all its residents, family members and servants alike, into the village byways as they run to rouse the villagers to action. Soon Rooster Village is a scene of pandemonium with people running about chaotically like startled ants.

In the midst of the confusion and turmoil, someone sneaks into the Liu compound and heads straight for the young master's bedroom.

When the door pushes open, Young Master's mouth expands into an "O", a prelude to a scream. The intruder throws a punch, slugging the lump of meat into oblivion. He turns to the woman, lying prone on another bed. In the cold lunar luminosity streaming through the lattice window, she resembles a beauty rendered in cool jade. He leans over the edge of the bed and smiles at her through his tears.

"Wukui, was it you who set the fire?" She is very perceptive.

He nods his head.

"You did that just to come and see me?" She reaches out her hand toward him. "You've got a lot of guts, haven't you?" She caresses his broad forehead and the bridge of his nose. "You better hurry up and get out of here before they discover you — they'll kill you, you know."

"I've come to take you away!"

"It's too late. Now I'm like this, I'm really already dead. I can't hurt you any more, Wukui. You'd better hurry up and go!"

He stands up straight: "If I want to take you away, I'm going to take you away!" He gathers the four corners of the blanket together, wrapping the woman up inside. With a mighty effort he hoists her to his back and supports her there with his arms wrapped behind him. Out the door he goes.

He bears her deep into the mountain forest.

The moon, distant in this night sky, is stingy with its light. The ascending mountain welters in the gloom, loathe to reveal its secret pathways. Wukui turns blindly into a ravine. As he traces his way along the bottom, the ridges on either side become lower and lower even as the ravine grows narrower and narrower. At last the two sides meet and form a block at the base of a mountain peak.

It's already noon of the next day. They revel in their liberty. As free as birds flown to the ends of the earth, they are; as free as fish swimming to the rim of the sea. Here the Lius will never find them.

Thoroughly fatigued, they sit down to rest. They nibble on cornbread that Wukui had stuffed into his shirt before he left home. The woman bombards him with questions about this place and what lies on the other side of the mountain that looms before them. No more apprised of this knowledge than she, Wukui casts his answer in terms of survival: Yellow soil, wherever they may find it, is capable of sustaining life, thus, the precise location is irrelevant.

He sets the woman down and goes off to relieve himself. He has chosen his privy well, for it rewards him with a pleasant surprise: There peeking through the splendid handiwork of Nature's vegetation sit the ruins of a temple to the mountain spirit. The four main walls are still standing. At the top of one of the walls, an ancient cypress clings to life, dismissing the fact that one of its sides is completely dead and decayed. Behind the temple a ravine slides down to the river that created it. The bridge that once spanned this topographical gash is now reduced to a few pieces of rotting timber tenaciously cleaving to the edge. A grey vulture is perched upon these old bridge-leavings, immobile as a rock — except for a string of liquidy white poop released with a flatulent spritz.

Wukui bounds back to the woman, leaping and dancing with juvenile joy: "We have a place to live!"

"Where?" Her eyes light up.

"There's a mountain spirit temple over there. That means people used to live here — and if people used to live here, it's because this place has things people can live on. We can stay here and we won't starve to death."

He takes her upon his back again and dives into the bushes and weeds. Profusions of beggar ticks glom onto her clothes, her blanket, her hair. He points out the old temple as he talks. The problem of the roof is easily solved. He can cut some trees and set them overhead for rafters and then cover them with mats woven out of grass. And look there — couldn't he get water from the river at the bottom of the ravine by way of that path behind the temple? Over there, that large expanse of grass and weeds used to be cultivated land, and if he brought it under cultivation again, couldn't he grow wheat and corn for them? "The birds of the forest will come to sing for you so you won't be lonely. And I'll pick wild flowers from the slopes and weave them into your hair. And the butterflies will come to admire your beauty. Here the grass is soft, and when the sun is shining I'll bring you out to lie on it, and you can watch the puffy clouds turn into little cats and dogs as they fly between the peaks. And we can raise some chickens and sheep and cows. You can lie here and watch as I urge on the cow and plough up the earth. And if gazelles or pheasants come by, watch how I'll bring them down and cook up a nice stew for you..."

His excitement is uncontainable. Before his eyes he sees not ruins and weeds, but a picture of the peaceful days that would be theirs from now on. Free of the proscriptions inherent to living among the Lius, his solicitous impulses toward the woman have reasserted themselves. He says, "You don't believe me? But you have every reason to, because I'm strong. I'm not going to die, and I'm certainly not going to let you die either, you'd better believe it!"

"I believe you, I do. But I'm starving. Is there any more cornbread?"

He feels around inside his shirt and brings out a dried morsel. He loosens his belt to make a more thorough search. To no avail. But a small hatchet falls out. He'd taken it along for self-defence, but the raid upon the Liu compound had gone smoothly and he'd forgotten about it.

In showering the woman with reassurances, he had painted such a rosy picture of the life they would have that he'd nearly begun to believe it was already realised. Such a foolish idyll! How could he forget he's brought her into the middle of nowhere? They are free, certainly, but the question of the moment is: What are they to eat now? And where are they to sleep now? Himself he's not worried — his needs are easily taken care of. But considering the kind of woman the young mistress is — and the fact that he has so heroically rescued her — could he just let her starve and freeze to death on the mountain?

She sees the shadow of worry take possession of his features and smiles her brightest smile: "Actually I'm not hungry at all. Really, I'm not hungry."

He doesn't believe her. For no reason at all, it seems, his heart begins to ache. Is this weakness? Inklings of shame. He camouflages his discomposure in a studied reconnoitering of the distant scenery. A patch of forest distinguished by a headdress of cloud catches his eye. He thrusts his hatchet back into his belt and says, "You sit tight and I'll be right back."

He returns with scads of peaches, wild, small pink succulents. Swamped by the bounty of the feral fruit, he had removed his outer trousers — those controversial trousers once owned by Young Master Liu — tied up the bottoms of the legs with vines, and filled them out with the peaches. The peach-stuffed trousers look like a gigantic character for "person". His illiteracy, however, deprives him of the propitious connotations of this. To him they look rather like one of those long bags used for carrying stuff on the backs of donkeys. So he drapes them around his shoulders and treks back, joking to the woman as he approaches, "I'm the Heavenly Queen Mother's donkey bringing the peaches of longevity!"

This double-horned cornucopia, though, is not for Wukui. As the woman slurps peaches, he throws himself into chopping down trees for rafters. He chooses a kind of evergreen that grows very straight and slim, like lodgepole pine. As his hatchet clangs away at the base, the sparse golden leaves at the top come fluttering down, imitating multitudes of frivolously arcing butterflies. This reminds the woman of when she used to play by the crystal pool as a child, dropping in stones and watching the ripples. She calls out, "Those leaves, I want them." He brings an armful for her. Still, she wants more, and he keeps bringing them and bringing them until she is buried up to her neck. She flings herself back into the pile and becomes an angel floating on a glorious rosy sunrise cloud.

He is charged, he is torrential, he is indefatigable. He amazes even himself. A dozen or so trees fall to his hatchet. In a trice, they are spanning the walls of the ruins. He lashes them down with kudzu vines. Across the tops of the walls and over the rafters he clambers as constant feminine admonitions to be careful spur him to do the opposite. Scorning the insurance of a good grip, he stands upright and walks across like an acrobat. He keeps losing his balance but saves himself each time by catching a rafter. These antics inflame the woman's fears. She yells, she screams, she's provoked to anger.

"I'm just teasing you!" he prods playfully.

Next come the wattles, which he fashions by intertwining branches and grass. He layers them across the rafters. Their little shelter is complete.

She asks him to take her in to take a look. He puts her off. There's no hurry, he says, and sets about cutting an abundance of slender sturdy sticks. These he inserts into the floor of the shelter, row upon row, in the form of a circle. Atop this foundation he weaves a web of supple criss-crossed branches. Over this surface he spreads cogongrass and leaves. Now he takes up the woman and tosses her on top. She bounces, and bounces. "It's springy!" she cries out in surprise. "Just like a rope-frame bed."

Pleased with himself, he sings a pleasant lilting little

tune. He winks and says it's only right you should have such a bed. When he was small his father told him a story about how in the old days an empress went wandering out among the common people. When the local official looked into it, he discovered there were three women claiming to be the empress. So he placed a pea on a bed and covered it with more than forty quilts, and each of the women slept upon it. The one who became sore from sleeping upon the lump was the one who was the true empress.

He picks up a stone and slips it into the cogongrass.

"I'm not an empress." She laughs.

"But you're a young mistress."

"I'm not a young mistress," she cries. "I'm not."

This pulls him up short for a second. Then he says, "That's right, you're not; you're not the Lius' young mistress. But you are an angel! Can you feel the lump?"

"My legs are totally paralysed. Even if you stick a knife in there, I wouldn't feel it."

This mournful fact sloshes over him, washes away his joy, returns him to the arms of melancholy. He bows his head, and time stops, stretches, accentuating the silence imposed by tragedy. Finally he stirs himself and goes out. The noise of furious chopping ensues. He returns with an armload of hewn branches. With them he erects a partition down the center of the shelter.

"Now what are you doing, Wukui?" she asks.

"That's your side of the room, and this is mine."

She flushes, the sanguinary hue flooding up and spreading with particular vehemence across her forehead. She is not, after all, Wukui's wife. Wukui is only a poor cowherd who has saved her. He's a bachelor. Yet here, even in the wilderness, he has taken the initiative to separate the sleeping accommodations. The decency of this man, his guilelessness, his utter irreproachability, move her even to the edge of rapture.

The sun, ponderous and red, dips behind the mountain. Crows, unwieldy black spectres, flap by in the incipient gloom. Darkness descends with discernable rapidity. Wukui settles the woman down for the night. He lights a pine torch and sits by her side, plumping up her courage and stoking her confidence with words of valour. Get a good night's sleep, he says. If any wolves or bears come snooping around, he will be right there on the other side of the partition with his hatchet keeping guard so they won't dare come in. She, though, is worried about his having no quilt. That's nothing to worry about, he says. He'll not be cold, he's used to sleeping in piles of cogongrass, done it since he was a child, and every time he sleeps like a babe and dreams the best of dreams. Anyway, tomorrow, he'll go down the mountain to bring back quilts and pots, dishes and food.

Her eyes are enormous and glittering as she studies the leaping, flickering flame of the torch. She turns them upon his swarthy face, glossy in the torchlight, and says, "Hurry and get some rest, dear brother Wukui!"

A dissolving sensation sweeps through his body, his sinewy strength, his massive bones, every seat of physical and affective function trembling indistinguishably into jelly. He stares at her. She stares at him. He opens his mouth, closes it again, no words uttered. His hands, shaking, reach out ... and tuck in the corners of her quilt. With swift precision he adjusts the torch. It flares up then gradually dies back, crouching ever lower in the darkness until completely extinguishes. Treading softly he withdraws to the other side of the partition. His own grass pallet awaits him, and he gratefully accepts its outstretched hospitality.

He does not relight the torch but savours, rather, the spaciousness of a world made bigger by blackness. Not only bigger, but fuller as well, teeming with substance, brimming with significance. Though he has no knowledge or understanding of that thing called poetry, his heart beats with poetic excitement and soars with lyrical joy. He is wide awake. Twenty-four hours of intense physical exertion have not weighted his eyelids with fatigue. He rises to a sitting position. It would be a waste to sleep: It would be unworthy of this night.

He luxuriates in the uniqueness of the day's experiences. Never has he done such audacious things. Never has he thought such stunning thoughts. The guilt that had been nagging him for months is gone — oh, miracle! What is there about today that has driven it off and freed him of its tyranny? Is it that he's liberated her from torment —and in the process come to know — really know — a man's ability to protect a woman?

Rustling, rustling, the sounds of her shiftings penetrate the partition as if there is none. They soon surrender to the quiescence of the night. Poor thing — the past twenty hours have been terrifying and exhausting for her. She needs a good rest. What perfection she is when she is awake — gentle and soft and amiable and kind; and when she's asleep, she's as peaceful and languorous as a cat, breathing in soothing rhythm, audible, but barely; unconsciously, unguilefully summoning admiration and fascination. And he is a man. Unwed. Uninitiated. Involuntarily celibate. And he has fallen in love.

Now here he is on this night of nights, enclosed in the same temple with the lovely, beautiful object of his affection with only a grass partition separating them. Her breathing, her scent penetrate that partition and caress his senses. His innocent, virginal sensibilities surge up from their slumber and glow and rejoice in the radiance of discovered sensuality. Breathless, measured, he turns his head and leans in close to the grass partition. All he need do is take his knife and ever so softly push aside some of the grass. Then he could peek through and see the sleeping beauty in the vague moonlight slipping through the cracks in the roof. The desire to do this inflames other desires, engulfing his entire body in wave upon wave of tremulous heat. He is drawn. His longing melds him into the golden molten tide of essential goodness flowing inexorably toward her. He rises to his feet. His feet move him toward the door: the other side of the partition, the source of his restless perambulation.

But that pool of white light, the moon's largess penetrating the roof and weltering at the entry to his quarters, disappears. As he had been lying on his grass pallet staring at it, it had appeared to him as a white rock, and then as the moon itself. Now as he passes over it, it vanishes.

A warning — this must be a warning.

What is this if not the light of revelation? The force of righteousness censoriously illuminating the dark intention in his heart? He reproaches himself: What in heaven's name was he planning on doing? Go over there and crawl all over her just like that? Or maybe kneel at the side of her bed and beg her favour? How on earth would he say such a thing?

And what would she have thought of him then?

Of course it would be very easy to get what he wanted through brute force alone. And then she'd be his. But that would mean he'd pulled off the daring rescue from the Lius simply for his own gain. He'd be worse than the bandit Tang Jing. Tang Jing and his men at least had been open and above board about their intentions — they were going to turn her into the bandit chieftain's wife and that was that. But he, he claims to be her rescuer, so it would be truly reprehensible of him to take advantage of her. Why he'd be nothing but a hooligan! Even if she took him with great delight, what kind of a way would this be for him to behave in light of his own scruples?

That white light has been keeping an eye on him in the night: the eye of Heaven, making sure he behaves. This he is certain of.

He turns back and sits down on his grass pallet. The patch of white light reappears. Its undiminished luminescence reassures him, calms him down. He feels as if he's crawled out upon the bank of an abyss of sin. Triumphant against temptation. As firm and tenacious men are. The air fills his expanding lungs with heady exultation.

Enthralling notions, ravishing conceits rush into his new expansiveness. Just think! A man like him, a man who has nothing, right now — this very moment — has a stunningly beautiful woman under his protection! No man before him has ever had such good fortune, not even Young Master Liu, the heir to a fortune. The woman is sleeping so peacefully. She's placed complete trust and faith in him. What is there that is of greater significance for a man than this?

A cricket, he notices, has jumped into the pool of white light, when, he doesn't know. Now it's chirping away. Is this little wilderness entity, this creature who's one with the spirit of the mountain forest and who's drunk its fill of sweet dew — is it singing a paean of praise for him, Wukui?

He lies back, nestles into the grass, and to the cricket's silvery Nachtmusik drifts off into the world of dreams.

There is a prickling sensation on his chest. It is this that draws him back into the mortal world. Instinctively he slaps at it. The slapping palm comes away viscous and smelling of blood even as the air erupts into that deafeningly faint, whirring whining buzz.

Mosquitoes.

So — they've finally discovered the presence of humans and how tasty their blood is.

He dabs his bites with saliva. The woman pops into his mind — the mosquitoes must be attacking her too. A bite on her tender delicate skin would surely leave more than a little red spot — more likely a bump the size of a chestnut.

Agonising deliberation. Finally he emerges from his snuggery and walks gingerly to the other side of the partition. He gathers together a pile of damp cogongrass and sets it alight with his flint and steel. It gives off a satisfying cloud of thick smoke. That'll keep the little buggers off her.

"Brother Wukui!"

Drat! He's awakened her in spite of all his efforts not to.

"I, I'm not ... I've come to smoke out the mosquitoes..." She can't, she mustn't, misunderstand his intentions.

"I know," she says. "I've been covering my head with the quilt — that way they can't get me."

"When did you wake up?"

"I haven't been asleep!"

What? She hasn't been asleep? How can that be? What's running through her head that's keeping her awake? Oh, no! — had she heard him get up before and approach her side of the shelter?

Fortunately it's dark, for his face is burning red.

"It's late," he says as he beats a hasty retreat. "You'd better hurry and get to sleep."

Silence reverberates in his ears. The woman and the nature of her thoughts revolve kinetically in his mind. Had she been thinking the same thing he's been thinking and that's what has kept her awake? No! Don't think such things! — you ought to be horsewhipped! For shame!

Ordering a thought to vacate the brain has no effect against the brain's compulsion to entertain it, especially in the middle of the night when its owner is wide awake and has nothing else to do. Wukui's brain at this moment is particularly given to defiance. It takes the forbidden thought of the woman and wines it and dines it and invites it into deeper, inner chambers. This evening, it now tells Wukui, she hadn't suggested they sleep on the same bed, but neither had she said that the two of them should sleep apart. Oh raptures! It's true then: Already she regards him as the closest person to her. Bring on the mosquitoes, then! There's smoke over there and they'll come swarming over — lucky he didn't light a fumigation fire on this side. A spot on his face starts burning and itching — ah, yes, there's one biting now. Maybe it's just bitten her over there on the other side, and now it's biting him; so though the two of them are apart, their blood is mingled together in its stomach — so bite away! Wouldn't it be great if he could turn into a mosquito? Then he could fly over and land on her face and bite her — of course he wouldn't hurt — and wouldn't it be wonderful? Or maybe she could turn into a mosquito and come over here, and no matter how hard she would bite and no matter how much it would sting, it would be all right — even if it was a poisonous bite, even if it gave him malaria — he'd be the happiest man alive!

When the sky fluoresces pale, he emerges from his retreat with his face smothered in little red bumps.

He announces he's going down the mountain. This elicits tears. He coaxes her with assurances that he'll return very soon. She says, "I'm not crying for myself; it's that, well ... I'm this half-dead ... thing that's causing you a lot of trouble!"

She pulls a decorative hairpin from her hair and removes a silver bracelet from her wrist and says he can exchange them somewhere for food and clothing. More tears — this time his. She kids him: "I've stopped crying, but now you're doing it — shame on you, you big strong man!"

He recovers his composure. His attention falls upon the wild peaches he gathered yesterday. One by one he wipes them clean and puts them on her bed. He goes out the twig door, latching it behind him with a sturdy stick, calls out, "I'm leaving," and sets out on his way.

All the way down the mountain he trots, steering clear of Rooster Village and taking a shortcut to Slacker Flat to see the woman's father. He finds him at home moaning and groaning because, it turns out, the Lius have already sent someone to check whether the young mistress had been brought there on the sly. Wukui's story incenses him. He starts ranting and raving about how his daughter had been married off to the Lius and that was that, and whomever a woman married that was her fate, and anyway the Lius were so rich and powerful she would have enough to eat and drink all her life, and wasn't that good for her?

Wukui, not in the least edified, decamps in the middle of the tirade. The old man chases out the door after him imploring him to stop. "Where have you hidden her?" he asks.

"I can't tell you that."

"Well, if you're not telling, then forget it. She was born under an unlucky star, my daughter was, and she'll never have a happy life, and there's not a damn thing I can do about it. So ... at least take something back to eat with you."

He turns the pots and urns upside down, but finds nothing to eat. Desperate, he raids his emergency savings: From a crevice inside the flue of the *kang* he digs out several silver dollars and gives them to Wukui.

The afternoon finds Wukui in a good-sized town, where he converts the hairpin and the bracelet into silver money at the going rate and makes his essential purchases: food, a pot, dishes, oil, salt, and a big hoe.

It is thus that he makes a life for the two of them deep in the wilds of the mountain. He devotes part of each day to taming the land behind the temple, cultivating it and sowing seeds. Then he digs up bamboo roots, picks wild haws and gathers all manner of wild vegetables. These he cooks up into a vegetable-rice porridge. Every three to four days he chops down a tree or bundles up some bamboo, hefts this mountain bounty onto his shoulder, and hikes down to one town or another to sell. With the money he buys more provisions. As the days pass, things begin to look up for them.

Though the woman's face has lost its former bloom, her bubbling spirit more than makes up for it. Each day he carries her out and sets her up against a tree to watch him as he works the land. Her very presence bouys him and charges him with energy when he otherwise would be dropping with fatigue. She glories in this fact. The physical damage that bars her from helping recedes in importance before the value of her moral support, reflected precisely in those things she does well. She chatters on endlessly to entertain him. She sings for him. Her hair, every bit the crowning glory attributed to the female sex, she fashions into every coiffure she can possibly conceive, using the new comb he bought for her. She has him pass judgement on the beauty of each one. He says, "No matter which way you comb it, you are beautiful."

He picks a flower for further adornment. She tells him to approach and add the embellishment himself.

He's abashed. He demures.

She pouts. She gets mad.

She lowers her head and ignores him vehemently.

He's trapped in his unsophistication. He's squatting there looking at her stubborn lowered head and doesn't know what to do. Just then, she looks up...

"Gee!" he breathes, "even when you're angry you're beautiful!"

Still she pouts.

He says, "You're not happy. I know — I'll turn a somersault for you, how about that?" He turns a chain of five somersaults. In spite of herself, she bursts out laughing.

One balmy day when he is excavating the earth to expand the garden, she calls out to him from her perch on the ground: "Brother Wukui, you should rest for a while!"

"I'm not tired."

"I want you to come here."

When he comes, she loosens her hair and allows it to float freely about her head. She rolls her high collar in, exposing her long slender white neck. "Part my hair for me," she says.

To decline would be gauche, a lesson well learned. He squats down behind her and begins to part her hair. It's soft, clean, shiny, silkening voluptuously through his fingers. His heart begins to thump.

"How's my hair?" she asks.

"It's ... it's ... very good."

"How good is it?"

He can not say. His eye is drawn to the nape of her neck, right at the gossamer featherly sculpted hairline that is always concealed, and then to the mellow fullness of the creamy-smooth neck itself. Still onward his imagination roves to where the unfastened collar exposes her throat and the little depression at the base of it, and then onward and ever downward toward that realm of gently swelling tumulosity. Her downy-soft hair catches the sunlight and scatters it into a halo — and he thinks of how that thing even further down must be springy to the touch and emanating a fragrance unimaginably sweet.

His entire body begins to tremble. The more he tries to control it, the more violently he shakes. The tremors transfer through the hair he's holding to the center of her sensibility.

"Are you cold?" she asks.

"No." He stands up. He is bathed in sweat. He comments on the glorious weather and sits down to the side. He occupies himself with picking the wax out of his ears.

This earwax picking is an invention of his, a self-administered therapy for jangled nerves and flare-ups of his own deep fires. Especially when he's afraid the woman will notice a certain intransigent and tell-tale bulge in that sartorial handiwork of hers does he discover his ears are in need of a major excavation, because it requires sitting, and if he's sitting her attention will be directed elsewhere.

He didn't expect that she would say, "So clumsy you are! Here, let me do it for you."

He declines. He'd rather do it himself.

She reaches out, grabs his ear, pulls him to her. She picks and picks. She has him move in closer. She has him lay his head on her bosom — to get a better angle, you know.

He sinks into another dimension as he sinks upon her bosom, all other reality dizzily receding just beyond his rational grasp. Hot gentle waves of fragrance inundate his senses. Right before his eye, up close and in focus, the sweetly plump hills covered unconvincingly with fabric blossom with two turgid little protrusions. He is deeply chagrined. All the rocks and all the trees around them suddenly seem like people staring at him. The ear getting picked glows as red as a hot coal.

"Okay, all done," he says as he pushes away her hands, extricating his head from her ministrations.

Her face turns crimson. She wants to tell him something but thinks better of it. She pretends to watch a pheasant spraying its colours through the woods as it flies unerringly among the trees. A soft yet unmistakable, eloquently protracted sigh whispers the secret of her languishing soul.

He discerns in this sigh the sign that they're long overdue for a change of subject. No time for consideration, he opens his mouth and out spill words and sentences and paragraphs that resurrect the scenes of the past, the old days when he had carried her as a bride. Drawn into his dreamy recollection, she suddenly blurts out, "Tang Jing was, after all, not a bad guy."

"Yes, that's true," he says reflectively, "he didn't seem like the bandit type."

"But why did he become a bandit then?"

This is the beginning of a series of conversations about the bandit that occurs in the ensuing days, almost always initiated by her. He surmises her praise for Tang Jing arises from a comparison that finds the young master sorely wanting. And he certainly can't take her to task for her judgement, for Tang Jing is undeniably a remarkable personage who's taken the world by storm and whom government officials don't dare provoke. Still, that face of his is just too pretty, and not only that, he was fooled by Wukui with just a few lies. It had been remotely possible that he would have released Wukui himself. But that he released the woman as well without touching her is just too ... incongruous. Though they bandy Tang Jing's name about like this, her interest in the bandit is conspicuous and remains unabated. This strikes him as odd, for in their isolation, the bandit is little more than a chimera, something very remote from them. Lying at the root of her fascination, he concludes, can only be one thing: loneliness. Cut off from civilisation like this, she must really ache for companionship, especially when he goes down the mountain to replenish their supplies or up the mountain to cut firewood and pick mushrooms, while she has to stay locked up in the grass hut for hours on end, unable to move and with no one to talk to.

For this reason, the next time he goes down the mountain, he brings back with him a dog.

It's a very beautiful dog with a tail that curls up and is so long it can touch his head. His yellow fur shines like gold while above each eye there hovers a round white dot. The woman names him Four Eyes.

Four Eyes, it turns out, is a high-strung, demented animal that tears and careens madly and mindlessly about. Afraid he'll run off somewhere and get lost, Wukui ties him to a rock, thus corking up an impetuous energy that explodes at the slightest provocation. The wind blowing through the trees sets him upon bouts of crazed barking as he jumps and leaps about yanking violently and vainly at the unyielding rope.

The woman unties him. She pulls him to her side and strokes his velvety ears and long luxuriant fur. She croons to him, "Four Eyes, Four Eyes."

No longer does Four Eyes thrash about hyperactively. Whenever she calls to him in that special high-pitched voice, he comes running. Even if he's already gone off with Wukui into the forest, he comes shooting back to her like lightning, tail irrepressibly wagging. When Wukui comes back from his labours, he more often than not finds the dog lying by her side just like a child, listening to her talk to him. He seems to understand everything she says to him. And she, expressing a newfound joy, laughs a sparkling laugh.

Wukui, inspired by this display, says, "Look at that! Four Eyes is just like a person."

"Yes, you're right. Four Eyes is just as a human. He has human sensibilities. He not only understands what I say, he can even guess what I'm thinking."

She pats the dog's head: "Go on, your daddy's back, go fetch him a cushion."

And Four Eyes does indeed fetch a grass-woven cushion and take it to Wukui.

Wukui says, rather disgruntled, "How can I be a dog's father?"

"Didn't you just say Four Eyes is like a person?"

"Then what are you to Four Eyes?"

"I'm Four Eyes' mother."

"Don't talk nonsense."

Uh oh. Mistake. Her tongue flicks out from between her teeth telling of her chagrin. Anything else she might have to say chokes on the embarrassment. But she keeps looking at Wukui, and Wukui keeps looking at her. Four Eyes, standing between them, raises his head to look at one and then the other. Finally he lets loose a bark — directed at Wukui.

This restores her power of speech. "Four Eyes is on my side," she crows. She calls the dog to her and hugs him to her breast. His golden tail wraps around her neck like a scarf.

No longer is she lonely. But now Wukui has something else to worry about: She's getting thinner day by day. In spite of his efforts to feed her properly. He always gives her the thicker portion of the rice and vegetable porridge, the part closer to the bottom of the pot, but she doesn't seem to appreciate it. Not really. She's always saying something like, "If the vegetables were stir-fried, this would really be tasty!" So these days, it seems he's in a state of perpetual disconcertion. Especially when he thinks of the fact that she never had to eat this kind of thin and watery fare at the Lius. He could never be the equal of the Lius in this regard, no matter how hard he tried.

Where is this all leading to? he wonders; what will become of her if they continue on like this? He'd rescued her way back when so she could enjoy the life she deserved, but now look at her — this is enjoyment? How many times when he's come back has he found she's been crying? Only she's been hiding it — she hears him coming and she wipes away the tears and puts on a smiling face for him to look at. She must be looking into the future and seeing nothing but a big yawning black hole. And then there's that Tang Jing — she's always bringing him up, as if ... as if.... Ah ... yes ... maybe that was a big mistake too — so you thought you were heroic, eh? Rescuing her like that? Rescue — ha! If only ... if only Tang

Jing would suddenly appear and kidnap her again! Yes! Maybe he's a bandit, maybe he's got the worst reputation in the world; but in comparison to you Wukui — a down and dirty bride carrier was all you were. You've got no money, no prestige and no military accomplishments. You can't even begin to touch the bottom of Tang Jing's shoes.

This is precisely the reason why he stands aloof from her, why he suppresses his own desire on that front. Tang Jing, bandit or no, is such a handsome man, and he's made his mark, and he's well-supplied with the material goods of life... Okay, then, since I love her and want to be nice to her, we'll just hide here for a while longer until the Lius have given up the hunt and things have quieted down. Then I'll take her to White Wind Village. I'll say I'm her elder brother and want to marry her off to Tang Jing. If he still thinks she's a white tiger star, I'll just tell him the truth and take what I've got coming. And if he quibbles about her being paralysed, well, that's easy, I'll just say she's a sleeping beauty, and where else in the world could he find such a beautiful woman? And besides, she's got a heart like an angel, and could there be another like her on the earth?

He keeps these thoughts to himself as he intensifies his labours. Now when he takes wood and bamboo down to the town market, he indulges less in food and drink so he can place more tasty treats before her. And while he's at it he makes discreet inquiries as to what's going on in Rooster Village and the news from White Wind Village.

His hard work begins to pay off — or perhaps it's the beneficence of a Heaven that has decided to smile upon them. At any rate, the mountain spirit temple looks more and more like a home furnished with the proper amenities. And the dewy rosiness returns to the woman's cheeks. At noontime he carries her out into the warm salubrious sunshine and sets her upon the lawn in front of the temple. He notes with satisfaction that her figure has retrieved the curvaceousness of that day when he'd carried her as a bride. Indeed, her swelling bosom is even fuller than before.

He by contrast has become pinched and dark, like a piece of scorched firewood. His mouth and nose and the whites of his eyes dominate his face. But he is happier. Decidedly happier — and pleased with himself. He feels himself a paragon of virtue, purged of all fleshly desires, marred not by a scintilla of selfishness nor the harbouring of an ounce of diabolic intent. Everything he does seems to glow with grandiosity, as if he's bestowing a moon upon the night or polishing up a fat red sun to confer upon the day.

For the first time in his life he calls her "Little Sister". Now he can part her hair without his body playing those nasty little tricks on him. He warms water for her and washes her hair, washes her neck, washes her feet. He vows that come the day when he can take her down the mountain, he will buy back her hairpin and her silver bracelet that he had sold so cheaply.

Winter dresses the landscape in white. Wukui builds a fire inside the shelter and goes off into the mountain to bag some ledge pheasants for dinner. His lack of gun or bow and arrow is not an impediment for he has figured out the habits and nature of the ledge pheasant and knows how to acquire these delectable birds bare-handed. He drops down into a ravine and ascending a slope, he now discovers in a sparsely wooded gully ten or so of the birds huddled upon a low, windward ledge. He scrambles over the rocks to the centre of the gully, picks up a stone and throws it at the ledge with a shout. The startled birds flap over to the opposite ledge on his right — ledge pheasants can fly neither high nor far — and they plop themselves heavily upon that narrow foothold. He repeats his stone-throwing and shouting, and the pheasants fly back to the left ledge. The clumsy birds, who can only lumber back and forth between the two ledges, do just that, over and over again, under the pressure of his relentlessly hurtling stones and his unabating shouts. Finally, three of four of them stop flying in mid-air and plummet like rocks to the bottom of the gully, dead from exhaustion.

He collects his booty and makes his way back, singing at the top of his lungs. On the final approach to the mountain spirit temple, he cuts off his song. He wants to surprise the woman. He can just see it now — he'll appear right when she's least expecting it, then whip the nice fat pheasants out from behind his back. And she'll be amazed and ask how on earth he'd managed to get so many. Then he, Big Brother Wukui, will put the water on to boil and pluck the birds and prepare the meat all the while recounting his exploits and how he had used cunning and skill, and of course he'll embellish a little bit here and magnify a little bit there and really lay it on thick, all to see the stars glittering and popping in her eyes.

However, when he draws near the shelter, he finds it

unusually, almost eerily still. Even Four Eyes doesn't come bounding over to greet him. Well, he'd planned to restrain his excitement anyway, and no matter what, he's still in that playful mood. He takes a mischievous peek through the cracks of the twig door.

This peek freezes him to the spot.

The woman is still asleep under the quilt. The dog is under there with her keeping her warm. So faithful is Four Eyes to his mistress, even warming her ears with a paw on either side of her head. Wukui never ceases to be amazed at how devoted this dog is to her. But wait — isn't that a movement? He looks more closely — and suddenly realises...

He bends down to pick up his hatchet, half buried in snow where he'd left it on the stoop. But it's frozen solid to the ground. He hesitates. Just as well, he thinks. He moves away from the door with deliberate steps and makes his way silently around to the back of the shelter. He begins coughing loudly and stamping his feet in the snow, as if he'd just returned from his expedition.

In the afternoon, after he cooks the pheasants, and the two of them have taken their usual repast, he announces he's going out to the back mountain to gather firewood. In fact he goes out to sit by himself in the snow and spill his grief into the barren white waste. He feels bruised. He feels mauled. The sight had been the cruellest of blows. Never had he imagined, not even in his most disgraceful of dreams, that she was capable of doing that. Good grief! Maybe there's something wrong with his eyes, maybe they're going bad. Yes, that must be it, he's getting near-sighted. Hadn't she risked her life to get away from Young

Master Liu's violations? And such being the case, how could she possibly do it with a dog? No way! — there's just no way!

His mind explodes as he strains for explanations, but nothing erases that nightmarish image, that expression of ecstasy on her face, her earnest unaccidental embrace.

Is she, then a lascivious female — one helplessly born to it! But if that were true, then why had she thrown herself into the jaws of death to come and beg his help to escape?

Every supposition leads to an impasse. He turns to combing over all their interactions, especially during their days in the temple. She had made many overt indications to him, and he'd have to be made of stone not to have been tempted. But he was all too cognizant of his status. He was even more cognizant — and fearful — of the guilt that would eat at him forever were the help he gave her to become self-interested. Could it be that his own self-discipline — the dire necessity of keeping a cold wall between them — had driven her to desperation? But even so, still, how could she have sunk this low?

In the depth of his anguish he questions — he demands — over and over how such a thing can be. He is devastated, his conceptions of women demolished. He, Wukui, who had prided himself on being the man most understanding of women, writhes in the grim truth that he understands them not at all — what, at the base of it, they are, what exactly makes a woman a woman. What before was perfectly clear has now become hopelessly enshrouded in mystery.

Finally, he comes to a conclusion: The source of this

abomination lies with the dog. Four Eyes — progenitor of evil and fountainhead of damnation! He had felt from the beginning this dog was different, and those dots above his eyes seemed to confirm it — that's why he had bought him in the first place. Now he knows just how different he is; he's not really a dog at all — he's a transmogrified spirit! No wonder he's got that extraordinary ability to understand people. No wonder he's so anomalously attached to the woman. He's bewitched her, that's what he's done. He mesmerises her, and while she's in a defenceless daze, he...

Wukui raises his fists and slams them repeatedly against himself. You idiot! You total screw-up! Who bought the dog and brought him here? — You! You! How many times already have you brought her pain and sorrow? And now you've done it again! — you've ruined her body, you've defiled her chastity, and now her moral character — her very soul — rests on the brink of eternal damnation, all because of you!

Gnashing his teeth he leaps to his feet. He'll go back right now and chop up that evil dog with his hatchet.

Between the crying ground and the grass hut, however, he has time to examine his options. It occurs to him that should he commit a bloody assassination upon the animal right before her eyes, the shock would be too great for her. Of course, he could pull the dog out of the shelter and execute him elsewhere, but if she should ask what happened to her pet, what would he say? Furthermore, if he does not rationally reveal to her the dog's iniquitous reality, and if she does not examine herself and show contrition for her error, then would he not have failed in his duty as an elder brother to cherish and protect her?

Three days later, the sun has munched holes into the silver-white cloak overlaying the land, exposing patches of black earth and entangled vegetation. He says, "Little Sister, the sun is really fine today. Let me take you out to have a look."

She agrees: "It's been very oppressive being snowed in all this time."

He carries her out and leads Four Eyes out as well. He takes them both to the edge of a chasm of vertiginous depth. Spanning this chasm are two bamboo poles. He sets the woman down on a pile of dry grass.

"Little Sister, this is really a wonderful place."

"What's so wonderful about it?"

"Look at how big the icicles are over on the other side of the chasm. Let's have Four Eyes cross over and bring one back, and we can hold it up to the sun and look at the beautiful colours."

He ties a rope around the dog's neck. The other end he forms into a loop, which he slips over the end of one of the bamboo poles. He points out to Four Eyes the icicles on the other side of the chasm and leads him to the poles. Four Eyes balks at the edge. Wukui pushes, but the dog won't budge. He appeals to the woman to tell Four Eyes to go forward.

"Go ahead, Four Eyes," she says to the dog in reassuring tones. "Don't be afraid. You can make it!"

As Wukui stabilises the poles with his hands, Four Eyes steps upon them and treads unsteadily across to

The Regrets of a Bride Carrier 303

the centre. The loop follows along with him. Suddenly Wukui separates the poles and Four Eyes goes hurtling down. The rope that arrests his fall tightens around his neck. He yelps and thrashes his legs in midair.

"Quick! Quick!" the woman shrieks. "Pull the rope over!"

Wukui, stock still, makes no indication he's heard her.

Four Eyes can no longer yelp. He stares at the woman with red pleading eyes.

"Brother Wukui! Please! Four Eyes will die!"

"This dog's a curse!" Wukui's voice rumbles ominously. "He must die!"

"Oh." A rush of understanding. A pregnant silence ... lengthening, lengthening. Wukui's breath knots in his throat. The world itself seems suspended in abeyance.

The woman speaks, in a voice that brushes the bottom of a remote abyss: "Wukui ... you've brought me out here just to see this?"

"No ... no! That's not the way it is." His denial can not disguise his agony. "Look over there on the other side — see how the branches are covered with ice? — see how the sun makes them look like jade? — see Little Sister?"

His heart is pounding. His voice is wavering. Not once does he turn his head to look at her — he's loathe to witness her moment of shame. Inwardly he's saying to her: "Forgive me, my good little sister, but I have to do this! You are a young mistress, you are my little sister. No! — you are a woman as holy and pure as an angel — so how could I ever hurt you?"

He hears a noise like the cracking of icicles. He looks up at the opposite side of the chasm. It's still scintillating in the sunlight, the icicles exactly as before.

He turns his head back — and discovers that the woman has dragged herself to the edge of the chasm. She is gouging her face with her fingernails. The gashes are deep and red.

He cries out in alarm and rushes over. Before he can grab her, she flings up her arms and topples backward into the chasm...

One year later, the grass hut in the mountain spirit temple has expanded into a mini-stronghold of multiple rooms, home to a small horde of bandits. Though this brotherhood of brigands is dwarfed by Tang Jing's veritable army in White Wind Village, its ruthlessness is unparalleled, its ferocity already the stuff of legends. With precious little interval between plunderous raids, these bandits come sweeping down from the mountain unencumbered with scruple or taboo; in all directions, everyone is their potential victim. Already they've kidnapped eleven women to be their wives. Wanted posters are plastered everywhere, the main street of the county seat bristles with them, they overlay the entryways to all villages in the vicinity. But heading the list of wanted men is not the notorious Tang Jing. Instead emblazoned across the top are the bold characters that scream: Wukui.

Translated by Josephine A. Matthews

The Monk King of Tiger Mountain

THE sun had spines that day. Like a balled-up porcupine it rolled across the sky, its light as bright and piercing as quills. The clouds bled red under its blazing brilliance. Billows of dust rose from the scorched earth like the residue of ashes from a defunct inferno. Upon Tiger Road a multitude of scuffing feet plowed through the dry dust in a cloud of exhaustion. These were bandits, warriors, though the scraggly column of men showed not one hint of prowess: to shove one man in the back of the knee would launch a toppling chain-reaction of collapse. There they would lie, embracing the dust, as if never to rise again.

The march had begun amid a soaring sense of accomplishment. The drum and bugle corps had set the pace with mercurial merriment, the horses were spirited, the men strutting their way in neat formation. Now the buglers' eyes bulged large with their final efforts, the fiery air stinging in their nostrils. The horn-blowers' cheeks strained, the veins of their thick necks squirmed fat and grotesque, yet the notes sounded grew ever fainter. Laboriously they wound down to a last desperate gasp. There was one that held out, a little private obstinate in the face of the inevitable, whose last defiant if wheezing "toot" impaled the ponderous silence.

They could hardly have been more disparate this

motley assemblage, wildly differing in age and dress. These were territorial bandits, vagrant and volatile the mood of their more recent lives, whose experiences were etched into their countenances, and now made all the more hideous and savage in the aftermath of a gruesome engagement. Victory had unleashed a frenzied rejoicing that resounded along the route of their return to home base until that vicious sun sapped the last of their energy. Still, they could appreciate the hilarity of that horn's last wail, its solitary swan-toot. Their faces wrinkled up into laughter, though not a sound issued from their lips. Barely had their amused aspects redrooped into the contours of fatigue when a convulsive burst of helpless mirth rent the air, drawing each soldier's open-mouthed attention toward the direction of its source.

The man from whom this eruction of humour emanated sat astride a silver-maned steed. Bai Lang was the unrivalled sovereign of Wolf Fang Peak, the archbrigand of a generation, revered among men, and now a prisoner of war. His head and hands were encased in a cangue, his body was swathed in ropes, he yet repudiated captivity with his ringing, unchainable voice. The row of round blue scars seared into his bald pate glinted in the sun as he rocked back and forth in laughter. These twelve marks — or perhaps there were twenty, the exact number was none too clear — signified initiation into Buddhist monkhood. It was possible that some of the marks were actually blood blisters raised by the sun. Sweat rolled off his face and plopped onto the saddle and from the saddle it splashed to the earth, raising little spectres of dust.

This torrent of amusement effected a commotion as it

floated over the ranks, striking each man's heart with dread and impressing upon them that this man with the delicate, even feminine features and the clear tenor laugh was not to be underestimated—nor misunderstood. With seven ropes they had taken him at dawn, a manoeuver calculated upon his state of inebriation. The dogface charged with binding his feet hadn't been quite quick enough or deft enough and succumbed to misfortune when he mistook the alabaster face and the branded, silken-smooth bald head for the aspects of a nun from the Buddhist convent. Unwittingly his fingers rose and pinched the cheek of this lovely vision — and Bai Lang's foot lashed out and struck him such a blow in the groin that the soldier fell to the ground and promptly expired. Oh, the stories were rife about the martial exploits of Bai Lang. Each time he locked horns with government forces, so they said, he would inevitably find himself rushed by laciviously leering men. Unperturbed, he would stand there, playfully tossing his handgun up and down as if it were no more than a spoon. Then he would raise his hand and, without even appearing to take aim, shout, "Left eye!" and the designated eye of the adversary would become an empty socket, as neat as if pecked clean by a crow, and all at a distance of a good hundred yards. Chuckling, he would amble over to the body, slice open the crotch of the dead man's pants, cut off the "family jewels", prize open the corpse's mouth, and stuff them in. It was thus that these soldiers had good reason to be nervous, and their hands flew mechanically to the hilts of the knives fastened at their waists. The litter carriers were seized with anxiety as well and their knees locked up making them jolt down from a rock embedded in the road, nearly spilling Heilaoqi into the dust.

"What's going on?" Heilaoqi opened sleep-locked eyes that registered fiery displeasure.

"Reporting, sir! He's been laughing!" One of the litter carriers pointed at Bai Lang.

The sound of laughter had indeed vaguely insinuated itself into Heilaoqi's dream. He turned his head for a look and noted that Bai Lang's face was still bathed in the afterglow of his great galloping guffaw, in contrast to his own men's abject consternation. The disgrace of their fear propelled him into rage. "All right, right, you punk monk," he roared, "what's — so — funny? You think you're sitting in your armed camp on Wolf Fang Peak, surrounded by all your flunkies?"

Bai Lang scrutinised Heilaoqi and said, "How astute you are: if indeed I were on Wolf Fang Peak, then I would be laughing now, wouldn't I?" He burst into a second round of unabashed merriment.

Heilaoqi's fury heightened to thunderous proportions: "You are in my custory now. You are my prisoner! And don't you forget it!"

"Then may I suggest that you enjoy your fortune and indulge in a good laugh?" Bai Lang said. "I've never once seen Boss Hei even crack a smile! Why, I remember that den in Seven Stars where you were really going at it, flinging the dice for all you were worth. Tsk, tsk, lost all your chips, didn't you? And you wouldn't pay up. Tsk, tsk, tsk. The creditor tried to discuss it with you, but you wouldn't open your mouth. That smack across your face was meant to loosen your lips up a bit, but it made you cough up, didn't it? You weren't laughing then — not a peep. Oh, no. Then you became a Big Boss, got yourself a tidy little mountain stronghold and came traipsing around to Wolf Fang Peak bringing me your tributes. I didn't treat you so good, did I, making you sit on that cold wood stump. You didn't laugh then, no indeed. And then when I passed out the cigarettes and didn't give you any, why, I never saw such a stony face. So, now, here we are — you're having a taste of good, sweet revenge for that stump and those cigarettes. Really, you ought to savour your accomplishment and have yourself a really good laugh, don't you think?''

Bai Lang spoke in a crisp, clear and tranquil timbre, his beautiful eyes sparkled with eloquent vivacity, his mild countenance radiated complaisance and bemusement. After dealing out this piece of advice he cocked his head to the side and eyed the youthful hornblower who'd rendered that last lingering musical blurt. He appreciated that lad's sense of humour, manifested further in his inventive headgear, which consisted of a band of dried osiers and peppermint leaves plastered to his forehead. He winked at the fellow. The youth for his part had absorbed Bai Lang's speech with a quiet contemplation that quite dissolved his image of him as Bai Lang the Terrible and convinced him of the monk king's amiable and salutary disposition. He knew well what Bai Lang was speaking about, from the feast that this, the fiercest of the twelve Tiger Mountain kings, had thrown in celebration of his victory over the government in wresting Salt Lake from its control. The youth, his fellow retainers and their chief had been the first to arrive on Wolf

Fang Peak, only to find themselves obliged to wait for the other ten mountain masters. Upon their arrival, each was shown to a round-backed armchair covered with bearskins. All, that is, except their own chief Heilaoqi, who'd been relegated to a wooden stump.

Bai Lang had burst upon the world with military eclat, the first to raise the flag of sovereignty upon Tiger Mountain, the sole and unaided conqueror of Salt Lake, acclaimed by one and all as the king of kings. Yet when he hosted that gathering of mountain masters, he was garbed in a dragon-embroidered robe of white, shod in thick-soled white shoes, and held a bamboo fan made of white damask. He was as immaculate as he was impressive and solemn. Indeed, the more he endeavoured to present an image of the unconventional scholar steeped in simple elegance, the more the world rhapsodised about the celestial genius who had created this dually virtuous man, the epitome not merely of martial brilliance but of physical beauty as well. His hearty laughter rang out then as now, even as he failed to return the courtesies of his guests and neglected to supply the standard amenities of proper entertainment: no smoking paraphernalia, no apportionment of the nirvanic opiate to quell the legion cravings. There was something new and different, he'd announced in sonorous tones, which he'd appropriated from the stores of the Salt Superintendent and which he now wished to share with each of them: cigarettes. The mountain masters had heard of these things called cigarettes, though they had never laid eyes on the new-fangled indulgence, let alone tried it and their eyes grew large in expectation. The chief of Wolf Fang Peak did not descend from his lofty stone dais, rather, he raised his hand, and the air was filled with streaking white lines that arced down to the tables below, whereupon each of the guests discovered planted before him one, and then two, paper-encased tobacco sticks rolled to precise uniformity end to end. Of the eleven mountain masters in attendance, ten rose to their feet and cupped one hand in the other before their chests in a dignified gesture of appreciation. Heilaoqi alone remained seated upon his stump, for his table was destitute of cigarettes. His fleshy face, shining under an oily film of perspiration, went from red to white, and from white to black as he collected a wad of saliva in his mouth and spat it out. The gobbet of sputum contained a tooth, a casualty of his gnashing indignation. The young horn-blower recalling this scene marvelled at how captivity had failed to erode Bai Lang's majesterial pride or diminish the magnitude of his charismatic presence. This was the incarnation of a real hero, one to emulate for all those who would be men. With this epiphanous thought, he winked back at the pale-skinned monk who loomed before him on horseback.

Heilaoqi noticed this intercourse between the two. He bellowed at the youth to step before the litter and gave him a violent box upon the ear, whilst barking out the orders: "Pull those ropes tight! I want to hear those drums and horns and I want to hear them loud! Let all those puny potentates on Tiger Mountain see just who is the king of kings!"

The four soldiers stationed on either side of the silver-maned horse threw their weight upon the ropes binding the prisoner's body, drawing them considerably tighter, so that even if he could surreptitiously spur the horse to bolt, Bai Lang would be slammed to the ground just as surely as if the ropes were attached to stone tampers. He was immediately set solidly on the back of the horse, the slightest leeway for movement now firmly denied.

The contingent of troops moved onward. Bai Lang sitting ramrod straight, had been moved into the center of the column as a precaution, and towered above it from his equine perch. Passing over the highest ridge of Tiger Mountain, the formation stood out in stark silhouette against the firey red hues in the sky. To the mountain people who lived sprinkled throughout the valley below, and to the brigands keeping watch on the stone or wooden battlements of their more distant forts, the commander of the troops appeared to be the chief of Wolf Fang Peak and not Heilaoqi. Eventually, this was the impression that seized Bai Lang's imagination as well. For many years, he and his tight-knit gang had scoured every inch and trod every stone of every valley for thirty-five miles around, slaughtering evil despots and carrying off their ill-gotten wealth. Once without warning, they had swept down upon a certain acquisitive official and pounded down his fancy double-knockered doors. Into the table top Bai Lang had stabbed his gleaming steel knife and watched as that lord and master carted his valuables out from behind his false walls and up from his cellar. They had snatched as well the scarlet headdress right off the master's head and peeled the tiny embroidered satin shoes off the feet of his concubines. Like celestial maidens strewing blossoms, they had scattered these personal items along with half the loot among the poor flanking the streets of the village.

What a thrilling exploit that had been! And then there was the time when dawn found them feasting beneath a restless, moiling sky, gorging on slabs of meat and guzzling bowls of wine, prelude to the raid of their lives. Bai Lang had led his men through the fortification's series of gates each swinging open in turn to his authoritative command. They marched out along the wall, down the hill and pounced upon the government's garrison of troops below. Through the congregation of barracks they sped with ruthless and irresistible deliberation, carving up men, hamstringing horses, and wantonly bathing themselves in a flow of acrid blood. With strings of twenty or thirty severed ears dangling from the tips of their knives, each man displayed back on the mountain slope the evidence of his prowess, and each man received the honour that accrued to him. How dazzlingly splendid, how utterly uplifting it had been, a matchless coup de main!

But to the magnificent spectacle of Tiger Mountain itself he had previously paid no heed, its powerful theatricality he had inexplicably ignored. Now as his horse advanced, myriad ascents and declivities performed an oceanic dance before his mesmerised eyes, a deep undulating liquidity that glowed red as an iron stove under the corrosive glare of the sun. Springs trickling through V-shaped ravines glared lustrously, like vivid rivulets of blood, evoking those slithering down the neck of Excellency Yao that day in Weijia Flat. Yes, it had been high noon then, just as now. The fabulously wealthy Excellency Yao was on the point of receiving a new concubine into his household and as the bridal sedan entered the gate, Bai Lang and his men slipped into the courtyard along with it.

Such a delicate beauty she was, the young lady in the sedan chair, truly the *crème de la crème*, and a shattering contrast to the toothless, dried-up bag of bones who intended to unite with her. Even he, Bai Lang, did not know why he had rushed upon the decaying old fossil and knocked him to the ground with one walloping slap. Then leaning down and grabbing a fistful of the old man's robe, he hauled him up and barked into his face his notice of the imminent transfer of his wealth. From the recesses of the sedan came a terrified shriek, drawing his attention just as the maiden within went into a dead faint. A wave of sympathy washed over him, and he bade his men, "Carry her into the rear boudoir!" Like a chicken pecking grain, old Excellency Yao abjectly knocked his head on the ground, all the while craftily signalling one of his own men to slip out and notify the government contingent in charge of local defence. Before he and his loyal men could touched the Yao treasure-trove, their lookouts at the village entryway were bloodying blades with the local guard. A visceral rage welled up in Bai Lang, an anger that ignited a pitiless extermination from which not one of the twelve Yao family members was spared. It was then that he had put his dagger to Excellency Yao's throat and sliced it with excruciating deliberation so that the blood trickled out and down like languorous red streams.

This poignant and orgastic image had lingered on in his mind's eye all these years, suffusing his dreams with an arousing intensity that would make him tremble.

With the massacre completed, the granaries were opened and the grain released into the hands of the people. Bai Lang was set for the triumphant return to his mountain fortress, when Liu Songlin, his sworn brother and second in command on Wolf Fang Peak, brought the little concubine out from the rear boudoir saying, "Brother, this one's for you!" Bai Lang regarded the maiden and discovered her beauty was indeed poetic; nonetheless he waved his hand and said, "Send her back to wherever she came from."

"What?" ejaculated Liu Songlin. "Then what was the point of sticking her in the boudoir? Okay, I forgot, you're a monk. You want to have nothing to do with women. In which case I'll take her!"

"The decision's already been made," Bai Lang retorted. "She's to go back home!"

Third in command was Lu Xinghuo, who now leaped forward and cried, "Take a look at this marvellous piece, would you? If we don't keep her for ourselves, then we can't have anybody else taking his pleasure either. I'll just open her up and be done with it!" and he ripped open the maiden's jacket, exposing an expanse of snowy flesh as smooth and fine as tallow. His impatient dagger was poised to split her from belly to breast when Bai Lang lofted a teapot and knocked the knife from his hand. He said, "We are brigands, that is true. But that doesn't mean we can go around gratuitously killing people. She's just a girl who's been forced to become a concubine by the Yaos. Since the relationship wasn't consummated, we can't treat her like a Yao!" He grabbed hold of Lu Xinghuo with one hand and led him outside.

This incident became a grudge that Liu Songlin and Lu Xinghuo held against Bai Lang over a period of years and led them to ridicule his principles regarding women. That is, not merely did he eschew marriage because he was a monk, already preposterous enough, but that he wouldn't visit violence upon a woman they claimed, because he looked like a beautiful woman himself! Nonetheless, no imagination would have been creative enough to envision that a few years hence it would be another altercation involving women that would bring an end to the great undertaking which these sworn brothers had so vehemently embraced, destroy a mighty military force, and bring down the inimitable Wolf Fang Peak!

Bai Lang shook his head to fling off the sweat that had collected on his brow and the vexation that had gathered in his heart. The monstrosity of colour ravishing Tiger Mountain under the perverse radiation of the sun had immersed him in dolorous memories of that young maiden and the lamentable ridicule heaped upon him by his own sworn brothers. He had never tried to hide his coenobitic origins, yet it didn't seem to strike them that his meticulously shaven head signified his pride — and his dispassion. To say that he wouldn't lay a hand on a woman because of his own feminine features was absurd! He could see back in the distant reaches of his mind that seven-year-old orphan, tiny little acolyte sequestered in the Monastery of Peace and Felicity. For ten years he pored over sacred texts under the cold, tranquil illumination of the oil lamp, his heart filled with the holy quest for Buddhist Nirvana. Then he discovered the abbot had installed a secret trap-door before the statue of Buddha which he would trip to have young women in the midst of their devotions fall into the dungeon below where they would be held in bondage, subject to his lacivious desires. Then he himself nearly became impaled upon that selfsame vile rod of flesh one evening after sutra recitation class at which point he had run out of the monastery bellowing deliriously to all and sundry of the evil within. As the villagers in their fury of abhorrence stormed the hallowed sanctuary and proceeded to reduce it to rubble, he slipped into that subterranean vault of iniquity and strangled the women confined there, putting them out of their misery; for the indignities of their imprisonment had destroyed irrevocably and forever their moral credibility, the *sine qua non* of their existence in society. Then he sank that abbot into the earth so that his head alone protruded above the surface and drove a horse hitched to an iron harrow over top, shredding the sex-fiend's brain. And that was how the Monastery of Peace and Felicity came to be known among the people as the Harrowed Head Monastery.

At that time, Bai Lang, had been all of eighteen years of age and suddenly found himself a wanted man to be seized and executed for the murder of blameless women, a charge devised by government officials bent upon avenging their friend the abbot's death. Thus forced to take to the hills, he embarked upon that furious anti-establishmentarian career which sent shock waves throughout the near world. None of this, however, could change the fact that he had taken his religious vows in earnest and had nurtured a devotion not to be compromised by the arbitrary whims of life's upheavals. "But you, Liu Songling, and you, Lu Xinghuo, what in Heaven's name have you done?" Bai Lang's eyes snapped shut in the wake of a surge of wrath.

The sun had by now reached its noontide perch. The shadows cast by man and beast had shrunk to virtually nothing, while the clamour of the drums and horns had died away again sometime during the haze of his retrospection. It was the sensation of something interfering with his stirrups, a persistent attempt to hang a bundle or something from them which brought Bai Lang back to the present. With each swish of the horse's tail these bundles would slip to the ground, and the sound of feet kicking them off to the side of the road would follow, intermixed with muttered curses. Pitiful were these soldiers charged with his transport. Each had started out with a bundle of plunder slung across his back, a silk gown and jacket, perhaps, or a pair of tiny satin slippers destined for mother, or a necklace, a turban, a copper basin, a pack of touch paper, or a teapot. To the sound of squabbling, the owner of a kicked item would retrieve his treasure, only to agonise again under its oppressive weight. Finally, staggering and dragging in exhaustion, he would gather the feeble remnants of his strength and swear, "Stupid idiot!" referring to himself, and "Rotten piece of junk!" reviling his cherished souvenir, which latter would receive an ignominious launch into the dust. This infectious disaffection spread like wildfire among the ranks, and soon a whole multitude of items was sailing through the air and falling forlornly to the earth. Only bags of silver coins were not discarded, each man tying his to his sweat-soaked belt, where they babbled the jangling, clinking language of cold hard cash. One determined soldier, however, retained his wine carafe, a delicately wrought artifact with its goose-neck spout and pinched waist, which jounced jauntily upon his cross-belt. His compatriots, galled that he should keep his loot when they had jettisoned theirs, pressed him to toss it away. This he protested vehemently, but in vain in the face of the majority against him. Finally he slammed it to the ground and stomped upon it, declaring, "If I can't have it, nobody can!" and with one kick he sent it flying into the rampant grass beyond the edge of the road.

The clanking, metallic impact of his vented grievance drew Bai Lang's gaze, which fell at once upon the object of the dispute. Though it had been shattered, Bai Lang recognised it as the vessel which had been used to fill his glass at Salt Lake. The idea of liquor sparked a craving for a deep draught of the voluptuous liquid. Its very bouquet was in his nose, a fragrance so heady, so redolent that he could swear it was real. Bai Lang swept his gaze over the convoy of soldiers and discovered no evidence of indulgence, only a portrait of desire as every head glued a pair of greedy, covetous eyes upon the occupant of the litter ahead. Heilaoqi, stripped to the waist exposing his hirsute chest, was drinking the aromatic contents of a calabash. He poured the liquor straight down his gullet, glugging inelegantly in thirst. One detail riveted Bai Lang's attention: those drops which clung to Heilaoqi's mustache and beard were red. Bai Lang blanched. For once in his life, he was visibly shaken. The scene inside Salt Lake's Trinity Temple returned vividly to his brain. He had ordered his men to relax, to live it up, to get steaming drunk, and in so doing, had inadvertently bestowed upon his former compatriot and now implacable enemy, Heilaoqi, the opportunity for surprise attack. He himself was drunk almost to the point of unconsciousness when one of his men reeled in to report that Heilaoqi's troops had surrounded the temple and killed a substantial number of Bai Lang's retinue. "What?" he'd had the presence of mind to exclaim, "are you drunk, too?" But Heilaoqi had already strode into his presence, and Bai Lang in his stupor was instantly bound with ropes and thrown to the floor. When he regained consciousness, Heilaoqi was clutching a human heart, crimson and dripping, and with his blade he was slicing it and trickling the drops of blood into the calabash, and the man who had come to warn Bai Lang of the attack was sprawled at his feet, chest a gaping cavern of gore...

As this scene flooded back to his mind, the horror vanquished Bai Lang's consuming thirst, and his eminent strength bowed to despondency. The very mountains themselves, those myriad age-old monoliths somehow became frail and insubstantial under the sun's incessant assault, turning into rising white wisps — like a clutch of diaphanous ribbons drifting off into the firmament. The boundless expanse of those awesome ranges, heaving up against the hazy horizion, made him sigh with sorrow, saturated with regret. Was that singular pinnacle jutting aloofly into the sky his own Wolf Fang Peak? He strained to pick out its distinctive features in the vaporous air. Yes, the vague form of his citadel's granite bulwark was still there, and so was the wooden lookout tower from which the surrounding strongholds could be observed and smoke signals sent. And there was the steadfast stone pagoda of the Temple of Heavenly Prime, rising majestically. Oh, such agony to think of it! He, Bai Lang, exalted luminary in a pantheon of heroes, unassailable Titan of righteousness for an entire decade, untouched by the burly arm of government authority, unscathed at the hands of ten mountain masters, each the consummate master of a singular and terrible martial art; he who held sway over them all, brought down from the heights of his splendour by the one whom he despised most, that contemptible knave who skulked behind the walls of Fort Pit, Heilaoqi. It was an ironic reversal of fortune, a betrayal made possible by the security that he Bai Lang had allowed the blackguard tenant of Fort Pit to install as he endeavoured to safeguard the entire range of Tiger Mountain. The searing torment of his indignation escalated, then dived into shattering grief.

Truly did he now rue the day he abandoned his citadel on Wolf Fang Peak in favour of Trinity Temple. A monumental mistake, that was, committed in the heady afterglow of his successful campaign against Salt Lake. Now he'd forfeited it all, from the start of his outlaw career when he'd absconded from Harrowed Head Monastery to his acquisition of a reputation that coursed throughout the realm, where everyone far and wide spoke in awe of a monk named Bai Lang. At first he'd been dismayed when his given name, Lang, which means "light", shifted in the popular mind into the lang that means "wolf", thus imposing upon him the sinister moniker, White Wolf, which usurped the original edifying nature of his name, that is, "White Light". Prompted by this development, he consulted an old woman adept in reading the Eight Character horoscope, who revealed to him that he couldn't hope for a more auspicious appellation than White Wolf and that if he wished to leave an enduring mark upon the world, he should occupy Wolf Fang Peak in the Tiger Mountains and consort with fortune; should he ever abandon the peak, he would certainly arouse the winds of calamity. And so according to the old fortune-teller's advice, he mounted Wolf Fang Peak and there pitched his camp. As she had predicted, everything he attempted he accomplished with facility. Furthermore, he found the environment to be exceptionally hospitable, for though the Temple of Heavenly Prime was in ruins, its pagoda still stood, creating an ambiance exquisitely suited to his spiritual sensibilities. For five hundred years this venerable ancient structure had tenaciously held its ground. Two hundred years previously an earthquake had split it in two. Then just at the time Bai Lang appeared to take residence, another earthquake struck, driving the two parts of the split pagoda back together again. The news of this miracle swept the countryside, spreading and consolidating his renown and sending his prestige soaring to incalculable heights. To look upon that pagoda was to be seized by a trembling that touched one's every fibre. Above his fortress he raised an enormous flag bearing the image of a white wolf's head and dressed his army, several thousand strong, in jackets emblazoned with the wolf's head insignia and rode enchanted wings of invincibility across the years and finally into victory at Salt Lake. The latter's enormous strategic advantage fired his ambitions. From Salt Lake he could drive the might of the government's forces further away from Tiger Mountain. In Salt Lake he could annihilate the tyranny of the Salt Superintendent and grant to the impoverished populace their rightful access to salt, both as a condiment and as a commodity.

Enamoured of these scintillating prospects, he forgot the old woman's exhortation and came down from the mountain to take up residence in Salt Lake, thus rendering himself vulnerable to Heilaoqi's treachery.

What was this Heilaoqi, anyway? Only a worm! A lowly, unworthy worm! The citadel of Wolf Fang Peak could never have been penetrated by the likes of him, even if Bai Lang, armed only with his trusty gun, had been its sole defender. Indeed, even in the alien confines of Trinity Temple, if he hadn't got drunk, or at least if he hadn't hung his gun up on that pillar, this Heilaoqi worm couldn't have touched him. Last night as he had lain bound in ropes, at that moment when he'd opened his eyes to the spectacle of Heilaoqi dissecting the heart of his loyal retainer, Trinity Temple had begun to shake, its door knockers rattled, its window paper split, and he sensed that they were about to be entombed together in the rubble of an earthquake. With what exquisite precision had Heaven timed its attack, and he'd laughed to think that Fate had favoured him with honour and revenge after all. But then, the earth settled down and everything returned to its normal state of equilibrium. Now from the back of his horse prisoner Bai Lang scanned the enduring form of the pagoda of the Temple of Heavenly Prime, and to his utter astonishment discovered it to be once again in halves, split saliently right down the middle nearly to its foundation and spearing the sky like giant twin swords. This, then, was the eloquent and compelling confirmation of the omen, an exclamatory rebuke of the fool who had forsaken Wolf Fang Peak. But — and this surely was significant — the pagoda hadn't fallen despite the severity and unprecedented depth of the split. Could this mean that the world had not yet seen the last of Bai Lang? Herein abided a gleam of redemption; a tonic to reinvigorate his battered spirit and lessen the burden of self-recrimination. Bai Lang silently swore his vengeance: "Heilaoqi, you wretched dog! What manner of man am I that you think you can destroy me? You may murder my men, rout my troops and empty the halls of Wolf Fang Citadel, but — and this I vow — as long as Bai Lang walks the earth, you will never know a moment's peace!"

The resurgence of his indomitable majesty revealed itself in a resurgence of pride. As his shoulders lifted and his spine straightened in an ardent display of dignity, the local inhabitants began to gather along the sides of the ridge-top highway and gawk. This was the formidable man whose sanguinary campaigns and stunning conquests had long fueled their passion for gossip and rumour, and suffused their minds with images brutal and terrifying. A savage fiend, they'd fancied him to be, and their nights would fill with trepidation at the bark of a dog, a warning, no doubt, of the demon in the vicinity. Murder most foul and unresolved became the grisly evidence of his handiwork, whilst the most malevolent and vindictive of curses rested upon the terror of his name; bawling children stopped instantly at the threat, "Bai Lang is coming!" Now the sensational news of the bandit's capture was sweeping through the population and propelling astonished and curious individuals to the roadside to witness his passage. Heedless of the soldiers' censorious shouts, they pressed forward insistantly, not to be denied their opportunity to lavish their eyes upon this ferocious and infamous super-bandit as he approached the moment of his execution. A mere glimpse, however, plunged them into disappointment, fed them doubt, and even provoked a measure of indignation.

"You mean he's the one who killed the Salt Superintendent? That puppy? He's not even dry behind the ears!"

"Well would you look at that, he's a goddamn monk!"

A woman's sharp-pitched voice sailed over the hubbub: "Look at that smooth forehead, that delicate nose, and those full, moist lips — a woman should be so lucky!"

"Oh, you don't say!" exclaimed an idler among the gawkers made jealous by her frivolous remarks. "Looks to me, Mrs Proprietress, like you're wishing to sleep with him!"

"And if I am — what's it to you?" the woman muttered, and she broke away from the crowd to stride alongside the horse and gaze up at Bai Lang. She pulled a wilted wild rose out of her hair, and when the horse happened to veer closer to her, she leaned over and tossed the rose up, hoping to hit Bai Lang's leg, or at least the horse's silver mane. But a soldier kicked her in the behind and sent her sprawling to the ground. Though Bai Lang could make out some of the comments coming from the crowd, he did not notice the woman nor the eyes she made at him as she stuck the tip of her tongue sensuously out between her lips. The wild rose, however, did enter upon his consciousness as it flashed before his eyes and fell to the ground. This act of adoration elicited Heilaoqi's gravelly bark: "Smear that face of his up! Get some mud and paint him up like a clown!" A dead silence fell over the crowd. No one dared to excavate a fistful of mud, let alone spread it on his face. Then suddenly from every which way there came a barrage of dust. Through eyes squinted into slits, Bai Lang surveyed the crowd. Both the soldiers and the lumpen loafers infesting the assemblage of onlookers were grabbing handfuls of dust and hurling it upon him. As the powdery dirt built up a crust upon his perspiring skin, only the woman sobbed for his plight, a wail that rose and floated above the commotion.

Bai Lang squeezed his eyelids tight against this humiliation and opened them again to the sight of a goshawk sweeping past, lustrous as if with the glow of a furnace. Having just pulled out of a power-dive, it now glided silently to a perch on a lofty cliff, where it took on the aspect of an inscrutable stump. With this hawk he felt a boundless sense of affinity, so that its very apparition caused him an agonising stab to the heart, a pain to rival the keenest of steel blades. Did this magnificent raptor mount the sky, its wings resplendent with the rosy radiance of dawn, to possess the airways and demolish the distance across that vast rugged expanse, that endless arpeggio of pinnacles and peaks, to its unfathomed destination? Did it scream its piercing battle cry and plummet from its mystic height to snatch a constrictor out of the grass, and did it climb again into the sky dome to drop the serpent to its death upon the rocks below? It now sat upon that lugubrious cliff, driven out of the sky by the pitiless waves of heat. And if it were to be injured and fall to the loathesome depths of the valley, how the hares would torment it, and how the ants would swarm upon its helpless mangled body! Just so, those curiosity-seekers who'd ardently joined the campaign to plaster Bai Lang's face with dust were now tagging along with the moving column of troops, gleefully raining mockery down on him: "King Bai Lang! King Bai Lang!" Insufferable anguish struck him, and yet a miraculous resilience of spirit tide bouyed him up until his heart became suffused with a sense of beatitude. He thought: these people are in fact not intent upon mortifying me. What they see before them in Bai Lang's sweat and dust encrusted face is the ferocious leonine image they'd expected to see in Bai Lang, the hero, insolent destroyer and intrepid defier of the Absolute — and this gives them enormous satisfaction. And he was absolutely right. To the command of his awe-enforcing war-machine that thundered down the mountain and poured with deadly savagery into government military camps, Liu Songlin and Lu Xinghuo had constantly entreated him to add the terrifying potency of a bizarre and hideous mask. Amidst the rise and fall, echoing and re-echoing waves of mockery, Bai Lang held his head even higher.

Eventually Heilaoqi ordered his men to drive the onlookers off. With no audience to goad them on, the troops once again became taciturn. The sound of desperate gaspings for breath once more rose from the ranks, mingled with the clink and jangle of their moneybags, and was rounded off with the effervescent whirr of cicadas ensconced in stunted, perishing trees. Searing, desiccating, the sun beat down until the men were delirious with dehydration and dreamed of nothing more than sinking into permanent sleep. As they watched their chief swig the calabash of bloody wine, someone cried out, "Look! Apricots! A grove of apricots!" Serried ranks of widened eyes and gaping mouths searched the distance. Despairing interrogatives punctured the air: "Where? Where?" "Up there. Just ahead." The idea of thirst-quenching apricots quickened their pace despite the fact that Tiger Mountain was bereft of apricot groves, and despite the fact that even if there was a whole swath of apricot groves, the fruit was out of season in July. The befuddled soldiers retrieved their senses after chewing up some three hundred yards of road, at which point they turned upon the hapless hallucinator and showered him with abuse. Several hotheads lay acrimonious hands and feet upon him, setting off a rash of violence that drew the body of soldiers into one or another of three or four separate brawls. Ad hoc willow-branch headgear, leaves long wilted in the heat, were flung to the ground. Fists landed unceremoniously upon chins, blood and broken teeth splattered upon the ground, and the moneybags fastened to the belts of the weak shifted to the belts of the strong. Just as like an ass taking an exhilarating roll in the dust, this flare-up of fisticuffs — the drawing of blood, and the forcible gains — wiped away their fatigue and restored their vigour. Heilaoqi saw no reason for reprimand; indeed, he looked upon this altercation with an air of satisfaction. The chief's continued disinclination to discipline his men had bred great unruliness. This became abundantly apparent once they arrived in a place called Hump Hill Cove, where there flowed a tenuous little spring, the only one for miles around. A great hubbub ensued, an every-man-for-himself rush upon the water for a tumultuous orgy of gulping. The spring emptied into a shallow mud-lined pool and reappeared where it poured out again to form a watercourse that continued on down the mountain. The edges of the pool and the watercourse as well to the end of its access now sprouted a flange of writhing humanity, teeming bodies stretched out to the lips of the reservoir like a bristling sheath of flies. Some conveyed the water to their lips with cupped hands, filling their gullets scoop after scoop. Others spurned dignity and plunged their heads into the water and drank with sustained ecstasy. Those unable to gain entree on the bank flung themselves over the first-comers — and over the second-comers — producing a pulsating pile-up that pressed those on the bottom into the mud. The latter, disgruntled at their predicament, drew up the mud and flipped it over their heads, spattering those who pinned them down. Still others leapt forward impetuosly, headlong into the pool, and stirred up the bottom with their lumbering feet, churning the water into an impotable yellow slurry. The soldiers charged with securing the prisoner meanwhile stood rigidly around Bai Lang's horse keeping the guy-ropes taut as they disconsolately sucked hollows into their cheeks. Burdened with the weightiest of responsibilities, they could on no account abandon their posts to slake their burning thrist. Bai Lang looked down at them: "Let go of the ropes and go get a drink. I won't make a run for it."

The four eyed him suspiciously. To take him at his word would be the height of folly. Each dug in his heels and increased the tension on his rope. One of them, as it happened, was the youthful horn-blower who'd received the brunt of the chief's ire a while back on the road. His face had taken a battering that rendered him unfit for blowing a horn so he'd been reassigned to the guy-rope detail. Now the gears of his mind were turning and he considered Bai Lang's proposal. Finally he said, "King Bai Lang, we know that you wouldn't do anything to get us into trouble, so we're going to tie you to a rock. Now, you promised — don't run away!"

Bai Lang said, "Very good. And tie the horse's reins to a tree while you're at it — for good measure."

Each secured his rope to a different rock; the reins, as suggested, were knotted around a tree, and the soldiers trotted off to refresh themselves. They waddled back supporting ponderous bellies with their hands. The young one, however — the horn-blower — cradled in his hands a giant leaf from a Mongolian oak folded into the shape of a dipper. Bai Lang's eyes moistened as he regarded the boy heading his way, water dripping profusely from his leaf-ladle. Though barely a swallow remained by the time the youth brought it to his lips, words of gratitude lumped in Bai Lang's throat. "Hurry and drink, before it all leaks out!" the young soldier exorted him. Bai Lang obeyed and wrapped his lips upon the edge of the "cup" but, alas, not a drop remained. The youth's ardent display of respect and admiration moved him deeply, however, and he uttered a thank-you as his right eye flicked him a wink.

"You know," the youth suddenly said in lowered tones, "yours was the army I originally set out to join!" He paused, then continued, "It was three years ago. I saw you right here in this very spot, and you were leading your men through that ravine and you went on down the mountain. I ran after you, but I couldn't catch up. After that, Boss Hei's troops passed by, and that's how I ended up with him..."

Three years ago? Bai Lang searched his memory, but this particular ravine failed to turn up in its recesses. "What's the name of the ravine that goes on down the mountain from here?" he asked.

"Sheep-Gut Gully. Don't you remember? It was in the evening, and it had just rained, and the western sky was full of red clouds. It looked like it was on fire." His earnest tones flowed unabashed and accented his ruefully shrugging shoulders.

A flash of imagery, thick if fleeting, inflamed Bai Lang's recollection. "This ravine," he asked, with a surging sense of excitment, "does it lead down to the western gate of Salt Lake?"

A particular day wandering now came flooding back to him unsummoned. It was indeed towards evening, and he and his men had been out to take the western gate — a mission ultimately doomed, for the patrols on the road around the lake had discovered them. All along the wall's three-mile length, columns of signal smoke belched forth from the beacon towers in unremitting succession, and thus the Salt Superintendent's army had been more than ready for them. It had taken three years to regroup, and it was only a short seven days ago had he and his men crept up under cover of darkness and as silent as shadows slipped across the moat, thereby keeping themselves concealed from the watchful eyes on the patrol road. They had then readied their ropes, and as each patrolman passed by they lassoed him off his horse. Thus did they break through the western gate unchallenged — and the eastern gate as well — and Liu Songlin and Lu Xinghuo were able to capture the cache of weapons in the military camp. Then they routed all the government troops out of their bunks and herded them stark naked into one of the quadrangular salt beds in the lake. Bai Lang had burst into the Salt Superintendent's house and performed upon him the closest "haircut" he would ever need. What a magnificent night it had been! The salt workers roused with a start from their dreams and to a man grabbed up steel shovels, wooden spades and brine dippers, and catapulted themselves into the fray on the side of the invaders. Raging conflagrations erased the night, ruddy radiances coalesced into a spectral glow that danced upon the government soldiers' ubiquitous rolling heads. The northern and southern gates succumbed without a whimper as the contingents guarding them panicked and scattered to the winds. From end to end, Salt Lake rang with raucous shouting, the crashing reverberations of gongs, the tireless gaudy staccato of exploding firecrackers and the beating of cudgels upon pots and basins, dust pans and planks of wood — a joyful noise that swelled and carried on until morning when the first rays of the sun brought the inhabitants of the surrounding villages and farms. They breached the wall in a dozen spots and swarmed upon the salt-drying flats on the levees separating the salt beds. They pushed aside the protective layers of mud and fell to an orgy of liberation, loading the chunks of white treasure onto the backs of donkeys, stuffing them into gunny sacks, throwing them into baskets. Tots in split pants and toothless crones requisitioned their share as well, five or six pieces at a time, tucked into the folds of their shirts as they trekked back and forth.

Bai Lang, high upon his mount, ambled through this congested hive of excitement, imbibing its free-for-all ambiance, soaring with galvanised emotions, riding a feverish tide of rapture. These were the indigenous inhabitants around the salt lakes and yet they barely knew the taste of salt. Salt workers by the hundreds, by the thousands, had been seized and confined within the lake's forbidding wall, slave-labour for life. Cartload after cartload of white, crystalline salt mixed with the sweat of their brow, departed the gates and headed not for the pantries of the people but for the county seat and thence to the capital. Salt could be had only for an exorbitant price to which was further affixed an onerous tax. The victims of this abomination now scurried about intent upon rectifying their years of deprivation, but not so intent that they failed to notice Bai Lang in their midst astride his steed looking like a god. To him they fell to their knees, en masse, and knocked their heads upon the ground, impelled not by fear of the notorious bandit but by gratitude, a beholden affection that glowed upon their features. Countless men and youths gravitated to him, anxious to pledge their allegiance and clamouring to join his army and return with him to live the life of an outlaw on the mountain. One particular old woman stood out in his memory, for she alone was uninterested in the pillage of salt. She and a young man were earnestly hacking with little hoes through the slabs of salt that lined a drained section of the lake. Then having made a package wrapped in an unwound turban, they approached him. The woman confided her age — seventy — and related how her son had been seized

seized ten years previously as a labourer, certain never to return home again. He'd been lost to her forever, she'd thought, and this unexpected reunion wrought by the conquest of Salt Lake had confounded the ferocious ascendency of her profoundest pessimism. "Bodhisattva King, I have found my son. He, too, wants to grab some salt. But I say, this is not the way. There is something much more valuable here, and I want him to take advantage of the situation to acquire it — salt root. He knows all about it. It's a medicine, and it will cure any disease. You just eat a little, and whatever is wrong with you goes away. Here, Bodhisattva King, we've dug up this bit for you!" He accepted this gift, then spurred his horse into a gallop and headed out upon the lake, where he flew swift and free and wild atop the levees, whooping with the intoxication of his success. The lake's scintillating spectrum — its riot of reds, yellows, greens, blues and whites vaunting the variant degrees of salinity in each quadrangular bed — stretched out before him unto the horizon, engulfing his vision and electrifying his sensibilities with the extravagance of its weird beauty. Ichor pounded through his veins, a manic rush vaulting to delirium as he revelled in the heroic signifiance — the supreme immensity even — of his earthshaking achievement. He lifted his face toward the sky and roared with gargantuan laughter. Then he tumbled off his horse. His image in the lake — that's what he wanted to see and he peered into the surface of the water seeking the knowledge, the confirmation, the certainty of his identity — was that man of monumental heroism one and the same with himself? Gazing back at him was one uncommonly fair of face, an avatar of true grace and beauty that evoked the old woman's delightful address — "Bodhisattva King" she'd called him! — and set it humming in his ear. And mingling with these thrilling reverberations were questions of wondrous felicity that throbbed in his heart: "How many of the great and mighty who have left their names in the annals of history had acheived as much as this? And which such hero had ever adorned the world with a face as beautiful as that of the Bodhisattva, the Goddess of Mercy?"

And yet as he feasted his inner eye upon the epic tableau of his fortitude, an ache gripped his heart. It grew and spread unchecked, until his elation was smothered in a sense of abysmal loss. The capture of Salt Lake had spurred his burning ambitions and presented him with the next inevitable step. His mind had long churned upon the strategies of his prospective exploit—how he could regroup his forces and accumulate the strength and wherewithal to broaden the territory under his sway; how he could unify the other eleven mountain strongholds and gather them under one flag; and how they could exert their unity in a military manoeuver that would wrest the county seat from imperial control. Out of the empire they would carve this chunk of territory, the entire county from border to border, and transform it into a whole new world. But his best laid plans fell to the havoc of whim, sacrificed ignominiously upon the altar of — of all things — womanhood!

Women! I can't believe it! Women! Bai Lang's rage careened throughout his inner recesses. Is that it then? Are women really the downfall of heroes?

He'd been out on the salt lake drinking in its

ravishing vista and revelling in his own martial pulchritude when Liu Songlin and Lu Xinghuo galloped up to him. They'd dispatched with all thirty-two members of the Salt Superintendent's household in Trinity Temple, saving only his daughters, two breathtaking beauties unsurpassed in the realm of feminine charm and exquisite as flowers and jade. They'd emulated Elder Brother Bai Lang's own compassion, his inability to kill such beauty, they said. And now they begged his permission to take those females as their wives. This was, of course, in Bai Lang's estimation, out of the question. He analysed the situation for them. The local authorities would most assuredly call in outside forces to recover Salt Lake, for the taxes on salt they exacted from the people amounted to their life-blood, making the loss of the lake tantamount to a hemorrhaging wound, which meant that one ferocious battle was in the offing. If they were burdened with worries about wives and children and preoccupied with erotic pursuits, they would undermine the morals and the morale of their subordinates, making it thereby impossible for Wolf Fang Citadel to maintain its momentum of victory. Wolf Fang Citadel had remained thus far undefeated not because of the numerical superiority of its forces, but because the men comprising these forces were so quick and fierce that one was equal to ten foe. Furthermore, since they had wiped out the Salt Superintendent's family save these two daughters, could they possibly bow their heads and submit to the conjugal embrace of their enemies and be the willing bearers of their children? But Liu Songlin and Lu Xinghuo had already succumbed to the tugging of lust. They refused to entertain his point of view. They droned on and on about the rare beauty of those girls. They demanded to know if they were doomed to remain unwifed all their lives simply because they'd thrown themselves on the mercy of the mountain and chanced its life of banditry. Their good names were already gone forever, officialdom naught but an elusive dream, and the only thing left to make life worth living was the gratification of the senses: to eat with prodigality, to drink with abandon, and yes, to luxuriate in the embrace of beauty! Onward did they press their case, venturing into the realm of Big Brother's coenobitic asceticism — a decade of vegetarianism, praying to Buddha, studying the sutras and meditating had naturally enough driven off his desires of the flesh. They could never compare to him, they for whom raw meat was a delicacy and hot blood, sliding down their throats, like nectar. For they, indeed, were like the devil incarnate. Then how, might they ask, could such as they endure the torment of that other kind of physical craving? He had refused to let them keep that beautiful maiden, delectible fruit of the Yao family massacre. Now if he denied them again this time, well, suffice it to say that he who was a monk could afford to forego sons and grandsons, but they could not leave this world without issue; they had to continue their lines to ensure that the incense and candles would be kept burning in the temple.

What outrageous insinuation! What intolerable presumption! A tempest of anger ravaged Bai Lang's usual equanimity as he took them to task. Just because he was a monk was he therefore assumed to be bereft of human emotions? What did they think he was, a eunuch? Were they saying his beautiful, beguiling face made him incapable, a bogus man?

He had tried to reason with them, but they were intractable. Now it was no more Mr Nice-guy! He issued his order: "Bring those two women here and cut off their heads where I and the whole world can see it — and I'll hear no more of this nonsense!" Liu Songlin and Lu Xionghuo, thoroughly wrecked by this exchange and the very picture of devastation and heartbreak, withdrew. And that was the last he'd seen of them. Instead of bringing the women to him, they each took one and flew off their separate ways to destinations unknown. Their departure had gravely threatened the might of Wolf Fang Peak and prompted Bai Lang to stage the feast at which he played tricks on Heilaoqi. It further figured in his surge of loyalty toward Salt Lake, a complex mixture of principle and emotion which had led him back there to view the statue of himself that the salt workers had erected in Trinity Temple at that crucial moment in time. And it was thus that he found himself here, prisoner.

"Liu Songlin, Lu Xinghuo — you two good-for-nothings!"

His quiescent exterior belied the cursing turmoil of his heart. A hundred thousand times had he thus silently reviled his sworn brothers, perfidious authors of his unassuageable grief, unforgiveable transgressors of his trust. He bore them an enmity that vastly outstripped his antipathy for Heilaoqi. Was it so long ago when the three of them had merged their destinies on Wolf Fang Peak? Together as the wind soughed in the pines and the cuckoo proffered its mournful cry, they had knelt to pay homage to its empyrean apex and make a pact among themselves: though they had come into the world each at different times, they would in death seal their eternal comradeship in one and the same grave. Oh, ye of the faithless hearts and of ephemeral promises! What was that rite anyway — the whimsical game of little children? Only this and nothing more? Arm in arm they had put down roots on Wolf Fang Peak, bearing countless hardships and wrestling relentless baneful elements until at last they had amassed a force of several thousand strong. Down from the tranquillity of Tiger Mountain they shot, armed, trained and ruthless, mowing down all opposition and capturing that prodigious strategic point, Salt Lake. Such a big noise they had made in the world of men, shivering the firmament and sending shock waves through to the bowels of the earth. What manner of man, after doing all that, would throw it all away for the sake of a woman? Think of the glory! Think of the power! What else could possibly compare to that! He who had never thought of himself as a *bandit* now slipped into rhapsodic admiration of the heights to which Wolf Fang Citadel had risen, the acheivements which it had wrought — yes, indeed, the men of Wolf Fang Citadel were what you call real bandits! Alas and alack, there exist in this world many who are capable of achieving greatness, but so often all that is destroyed in a moment for the sake of money, position, women or petty loyalties!

Gripped in the throes of his depressed turmoil, our jade-faced hero twisted his neck as far about as he could to catch another glimpse of the mountains undulating in silhouette on the horizon. There was the pagoda of the Temple of Heavenly Prime, rearing up from within the Citadel, wrapped in its diaphanous raiment, the mist that grazed the atmosphere weltering under the brilliant sky. And at the bottom of the mountain: the liquid gleam of the salt lake. A rush of emotion ravaged body and soul. He wanted to shout and vent his spirit surging with the substance of heroism, but a big hot tear rolled down instead.

2

The next day Bai Lang awoke to a tall red glow — the rays of dawn pressing through the thin jute paper of an elongated six-foot quadrated window. He found himself in an immaculate room, all four walls of which had identical windows. He lay fully clothed on a mat of split bamboo spread out upon a large tiger skin. An eared urn of blue and white porcelain on a table at the head of the bed, a tell-tale rivulet of half-evaporated wine trailing out from its gaping mouth. From the foggy reaches of his mind he dragged up a tenuous memory of having been hauled in here around midnight, and of a reticent figure gliding into the room, depositing the urn, and gliding out again. This place, he assumed, was Heilaoqi's lair, Fort Pit, though having no idea precisely how he had come to be here, nothing of its nature or design had made an impression on him. Now, however, his first priority was to obey the commands of his thirst. He seized the urn and gulped its contents greedily, swiftly inducing a vertiginous haze. Endeavouring to draw himself up into a sitting position, his attention was then arrested by a metallic sound, as of shifting chains. Looking down he found his wrists and his ankles were enclosed in shackles to which were attached lengthy chains contrived to allow freedom of movement while removing the possibility of making a leap for it and escaping. He regarded them with satisfaction. Here he was, an empty-handed prisoner hopelessly immured behind the alien walls of Fort Pit, yet he'd evidently been plied with wine then bound in incompacitating chains.

Obviously Heilaoqi was still deathly afraid of him.

He took up the urn again and drained the remaining wine, which ironically cleared the passageways of his mind. Chains rattling, he moved about the room flinging open the window casements and scanning his confines. His quarters occupied the top level of a three story sutra-chanting tower and afforded a view that revealed the origin of Fort Pit's name: it really was ensconsed in a pit. Here Tiger Mountain shot its projections to spiring heights, layer upon layer of peaks and slopes which, upon approaching their base, suddenly and starkly descended to form an ovoid pit eighty to a hundred feet deep, four hundred and fifty yards wide from east to west, and nearly two-thirds of a mile long from north to south. The sharp loess descents on all four sides were devoid of vegetation, and even the tiniest blade of grass where the most agile and ingenious of hares could gain no foothold. Perched atop the edge of these remorseless inclines was a high wall about nine feet thick crowned with a crenelated parapet with projections each supporting a knife-wielding sentinel. Beyond this wall in every direction loess hills capped with lookouts rose to a goodly height in the distance. Bai Lang had heard that Heilaoqi's lair had been the retirement retreat of a member of the Imperial Academy in some former dynasty, a sanctuary not nearly as remote and secure as Wolf Fang Peak with its inhospitable mountain passes so narrow that one man could keep at bay ten thousand. But now he could see this was a most excellent fortress: in seeking height by creating depth, by tunnelling aslant through the southern end of the depression, once the granite gate was closed, its inmates had themselves a virtually impregnable refuge. The buildings within formed a complex of seven connected courtyards. There was a gazebo with a spring and a waterfall, a Buddhist chapel, and a family ancestral hall. As for the sutra-chanting tower itself, it was of a grand old age, yet its eaves and roof corners were all intact down to its aeolian bells. Bai Lang's room harboured the accoutrements of sacred recitation: a niche for the statue of Buddha and a long, high altar table, along with an incense burner, a kneeling mat, a lamp, a tribute dish, praying beads and the stone bowl which were heaped in a corner. In Bai Lang's eyes the place altered his perception of Heilaoqi, burnishing it slightly on the one hand — for an uncouth illiterate, he did manage to make himself look a little more refined than most of the other bandit chieftans on Tiger Mountain — while introducing a note of comical incongruity on the other. This light-hearted thought, however, gave way to puzzlement. Logically, Heilaoqi would have been most anxious to remove him from the face of the earth; or, given the impracticality of this option for whatever reason, to at least humiliate and torment him by stashing him in a cold hole of a dungeon. Instead he'd alloted him quarters in the most scenic edifice in Fort Pit, complete with creature comforts. Why, it was practically like the old days when he was pursuing his career as a monk! He scrutinised each of the compounds in the fortress, wondering which courtyard Heilaoqi claimed as his own. Down below, the tower was surrounded by three tiers of armed soldiers, obviously a special guard detail for his benefit. He snorted in contempt. Heilaoqi, here I, sovereign of Wolf Fang Peak and the king of kings, have become on this day your prisoner, and still you are constrained to accord me worthy accommodation and to look upon me as a god, he thought with triumph.

He felt the thrill of his own immensity blooming — a burst of pride in fact unsustainable under the circumstances. A seasick misery began to ebb through him as he gazed down upon the enemy camp, after all, he'd not come here as a guest. The mountain king and hero of his age was now the victim of concerted mortification, pitifully enchained and shut up in an isolated tower. Even the tower's sacred provenance could not compensate for his predicament, for he was no longer a disciple of Buddha. The gore and violence of the killing fields had warped his consciousness and hammered him into no less than a crazed barbarian incapable of savouring the peace and tranquility of the place with the appreciation that was the birthright of, say, an innocent young girl. What was this but a snuggery, a cozy little nest fit for the puny ambitions of the sparrow and the swallow? What headstrong hawk would condescend to perch in such insipidity when its true element, the vast and boundless sky, beckoned with all its infinite grandeur? Clouds of shame collected upon his face. He raised the clanking chains that conjoined his extremities and poised himself for the nullification of this intolerable abasement: he would smash his unbowed head on the brick wall.

He bent forward and launched himself toward destruction. The interminable milliseconds prior to impact regaled his senses with sounds and visions palpable and immediate. With a reflexive jerk, he pulled up short. The imagined splat of his own brain hitting on the floor lingered on in that auricular aura, as did that of the nebular figure of Heilaoqi entering the room, kicking his dead body, and laughing with gloating insanity. "So this is the king of kings, eh? What a way to go! If I had known you were to die like this, I would have immortalised your heroic name with my dagger in Salt Lake! His withering judgement resounded with a terrible finality that pounded mercilessly upon Bai Lang's thoughts and emotions. In the harsh light of afterthought, the truth glared brutally unvarnished: to end one's days in such a manner was despicable self-humiliation. All those ancient heroes who cut their own throats in the name of martyrdom on the battlefields of their defeat had actually effected cowardly escapes, while the encomiums upon their noble sacrifice in later ages were nothing more than pathetic extensions of pity. Surely after they had done the deed, in the waning moments of life, they conceived the same thoughts that Bai Lang had; but by then it was too late. But at least theirs was a foolishness committed with precipitous haste as the enemy closed upon them. I who was taken while bewildered with wine had no opportunity to slash my own throat, nor even had the question of suicide been suddenly thrust in my face. To do it now only after having been brought here in disgrace before the eyes of multitudes would be vastly more cowardly and stupid. People could only conclude that Bai Lang was weak before adversity and couldn't take humiliation and so he killed himself. Truly, now, is this the way the resilient hero comports himself and pays homage to his own worthiness?

He returned to the bed and sat slumped in an aspect of dejected contemplation. He reached out for the urn to test it for more wine. There was a sound at the door. Someone pushed it open. Bai Lang's hand froze in its position upon the table, his eyes fixed before him — a dagger stare. His face he composed into a mask of forbidding arrogance. Hesitation at the door. Then the sound of light-footed steps and the rhythmic creaking of the wooden floor. A disagreeable odour assailed his nose — perfume. A woman? The possibility hadn't occurred to him.

He'd anticipated Heilaoqi, attired as the aggressive warrior, intimidating blade at his side, exultantly holding the gun that used to be his. But even a gentler Heilaoqi turned out in the capacious shirt of the country gentleman and bearing a porcelain teapot would not have received the courtesies of Bai Lang. At this moment Bai Lang would have leapt to his feet and denounced him in no uncertain terms. He may have even flung his long chains upon him and pulled them tightly around his thick stubby neck and watched him slowly swell purple and behold with satisfaction his tongue come lolling out in the throes of death by strangulation. But these savourings of the imagination he had to set aside, for his visitor was clearly not Heilaoqi. She presented him with an entirely different problem. The monk who he no longer was would have bowed his head and intoned "Amituofuo" (Praise be to Buddha). Now he simply felt awkward. He went rigid as a statue. Only the slight quiver of his eyelashes betrayed his mortal being.

"Did Your Grace have a good night's sleep?" The woman placed herself directly in front of him. The sugar of seduction inflected her voice. She bowed to him deeply, hands reverentially pressed to the lap of her dress.

Bai Lang disdained to dignify her with an answer, nor did he direct his gaze upon her. Only a vague jade-green form played upon his awareness. A slave girl. Heilaoqi didn't dare ascend the tower to face him. A slave girl to attend to the tower room was all he could muster. It was she who'd brought the wine last night. She even calls me "Your Grace" and bows!

"Oh my!" the woman cried out in surprise. "I had heard Your Grace was a great drinker, but I had no idea he could finish a whole urn in one night! If Your Grace should finish this new one, all he need do is call out and I'll bring another. Will this plate of beef fulfil Your Grace's requirements for breakfast?"

Bai Lang still deigned not to pay her any heed. He poured his attention upon a spider industriously weaving its web in a corner of the room. The woman quite perversely inserted herself between his line of sight and that very corner. The reek of her perfume thrust itself with renewed strength into his nostrils. He snorted and shifted his gaze to the ceiling. An unusual warbling laugh emanated from her. She picked up the empty urn and set the full one in its place. As she did so her wide silken sleeve, then her lovely tallow-smooth wrist, brushed upon his hand which was still riveted to the edge of the table.

"Your Grace truly regards everything with a supercilious eye," she ventured to observe. "Here you are a prisoner, and yet you refuse to look upon such as me." She walked toward the door, her light footfalls caressing the creaking floor and gradually fading away. Bai Lang broke his frozen pose and gave his nose a vigorous rub. In the wake of her lingering fragrance, he was seized by an overwhelming desire to look at her, for during his sacral sojourn at the Monastery of Peace and Felicity, he had never cast an indecorous eye on a woman. Then when he mounted Wolf Fang Peak, he had barred the entry of the weaker sex into the citadel, in contrast to Heilaoqi, who kept slave girls to minister to his needs. He could hardly bear to think of the ugly Heilaoqi pursuing the Priapean rites. Judging by his appearance, the slave girls were really to be sympathised with! He turned his head and glanced toward the door, and to his consternation his eyes landed right upon hers. She hadn't left after all but stood in the doorway devouring him with bewitching eyes. She broke into a smile, which he, despite himself, perceived to be delicate and charming.

Instantly he felt dirty, as if he were a crucible of obscenity. He averted his eyes as his astounded heart started thumping wildly. But he had taken in everything. Her hair was dressed in a high coil and adorned with a silver phoenix-head hairpin and a long sprig of crushed pearls which quivered with every move. Her long sheath of cobalt-green silk brocade hugged her body sensuously, accentuating the swell of her bosom and shapely hips, showing off a waist so slim that one could encircle it with one's hands. Her dimpled face, refined and vivaciously alight with her smile, had struck him with a particular thrill, for celibate though his life was he had unavoidably seen many women in passing, but never one this beautiful!

"Did Your Grace wish to say something?" The woman addressed him with particular solicitude.

He steeled himself, turned away, and resumed his posture of proud aloofness. Where there had been a man there now sat a statue of stone.

"Well, I'll be leaving then, Your Grace." And then she was gone.

Bai Lang finally recovered from this novel encounter when his stomach began demanding breakfast. He turned his attention entirely to consuming the plate of meat, and half of the wine to wash it down. In his plenitude of idleness, time and the wine weighed heavily upon him, and he lay back upon the bed in a haze, partially paralysed. His mind, nonetheless, did not sink into sleep but instead wandered the labyrinths of brotherhood. What, he wondered, were Liu Songlin and Lu Xinghuo doing right now? Did they know their elder brother was in this place and that the power and prestige of Wolf Fang Citadel had been annihilated? How pitiful it was that his own younger brothers should fall down in worship of pomegranate skirts. And speaking of women, there was something about that slave girl — what was it? He was struck with the feeling that he'd seen her somewhere before. But where? He delved into his memory, rifled through the records of the past but came up blank. But what's this? What's this shameful train of thought have you embarked upon? How come when a beautiful woman presented herself before you, you didn't rise up in righteous rage and put her in her place? How come you just sat there all stiff, wallowing in a false sense of pride and pretending aloofness from the sordidness of the world? If it were true, if you really were, as the slave girl said "unwilling to look upon such as me", then how come you just had to take a look as she was leaving? And not only that, you drank the wine she brought, and now you're thinking about her and wondering where you've seen her before!

He thought of a story he'd once read in the books of Buddhism in the Monastery of Peace and Felicity about an old monk and a young monk who were about to cross a river when they saw a woman standing disconsolately on the bank looking at the rushing flow of the water. The old monk volunteered to carry her across. Quite some time after the two monks had resumed their journey on the other side of the river, the young monk asked the older one: "We who have forsaken the world are not supposed to get close to women, so why did you carry that woman across the river?" The old monk replied: "Are you still thinking about her? I'm the one who carried her, yet I left her where I put her down on the bank!"

Consternation. A moan of despair. You! You're just like that young monk! And steeped in the shame of this blot he had smeared upon his own heroic soul, he turned his fists upon himself, slamming them over and over onto his head until his anger turned into despondent blankness.

That afternoon, the slave girl reappeared with a plate of meat-stuffed buns, a bowl of shallot and beancurd soup, and another urn of wine. He sat as before, eyes firmly cemented in their sockets, body an immovable monolith, obdurate against temptation. In the ensuing days, always it was she who brought him his sustenance, and each appearance brought a different incarnation of herself, each more beautifully dressed, ingeniously coifed and sumptuously adorned than the last. Her voice washed over the planes of his secret inner terrain, words sweet, emollient and disarming, until gradually he grew accustomed to her presence and dispensed with fixing his eyes upon the ceiling. Instead he stared at her in cold, determined silence. With gentle deliberation she would set down his repast, then take a seat in front of him and watch him wolf it down. Or prior to taking her leave, she would sweep the dust from his bed mat with a palm-fibre whisk, at which time he could not help but notice that her intricate hairpins were forged from pure silver and that the bracelet encircling her jade-smooth wrist was fashioned from agate. To her laughing lips — for in attempting to amuse him she would end up amusing herself — she would apply a perfumed handkerchief, an exquisite piece of Suzhou embroidery, rare in these parts. He had seen one before, in the boudoir of the the Salt Superintendent's wife. And so he began to doubt that she was Heilaoqi's slave girl. But if she wasn't a slave girl, then what was she? Surely not the bandit's concubine or daughter or some other such intimate relation — such a woman would never condescend to serve a prisoner twice a day, let alone do it with her measure of grace and solicitude. He who prided himself on his unfailingly accurate readings of others found himself swimming in doubt and uncertainty.

There came a day of torrid heat, stifling and predacious, when the roof virtually glowed with the sun's malevolent radiation. Bai Lang threw open all the windows of his tower room, seeking the cross-breezes of their gaping accessibility, but the air remained unstirred, as stuporous as a stagnant pond. His noonday meal beckoned him despite the blasting heat, and upon consuming the food and wine, he felt himself akin to a piece of roasting flesh. Seeking relief, he walked out the door and followed a winding corridor to a stairway of thirty or forty steps. Iron bars had been thrown up around the landing below, and outside this cage three menacing armymen bearing daggers stood guard. He returned to his room and closed the door. It would be some time yet before his next mealtime, he calculated, so he peeled off his shirt and stepped out of his trousers. Clad only in his underwear he lay spread-eagled upon the bed's cooling mat. With uncanny timing did the door push open upon his vulnerability, producing the presence of the slave girl beaming the smile of seduction. He clapped his legs together and bolted upright and hunched himself into a tight ball. "Get out!" he screamed at her with frantic rage. "Get out!"

She, however, leaned against the door, pushing it shut with her weight. "So, Your Grace can speak after all!" She ogled him with lacivious eyes. "But, as you can see, I'm not getting out!"

"If you don't get out, I'll throw you out the window!"

"Be my guest," she replied, unperturbed, as she moved toward the bed. "Come, take me up in your arms and toss me right out." Step by step, inch by inch, she advanced, her full bosom leading the way, the two large breasts jiggling under her garment.

Seething with rage, he wanted to rush upon her, whallop her across the face, seize her around the middle and hurl her out the window. But he was held back by a power with which he could not contend: her mesmerising, heavy-lidded eyes, waiting for his naked body, prepared to sink langorously into his arms the moment he touched her. He leaped off the bed like a lion and froze in a daze of terror, then in desperation he grabbed his long chains and flung them at her. Long as they were, they were still too short to reach her. Instead their impetus dragged him forward a staggering step. Startled at the swift ferocity of this move, however, his adversary shrieked, and with a face blanched into a ghastly white, she turned and fled.

And now Bai Lang knew hunger, for she did not come at the designated time, and when the sun had slipped behind the mountain with yet no sign of provisions forthcoming, he rent the air with profanity and glumly listened to the rumblings of his stomach. Still, he congratulated himself on having avoided a most uncomfortable and compromising encounter. A gastronomic drought was truly a small price to pay, particularly considering that now she'd been frightened off, Heilaoqi would have no choice but to mount the tower himself. This night he allowed the tower to remain dark as he dealt with his gnawing hunger and gnashing thirst, putting them and his fully clothed body to bed. Early retirement. Beat the heat in modesty. And don't waste precious energy. But if he sought the depth of the darkness and its heightened sense of solitude, it was not to be. Footsteps sounded in the stairwell and a whisper of light grazed the corridor outside his door and grew and ever grew in intensity until the slave girl entered with a gleaming polished lamp whose wick had been pulled up very high.

"Why hasn't Your Grace lit the lamp? Is it out of oil?"

Her voice so calm and gentle, her demeanour so serene, betrayed no trace of the fright he had given her. Extraordinary, this woman. And this thought exploded upon the secret crypts of his heart, where no one — but no one — was given leave to look. As she placed the lamp upon the table, its incandescent glow bejewelled her face, imparting a soft warm sheen that was not the province of day, heightening its already impossible beauty. Again that aura of *déjà vu* enveloped him, insistantly pressing upon his consciousness, yammering that though her beauty was unique in his experience, there lay beneath its lineaments something keenly familiar. A slave girl, she? Even a housemaid — something in his intellect rebelled at the likelihood.

"Your Grace must be starving! To think he has such a mild scholarly mien, but my, how like the devil himself when anger invades it! I'm an ugly woman, truly maddening to look upon. But if you had actually smashed my head this afternoon, most likely you wouldn't be getting anything to eat and drink tonight." Provocatively she looked straight into Bai Lang's eyes and withdrew from her basket an urn of wine, a plate of beef, and three steamed buns. These she pushed before him and said, "Don't look at me so ferociously, like you still want to beat me. I'll bet right now Your Grace hasn't got an ounce of strength left to do it anyway!"

A most astute observation — and he wasn't about to allow her the satisfaction of capitalising upon it. He would refuse her largess. He would make her know he was a force to contend with, a man of hard determination, unyielding to the end. He had his heroic code to live up to, the code of brotherhood, the code of undying loyalty to the fraternity, and for the sake of this code, if necessary, he would never eat or drink again. But no sooner had this self-immolating impulse entered his mind when he realised it contradicted his own philosophy of conduct as well as threatened all that he would achieve. That is, he had vowed not to allow women to affect him, so why should he waste energy contending with one? Wolf Fang Peak had been annihilated, all his brothers in banditry killed or injured or scattered. He, though, was still alive, and this meant that he would one day rally his forces and retrieve his rightful status as a true man. Wouldn't it thus be childish to go on a hunger strike just because of a woman? Wouldn't it merely amount to the futile, puny protest of an impotent, half-baked scholar? Precipitously he opened up his arms, encircled the comestibles on the table and swept them toward him. Paying her not the slightest heed, he hunched over his "kill" and started to eat, a juggernaut of gluttony assailing the food with a "take no prisoners" attitude. The woman regarded him in extreme astonishment. Then guttural laughter arose in her throat, derisive and unrestrained. What atrocious manners! To think that one of looks so refined and airs so intellectual should eat like that! He ignored her. She was but a wooden carving, a clay statue, an inanimate object... He increased the furore of his ingestion, brutishly cramming in mouthfuls, guzzling the liquid and releasing big revolting belches. The woman said, "Okay, you've made your point. Yes, that's just the way the king of the mountain would eat. But if I were to say just one certain sentence, you wouldn't be so gleefully stuffing your face!"

Bai Lang took up the urn and poured its contents down his gullet, noisily smacking his lips.

"Yesterday," the woman said with an informative air, "the seventh day since Your Grace captured Salt Lake, and the fourth since you've been locked up here, the government deployed five thousand troops and took the lake right back."

The urn froze mid-air. Bai Lang choked, spewing out his latest swig of wine. He stared at her agog. "Is this true?" he demanded.

"See, I told you you'd have a fit. What do you say to that?"

"If you keep making a fool of me, I'll smash this urn over your head!"

"Come now, is that the extent of your capability — wreaking revenge on a woman within the confines of four walls? I was going to tell you earlier today, but you practically blotted me out. This time I'll not retreat — come on, smash your urn!"

A second of silence, ratifying his realisation, terminating this interview. "You goddamn beggerly thief!" he suddenly roared. "Heilaoqi, you goddamn beggerly thief! Now you see what evil you've wrought? Destruction, that's all you know! You've destroyed Wolf Fang Citadel, so why don't you go fight and kill the troops of the realm? Where are you? Where have you hidden yourself, you yellow-bellied son-of-a-bitch!" From his hand the wine urn flew, sailing high over the woman's head and out the window — a tic in time — then an explosive thud from the dusky fathoms below, ceramic shattering into smithereens. This raised a din of shouting down below, the riotous thrumming of running feet, the clank and rattle of slavering blades drawn for a fight, the cracking discharges of a single firearm. Bullets grazed the upper frame of the window, sending pieces of broken brick spattering into the room.

The gunfire pitched Bai Lang into a frenzy of rage. Of the twelve Tiger Mountain masters, eleven brandished the authority of a rifle, while he alone possessed the superlative of firearms, that pistol of perfect alignment and handy accessibility. With it he'd decimated the ranks of the filthy money-grubbing gentry, those worshippers of despotism, and liberated all in the shadow of Tiger Mountain from the scourge of exorbitant taxes and levies. This was the weapon that had shocked the Salt Superintendent as Bai Lang picked off countless government soldiers like sitting ducks. But now it had fallen into the hands of Heilaoqi and was being aimed at none other than Bai Lang himself! He rushed to the window and poured a stream of invective toward the buildings indistinct in the gathering darkness and toward the moving shadows below: "Heilaoqi, you bastard! Go ahead and fire away! You still haven't learned how to shoot straight! You only hit the window frame! You've lost Salt Lake, and my scattered men won't let you get away with it! The other mountain masters won't let you get away with it! Heilaoqi! Heilaoqi, you fucking son of a bitch!"

In the darkness Heilaoqi shouted abuse back at him: "Monk Bai Lang, I may not haven't mastered this gun yet; Heilaoqi may not be as smart as you, but the smart bandit chief of Wolf Fang Peak is my prisoner locked up in my tower! Believe me, the other mountain masters will think twice before they ever dare offend the new king of kings again!"

When Bai Lang heard this, he began to grind his teeth, but what could he do about it? He whose ambitions had been so cruelly thwarted shook to his very core. He collapsed limply away from the window, voice abjectly raised in bitter lamentation as his heart cracked with pain. Salt Lake lost! Himself dealt a fate so wretched! Men's aspirations in the world were never destroyed at the hands of his avowed enemies, but by his own so-called allies, the very ones he neglected to take precautions against! Another wail wrenched out of his throat. Then he noticed the woman staring at him, wide-eyed. She'd seen the whole display. His wrath veered and looped and zeroed violently in upon her. Why are you still here? he screamed, hysteria rising. Leave! Go away! And he grabbed up the plate of meat and the steamed buns and smashed them against the door.

The night was jet black, the moon snuffed out behind a thick phalanx of racing clouds. Throughout the interminable hours of restless stygian gloom a raw, piercing and terrible agony emanated from the tower. Bai Lang slung invectives at Heilaoqi, guttered obscenities that had never before crossed the threshold of his lips, bellowing and howling at the night with fury and heaving up the strangling ravages of his heart. Heilaoqi, too, cried out, ordering the men that were stationed around the tower to stuff their ears with cotton, a precaution against the influence of Bai Lang's imprecations. "Let him carry on," he said. "Let him empty his guts into the vacuum of the night." And to a vacuum, indeed, did Bai Lang commit his anguish, and time stretched and he was like the ferocious lion caged, futilely roaring monarchical rage into a seamless sea of apathy, the last soul in eternity condemned to the ridicule of resounding silence. Gradually then did his maniac vociferation yield its tones of powerful and lordly certitude to the creeping inflections of despair, and his voice began to falter and grow hoarse, and further yet did it decline until reduced to a thin and feeble twittering. And thus voiceless and spent, engulfed in impotence, he turned his passion upon himself, slapping himself upon the face.

Dawn found him slumped upon the floor underneath the window, breath rattling in his chest, sleeping the sleep of the dead.

The next time he saw the light of day, nothing much had changed. At the appointed hour the woman entered with a sumptuous array of food. He spoke to her, words stiffly circumscribed in formality. "Have Heilaoqi come up here! I demand to see him!"

"He will not come to see you."

"He won't see me?" Anger. "The son of a bitch. The coward. He doesn't dare to come and see me!"

"You are certainly right about that — Heilaoqi is indeed afraid of you. He's got the base of the tower all wrapped in wire, and he's got men on patrol day and night."

"Then why doesn't he just kill me and be done with it? Why do you bring me this stuff every day?"

For this she had no ready answer. She lowered her head in a lengthening period of silence. Finally she said, "Is that what you want — to die? If so, there is a very fine death waiting for you, but you insist upon putting forward such a ferocious face..."

Ferocious, she'd said. Well, he hadn't been exactly conducting himself like a gentleman. His anger dissolved into a helpless sorrowful sigh. Remorse. But then his mind flashed onto her ambiguity. Her face had changed, there was no doubt about it. She'd come in with her usual kind and pleasant aspect, but at that moment a subtle eeriness had brushed across her features. Was it deceit? And there was something very peculiar about her words: "There is a very fine death waiting for you" — what did that mean? He searched her countenance. Was she deep or was she shallow? Was she good or was she evil? He could not decipher her.

Later when she brought his dinner, he deliberately limited his remarks to the precedent of cursing Heilaoqi and demanding that he make an appearance. It was a test. He wanted to measure her response and from it glean some understanding of what was going on outside. His efforts did not go unrewarded, for she revealed that Heilaoqi had suffered a leg injury and was using pumpkin pulp poultices on it to effect a cure.

"Has the government sent troops up here on a suppression campaign?" he hastened to ask.

"It's not as serious as that. Does Your Grace know a bandit named Lu Xinghuo?"

Lu Xinghuo, his sworn brother, that fellow who ran away on account of a woman! "Don't mention his name to me!" he bristled. "Are you trying to mock me?"

"I'm trying to tell you it was a dart of his shooting that caused the injury to our chief. But our chief in turn broke one of his arms with a gun. Without the use of his arm, what kind of a Number Three King can he be? They say that he ran off because of a woman — so what I'd like to know is why, since he was so fond of sex that he abandoned you, his own elder brother, how come he was so ruthless toward me?"

"He's been crippled by Heilaoqi!" This Bai Lang literally shouted in his excitement, and he broke into hearty laughter. How ironic! Heilaoqi had ambushed him right at the moment when Lu Xinghuo and Liu Songlin had made their sudden departure—undoubtedly a deliberate calculation. So if anything, Heilaoqi should be grateful to Lu. And yet he's repaid him with murderous violence! Good, very good, Lu Xinghuo has been laid low — serves him right! But what of the mystery she'd injected into her account, that last sentence of hers? He asked, "Do you know Lu Xinghuo? When did he try to kill you?"

She looked at him, plainly astonished. "Your Grace, have you been playing the fool all along, or have you really forgotten?"

He had no idea what she was talking about.

"You really have forgotten!" She sighed and muttered something, as if in self-reproach. "You are indeed a monk, not paying heed to any woman! You obviously don't recognise me, but I know you, quite well. Surely you can at least remember that year at the Yao's house, when Lu Xinghuo was itching to cleave in two a little concubine who'd just arrived in a bridal sedan."

Instant enlightenment. No wonder she looked familiar! He should have known, but who could have thought that the Yao's little concubine whom he had saved from Lu Xinghuo's knife would show up in his cell in a prison tower? Now he scrutinised her exceedingly beautiful face and remembered the shy and terrified girl whose features had been suffused with anxiety. Though those vulnerabilities had disappeared, the memory of that pitifully young little concubine made him more disposed to sympathy for this woman of Fort Pit.

He let out a gasp. "Now I see! You've been showing me all this kindness — bringing me food and wine all this time — to repay me for saving your life. But you should know that although Lu Xinghuo is not a true hero, the fact that he wanted to kill you doesn't mean he felt nothing for you. In fact, he wanted you for a bride, but for your sake I refused him. And it's precisely because of that refusal that he turned his back on me when he saw another beautiful woman."

"He forsook you, and yet you defend him? No matter how much you defend your former brother, I still hate him. Heilaoqi really is very inept with a gun — if he had killed him, then I should have had my rancour satisfied at last."

It was far from Bai Lang's intent to absolve Lu Xinghuo. For the latter's defection, he had cast him completely from his heart. No more "younger brother" ever. Only his belief in giving credit where credit was due had given rise to this single consideration and resurrected for a fleeting moment the one who was dead to him. He bent the woman's conversational propensity toward that which was consuming his mind — the state of affairs beyond the confines of his cell. The news that Salt Lake had been retaken had reached Lu Xinghuo's ears the same day it occurred, she told him, along with belated tidings of Heilaoqi's imprisonment of Bai Lang, and that very night he and his men headed for Fort Pit. That was the night Heilaoqi had been under assault from Bai Lang's storm of damnation, his anthem of curses. Heilaoqi feared that the situation was ripe for a government attack, so he set out with his men for a village about six or seven miles from the fortress to set up a line of defence. As luck would have it, they ran right into Lu Xinghuo, and in the ensuing battle Lu Xinghuo cut down twelve Fort Pit men and pierced Heilaoqi's right leg with a dart. He fell from his horse and was in imminent danger of capture. Only his gun saved him. He fired it and fired it — he's such a bad shot — and finally after about ten shots he managed to hit Lu Xinghuo in the arm, and the impact of the bullet broke it.

After hearing this account, Bai Lang leaned in silence upon the windowsill and looked out at the mountains stretching to the horizon beyond the fortress wall. He raised his hands before him, one fist in the other, and prayed to Heaven on behalf of Lu Xinghuo. He was moved beyond words, at the selfless actions of this man who had suffered an injury in his attempt to save him. And there came flooding back to him the renewal of his faith in promises. Just think of it! Sworn brothers are brothers after all, and they are the true heroes of Wolf Fang Citadel after all, and they didn't forget their big brother Bai Lang after all! They'd fallen in love with women, but they and the government were still irreconcilable enemies. Yes, it was true, Lu Xinghuo had been forced by circumstances to act as he did. Just look at what he'd been up against. He'd been one of those extraneous, unemployed young men in his village, all alone in the world and with no training to do anything. He'd had to carry brides to survive, twelve long years of facilitating other people's weddings, always the bride carrier, never the groom. So it was understandable that he should run off once he got himself a woman. And Liu Songlin, too, had not had it easy — growing up in a theatrical troupe, raised to be an actor. And they'd gotten him hooked on opium, too. He was emaciated like a skeleton, and still he couldn't free himself of the drug's insidious hold. He'd be all decked out in his performance regalia, standing behind the curtain ready to go on, and then simply have to have a smoke before he could truly transport himself back to the Three Kingdoms, to transform himself into Zhou Yu and play that role with all the vivacity it demanded. Then the Salt Superintendent raped his wife, and he was so enraged that he killed that wife, and then he escaped into the mountains. Could you say, then, that when he snatched the Salt Superintendent's daughter there was no element of revenge in it for his former wife? And now Lu Xinghuo has been trying to rescue him, and although one of his arms has been broken, that only means he'll be more determined than ever. Meanwhile, if Liu Songlin should hear of this, do you think he'll just stand by and do nothing? Ha, ha! With these two brothers of his raising once again the banner of Wolf Fang Peak, all his scattered men will descend in an endless stream upon Fort Pit looking for him!

His heart swelled at the thought, and his blood quickened, and he felt the resurgence of that fiery energy, that elegant mettle, and the inextinguishable essence of his heroic spirit burst through the walls of incarceration and billowed out toward victory. He turned back from the window, his face transformed with the light of elation. Jubilance personified. Skimming atop the waves of ultimate triumph, he indulged in a little light raillery. "Now I know why Heilaoqi doesn't kill me," he said to the woman with a wicked glint in his eye. "He fears Wolf Fang Citadel! Just look, Lu Xinghuo has injured his leg, while the punishment of the ten thousand cuts still awaits him!"

The woman regarded his air of satisfaction with equanimity. She gave a laugh. "And what else is it Your Grace has come to realise?"

"That Heilaoqi is using you to get to me. It's the classic trick: deploy the wiles of a woman to exact surrender from the enemy. At the very least he's trying to get me to keep my men out of his hair!"

A gurgling laugh from the woman. She leaned against the wall and gave him a jaundiced look. "Is that so?" Lips twisted into a sneer, laughter turned to ice. This was an aspect of her he'd never seen before, and it unsettled him. "Am I not right?" he asked.

"You hero types are all alike! Your analysis may be appropriate for your run-of-the-mill adversary, but our chief is not at all what you take him to be!"

It didn't really matter what the woman said, however. Bai Lang had taken the high road, and he was not to be daunted. From this day forward the tower cell was host to an unusually active inmate. Every day he arose early and exercised, and here the weight of his chains proved beneficial as he lifted and stretched his arms and legs. Then he would move from window to window and lean on the sills and gaze into the distance, ever on the lookout for a churning cloud of dust skimming over the hills and a white wolf's head banner fluttering over it in the wind. The zeal and patience he devoted to this vigil were attenuated only by its tendency to inflict upon him a stiff neck. It was then that he began keeping an avid ear open for footfalls on the stairway. And he would rush to welcome the woman bringing him his meal and pump her for information about what was happening on the outside. The woman for her part demonstrated an ever-developing sartorial sophistication and chose ornaments ever more dazzling and brought to him ever more and newer news. And each day he felt nurtured by her graciousness and solicitude. She told him that on a certain day a contingent of twenty combatants from Wolf Fang Citadel had attacked Fort Pit, that on another certain day some Fort Pit soldiers who'd gone down the mountain to gather the harvest had all been slaughtered by three men wearing white clothes with the wolf's head insignia, and that Lu Xinghuo with his broken arm had indeed made a second and a third attempt against Fort Pit, so alarming Heilaoqi that he decreed a reward for whoever could bring him Lu's head. Oh, how Bai Lang thirsted for such accounts. He would listen to her, unblinking and rapt, devouring every tidbit with the ardour of the starved, and the woman to him was so utterly amiable — yes, lovable — and he grabbed her shoulders and shook her and said, "Tell me some more, tell me some more!"

"Your Grace would have me commit treason?"

He froze. And his hands were still on her shoulders, and it struck him that this was so. Aghast, he jerked them away as a crimson tide swept over his face.

She, however, missed not a beat. Upwards tilted her chin so that her gaze filtered out from lowered lids. "People often say that when the tree falls, the monkeys scatter. I would like to know what it is that people find so attractive in Your Grace that though he be imprisoned they risk their lives to come and rescue him?"

"What do you think it is?

"I think it's your face."

Bai Lang's expression underwent a transformation, but then he laughed. "Why don't you go ask your chief? He brought me here — can it be that he too has a thing for my face? In which case, why has he refused to come and see me all this time?"

"You've got a point there... but I've come, haven't I?"

"How can a little slave girl understand the affairs of men?"

"Of course women can't understand the affairs of men, but do men understand the affairs of women? Especially you, a monk king — as is obvious by the fact that you have mistaken the First Lady of the fortress for a slave girl!"

"The First Lady?" Like a sudden blow to the solar plexus did this intelligence hit him. Sitting close beside him, she cooly extended her hand to pick from the back of his head a speck of dust that had fallen from the ceiling. Instinctively he gained his feet and backed away, reiterating the burning question, "You are the First Lady?"

In the days that followed Bai Lang struggled with the implications of her revelation. Immediately the alarm bells had gone off, and he had sought to distance himself from her. Yet he was far from attaining lucidity in the abyss of contemplation into which she had plunged him. His head teemed with doubt and disbelief — was this female pulling a fast one on him? But she'd subsequently confided facts that could not but indicate otherwise. When her concubinage to Yao had been subverted, she'd been married off to a rich merchant. Heilaoqi, though, had taken a shine to her and pulled off a caper in which he kidnapped her husband for ransom and carried her off to Fort Pit. It would certainly seem there was no reason to doubt she was the First Lady, and once he had accepted this at face value, a great wave of sympathy washed over him for all the adversity she'd had to endure. In this world, beauty was misfortune, the root of a fate steeped in bitterness, and she in her feminine fragility had become like a hunted creature to be snatched, abducted, shanghaied with impunity by vile, repulsive men. Even he, a man, had been subjected to the abbot's abominable attempt to befoul him in the Monastery of Peace and Felicity, all because of his comely face. Nor had escape into the mountains freed him from the filth of people's minds, for he often found himself the object of derision among those who frequented the highways and byways of this untamed realm. How much the worse for her, she to whom respectable family stability was denied and who had changed hands several times like a piece of chattel only to end up living in the midst of knives, guns, death and flowing blood in a bandit's mountain stronghold! But, and this Bai Lang found strange, she did not carry in her appearance or demeanour the anxieties and stresses that were ordinarily the lot of a bandit chieftan's wife. And she wore gorgeous, luxurious clothing and bedecked herself with rare jewels. Was her motivation to please Heilaoqi, or was she trying to alleviate the tedium of her isolated life, to extract a little pleasure from spiritually impoverished circumstances? Bai Lang could only lament that having entered the monastery at such a tender age, he was woefully ill-equipped for the task of knowing women. Marry a chicken, follow a chicken; marry a dog, follow a dog, they say. And so she who'd perhaps once timidly peeked out upon the world, an innocent creature so delicate and soft, kind and good, has been as Heilaoqi's wife constantly bathed in the bandit's brutishness and malignancy, and so inevitably will change someday into someone entirely different. In which case, how could Heilaoqi set his own wife to the exclusive task of bringing food and drink to an enemy, and catering to that enemy's every need? Did he have another ulterior motive — and if that motive wasn't to get him to surrender to him, then what was it?

Baffled, he was beset by this enigma. He would have to probe the depths of the First Lady's mind to discover the intentions and objectives she harboured there. And thus it was that Bai Lang for the first time in his life began pondering what it must be like to walk in the shoes of a woman.

It was midday, another scorcher, and the woman came to him in new guise. She'd taken a bath, and her hair was fluffy and tumbling loose past her shoulders. Her long body-hugging sheath had been supplanted by a tunic that revealed the jade-white sheen of her limbs, and from inside a high but carelessly unfastened Mandarin collar the base of her throat peeked mischievously. A rose, velvet and vivid, glistening with droplets of moisture, provocatively clung her bosom, drawing attention to the exceptional fullness there. She came and sat in front of him and cooled herself with a round fan, its breeze animating her hair and setting the petals of the rose aquiver. She was ravishing. Radiant, exotic. And Bai Lang, innocent Bai Lang, found himself inflamed. Furtively, he cast his eyes over her face and just as quickly glided them away. Sheets of light glanced off his skin; drenched, he was, in sweat.

"Your Grace, aren't you hot?" she asked. "Maybe you should take off that gown."

He wasn't hot. Definitely not. But what about Heilaoqi — what was Heilaoqi going to do to him?

"Don't you have anything to talk about? You say you're not hot, but your face is redder than a blushing girl!"

She extended her fan out to him and bestowed upon him her gaze, unabashed and lingering. Luminous were her eyes, luminous and sultry, uncommonly alive, and she spoke to him in molten tones unfamiliar to his ear and singular to his sensibilities. And his thoughts were spinning, flashes of mute pictures recalling to him that mysterious serene reflection at the bottom of the well on the dry plateau when he had looked in over the edge, and the small shepherd he once was, leaping joyously into the limpid pool nestled in downy waterweeds and swimming happily around, and his rambling treks through the mountains under a September sky when a flaming orange persimmon, lustily ripe, beckoned him from its branch and he climbed after it, bit into its tapered end, sucked out the sweet pulp and forced his breath into its tough empty skin puffing it out fat and round. She said something that he missed in his reverie, and then her soft hand was lying in his. A thrill trembled through the two of them. Silence, sweet silence as they gazed into each other's eyes. Vanished were the sun's rays glaring through the window, and in the crooked willow just outside, the shirring of the cicadas turned the noontide into a glimmering void of peace. She began to melt. A tide of red suffused her face, livid became her lips, moist and round her little mouth, luscious like a cherry. And her dimpled cheeks and tender throat and soft swelling bosom pulsated ever so slightly with the raging life within.

Bai Lang, virginal Bai Lang, took her into his arms and breathed her fragrance and felt her soft voluptuousness. As he looked into her eyes, he bent his head lower and lower until his quivering tongue could nearly reach that red fruit and he could see in her eyes the tiny reflection of himself. And the blood boiling and coursing through the veins of this youthful king at once stayed its momentum, spreading a wave of languor throughout his body. It was like floodwater ravaging a shaky dyke suddenly receding. It was like holding sleep at bay an entire night and the hours tick by in excruciating fatigue, one o'clock, then three, then finally five o'clock, ticks around and the weariness retreats irrevocably. It was like coming to the end of one's rope only to emerge into an entirely new world of possibilities. He placed her gently on the bed and then — what? What was he to do? He felt himself an alien in unexplored terrain, bewildered, hampered with ignorance, movements clumsy and miscued.

She was like Woman, the feminine paradigm, this

First Lady of Fort Pit. She had entirely altered his view of the "weaker sex" and freed him of the monkish notion that to look upon women was evil, salacious and criminal. But neither did he countenance those brigand overlords of the mountain who regarded women as tools for sex, mere vacuous receptacles for mindless bestial lust. Restraint was the watchword, this he knew. In restraint lay the path to true greatness, and he who eschewed self-discipline compromised his ambitions. And yet this woman had lavished him with comfort, consolation and countless moments of soul-strengthening delight! If he were a literary man, it might be different for him. He would pour his soul onto the page and fill reams with words surging in intricate arabesque, images and ideas boundless and extravagant, opulent and vividly flamboyant. But he was a warrior, a military man of righteousness who thrived on action, one for whom imprisonment meant wasting tragically into oblivion. And the reason why his mood had not plummeted to the depths and his health had not deteriorated and he retained fire in his belly was most basically and undeniably due in no small measure to the efforts of this woman.

The truth of this bore into his consciousness, and his heart brimmed to think of it. Yet in consonance with this insight there came the flash of caution: he could not, must not, become mired down in the sinkhole of lust. But what of love, true love, untainted by concupiscense? Could a bandit chieftan's wife surrender her body and soul to a man such as he? Then there it was: gently laying her down upon the bed and looking into her languid eyes, he knew she'd slipped into a realm of ineffable subtlety. What he ought to do was garb himself in gallantry and say: Madam should go back for her afternoon nap! But he couldn't bring himself to say it. For he could discover in her no evidence of malice, nothing to feed his suspicions. Even if it were all a sham, an elaborate masquerade behind which lurked some hidden agenda, she clearly, at this moment at least, had some genuine feeling for him, and for this he was grateful. Monumentally unbecoming it would be for him to repudiate her. What would he do, now, leap up and rant and rave about virtue and chastity, curse her as a jezebel, beat her half to death? Especially now that he himself had taken her up and laid her upon the bed, and she was like an opening flower waiting for rain — wouldn't it be simply too ruthless, too cruel, to just drop her? Was that what it meant to be a true man — to be ruthless and cruel?

Bai Lang stayed; he didn't turn away from her. He stretched out his open hand and delicately, tenderly caressed her hair. Downward his hand slid to her swelling bosom and onward to her belly. Suddenly her eyes snapped open. In great agitation she pushed his hand away, wrenched herself toward the other side of the bed and gained the floor. "No! No!" she cried. "You mustn't do that! You mustn't!"

He gawked at her in dismay, thoroughly flummoxed! Shame commandeered his face in deepening crimson hues, and he snatched his terrified eyes away from hers and hid them in the yawning depths of his disgrace. Quietly, her head drooping abjectly, she withdrew from the room. And he flung himself upon the bed and hid beneath the sheets, where torrents of inner heat soaked him in the salty sea of his humiliation. Hours passed, torpid noontide hours, and he was aware yet unaware, benumbed and bereft of will, suspended in a leaden narcotic swoon.

The return of his senses impressed upon him the sensation of something cool and slippery. Down there. He'd had a dream. Yes, he remembered it — an exquisite blissful dream. Alarmed, he took a look and saw the spots, upon his undergarment, upon the sheet. Odiferous, musky. He studied them for a lengthening time in mute solemnity. Then, with calculated calm, he arose and thrust the soiled areas of the linens into a bowl of cool water, scratching at the spots until they disappeared. Then he raised the bowl to his lips and drank. At the Monastery of Peace and Felicity, the abbot had stressed to the postulants that they were to examine their bedclothes every morning, and if they discovered such spots they were to scrape them off into water and then drink that water. This was a penalty that would help those beset with physical cravings to remember the convictions and beliefs of their vocation. From that time Bai Lang understood the basic essence of monkhood and knew that the cultivation of character lay in the struggle against sexual desire. It was a struggle that spilled no blood, took no life and consisted of meditating under the oil lamp and thinking deeply to the resonance of the "wooden fish" which was much more soul-stirring than bathing oneself in gallons of gore! After completing this ritual, Bai Lang felt himself purified, cleansed of passion and transported into the realm of the heroic; a true monk. The true hero and the true monk was not one who had no sexual desire, it was one who conquered sexual desire. Monkhood called not for forging oneself into an unfeeling rock or a block of wood, but rather required self-control and self-discipline. He, Bai Lang, was subduing Heilaoqi with his nobility of spirit, his unyielding excellence, his transcendent virtue. And through the principles of charity and righteousness that inhered in the character of the true man, he had won a woman's love without having wallowed in depravity before her eyes!

For two days after this, the woman did not return, and his meals were brought to him by a soldier. He would spend his time standing before the window, a solitary figure wistfully pondering upon her absence. This was how he came to notice the approach of men from Wolf Fang Citadel. They threw themselves into bloody battle on the loess expanse beyond the gate of the fortress. Few in number they displayed middling martial skills, and were obviously outclassed as they rushed in earnest upon Fort Pit. Yet dauntless they were, launching three courageous if hopeless attacks. And each and every soldier in the throes of death went down shouting zealously, "Give us our chief! Give us our chief!" Bai Lang witnessed these heroic acts through hot streams of tears, and he fell to his knees before the window, the names of his men strangled in his throat, and he could only beat his fists upon the floor swearing he would avenge them as he prayed that the souls of these men who had died for him would find a peaceful resting place in Heaven.

Then later that day a great din and commotion broke out below that sent him flying again to the window. Within the walls of Fort Pit two lines of soldiers in full battle regalia extended from either side of the cavernous gate forming a militant path all the way to a sizeable courtyard mansion. He watched in growing curiosity. Finally the gate opened, and a man dressed in nothing but a pair of red shorts walked in. He held at chest level a wooden tray upon which rested a bloody human head. Bai Lang's eyes nearly popped in astonishment, for that man was none other than Liu Songlin! This Number Two King of Wolf Fang Peak looked like a hungry ghost. If he had come to rescue Bai Lang, then why was he alone? Why was he naked and unarmed? Why did he appear to be in a trance as if he hadn't had his opium fix? And whose head did he have on that tray? Then all the soldiers in both lines solemnly raised their voices in unison: "Liu Songlin presents the head of Lu Xinghuo!" What! Bai Lang screwed up his eyes and scrutinised that head. It was indeed Lu Xinghuo's. So that's what Liu Songlin is up to! A volcanic rage boiled up in him and shot out his lips in stentorian rebuke. "Liu Songlin, you shameless traitor!" he thundered. "Did you kill Lu Xinghuo? Have you come here to surrender?"

His fury rolled mordantly across the array of warriors and drew banks of eyes toward him. Liu Songlin in the midst of his solemn march down the path that bristled with unsheathed sabers hesitated and swayed. He looked up, saw Bai Lang and fell to his knees, calling out, "Big brother! Liu Songlin at last is able to see you!"

"You disgusting dog!" Bai Lang roared back. "I won't have the likes of you kneeling to me! Brethern we are not!"

Liu Songlin regained his feet and burst into plangent laughter. "Very good, then, Monk Bai Lang. You are already King Hei's prisoner — would you have me throw away my life as well? Lu Xinghuo was out of touch with the times and so opposed King Hei. His head is worth three hundred taels of silver. Now all the opium I need is mine!"

"All right then, go ahead, throw yourself at Heilaoqi!" Bai Lang ranted. "But remember, one of these days I will chop you into mince meat!"

"Ha ha! Don't be so sure! King Hei may see fit to bestow upon me more than just silver. He may well make me a chieftan! And then I'll come to finish you off. So, Monk Bai Lang, just relax up there in your tower. King Hei summons me!"

Whirlwind of fury, explosion of ire, assaulting fragile flesh, careening through delicate veins, to extinguish all senses. Bai Lang collapsed into a swoon, nearly tumbling out the window. He hit his head on the frame and crumpled unconscious to the floor.

When consciousness returned to him, he clung to his inertia and the private world of darkness underneath his lids. Nonetheless, the swirl of recent events flooded back to him. He'd been counting on Liu Songlin to rally the troops in the aftermath of Lu Xinghuo's injury and descend like a cloud of death upon Heilaoqi and rescue him. Instead Liu Songlin had turned on him and dealt him another devastating blow. Oh, the pain, unbearable pain, right in the centre of his chest. How difficult people were to fathom, though their hearts lay under a mere layer of skin and meat! This melancholy thought throbbed in his brain and maddened him. He swore: Damn you, Liu Songlin! Blind-hearted you are; thoroughly blind-hearted! And damn you too, Bai Lang: you are blind!

A voice came sailing into the mists of his misery, calling to him. He opened his eyes and discovered himself on the bed. Sitting on the edge was the First Lady of the fortress. He squeezed his eyelids back together and turned his face toward the wall. "Your Grace," he heard her say, "can you bring yourself to look at me? This is the last time we'll be able to see each other. Will you refuse to look at me one last time?"

He sat up, his movement sudden and violent. "Is Heilaoqi going to kill me? Tell him to come and do it now! And Liu Songlin — tell him to come and do it too!"

His splenetic outburst foundered, however, upon the shoals of astonishment, for the woman was completely altered. He stared at her in disbelief. What time hath wrought in just a few short days! Her nose was enflamed, her eyes dull and heavy, her raven mane limp and thin, leached of colour, dry as straw. He gulped and jerked his gaze away, dropping his head, appalled.

"Does Your Grace perceive that I am become ugly?" the woman asked in a welter of tears. "Finally you deign to look at me! This is not an opportune time for me to come, I know — you can't have much to say to me. But I had to come. I had to tell you about your brother, Liu Songlin."

"I never want to hear his name again!"

"Okay, then. In that case I'll tell you about myself, how about that?" She was seized by terrible spasm of coughing. When she recovered she asked, "You must tell me — have I really become ugly?"

It was true, she looked ghastly. How could such a

stunningly gorgeous person have changed so radically, literally overnight? "What's happened to you?" he asked.

"I'm going to die," she said with stark simplicity.

"Die?" Bai Lang said, incredulous. "Did you say die? What kind of a joke is that? Heilaoqi doesn't have a credible adversary left — Lu Xinghuo is dead, Liu Songlin's surrendered, and Fort Pit has nowhere to go but up — and you, the First Lady presiding over it all, tell me you're going to die?"

"I know that you've regarded me with distrust all along, and — it's true — I've not been forthcoming with you. Now I'll tell you everything. The reason why the First Lady of the fortress would trouble herself to personally bring your meals — like a slave girl, as you said — is that she has contracted leprosy. Don't interrupt — hear me out first. It's essentially an incurable disease. 'Essentially' because there is one way to purge myself of it, and that is to sleep with a man and transfer it to him in the process. Ironically, at its most virulent stage it makes its victim stunningly beautiful, and so it's easy to incite a man's purient desires. After Heilaoqi learned of my condition, he naturally shunned conjugal relations. But at the same time he regretted the loss of my beauty to an apparently needless death, so he pressed me to transfer the disease to one of his low-ranking soldiers, and afterwards he would put that soldier to death. But the thought of sleeping with such a person was revolting. I've already been subjected to enough humiliation just in having been brought to this ... this ... lair; and if I have to do that with someone I don't love, then I'd rather die! Then you showed up — or rather I should say were dragged in. Heilaoqi's plan was to display you

The Monk King of Tiger Mountain 379

before all the kings of Tiger Mountain to signify his power and prestige, and then to kill you without further ado. But I liked you from the moment you arrived and so Heilaoqi agreed. He said, 'You can be with him one time, and when the thing has been accomplished, you let me know right away — because I'll not allow any man who's been all over my woman to live one hour longer!' So that's why I brought you your meals, and why I came in all manner of beautiful dress and ornamentation. So you see how terribly vicious and evil I've been? But then in the process, I discovered that you were a person of truly heroic stature. You have a face and a body that far exceed the average man. But it wasn't just a matter of physical beauty. No, you have something far more important — a heroic nobility all too rarely seen. You're not a lacivious person, you don't play on your good looks, you don't act like you have the right to do anything you want with a woman who's been handed to you on a silver platter just because you are a person of note, the king of kings. It's precisely because of this that I loved you even more. And then I finally realised just precisely who it was you were — the very one who had saved me that time — my benefactor. How could I possibly proceed with a plan that would hurt you? But then again, I am a woman, beset with womanly desires. I loved you so much and I longed to win your love, to be held in your arms and receive your caresses. And I wanted to give you some moments of happiness so you could forget for awhile your misery here as a prisoner, and I wanted you to let me die happily in your arms. But when I thought of you catching the disease like that and dying, then I had to stop you. I just couldn't let it happen. You know, every time I left you, Heilaoqi would ask how it went, and I would stall him and say the right opportunity hadn't presented itself yet. He didn't believe me. He said that would be like a cat turning up its nose at fish, and he suspected that I had fallen in love with you. In fact I had a huge war going on inside me, and I would lie awake at night trying to think what to do. That's why I didn't come for the last couple of days. Then it turned out that all this turmoil aggravated the disease and my nose started to get red. I knew that once it started to fester, my hair would be next — it would start falling out by the fistful — and my skin would start to putrify and fall off. By that time I would be a horrible sight and I certainly wouldn't want the one I love to see me like that. The disease is swift and fatal. No matter what, I had to come and see you for one last time! When Heilaoqi saw that the disease had already advanced to this point, he knew that it was not necessary to keep you around, and he started ranting and raving about how he was going to kill you. But at the moment he's not feeling very well. In fact he's quite ill, and all day long he lives in mortal fear that someone's going to come and kill him. And he's changed toward me too, I'm banished to an empty house to die. I sneaked over here to see you, to warn you he means to kill you tomorrow, or maybe even today; so whatever you do, don't fall asleep, you have to defend yourself. I came for another reason too — to beg you, to entreat you, to let me die by your hand!"

The words tumbled from her mouth, an avalanche of urgency, as if she feared that to stop for breath would be to forfeit her chance to say all that had to be said. Now she knelt before Bai Lang and looked up at him in abject supplication. He returned her gaze through rivers of tears. His head was reeling with her stunning testimony, his throat was knotted with emotion, his entire body trembled with compassion for this woman before him. Merciful Heaven! So this is what's been going on! His heart went out to her, she so grievously deserving of sympathy, even as it sang and leapt at the thought of her sincerity and devotion to him. Forgotten was his vexation over Liu Songlin. He'd arrived at an essential vision. Here was compelling evidence that heroism was not exclusive to men. Soft and delicate, yet this woman, too, had had the fortitude to make the ultimate sacrifice. Never had he taken women seriously, and now in this signal moment of his life, the one to deliver him from destruction was not his one and only sworn brother left in the world, that unsurpassed performer in the theatre of war, the Number Two King of Wolf Fang Citadel, Liu Songlin, but rather this woman so frail she could be blown away by a puff of wind! He gathered her up in his arms and held her tight with all the tenderness his heart contained. Absolute conviction suffused his voice as he said, "You will not die, I will not let you. As soon as I get out of here, I'll find the best doctor in the world to cure you."

Like a slim willow buffeted by the wind, she trembled in his arms, a shaking violent and convulsive. Enormous tears spilled from her eyes, and she said, "It makes me so very happy to hear you say that, but it is impossible, just impossible."

Bai Lang, rent to his very core with grief, felt his

corporeal fibre, muscles and sinews capitulating to the pull of the earth. He slumped on a bench, aware momentarily of a creeping consuming thirst. He reached for the urn. It made a noise. There was something in there besides wine, something metallic — a snub-handled knife! He snatched it up and turned to look at the woman. She was lying on his bed, clothing arranged demurely. With a tragic smile, she said to him, "Your Grace, please come and free me from this life."

Still holding the knife, he walked over. His hand was shaking. Countless times had he killed before and never had his hand shaken like this. "How can I kill you? How can I possibly kill you?"

"If you do, I will at least die happily! I beg you, My King!"

Her face was composed in serene resignation, eyes veiled beneath closed lids, a smile adorning her lips. As he looked upon her, horrifying images flashed before him: the knife descending and severing her throat; the knife plunging into her breast, a fountain of blood spurting up and spattering the ceiling and the walls... and then, and then, could it be — a woman who'd walked in goodness and beauty and showered him with the mercy of passion will have departed forever from this existence... He turned his head and looked out the window. As grim as his heart was the picture it framed, grey and unsunned, the solar orb blotted out by a tyrannous sky-wide nimbus and its dreary rain. The shimmering soaking silence lengthened, and then he said, "Okay, I'll do as you ask." He bent down and kissed her on the forehead, on the nose, on the lips. "Rest your left hand on the edge of the bed.

I'm going to cut open a vein so that your blood will drain out."

Obediently, without opening her eyes, she placed her right hand on the edge of the bed. Serenely, she lay there in elegant expectation. Bai Lang took the knife and drew the blade across her wrist, then shifted over to the side and sat, head bowed, in the muted atmosphere of irrevocable transformation.

Silent was the tower cell as she drew into herself the pattering of the rain and it became in her consciousness the dripping of her blood, her vital vermilion humour departing steadily, rhythmically, soothingly... painlessly. She belonged to Bai Lang, and if in this life they could not be one, not even in surreptitious ecstasy, then dying by his hand like this remained the sole avenue of the boundless joy she would otherwise never know. Life was dripping, dripping away and death was at hand, carrying her off in a rapturous dream, he and she again someday, free together in another world.

Bai Lang raised his head and watched the rise and fall of her breathing as it gradually subsided. He stepped over to her... and she was already gone! Peacefully she lay there, the smile still upon her face, the luminous serenity in which she'd breathed her last. Unblemished by wound or drop of blood, she looked the perfect alabaster likeness of the sleeping Bodhisattva. Thus did Bai Lang gaze upon her, and as he looked, her remains became to him the very image of sanctity, a holy relic not to be defiled by those still wedded to the flesh, and he dared not to touch or caress her. He kept vigil over her, steeped in meditation upon her saintliness, abstracted throughout the passing hours until day faded into night and night once again relinquished itself to dawn.

In the early morning light, he roused himself from his trance, took up the urn and drained its contents in great needy gulps. Instantly drunk yet thirsting for more, he shook the urn as if hidden reserves might be jarred loose. And lo and behold, there was the sound of something else rattling around. Definitely not wine. He upended the urn and the thing fell out. A key. Sobriety rushed back to him. He picked it up and tried the lock on his chains. The lock opened. Tears welled up in his eyes. He wiped them away and still more flowed. Ministering angel of mercy she was, who had taken care of everything! He knelt before her body and exclaimed, "My Lady! My Lady!" over and over, heart-rending homage to her sublime virtue. And through his copiously flowing tears a laughter arose — a manic satisfaction at the fearsome solidarity their spiritual union had created.

As if on cue, up from below drifted a ringing melange of shouts and crys dominated by one hoarse and grating roar: "Stand our ground, men, we must stand our ground! Today, whoever kills their leader will win the hand of the First Lady of the fortress!" The unmistakable voice of Heilaoqi who then called out for the First Lady and swore at her lack of response. Where the hell had she got to? A soldier informed him: "The First Lady went upstairs yesterday and hasn't come back down." Heilaoqi swore again: "The bitch! Who told her she could go back upstairs?" Bai Lang looked out the window and saw the source of the excitement: several wolf's head flags had sprouted on the expanse outside the fortress gate, bearing glorious witness to multitudes of Wolf Fang

Citadel men engaged this very moment in pitched battle with the Fort Pit enemy. His first instinct was to lean out the window and rain derisive laughter down upon Heilaoqi, but a clatter of footsteps resounded in the stairwell. In a trice he regained the bed, sat himself down strategically, artfully redraped the chains upon his wrists and ankles, and slipped the knife under the bamboo mat just within reach of his fingertips.

With a bang the door kicked open, and Heilaoqi and four guards brandishing long, thin knives entered the room.

"Monk Bai Lang!" Heilaoqi addressed him pugnaciously. "You've been demanding to see me, right? Well, here I am! How about it, eh? The treatment you've received at Fort Pit's not been too bad — a nice tower room, all you can eat and drink, and pussy to boot!" Then his face transformed horribly, and he roared: "Okay, boys, run that stinkin' bitch through!"

Bai Lang said, "Not so fast! She's asleep!"

The four guards froze in rank embarrassment. Yes, the First Lady of the fortress was indeed asleep, right in the bed of the prisoner. They turned anxious eyes upon their master. Heilaoqi laughed boisterously: "Monk Bai Lang, you think you've got one over on me, don't you? Well, let me tell you, that stinkin' bitch's got leprosy, and I sent her here to you just for the purpose. I don't have to kill you — you're already good as dead!"

Bai Lang sat unmoved, regarding Heilaoqi with a cold, imperious look. "Is that so?" he said with mock incredulity. "Then what the hell are you doing up here! Maybe you've come to ask me to go out and play host to my men amassing at your gate! To invite them in — is that it?"

"It's just as you say, Monk — there's quite a battle raging out there. Ever since you've been here, Fort Pit hasn't had a moment's peace!"

"That's pretty obvious — you're a lot thinner, and you don't look so good. Tsk, tsk. From morning to night — and from night to morning — every little sound makes you jump, isn't that so? And behind every tree there's an enemy soldier lurking, right? You go on like this much longer and you might just drop dead of fright — either that or you'll go out of your mind! Don't you think?"

"Oh, you are so astute, aren't you? So perceptive! Well, it's just for that very reason I've come to borrow something from you."

"And what might that be?"

"Your head! Once they see your head, those people out there will have nothing to fight for and they'll stop coming here and bothering me!"

"Ho, ho! You don't say! Well, then, come and get it!"

"Take him, men!" Heilaoqi shouted, but before the guards could act, Bai Lang leaped up into the air, whipping the knife out from underneath the mat. In a flash he had the blade at Heilaoqi's throat, while his free hand gripped his arm like a vise. "I'm truly sorry, Heilaoqi! Tell your men to be good little boys and lay down their knives and lead us out of here!"

The situation had changed so fast that the four guards stood stock still, dumbfounded. Meanwhile Heilaoqi's face looked like death warmed up. He had no choice but to order his men to put down their knives and proceed them out the door. Step by step Bai Lang escorted the hapless Heilaoqi down the stairs, knife still riding his throat. Emerging from the portal of the tower, this little hostage party immediately attracted the attention of those warriors manning the fort. The latter launched themselves to their master's rescue, then froze at the sight of the knife drawing his blood. Heilaoqi shouted in his strained hoarse voice: "Nobody move! Nobody move!" The men battling outside the gate noticed this crucial turn of events. Fort Pit combatants hesitated, and their Wolf Fang Citadel adversaries took advantage of their distraction to run them through. Having dispatched the resisters, the men of Wolf Fang Citadel swarmed to the gate and set about pounding it down. Bai Lang tightened his grip upon Heilaoqi and increased his pressure upon the knife. "Order your men to open the gate!" he said.

All the soldiers of Fort Pit were rounded up, disarmed and herded into an empty space. Bai Lang now returned his attention to Heilaoqi. "You tell me how I should punish you!" he said. Heilaoqi's face was bathed in tears. "A tooth for a tooth," he said. "Parade me as your prisoner all the way to Wolf Fang Citadel and lock me up!" Bai Lang drew out his revolver from Heilaoqi's belt and shoved him off to the side. He lowered his head, opened the gun's chamber and blew upon its barrel, then stuck it into his own belt. He raised his face toward the sky and laughed. "Heilaoqi," he said, "you're a real character! Now why would I want to escort you all the way to Wolf Fang Citadel? Why, if I even raised my little finger to kill you, it would be at the risk of sullying my good name!" Then he shouted out: "Who will come to dispatch him?" From among the crowd one man strode out. He was wearing the wolf's head uniform and was holding a humongous hay chopper. Bai Lang did not recognise him.

"Who are you?" he asked.

"Your Grace does not know me. I'm a new volunteer."

"Can you take care of this bandit?"

"I come from just north of Salt Lake, and when Heilaoqi ambushed Your Grace and the government snatched Salt Lake back, they killed many of those ordinary folk who had plundered the salt, including my mother and father. So yes, I can certainly do away with this troublemaker — and gladly!"

Under the brilliant rays of the sun, the hay chopper cut a wide swath and cut Heilaoqi clean through the waist. As the top half of Heilaoqi went crashing to the ground, he was still alive, and wailing: "I shouldn't have sought to be the king of kings!" and he died with his eyes staring wide.

3

Bai Lang mustered his remaining troops and returned to Wolf Fang Citadel. Once again he reined as the unchallenged gallant of the age and the king of kings on Tiger Mountain. Everywhere there spread glowing tales of the hero who had survived calamity, the hero who could not be vanquished, the hero who had defied death. Imprisoned in the ancient Sutra Chanting Tower, he had been by day a handsome, dashing, jade-faced monk, but by night he'd changed into a white wolf that bayed at the moon and incited the wolf packs roaming throughout the wilderness. Bai Lang's evanescent chanting exalted the tower's aeolian bells which rang in the dawn, and white cranes and swans otherwise fiercely attached to Salt Lake would come flying through the sky and perch upon the tower's roof and stretch their necks and unleash their haunting cries. Tales such as these began circulating among the mountain folk, then spread to the ranks of the Tiger bandits, and to the shopkeepers and artisans in the county seat. Even the valiants in the government garrison bandied them about. Then printed portraits began to appear. One depicted him with a human body and the head of a wolf and was sold in the market as a magic charm that warded off evil. A second one showed him with a face as beautiful as that of a painted woman and was entitled "Monk Bodhisattva" and was relinquished for a substantial sum to those who sought to "invite" it into their midst, it being an image that could not be "bought". This people would hang high on their walls or in their ancestral shrines, where they would burn incense before it day and night and kowtow and pray for riches and advancement.

With Heilaoqi eliminated from Tiger Mountain, there were now only eleven mountain strongholds left. When Bai Lang had been taken prisoner, it had come like a bolt out of the blue that truly shook up the other ten mountain masters. They lamented Bai Lang's demise — the majestic eagle that had broken its wing, the gallant steed that had lost its footing — and they sorely empathised with him for this tragedy of a lifetime and the galling shame and humiliation he had to suffer. However, each of these mountain masters had as well tucked into his heart a measure of secret glee, a tiny modicum of gloating satisfaction at his misfortune. When Bai Lang had been present, Tiger Mountain had of course been secure and safe; they'd collected the taxes the government would normally collect, and they'd received the grain the government would regularly receive. There'd been plenty of wine and an abundance of meat and they'd enjoyed wealth and happiness. But also with Bai Lang present, the highest position of command had always accrued to him. Therefore, when Heilaoqi destroyed Wolf Fang Citadel, they had all mouthed platitudes to the effect that Heilaoqi was vicious and brazenly insolent, but not a one of them raised the possibility of storming Fort Pit. In their eyes, Heilaoqi had always been a nobody whose strength and ability only called for minor increases in vigilance and measures of defence, and they saw fit to simply concentrate upon the management of their own strongholds with an eye to someday taking over the sovereignty of Tiger Mountain. But now Bai Lang had miraculously returned to Wolf Fang Citadel, and the woefully over-ambitious Heilaoqi and his stronghold had been ignominiously eliminated. It was thus that they all sang the praises of Bai Lang and eulogised him as the greatest hero of all times.

Atop the pagoda of the Temple of Heavenly Prime, split in two like the open blades of a scissor, the white wolf's head flag once again flapped in the wind, signifying that the territory within a hundred mile circumference remained the realm of the mighty mountain kings. Off in the county seat the garrison lieutenant redeployed his watchmen and beefed up security at the drawbridges of all four city gates. Everyday at dusk the drawbridges would be raised up high, while plans to suppress the Tiger Mountain bandits were quietly rescinded. Soldiers and new recruits and various civilian militias, all mustered for the purpose, dug in at Salt Lake. On Tiger Mountain, the eleven strongholds were like eleven tribes, each tending to its own affairs within its own sphere of influence. Warriors patrolled the strongholds and at road intersections, confiscating the transports of cash and grain belonging to merchant princes and the lords of wealth and power, killing any government soldiers caught snooping around. From mountain to mountain, signal smoke and bugle calls kept them all in touch, though each stronghold jealously guarded its own autonomy and power. Only men of Wolf Fang Citadel wearing the wolf's head uniform or sporting a wooden wolf's head badge could move freely throughout the domains of all the other strongholds. Though this practice was not founded upon law set down in black and white, with the passage of time it earned the sanction of tradition. And it came to pass that when people walking by in the middle of the night were asked to identify themselves, they would claim the mantle of Wolf Fang Citadel, and true or not, it was awkward to question their word. And when clashes would occur over a beautiful woman or a load of merchandise, the parties involved would be heard to boast; you'd better watch out who you're tangling with, because I'm from Wolf Fang Citadel! Thus it was that bogus claimants to Wolf Fang Citadel gained illegitimate advantage, while the genuine men of Wolf Fang Citadel were taken for imposters, and not a few bloody incidents occurred. In view of this, Bai Lang sought to send a strong message to the other ten strongholds, and to this end he invited all the other mountain masters to a conference to discuss the matters concerned.

When the mountain masters received their invitations, none dared neglect to prepare bountiful and luxurious gifts. Bai Lang was more powerful than ever, and well they knew his "invitation" to Wolf Fang Citadel was actually a summons to pay him homage in the wake of his stunning comeback, as well as a subtle warning to those who would appropriate the name of Wolf Fang Citadel. Thus they proceeded in a steady stream that day toward the pagoda of the Temple of Heavenly Prime.

The mountain masters' suppositions in this regard were absolutely correct. Although the youthful monarch had had Heilaoqi cut in two and reduced Fort Pit to flying ashes and smouldering smoke, nonetheless he had first been cangued and guy-roped and paraded like a common criminal for miles all the way to a tower cell by the most unworthy of the mountain masters, and this was an insupportable insult. He had contrived this occasion deliberately, to impress upon all that he, the king of kings, would not tolerate attacks upon his person. To assure the success of the assemblage, he had the crumbling walls and ruined palisades of the citadel restored; all the towers, pavilions, and domiciliary buildings whitewashed; and sought to effect a reassemblage of his scattered men, as well as recruit new warriors. The last of these endeavours, however, proved a disappointment, for though he had notices posted and sent out recruiters broadcasting the message with the glamourous clamour of drums and gongs, pitifully few men showed up on the mountain, and most of those were former Fort Pit soldiers, indigenous inhabitants of the mountain environs, or salt workers who'd escaped the confines of Salt Lake. These new recruits donned the wolf's head uniform, wrapped their heads in yellow turbans, and trained in the art of wielding the cudgel and the knife, and whenever he appeared they would all prostrate themselves and shout out their allegiance. Your Grace! Your Grace! But he didn't know these new faces and missed the old familiarity and intimacy he'd enjoyed with his brethern of old. After an interval he sent a chieftan who'd served under Lu Xinghuo back down the mountain with the order to find at all costs all his former men and have them return. To them he sent a message suffused with passion: "Wolf Fang Citadel suffered a catastrophe, and I, Bai Lang, failed to protect you. But now that Heaven has seen fit to spare me, the men of Wolf Fang Citadel will share and share alike its fortune and prosperity!"

Toward the mountain portal to Wolf Fang Citadel the mountain masters rode. When they arrived they saw looming before them two thousand stone steps mounting the lofty ascension of a lateral ridge, and they had to abandon their horses. Climbing higher and higher they gasped for breath, and then they were confronted with a series of barred gates set into wall after encircling wall. Warriors wearing straw-coloured turbans and knives that gleamed at their waists were waiting for them, and these shouted out each time for a gate to open and shouted again for it to close behind them. What a forbidding display of strength it was! The grueling trek to the top of the ridge, however, did not yet bring them to the citadel proper. Instead, a sheer wall of rock rose before them, capped with the pagoda of the Temple of Heavenly Prime. Waterfalls spilled over either side of the precipice and shot straight down, smooth as two silk curtains. The path they were obliged to follow curved behind the cataracts to where the cascading water separated into enormous liquid crystals that sparkled like a shower of gems in the sunlight. There the rock face was pitted with caves, and looking straight up they saw it was embellished with dense growths of dark green moss that humped up like the shoulders of a wild sheep. They had left the scorching heat of summer far below, and now they bore the discomfort of an unseasonable autumnal nip. Bai Lang, the perfect host, met them at the path's pinnacle, one hand cupped graciously in the other before his chest. And just as in those days gone by he was dressed fastidiously all in white and his head was cleanly shaven in the coenobitic tradition. To each he extended effusive greetings and from each he received a resoundingly profuse reply. Sixty-four laquered tables for eight and eighty-one cushions with rush mats had already been set in place by a score or so of young disciples with classically topknotted hair. The guests of honour and their respective entourages moved toward their places at the table, but the mountain masters deferred taking their seats. Rather, they walked about ogling the time-honoured architecture that surrounded them: the gateway arch with its three big pillars, the ceremonial gate with its three massive pillars, the main hall with its five humongous pillars, the west and east wing rooms each with their three enormous pillars, the side doors to the back hall, the armory, the kitchen and the utility room, the three-pillared drawing room, the spacious rooms along the east and west side of the main gate, and the covered promenade fronting all twelve rooms. All had been renewed and refurbished and were completely transformed, and lanterns and festoons enriched their reborn opulence. Meanwhile, the twenty newly constructed out-buildings, the four watchtowers, the six massive defence towers, together with the wooden sentry platform and the pagoda were all topped with brand spanking new wolf's head flags. Overcharged with awe were the ten mountain masters at the palpable grandeur of this display, and the fierce driving currents of their own ambitions evaporated, replaced by the clammy sensation of inferiority. They straightened and smoothed their clothing, adjusted their hats and did their best to keep smiles pasted on their faces. Then to the booming cadence of giant drums, thundering tympanic vibrations, their attendants presented their host with tribute: tiger skins and bear meat, smoked fowl, red-cooked duck and jug upon jug of fine wine, bolts of silk, reams of touch paper, salt, soybean oil, black fungus and mushrooms. And these they disparaged as mere pittances, trifling little tokens to symbolise their respect. Then they bowed to Bai Lang and congratulated him, and one by one regaled him with the most elegant phrases composed under the sun, extolling his heroism in euphonious and sonorous tones. Thus it was that at this moment Wolf Fang Citadel flew its flag of triumph over all of Tiger Mountain, and Bai Lang reigned as the sincerely admired paramount of all the mountain masters. And from this time Tiger Mountain would be invincible and the recapture of Salt Lake was inevitable and close at hand. The county government troops were inconsequential pests, and the territory within a hundred mile circumference would ever be a kingdom unto itself, a luminous enclave of peace and tranquility.

The consensus upon his illustrious achievements and exalted leadership — as well as the spirits he'd been sipping since waking that morning — soon had Bai Lang's cheeks aglow. He strutted before his assemblage of guests, radiant and ebullient, the image of vitaliy. And as he considered the vicissitudes and victories of his life, the heady heights to which he had risen this day amazed even himself. Indeed, how often is it that one captured, shackled and condemned to die subverts his fate with such sweet revenge and returns to the seat of power stronger than ever, exuding a charisma that draws adoring multitudes with just the wave of a hand? What captor has ever shaken in his boots just to behold his hopelessly encaged prisoner, as had Heilaoqi? And while in the realm of the miraculous, what man fallen into such dire straits has had a woman as beautiful as a goddess fall in love with him right in his prison cell? Oh miracle of miracles! All had been subjugated by his own heroic nobility! Who else on Tiger Mountain could even begin to approach the magnitude of his lofty excellence, his nobleness? Perhaps there was extravagance in the accolades the mountain masters and his men heaped upon him, and yet who else could dare assume the mantle of a god?

And Bai Lang, in the true spirit of his heroic rectitude, quelled the lambent roar of acclaim rising from the crowd to pay solemn tribute to all who sacrificed their lives for him: those departed souls he could not and would not forget even in the swelling exhilaration of this, his finest hour. For his sworn brother, Lu Xinghuo, he reserved his premier salute. He told of

Lu's valour and from an exquisitely fashioned wooden box brought forth a human skull and set it upon the table up there on the dais upon which he stood. Before it he poured out a libation of wine, then he knelt before it in reverence and stood up and bowed twice, fists clasped in veneration, a ritual of homage he repeated three times. He announced that he would build a tomb and erect a stele in honour of Lu Xinghuo and that every month of every year he would offer sacrifices to the spirit of this man who inspired in him deepest respect and affection.

Next he turned his attentions to the memory of a woman. This he knew was risky business, he of the monastic persuasions raising on this day of days the spectre of a woman, particularly one who'd been Heilaoqi's First Lady. People undoubtedly would look at him askance. And they did. As soon as he opened his mouth to tell of her deeds the crowd broke out in uproar, the mountain masters and his men alike murmuring resentment and sneering in shock. What's the matter with him? Has his brain gone soft? Totally inappropriate! But he made them hear him out, and he told of how she'd taken care of him in the tower cell and clandestinely slipped him the key and the knife. None in his audience had ever heard tell of such things, and all listened in growing wonder and admiration for this incomparably stunning person whom they had never seen or heard of before. Surely it had been written in the stars that she and Bai Lang would meet. And their minds lit upon the possibility that he and she may have embarked upon that kind of a relationship. And they sighed with tiding emotion to think that a delicate fragile woman who'd been none other than Heilaoqi's First Lady would fall in love with Bai Lang, positive proof of his extraordinary power to inspire courage and virtue in even the unlikeliest of hearts. The world was witness to great heroes, and he abided among them! Piously they followed him in pouring copious amounts of wine out on the ground, inwardly praying that they too might meet such an extraordinarily beautiful woman, reap such extraordinary fortune and become distinguished and admirable heroes for all time!

Then Bai Lang mourned the deaths of his men who had laid down their lives to rescue him and eliminate Heilaoqi. This he concluded by shouting the signal for a thirty-six cannon salute. Then he had forty-eight soldiers carry in plate after plate of meat—chicken and duck and pork and beef — and fill everyone's oversized bowls with the contents of urn upon urn of distilled white spirits. And he proclaimed the start of a bacchanal feast to end all feasts, a great engorgement, a riotous drunken bash which knew not the meaning of inhibition and restraint, for without Heilaoqi around, they need not fear a sneak attack. And all who would pass three days in a stupor would be Bai Lang's friends. However, someone in the crowd called out: "Your Grace, you have neglected a person who was also responsible for saving you and also died in the process!"

This was a very sonorous voice that had the ring of youth. Bai Lang, who had already sat down, stood back up and asked: "Who is speaking; and whom have I forgotten?"

A tiny young soldier stood up in the midst of the crowd. He was wearing an outlandishly large wolf's head uniform that hung well past his knees, making his legs look peculiarly short. But his eyes were delicate and pretty and had an endearing look about them. Bai Lang recognised him as one of Heilaoqi's former soldiers, the one who had played the horn and who had later been put on guard duty at the Sutra Chanting Tower. He moved to the front of the crowd and made an obeisance to Bai Lang, winking at him with his left eye. Bai Lang found this charming and laughed and winked right back at him. The young soldier said, "Your Grace has just spoken of Heilaoqi's First Lady. She was, in fact, none other than my cousin, and all that Your Grace has said here today I have heard before from her own lips. Because this involves the affairs of women, I would not have ventured to speak of it today if Your Grace had not already brought it up. But Your Grace can little imagine that her own personal maid also died for Your Grace! After Lu Xinghuo and Liu Songlin died, few of those who came to Fort Pit to rescue Your Grace were a match for Heilaoqi, yet he was very nervous because they kept coming in droves. My cousin and her maid sought to push him to a nervous breakdown so he couldn't execute his plan to kill you, and to this end they secretly wrote a lot of notices that said, 'We're coming for Heilaoqi's head!' In the middle of the night she had the maid go out and stick them up all over the place — on the walls, on the trees, in the toilet. This made Heilaoqi think that people from Wolf Fang Citadel were sneaking into Fort Pit or had infiltrated the ranks of the Fort Pit soldiers. He investigated and he searched and he killed many of his own troops, but every day he would still find those notices plastered up all over the place. So he didn't dare to sleep at night because he was afraid that someone would come and take his head. In the day he didn't dare to eat without having someone sample the food first, because he was afraid that it might have been poisoned. Anyone living like this is bound to get sick, and that is what happened to Heilaoqi. The wind rustling the tree leaves would startle him, and shadows cast by the sun or by lamps would make him jump out of his skin. This happened so often that he began to suspect those people closest to him and he would torture them cruelly or kill them. Just think, Your Grace, he had your pistol, and from Fort Pit's gate tower he could have easily picked off the attackers. Even if he couldn't aim well enough to get one man with every shot, he could have gotten one in every three. But he never went up into the gate tower, because he was afraid that if things got out of hand, one of his own men would stab him right in the back. Wasn't this the effect of those notices? He was going out of his mind. He was in terrible physical shape, so in the end when he went up in the tower to kill Your Grace, Your Grace could certainly see that he was completely changed. Here Your Grace was able to take him with a tiny knife without the least bit of a struggle. When my cousin's illness flared up and she knew she was going to die, she kept exhorting her maid not to breathe a word of it, and the maid agreed, but in private she cried and she thought my cousin didn't trust her. And it was no wonder, because she was the daughter of Manager Yang in Seven Stars. Manager Yang had once given Heilaoqi refuge, and after that Heilaoqi became a regular visitor. He took a fancy to her but he couldn't openly snatch her away, of course, so he used devious methods to seduce her. In his younger days, he'd been very capable when it came to hopping from bed to bed and getting the prostitutes in brothels to keep him in style. He knew how to get a cat to pee in a handkerchief, and he would take the handkerchief and stick it in front of a snake hole, and the snakes would mate on it and leave traces of semen. Then he would take the handkerchief and wave it before the face of a woman he wanted, and the woman would do his bidding as if she were hypnotised. That was how he got Manager Yang's daughter into bed. Then afterward when he got tired of playing with her, he made her become my cousin's maidservant. With a background like this, she thought my cousin doubted she was capable of carrying the plan through, and so that night she hung herself from the doorframe of an empty domicile. And before she hung herself, she pasted up her last notice — right on her own body. Of course it didn't occur to Heilaoqi that she might have been up to anything and he thought she'd been murdered, and he thought this murder was the prelude to his own. Your Grace, her contribution was no less than that of the soldiers who came rushing upon Fort Pit. In fact she was the equal of ten soldiers, twenty soldiers. But Your Grace hasn't mentioned her."

When the young soldier finished speaking, he withdrew to his seat. Bai Lang picked up his wine with both hands. Ah, little maidservant! Wouldst thou had made thyself known to me! Lips atremble, tears aplopping into his bowl, he lurched to his knees and the impulse to call out skyward to her soul wandering desolate in the netherworld. The sound of loud and bitter lamentations broke out. Grievous and heart-rending, this crying permeated the noonday warmth and pierced the manly viscera of all in congregation. The crowd was seized with a trembling to rival the convulsive tics of fever. It seemed to be coming from the sky; the soul of the anonymous maidservant wailing her piteous plaint at this moment of revelation. But, no! It was Bai Lang, the heroic Bai Lang, weeping with grief over his own guilt! But when all the mountain masters and all the warriors looked at Bai Lang, they saw that he too had lifted stupefied eyes toward Heaven. And then the plangent ululations drew their focus at last upon the flat-yard tucked in the northern corner. It had sprouted a milling mass of locals come to watch the excitement, and from the midst of this humanity a figure had emerged staggering toward them. And Bai Lang's voice arched in astonishment over all the steamy commotion: "Liu Songlin!"

Bai Lang's personal attendants bounded away from his side and descended like a pack of flying tigers upon the staggering man, flinging him heavily to the dust. Bai Lang, livid of face, smashed his bowl upon the ground. "Liu Songlin, you shameless traitor!" he screamed. "You dare to show your face here today! Good! I need your villainous head as offering to the spirits of Wolf Fang Citadel's valourious dead!"

Through the constricting sinews of his stiffened neck, the man on the ground strained to speak. "Your Grace!" he rasped. "Take another look and see if I am Liu Songlin or not!"

Fury could not contain Bai Lang's consternation. He eyed him up and down. Remarkably did he resemble Liu Songlin, only he was a little shorter and a little heftier, and his complexion lacked the leaden tones of the opium addict. What was going on here, anyway? "You're not Liu Songlin?" Bai Lang asked, perplexed.

"I'm not Liu Songlin. Liu Songlin's my brother. Today Your Grace reigns again, and Liu Songlin is your number one enemy, a man whom you would slash to a thousand pieces for treachery. But in fact, the first person to whom Your Grace should make offerings and sacrifices is none other than him!"

Pandemonium erupted among the mountain masters and the remnants of Bai Lang's old troops seated on rush mats. This guy is talking bullshit! Liu Songlin is a heinous traitor! He murdered Lu Xinghuo! What a travesty — him a paragon of fidelity and outstanding service?

But Bai Lang waved his hand and had his men release the object of this stream of anger. He looked at him cold and hard. "Liu Songlin is dead?" he asked.

"Yes, he's dead, Your Grace. There is no body and there is no grave."

"He's dead?" Bai Lang repeated. He advanced brusquely upon him another step. "According to you, he's the primary person to whom I should make offerings and sacrifices. But what is he before Lu Xinghuo? What is he before that lady of Fort Pit and her maidservant?"

The man stood up, looking wounded to the quick. Under the blazing sun he wiped his tears and said, "Lu Xinghuo was a faithful and loyal martyr to your cause, and that lady and her maidservant have joined the ranks of chaste and virtuous women who chose death over defilement. And I don't need to tell Your Grace of Liu Songlin's achievements and contributions when he was at Wolf Fang Citadel. All of this is knowledge that abides in your heart. Everyone here is very clear about this. And what was his greatest mistake? To run off with a woman and abandon Your Grace, right? But when he found out Your Grace had been taken prisoner and Salt Lake had been lost, and Lu Xinghuo had broken his arm trying to rescue Your Grace, he shed not a few tears. He stained his knife red with the blood of that woman and rushed to Fort Pit, though after he'd left Your Grace all he'd thought about was living in cosy retreat with her. That and the opera — his role as Zhou Yu on the stage was drawing him again. Therefore, when he went to Fort Pit there were only two other men around to go with him and he wasn't very skilled in the martial arts, but he went anyway. When he got there he found it was very heavily guarded and there was no way he could make any headway, so he retreated and went looking for Lu Xinghuo. Lu Xinghuo was still leading his men to attack Fort Pit despite his arm, but by this time almost all of his men had been injured or killed. That night the two of them stayed at my house. They talked the whole night and drank a whole jug of wine but could come up no good strategy. They put their heads on the table and cried. Then just before dawn Lu Xinghuo finally thought up the idea of having Liu Songlin cut off his head and pretend to surrender to Heilaoqi so as to get into Fort Pit and kill the evil Hei so as to avenge Your Grace — just like in the ancient story of Jing Ke and his plot to kill the king of Qin. While this was a good method, Liu Songlin couldn't bear to have Lu Xinghuo die like this. So Lu Xinghuo said don't argue with me on this matter, because if it were you who supplied the head and I who went to present it, Heilaoqi wouldn't believe for a minute I was being sincere; and besides, I haven't got enough strength to kill him with just one good arm. Then he excused himself to go to the outhouse, where he cut off his own head with his knife. At that time Liu Songlin didn't cry. He sprinkled the blood from Lu Xinghuo's head into his wine and drank it, saying, 'Brother, Liu Songlin is no longer only Liu Songlin. He is now both Lu Xinghuo and Liu Songlin!' Then he took the head to Fort Pit. Just as expected Heilaoqi took it as a bona fide surrender and had him carry Lu Xinghuo's head into his residence. The first thing he wanted was for Heilaoqi to take out the three hundred taels of silver and lay it aside, and then he wanted him to get the raw opium ready because he was going into withdrawal and needed a smoke. Heilaoqi complied with each of these requests, and he wanted him to bring Lu Xinghuo's head to him, but wouldn't let him just walk right up to him. Since he wouldn't let him get close, then what was to be done? There was a short knife hidden under Lu Xinghuo's head, so he said, 'I have another request. Master Hei must promise to grant it!' He said that Lu Xinghuo had a gold tooth in his mouth, and requested he be allowed to pry it out! Heilaoqi laughed and had someone hand the head to him. As Liu Songlin walked toward him, he opened up the mouth of the head, then suddenly drew the knife out from underneath. But then just at that moment he stepped on a piece of melon rind and slipped and fell. He went to get up, but it was already too late. Your Grace, as you know, Liu Songlin was addicted to opium, and when he didn't smoke he didn't have any strength or energy. When he left my house, he'd been smoking the whole night through, but by the time he got to Fort Pit, the effect had already worn off. He couldn't get up, and the soldiers on either side of Heilaoqi pounced on him and chopped him to shreds. After this incident, Heilaoqi was terror-stricken. Just now that young man told of how the maidservant's notices had driven him nearly crazy, but Liu Songlin's plot to assassinate him certainly had something to do with it as well. Such a valiant person he was, and yet Your Grace not only fails to eulogise him and make offerings, you curse him as a heinous traitor. My brother can find no peace in the underworld."

Here the reins upon his composure snapped and the man fell into a fit of weeping. Bai Lang, too, could no longer contain himself. He dropped numb onto a bench, repeatedly addressing his stunned sensibilities. "Can such things be? Can such things be?"

"Yes, such things can be, and are, Your Grace. If I have said one false word, Your Grace can cleave me in two right now. There are those who can corroborate what I've said."

Two men emerged from the crowd of curiosity seekers and knelt down and identified themselves as Heilaoqi's right and left hand attendants. They had personally witnessed Liu Songlin's act of valour. After Liu Songlin perished, they said, Heilaoqi sealed the main gate to his residence and suppressed intelligence of the event, thus keeping all his other men in the dark. By the time he met his demise as well, both men had lost their stomachs for banditry and returned to their farms and wouldn't have even been here today if Liu Songlin's brother hadn't asked them to come and bear witness.

Bai Lang's complexion took on a sickly greyish hue. Without offering further libations, without even a tear, he dismounted the dais and approached the mountain kings and his soldiers, addressing them in muttering tones. "Is there anyone else unbeknownst to me who I ought to remember for their ultimate sacrifice on my behalf?" Piously he walked among them, yet he was terrifying to behold, and when his gaze fell upon the mountain masters, two of them went gastly pale, crumpled up upon themselves and slumped lifelessly to the earth. The hot miasmic atmosphere quavered with the agitation sweeping the crowd. A soldier hurried to ladle out cold mung bean soup to revive the two heat-swooned kings, but their eyes remained implacably closed. Even more alarming, they began to make utterances in eerie high-pitched voices. One said, "Well, what are you waiting for — go on, speak up! You said no one nowhere would listen to you, didn't you?" The other one said, "I'm afraid." The first one said, "It's His Grace, Bai Lang. What are you afraid of? He's not a real white wolf who's going to eat you." The other one said, "I don't care." The first one became angered and said, "You're a hopeless excuse for a man! The day I got together with you I was cursed with enough bad luck to last eight lifetimes. If you won't speak up, then I will."

Neither of the bickering kings looked at the other as this conversation proceeded, yet their dialogue was uncannily coordinated and intonated in the patterns of a married couple. "They're possessed!" somebody yelped. "That's not them talking — that's spirits! Quick, get some winnowing pans and cudgels — we'll cover them up and beat them out!" The king speaking like a woman clenched his eyes and said hotly, "Beat me? Beat me? I've come to tell His Grace our grievances!" Somebody asked: "Who are you? What grievances do you have to raise with His Grace? If you have grievances, then go to the court in the county yamen!" The one with the woman's voice said, "I'm the proprietress of the Inn of Exuberant Prosperity in Seven Stars. He's my husband. We put some Wolf Fang Citadel warriors up at our inn — twenty men — and when they said they were going to fight Heilaoqi and rescue His Grace Bai Lang, we gave them their meals and drinks for free. But no sooner had they left in the morning when they ran into men from Fort Pit. There was a battle and they were all annhilated. Then the Fort Pit men came looking for us. They stabbed my husband in the courtyard, then went into the kitchen after me. I jumped into a water urn and covered my head with a gourd ladle, but they found me anyway. They accused me of being a Wolf Fang Citadel sympathiser. I said I wasn't but that I didn't think much of Heilaoqi either, because instead of going to fight the government soldiers, he turns Bai Lang into a prisoner. He's nothing but a little wiener. They asked me what's a little wiener? I said it was a baby's dick. So they whacked off my right arm. I knew they were going to kill me, so I cursed Heilaoqi. They said if you don't shut up, we'll cut off your left arm too! But I went on cursing, and they cut off my left arm. I fell to the ground, but I just went right on cursing. So they cut out my tongue. Then they sliced off my breasts, and down there —" Here the other one broke in: "That's enough! Now I'll say what I have to say to His Grace. Your Grace, we were not of Wolf Fang Citadel, but we died for Wolf Fang Citadel. In which case, we came to tell Your Grace about it. If Your Grace is unwilling to pay us any heed, wouldn't that means we died utterly grievously, all for nothing? If Your Grace can understand us, then consider us to be of Wolf Fang Citadel, and if Your Grace pours us a libation, then we can enjoy a mouthful."

Bai Lang, whose complexion was becoming more and more ghastly, was stymied by this situation, concerned about the welfare of the two mountain masters, yet dumbfounded by the strange voices coming out of their mouths. He gathered his presence of mind and said, "Whoever died for Wolf Fang Citadel of course deserves a libation."

"Wife, did you hear that, did you hear that?" Then both of the voices spoke at once: "Thank you, Your Grace!" And at that moment, the two mountain masters opened their eyes and sat up. They were bathed in cold sweat and totally spent, as if they'd just made a tremendous physical effort. When people asked them what happened, all they said was they'd heard a buzzing in their heads and then everything went blank.

Hair stood on end as everyone stared each other in dismay. There was no doubt about it — a possession had taken place and the spirits had spoken through the mouths of the possessed. On this glorious day, Bai Lang had made libations of wine as offerings to the departed souls, and in so doing had precipitated an invasion of ghosts and spirits. How many others like the couple from the Inn of Exuberant Prosperity were floating around in their midst? And would they all try to possess the bodies of the living and speak through their mouths? Everyone, mountain masters and warriors alike, looked waxen and yellow with terror. An older, more experienced soldier hurried off to get the touch paper that had been brought in tribute. With a copper coin he struck a spark and set the whole mass a light to provide all the haunts with netherworld money so they could rest in peace. The huge bonfire billowed and sent paper ashes into the air until it looked like thousands and thousands of black birds were hovering all over the sky. Bai Lang, who lifted not a finger to discourage this activity, raised his head to watch. For a long time he fixed his gaze upon a large paper ash that floated erratically here and there on the currents of air. It finally landed right on top of his head but he made no effort to brush it away.

At this time, a group of newcomers entered into the arena, apparitions with pale pinched faces and bodies hung with rags. In the lead was the chieftan whom Bai Lang had charged with the mission of gathering up his old troops. With startled countenance the chieftan surveyed the scene of chaos and terror presided over by a Bai Lang clearly in distress. He knelt before his king, as did his bedraggled companions. In fact, all the soldiers of Wolf Fang Citadel knelt as a body and intoned: "Your Grace —"

Bai Lang looked at them woodenly. Finally he lunged forward to raise the chieftan from his knees and ask him: "Are these all you've brought? My confreres from the old days didn't want to come back?"

The chieftan said, "Reporting, Your Grace! All your confreres from the old days have come back!"

"But there were three thousand of them!"

"Yes. All the others are dead."

"Dead?"

"I went everywhere looking for them, to all their homes, and it's true — they're dead. Some perished when Heilaoqi attacked Salt Lake — three hundred and seventy were killed that time. Some were scattered when Salt Lake was retaken, and they were rounded up by the government and executed —that was seven hundred and twenty-one men. Some died outside Fort Pit trying to rescue Your Grace —six hundred and thirty-nine men. Only thirty-eight of the survivors didn't come back with me, men injured in the campaign to save you: both legs rendered useless, or eyes blinded, or so seriously wounded that they had to be carried back home and were virtually paralysed."

Bai Lang said nothing. He turned his head and called out, "All of you my old confreres, stand up and come over here!"

Half the soldiers squatting on the ground stood up and gathered in one spot. This was a crowd of about a thousand, a third of which had injured hands or broken legs, while many more had their heads or their shoulders or their legs wrapped in thick bloodied bandages.

Bai Lang raised his head toward the sky and erupted into insane laughter. "This is victory?" he cried, voice cracking and rising toward hysteria. "I'm the hero and the king of kings?"

Shivers of fear ran through the crowd. Everyone's

skin crawled. He sounded demented, demonised. Ten Tiger Mountain kings and a dense mass of soldiers all watched in horror as, under the fiery sun rolling across the sky, Bai Lang's face surrendered its glow, his lips became drained of colour, his eyes went dead, his skin went slack and a pasty canescence creeped over his countenance, and all at once he was old. From being absolutely still, his body began to sway, slowly back and forth, back and forth, in an ever widening arc until he crashed to the ground. In the distance, the pagoda of the Temple of Heavenly Prime, with its two sword-like halves thrusting into the sky, gave an oppressive rumble and collapsed...

And it came to pass that three days later the little spring in Hump Hill Cove gave of its pure waters to a group of women on their early morning errands. By and by, they noticed a man proceeding down the road and toting a gun. A roving bandit or a government soldier looking for trouble, surely. Frightened, they hid themselves in the sheltering grass. The man approached, and they watched between the grassblades until one of the women gave a gasp. She leapt up and cried out in piercing tones — for she was a woman of uncommon courage — "Isn't that Bai Lang?"

Sharp indeed were her eyes for the peregrinating figure bore the aspect of long years of tribulation. No dashing youth in white dragon-bedizened robes and thick-soled shoes was he. Quite the contrary, he presented the image of old age in filthy and abbreviated garb. No shoulder holster decked his person. No jaunty waistband addenda either, that gun of his simply dangled from his hand, besmirched with dirt, the barrel plugged with mud. He was clambering up the bank, then as his name rang out over the landscape, he came to a standstill and saw the woman before him. He looked at her uncertainly.

"Your Grace doesn't recognise me," the woman said. "But I know you. Remember when Heilaoqi had you cangued and wrapped in ropes and you were driven past that peak right up there? A woman in the crowd was raving over your beauty and tossed you a wild rose and then Heilaoqi's soldiers kicked her. That was me!"

A look of delving deep into memory passed over his face. Then he shook his head.

"Well, I'm not surprised. Why should the fabulously famous king of kings remember the likes of me? Why should the epitome of masculine magnificence, ever mobbed by feminine youth and beauty, take notice of the age proprietress of some shop?" She gave a dissolute laugh.

"Is that a proper way for a woman to talk?" one of her companions interjected.

"Well, it's true, isn't it? Who among you has not dreamed of Bai Lang? I've heard tell that loads of people have enshrined his portrait in their houses and they worship it everyday. And you can bet the women in those houses dream of him and fantasise about him and long for him in the night until they go quite out of their minds."

Thus enamoured of her own sauce and emboldened to further irreverance, she turned again to him of sorry countenance and said, "But Your Grace, I find myself compelled to say something that you might find rather offensive — you won't shoot me with that gun of yours, will you?" — she regarded the abused weapon, which looked anything but cocky — "You've really — ah — aged. A handsome, dashing hero like yourself — it's such a pity — you really oughtn't to run yourself down like this for that bunch of hussies. No offence, but it's really disappointing to see you this way!"

This brazen and intrepid speech, however, elicited from her "interlocutor" only a stupid stare. At last his lips moved and from them came the request: "You've got a water jar there — can you give me a drink?"

"Your Grace, what's the matter with you? You're standing right beside a whole spring of water, and still you beg me for a drink?"

Whatever the genesis of his distraction — the brassy flamboyance of the woman or the absorbing train of his own thoughts — the spring bubbling out of the side of the mountain had, in point of fact, escaped his notice. Now he approached it, lay down his gun, and stretched out upon the ground to drink. He drank as if assailing an unquenchable thirst, even plunging his branded head into the water. When he finished, he stood up, muttered something, then walked off, reassuming the same wobbly if determined gait as before — step by step, step by step, inevitably onward. The women, speechless, watched his relentless retreat, his figure whittled smaller and smaller by distance. Then they espied his gun still lying on the lip of the spring, and they called out after him: "Your Grace, Your Grace, you forgot your gun."

He may not have heard. Or he may have ignored them.

The gun drew the women back to the edge of the spring, where it sat, mute and sombrous, in the scorching sun. Succumbing to the urge to pick it up, one of them extended her hand and grasped it only to release it again with all the speed her reflexes could muster. It fell into the water with a hiss and a poof of steam and vanished. They peered into the water and saw hovering on the bottom a silver fish with a black back.

Whence came this silver fish? And where had that gun gone to? And now a web of tangled emotions ensnared them: consuming infatuation, frustration, anger, fear, vindictiveness. This man whose ethereal essence had long coursed through their veins and penetrated their very cells —though none but one had ever seen him — had stood in almost intimate proximity to them, and in those moments, his exhilarating heroism and his legendary beauty excited them to frenetic adoration. It mattered not that he had aged, nor that he showed no interest in them. They longed for him with all the aching yearning of raging adolescent love. And if they couldn't have him, they would have at least the very same water he drank, and that would be like kissing him on the lips and absorbing his courage and uprightness. But now there was a fish in the water, and it was stirring up the sediment with its maddening tail, contaminating it and dispersing the precious essence he had left. And as their passions hung in tortured abeyance, they began to consider the disappearance of that gun, and then to doubt that it had existed, and then to wonder if they had only seen Bai Lang in a dream, a vision of mass hysteria. "No! This was not a dream!" said the bold and raunchy one. "There was a man here, and that man was acting like an evil spirit. He couldn't have been Bai Lang. Not in a thousand years. I saw Bai Lang when he was a prisoner, and I tell you, in spite of everything he was still very heroic and very handsome. Now that Wolf Fang Citadel is strong again, how could its king look like that guy?"

And so they concluded they had been subjected to humiliation. It was a coward they had encountered, a craven imposter. And they set out down the road after him. They would catch that dastardly vermin and teach him a lesson. They walked for quite a distance on the mountain road and finally found him sitting in a cave beneath an inconspicuous cliff. His legs were crossed in a yoga position and his eyes were closed. This strange apparition confirmed their suspicions that he was indeed not Bai Lang but only a wandering hermit in pursuit of the arcane secrets of mysticism, magic and immortality. The cave was slanted precipitously downward, frustrating their impulse to enter and pull him out and dish him out a most deserved lecture on on propriety. So at the mouth of the cave, they demanded: "Do you still dare claim to be Bai Lang?" The man looked at them and said, "Yes, I am Bai Lang." The women could no longer contain their rage, and they threw clods of dirt into the cave and yelled: "How can you be Bai Lang? We won't permit you to be Bai Lang! You are not Bai Lang! You are not Bai Lang!"

Translated by Josephine A. Mathews

图书在版编目(CIP)数据

贾平凹传奇小说选: 英文/ 贾平凹著; 马若芬等译.- 北京: 中国文学出版社, 1996.5
ISBN 7-5071-0346-3

Ⅰ.贾… Ⅱ.① 贾… ② 马… Ⅲ.中篇小说-作品集- 中国- 当代- 英文 Ⅳ.I247.5

中国版本图书馆 CIP 数据核字(96) 第02519 号

晚 雨

贾平凹

熊猫丛书

*

中国文学出版社出版
(中国北京百万庄路24号)
中国国际图书贸易总公司发行
(中国北京车公庄西路35号)
北京邮政信箱第399号　邮政编码100044
1996年第1版(英)
ISBN 7-5071-0346-3

34.00